EVG. MYRTHA A. HEROLD

Editors:
Professor Rocco Dormarunno
Stephen Levien—Writer/Filmmaker
Pierre Andre Cadet— NYPD Sergeant

WORKBOOK PRESS LLC
187 E Warm Springs Rd
Suite B285 Las Vegas NV 89119 USA

Website: https: https://workbookpress.com/
Hotline: 1-888-818-4856
Email:admin@workbookpress.com

Ordering Information:
Quantity sales. Special discounts are available on quantity purchases by corporations, associations, and others. For details, contact the publisher at the address above.

Library of Congress Control Number: 9781961845022

ISBN-13: 978-1-963718-42-3 Paperback
        978-1-963718-83-6 Hardback
        978-1-961845-05-3 Digital

REV. DATE: 07/08/2024

Can I be the One?

God's Intent for the Given Gifts

MYRTHA A. HEROLD

Can I Be *the* ONE?

God's Intent for the Given Gift

Evg. Myrtha A. Herold

Myrtha A. Herold

Other Inspirations
by Myrtha A. Herold

Can I be the One?

"The Album"

DEDICATED TO

To the **K***ing of my life* who has given me this vision and mission:

Lord **J**esus, seeing the outcome of this work fills my heart with joy for this moment. It is only right that I should give You, my Heavenly Father, reverence, blessings, honor, glory, and thanksgiving for choosing me. You are the Potter that has transformed me into a vessel of honor in your Kingdom. You give me the opportunity to expose such a marvelous teaching to the world; that is more than I ever expected. Father, I bless your name for breaking down every stronghold that opposed my ministry so I could make it this far. I will always have a sense of gratitude towards You for my discoveries in the inspiring songs which are extended into this manual; a tool to open the eyes of many about your intents for the given gift (s). I am amazed by the outcome of your revelation to me!

Thank You for answering my prayer for making me ONE of those that You could use.

Your humble servant, Myrtha Herold

ACKNOWLEDGEMENTS

I am very thankful to all my partners and friends who never give up in waiting patiently until the achievement of this work, such as:

My daughters: Jennesa for letting me know how proud you are of my accomplishment. Your words of encouragement mean a lot to me, Justine, my Little Treasure Box. I thank you for believing in me, for taking part in the recording and for giving me hints about the music industry.

My dear friend, John Patrick Honoré: for never stop to trusting God and believing in my ministry as to be something very special from the Lord.

My beloved friend, Esther Reynold, for allowing God to use you in declaring God's prophetic words over my life.

My dear sister and old-time friend and prayer partner Minerva Morisseau, for support and sincerity.

My precious friend Junie Pelissier, for being a loyal servant in supporting most of my events.

My beloved friend, Rev. Dr. Ghislaine Renazile Herard, for your faithfulness to God in counseling and interceding for my breakthrough.

My precious Stephanie Jeanty: for believing in the outcome of this work. God has given you the privilege to get the first bite out of this teaching.

My Friend, Sister Anna Clermont: for your words of encouragement and general support.

My brother in Christ, Milot Eliassaint, for working diligently on the musical production of "Can I be One?" which is the root of this manual.

My brother in Christ, Pastor Joseph G. Duvert, author of "The Blame Game": for being a long-term friend and supporter to me.

My beloved friend, Sister Mirlaine Doriscar: thank you for your words of knowledge and feedback in this teaching.

Great big thanks to my friend, Pastor Rousselin Allonce, one of the partial editors and reviewers in the outcome of this manual.

TABLE OF CONTENTS

Mission Statement

The number one mission of the author is to establish a Godly standard in the mind of the People (ministers) when presenting the gospel of Jesus Christ. In addition, she wants to encourage today's recording artists, and all those that come not to trade their gifts for temporary happiness. Furthermore, she wants to bring spiritual guidance to all who possess any types of gifts to develop gratitude towards God for their given gift (s). Much more, she wants to break the cycle from vain performance in exchange for service, as it was intended to be by God our maker.

This Manual is designed by the Holy Spirit to:

- Alert people about the misuse of the assigned gifts and teach them and teach them how to overcome challenges of worldly conformation.

- Bring improvement and change in how we write Gospel songs.

- Bring to our attention the responsibilities with the given gift(s).

- Persuade people about how to successfully use their gifts in God's intent.

- Provide information that would build stability in fatih and restore higher values in people's minds for service.

- Restructure peoples' perceptions about their official ministry and teach them how to be loyal to God while using their gifts.

- Teach the certainty in how to use their gifts in a way that would honor God.

- • Teach the principles that are attached to the gift and
  how they should be applied when pertaining to a specific audience.

NOTE:

- • This manual is highly recommended and useful for the followings:
- • Bible Schools, Sunday Schools, home groups, and personal and
  group studies.

Foreword

When we are toddlers, we rely on our parents and guardians to provide us with ways of knowing the world in which we live. These providers show us how to put on our sneakers, how to make a sandwich and how to avoid danger. They tell us why the sky is blue, why thunder can't hurt us and why we should stay away from that bad street corner. At a certain age, however, these guardians send us to school where someone else would take over some of these tasks, would take over the process of teaching the more specific aspects of the world: its sciences, its history, its languages, and its mathematics. When the child becomes an adult, and if that adult is interested in furthering his or her education, the college professor takes over. In a way, the teachers and professors had become second-tier parents over the course of many years.

I have taught at several local colleges and universities for the last three decades, including Brooklyn College, The College of New Rochelle, and Rutgers University. It may sound altruistic, but I enjoyed (and still enjoy) seeing that "light" come into students' eyes. I celebrate the acknowledging nod of a student that says, "Okay, I get it now. I see."

Myrtha Herold was one of my students during my years at The College of New Rochelle. She was one of those students who wanted to learn. (Sad to say, this is not as common as I would want it to be.) Myrtha worked very hard. She volunteered to take on extra work and sought guidance from the college's tutoring center. When the unspeakable horrors of the 2010 earthquake struck Haiti, there was nothing Myrtha would not do to assist its victims, including traveling there on a mission of mercy. It was then that I knew something deeper, and more meaningful than anything I could teach her, was going on in Myrtha's life. And this was her irresistible, unstoppable, and sincerest devotion to The Lord.

This manual is but one expression of her love for God, and how better to express that love than to teach someone else how to praise Him? For those who are musically inclined, Myrtha guides the student along the path to successful gospel songwriting. At the same time, we are admonished, both by her experiences and the experiences of those around her, that many defects may prevent us from being true "instruments": pride being the most dangerous and deadly. The manual also includes several samples of Myrtha's creations. Each song stands alone and yet, each song is part of a greater whole.

Writing gospel songs is extremely difficult. Myrtha, however, is a patient teacher with an impressive background in the craft. She encourages the songwriters while instructing them. She guides them with expertise and leads by example. When writing about artists, Jovette Elise Cutaiar once said, "We lead by example, we love by heart, we write by soul, we play by ear." Nothing better expresses what Myrtha Herold does in this manual.

Although I am no songwriter, I learned some things as I edited this manual, and the things I have gleaned will lead me along my own spiritual journey. In this manner, the student became the teacher, and the teacher became the student.

Professor: Rocco Dormarunno

<u>*Preface*</u>

There are many to whom the gift of salvation is a common misapprehension. They believe that having been born into a Christian family automatically makes them born again Christians. When Christ dwells in the heart, the fruit of salvation is evident. A friend of mine asked someone very close to me this simple question, "Are you a born-again Christian?" The person of course felt offended by such a question and replied "What do you mean? I was born a Christian!" Listening to her remarks, I thought, "What a defensive answer." I suppose that could have been my perception, if God had not proven me wrong in His letter to us, the Bible. Some people could grow up in a religious environment where they attend church on a regular basis, and yet never profess having accepted the gift of salvation. They perceived salvation as some type of automatic inheritance. I was one of those people. As a religious person, I was trapped in worldly desires, and bound by generational curses. Being in that situation had left me in spiritual obscurity and darkness. I was far from understanding the gift of salvation. How then, could I understand the purpose of my inner gift if I did not understand the gift of salvation?

Longing to be used by God, I raised the ultimate question in my mind. That question was "*Can I be the one?*" That question links to my desire to serve God for all that He has done for me. I desired to be the one that He can use as a vessel of honor.

My love for service is the evidence that God had heard and granted me my request. He has equipped me with both the gift of singing and writing songs. He delivered me from religious corruption and turned me into one of His followers. He opened the door to a broadcasting ministry where my husband and I preach and teach the gospel of Jesus Christ. God also reversed generational curses into eternal blessings. Now, I can boldly pray for the salvation and deliverance of others and invite them to become followers of Christ. That is why I want to publicly share my appreciation to God for allowing me to hear the call and delivering me from all snares. After all, I am not the only one that God has called, but I am among those who were fortunate to hear the call, and I gladly said yes.

Being restored by the gracious love of God leaves me with a thirst that subdues my heart. That thirst constantly refreshes my memory about the prophetic word of God over my life. That prophetic word was that "I would be one to tell many stories;" (my stories). Writing this manual is not based on my own choice, but it is an act of obedience to God who said that **"I will instruct thee and teach thee in the way which thou shalt go: I will guide thee with mine eye" (Psalm 32:8)**. Because I am a divine partaker of God's nature, I believe that I can be anything that He wants me to be. I can use my precious gift, my voice, to honor Him. I can be the one to tell the story of salvation. I can be the one to stand for righteousness. I can be the one to share my testimonies. And I can be the one to bring significant change into one's life.

This is no superstition. For more than two decades I desired to record Gospel songs. I never thought that it would take me this long to accomplish this vision. Throughout my life, I have always wondered: Can God find in me one He could use to bear light to people through music. As the years passed me by, I could not comprehend the heaviness of this desire. Being able to move forward with this project is a total breakthrough for me. I suppose God was still preparing me for a greater experience. This long journey also prepares me to receive greater anointing from God. Through this experience I discovered my purpose through spiritual sight which has strengthened me to approach my ministry with confidence.

This teaching is about the real conflict that most ministers encounter when using their gifts. It is also about those who have not yet discovered their gifts. As I gathered the information to write this manual, I devoted special time to seeking, listening, and following the voice of the Holy Spirit. I am thrilled about my findings in God's word, and I want to exhibit them inclusively; even though it is primarily addressed to Christian artists or ministers, one does not have to be a Christian to participate in this teaching. My alternative is to make this teaching enjoyable, interesting, easy to grasp and practical to all, but excluding personal drama. The resulting process to my alternative was to use specific relevant experiences, to unify and to capture the reader's attention. So, to make this teaching come alive and at the same time be transparent, I will be using both questions and answers to these questions.

When gospel artists refer to *singing* as a ministry, several questions jog my mind. I always wonder if they really understand the characteristics that support such a statement. They need to understand that one cannot have a ministry without becoming first a minster. Based on what I learned, a minister is one who serves in diverse areas such as assisting one another and attending to a task. As for me, I could not pass over these concerns, because I believe that it is essential for Christian artists and all who possess inner gifts to know the basic objectives of their ministry. In view of these objectives these questions arose.

> *Why do we sing, write songs, and compose gospel music?*

> *How do we write gospel songs?*

> *How do some of us perceive talents and gifts?*

> *Are there principles that follow the gift?*

> *If so, what are these principles, and how can we apply them?*

> *Are there standards to keep in terms of gospel performance and activities?*

> *What should we expect in the singing or music ministry?*

> *Does music have a language? If so, how does it communicate to us?*

> *What roles does gospel music play in a Christian's life?*

> *What does God approve or disapprove in the operating of the given gift?*

> *Can the gifts become ineffective?*

The answers to these questions will be addressed while I present the teaching about the principles and the standards that follow the given gifts. Also, the detailed definitions about the intent of the gift will be fully developed throughout this teaching. In the context of the title, I will clearly explain both the importance of the theme and my responsibility toward my audience. I will detail the prerequisite in the application of the principles by using scriptures from the King James Version that support the teaching. The foremost will be God's purpose for the giving gift, talent vs. gift, entertainment vs. ministering; the role gospel music plays in a Christian's life, and the boundaries that ministers must apply when using their gifts.

In addition, together we will learn about how God uses music for different purposes and about the importance of being submissive to the Holy Spirit in the process of using the gifts. Much more, I will share some principles about writing Gospel song lyrics and how to focus on the theme.

Furthermore, together we will see about three specific types of audiences that we tend to minister to. Along with that, I will use some of my inspirations as examples to show you in which category of audience that I place each of my songs. I will also discuss how hiring a non-Christian to produce your gospel songs could affect your inspiration. I have also included a list of Biblical warnings about obstacles that could hinder our gifts.

There is much more. I will also discuss God's expectations in terms of ministerial work. I will share my view about Performing VS. Ministering and the Ministers' contributions to the development of the given Gift. I will also express my love for God and my experience about trust and obedience as a minister. I will share some true stories about the motive outside God's will and the discovery of how the Gift could be more effective.

After all, it will be good to know God's purpose for the giving Gift. Next, we will look together at the establishment of the principles and the beneficial attributes of teaching lyrics to the congregation, by understanding God's beneficial attributes of teaching. I will share some of the ways we can express our gratitude to Him. We will learn how to appreciate God's promises with the Gift so we could overcome Satanic challenges, such as the controversy between Satan and God, and the contest between Satan and the believer. In conclusion, I will share with you a glimpse behind the victory of opposition and persecution in my life and encourage the born-again Christian in the hope of eternal rewards.

Introduction

First and foremost, I want you to know that I never thought that God would select me to teach about spiritual gifts. That blows my mind. Since God anointed me to teach, I am going to tell you like it is. The subsequent songs that are used as examples in this teaching are my specialties. Though these songs were rooted in the circumstances of my life's journey with the Lord, but my Gift was congested because they did not reach as far that I would like them to. Each time I would go through some type of trial or victory, a theme just popped into my spirit. Moving forward with the Gift, my assignment is to clear the eyes of gifted people about the importance of using their Gifts in uprightness. God loves us so much that He would take the time to forewarn us. God gives us Biblical principles to alert us from the danger in operating in the Gift outside of His intent. As one of God's elects, I could not hold my peace.

For many years I struggled to become a recording artist. Under false appearance, I pretended that I did not care to be famous. God knew all alone what my desire was; I wanted to be a celebrity. I failed to understand that Jesus should be the star and not me. Much more, my insecurity caused "Can I be the One?" to take me over twenty years before it was finally released. In my silent struggle, I could never have a valid reason to explain such a delay to those who acknowledged my Gift. Waiting for so long, on October 1, 2011, at 2:00 pm the idea appeared to me. My heart led me to write a short booklet about the reasons for my lyrical inspirations. With an open heart, I accepted that thought. Unknowingly, God had something else in store for my ministry. Let me tell you, the Holy Spirit took this idea to a higher level and turned this idea into a greater assignment. That is why you have the privilege to take part in this great teaching today. Is not God amazing?

The Bible is not an ordinary textbook that one can understand without divine revelation. Because I depend on God's wisdom in me, I can declare that: ***"My words shall be of the uprightness of my heart: and my lips shall utter knowledge clearly" (Job 33:3).*** As I invest time in God's word seeking answers, the Holy Spirit opens my eyes, and I begin to understand these principles. I am convinced that God does not play favors when it comes to supplying knowledge to His children. These principles are not a model solely for me but are available to whoever yearns to learn them. This is why this manual is designed as a teaching tool, so all can get familiar with God's plan in the principles that are attached to the gift. You will soon see why it is necessary to know about the principles. For instance, a detailed description of the principles will be discussed extensively in this teaching. Readers, I do not know about you, but this is good news for me.

Before we go further, we must agree that it is well for anyone who has a ministry to develop a dependency on God. Come to think of it, it is impossible for us to stand alone in our ministry. The reason is that we are limited in knowledge. We know about what we desire, and our desires most likely do not correspond with those of God. Therefore, we are in great need to rely on God to extend our knowledge because ***"Not that we are sufficient of ourselves to think anything as of ourselves; but our sufficiency is of God" (II Cor. 3:5).***

Singing, which is one of my gifts, to me, was nothing else but a talent that can be used for both pleasure and fame. I spent a great deal of time using singing in the church outside God's intent. I specify the church because performing in the church does not mean that we have the right motive. I say this because of my own experience. I was trapped in a religious world where I was singing for all the wrong reasons, such as pride, fame, pleasure, etc. But when I responded to the calling of God in my life, I realized three important things that He wants me to know: *(1) God is seeking to direct my mind to focus on*

His principles; (2) God wants me to know His purpose for giving me the gift of singing so I can appreciate and use it correctly; and (3) my gift will not be fulfilling the will of God without the act of obedience. My obedience to fulfill God's mission will be followed by great rewards. One of the greatest rewards will be to bring souls to Christ. As the Holy Spirit guides me, the teaching will be honest, and simple.

This manual is not written independently. I consider myself to be in partnership with the Holy Spirit in the accomplishment of this work. ***"But the Comforter, which is the Holy Ghost, whom the Father will send in my name, he shall teach you all things, and bring all things to your remembrance, whatsoever I have said unto you" (John 14:26).*** Keeping that in mind, I will properly direct the praise to whom it belongs. Therefore, the marvelous works of the Holy Spirit will be displayed without limitations throughout the entire sessions. Furthermore, because the love of God is stronger than anything in existence, the word love will be the pillar of this teaching. I guarantee you that this teaching will be practical and supported with Biblical texts. So, I urge you to approach the rest of this reading with an open mind. Take some time to listen to the voice of the Holy Spirit as He ministers to your spirit during the reading of this manual. What you are about to learn could change your objective about your given gift and create a door to enhance your relationship with God.

Thinking about my personal condition prior to my understanding of God's view for the given gift, I came to understand that there is a contrast about the use of our gifts in the Gospel ministry. One can only bring out what is inside. In other words, you give what you have. With that in mind, I conditioned myself so that God could use me to settle this matter. It is not with pride that I make mention of this problem. Rather, it is to apply one of the greatest principles of Paul's teaching to the church. He encourages us to ***"Study to show thyself approved unto God, a workman that needeth not to be shamed, rightly dividing the word of truth" (II Tim. 2:15).***

Therefore, the teaching of these principles will be presented to you shamelessly, in compliance with the command of God. I also urge you to unlock the door of your heart and allow the truth to penetrate deep within you so you can have the full benefit of this teaching.

Let us consider for a moment the term "*principle*." We learned that a principle is a source of origin and a fundamental truth or doctrine. We might want to know the essentials of its existence. There is no doubt concerning the existence of principle. This fundamental truth of doctrine is basically a guideline to answer our questions and to follow Jesus Christ's examples. What is even more astounding about principle is that trying to operate outside its order is to operate outside the guidelines of God. Most importantly, God does not want His followers to operate outside His principles. So, he gives us the Holy Spirit to teach us how to follow the principles in His word. So, those who sought to obtain knowledge about the principles will diligently work to apply them. Isn't this a tremendous reality of God's faithfulness towards us? This is why I encourage you to note carefully how God has pointed out the principles concerning the gifts He has entrusted you with. You can begin by acknowledging that God was generous to have given gift(s) to you.

PART- I

SESSION ONE

In this Session, you will learn about:

- *My objective behind the theme of this manual.*

- *The advantages and the disadvantages of using the gift.*

- *My disclosure of temptation and God's destiny for my life.*

- *Prevention for yielding to lustful temptations.*

- *My responsibility and my sentiment in delivering this work.*

- *The difference between talent and gift.*

Behind the Theme

My devotion toward the theme **"Can I be the One?"** is to stay focused in compliance with God's words as my guide and influence in this teaching. **"Having then gifts, differing according to the grace that is given to us, whether prophecy, let us prophesy according to the proportion of faith; or ministry, let us wait on our ministering: or he that teacheth, on teaching..." (Rom. 12:6-7).**

The Psalmist said: **"My heart is indicating a good matter" (Ps. 45:1).** This means that his heart is overflowing with a good theme. I can relate to this excitement when I think about *"Can I be the One"?* The awareness of the meaning of the theme is a great discovery to me for these reasons: it reveals the secret about God's design and destiny for my life; it shows me the areas of effectiveness and ineffectiveness in the use of the gift; it connects me to the service that I am assigned to do; it restructures my perceptions and officiates my ministry; and it allows me to discover the *advantage and the disadvantage in using the gift.*

There is no controversy about how God designs each one of us so differently. Regardless of how different we are, we all have one thing in common: that is, we were all *designed to serve and worship God, our Maker.* Even though, we perform in the contrary of God's intention, it does not change the purpose of God's design. He declares that we are His, and no other should have our primary service but Him. That settles His ownership. If I had comprehended that concept a long time ago, I could have avoided the pain of my foolish actions in using my gifts. I don't know if this is any encouragement to you, but I am astonished by the fact that such an insubordinate like me belongs to God. If I could go back and regain the times that I wasted trying to figure out my destiny, I would have allowed God to use me as He saw fit. Since I cannot change the past, I would rather take advantage of the remaining time to focus on God's destiny for my life. Therefore, it is imperative for me to spread this vision about the advantages and the disadvantages of the given gifts.

The *advantage in using the gift* depends on my knowledge of God's purpose and how I use it today. As I devote my heart and make myself available for the use of the gift, I have peace within me. Not only that, but I also live each day expecting a new inspiration from God. My greatest advantage is my resolution to explore the gift in its wholeness by leading others to the light of truth. It is advantageous to have the opportunity to openly share my knowledge, and in return leave a legacy behind. Discovering my true self is specifically advantageous to me. I can now boldly declare that I know who I am. **"I am the righteousness of God in Christ Jesus" (II Cor. 5:21).** The fact that I know who I am in Christ Jesus today motivates me to take advantage of my heritage.

Excellent service is what my heavenly Father deserves; and what I desire is to deliver that kind of service. The desire is already established in my heart through the expression of my love for God in this teaching. The fragrance of my desire draws me closer to the reality of the holistic view about the given gift. The immediate view is how He broadens my vision to receive greater revelations in the process of this teaching. As I present my excellent service to Him, I also embrace my desirable promise to Him. I intend to obey God's principles because I would like to continue to prosper in knowledge. **"If they obey and serve Him, they shall spend their days in prosperity, and their years in pleasures" (Job 36:11).** With these promises in mind, I am convinced that I am heading towards the destiny He has prepared for my life.

Conversely, the *disadvantage* in comprehending the theme arises when I become dependent on others to create a fairy-tale destiny for my life. Expecting the world to provide limited resources to fulfill my destiny, through selection is experiencing a *fairy-tale destiny.* Take for instance, "The American Idol Show." Many gifted people are falling for this intense temptation because they don't really know the true advantage of using the gift for God's glory. They go after fulfilling their destinies the wrong way by expecting the world to lead them to it. Consequently, they drift away from God, who gives access to all good things.

The *destiny* of God's children is already planned by Him. But we will never know unless we follow the map in God's Words to us (The Bible) that leads us to the calling of God. **"For I know the plans I have for you,' declares the Lord, 'plans to prosper you and not to harm you, plans to give you hope and a future" (Jer. 29:11).** Some Christians tend to be pulled away by temptation and misuse their gifts. I have had to say this because many of them started to develop their singing gift in the Church but later deviated from singing gospel to singing secular songs. I have heard some of them justifying yielding to temptation by blaming the church saying, "The church does not support them; so, they had to go outside the church to get it." We could always find many reasons to justify our willingness to fall into temptation. Just know that these excuses will never serve as righteous. Neither will they make God justify our shortcomings.

Temptation is a part of everyone's life. Even Jesus Christ faced temptation. He overcame Satan at his own game using the Word of God just to show us that there is a way of dealing with temptation. We know for sure that temptation is the work of the devil. The Bible makes it clear that: **"Let no man say when he is tempted, I am tempted of God: for God cannot be tempted with evil, neither tempteth he any man" But every man is tempted, when he is drawn away of his own lust, and enticed. (James 1:13-14).** Yielding to temptation burdens us and impedes our reaching our destiny. So, there are no spiritual advantages in surrendering to temptation.

I can testify to the magnet of temptation in the world. There is no place where the temptation of fame more generally displays itself than television. I know the feeling and the intensity of its magnetic attraction. I used to spend so much time in front of the TV screen as I sought to fulfill my destiny. Exposing my mind to this type of environment daily had built up in me some type of fantasy about the world of fame. I could have watched anything else on TV, but I was always tricked by the beautiful appearances of fame.

Addiction to fame is just as bad as any other addiction. Its horrible result would inevitably lead to sin followed by disaster and even destruction. Let me shed some light on this. Fame itself is not an ill but pleasing God must be the primary goal in its productions. The unique fame of Jesus was about "His Father's business" because Jesus' works exposed light everywhere he went. **"And immediately His fame spread throughout all the region around about Galilee" (Marc 1:28).** As Jesus perused His assignment, the Holy Spirit revealed His power throughout the world. He did not need television to become famous. This is the example that we need to follow.

The Holy Spirit is the blinking red light that alerts the door of my eyes and my ears. Ignoring the Holy Spirit was not in my favor. This will only cause a deeper lapse in my condition. ***"Then when the lust hath conceived, it is finished, bringeth forth death" (James 1:15).*** When I understood the influence of vague fame, I was determined to combat these forces. I was urged to take measures by the conviction of God's Word as my refuge. Through fasting and prayer, the LORD graciously delivered me from this entanglement. Presently, I no longer focus on what makes sense, but on the real. God's purpose for my gifts is real. It is with immense joy that I appreciate my letting go of the desire for shadowy fame. Jesus is the star of my life and always will be. Now, I consider myself as content, satisfied, and blessed because my mind is focusing on God's purpose. I know where I have been, and I will continue to use my testimonies as a frame of reference for others who are struggling with that sort of temptation I was.

Visualising ourselves outside God's purpose is yielding to temptation. And when we yield to temptation, we give priority to what the Bible calls *"lustful sin,"* which is the product of the work of the flesh. Some people think that lust is based only on sexual immorality. Let me tell you, the lust list has far more items than that. *Lust is anything that one craves for*. Fame just happens to be one on that list. Take notice that the temptation of making a name for us will be a birth sin. If we abort temptation, the result is sinless. Satan's strategies to keep us bound will have no effect on God's glorious promise to us for: ***"He will make our names to be remembered in all generations..." (Psalm 45:17).***

For the new generation who are struggling with craving for worldly fame like I was, God wants you to know that you no longer must create a worldly profile to present your gift. Your profile is in Jesus Christ. What the world offers is temporary. To be attached to the things of the world is warfare against one's soul. God has much and, bigger plan for your life than that of the world; and nothing less. ***"Dearly beloved, I beseech you as strangers and pilgrims, abstain from fleshly lusts, which war against the soul" I Pet. 2:11).*** It is worthless to allow temptation to dissuade you from your conviction and allow man's glory to take control of your hearts. For the Word of God says, "let no man ***glory in men..." (I Cor. 3:21).***

How do we prevent ourselves from yielding to lustful temptations? The best prevention from my personal experience is to put a limitation to this temptation *by making a firm decision to surrender to God.* We cannot continuously take the risk of exposing our minds, ears, and eyes to the system of the world, and expect to have a positive outcome. The next step is to *transfer our minds to Godly fame by making Jesus the bright star of our lives.* This will secure our blessings in the use of the gift. We should never try to convince ourselves that our corrupted desire will bring forth good fruit. ***"For a good tree bringeth not corrupt fruit; neither doth a corrupt tree brings forth good fruit" (Luke 6:43).*** What your soul desires will determine the fruit you produce in your ministry. Be mindful that temptation, pleasure, profit, and fame are all temporary, but the consequence is a long-term agony.

To honor God in my teaching, I also had to make a choice. My choice caused me to become intolerant of lustful desires. I find myself continuously sitting in the classroom being taught by my great professor, "The Holy Spirit." I was convinced that succumbing to the world's pressure and swerving from my focus on God's work, was not acceptable to Him. I did not impress God, but my obedience in shifting my mind to Him did. For my work to be acceptable to God, I needed to open my heart, repent and receive God's forgiveness. After my graduation from the class of repentance, my study took a higher state. This was done gradually. I went back to study the book of knowledge and wisdom "The Bible," and approached it with a different attitude. Again, I graduated from the class of ignorance and received my diploma for stewardship from God. He empowers and qualifies me with multiple gifts as channels to please Him and thus spread the gospel of Jesus Christ. You too, my friends, have the same privilege to attend the college of Jesus Christ. I encourage you to register today while you still have a chance. There are no preparation tests, no registration fees, and Jesus already covered your tuitions entirely. Therefore, you are the only one who can stop yourself from moving forward. It all depends on who is the directing of your decision.

The Word of God is a loaded weapon; all you must do is to learn how to pull the trigger against your enemies. The best result in learning how to pull the trigger is to have the Holy Spirit as your mentor. This weapon is designed to detect your enemies from every direction of Satan's attacks. It requires serious training to attack your enemies with precision. Your enemies are the devils in your life.

What devils do you ask? Your devils are the obstacles that you are attached to; those that hinder your gift or your ministry. Your enemies are too personal for me to address. However, I am sure some of them may show up in this teaching. If the Holy Spirit points them out to you, be courageous and make the right decision to follow-up with your responsibility.

Carry On the Responsibility

Being called by God to become a bondservant, I was also made aware of my responsibilities. My mind is made up to make my boast about Him. As I make myself available to work for the King, my priority is to achieve whatsoever He desires as a diligent servant. None of us could ever deserve eternal life from God by doing good deeds. The word of God teaches us in the *second chapter of James* that faith without work is dead. It is by faith that I am approaching this teaching with confidence to reach many. God's grace is the ultimate *gift* that brought about a spiritual change in me. That change compels me to carry the torch of my responsibility and pass it to another.

I take seriously my responsibility to carry out the "great commission." The goal is for me to take this teaching to a world-wide dimension as Jesus did. He was obedient to carrying out the work of the Father. Christ's work was to *teach, preach, and heal,* and there is no greater work than that. Therefore, I have strong reasons to conduct this teaching in the fulfillment of these aspects: ***"And confident that thou thyself art a guide to the blind, a light of them which are in darkness, an instructor of the foolish, a teacher of babes..." (Rom. 2:19, 20).*** This scripture helps me to examine God's purpose for my life, enter a deeper relationship with Him and activates my passion to touch the world using my gifts without limitation. I am ready to explore the principles that completed the "Great Commission" in this teaching. As I learn more about the principles, I desire to share them for the improvement of God's gifts to us.

Some of us possess the gifts of writing, singing and composing music, but do not really know how to use them effectively. Looking into the principles that are attached to the gift (s) I come to realize that for us to use our gifts effectively, we must be exposed to some type of teaching. I cannot delay my responsibility concerning teaching about such an important subject, because reluctance is a sign of being irresponsible, rebellious, and unreliable toward my heavenly Father. I am relying in Jesus' strength to confess this teaching before men. ***"...Whosoever shall confess me before men, him shall the Son of man also confess before the angels of God" (Luke 12:8).*** This teaching will also include several stages that pertain to the use of the given gift (s). However, I do believe that in the process, some people might feel offended before becoming convicted. We must admit that sometimes, these feelings come from an unwillingness to let go of the things we perceive as our truths. These feelings are to be subjective by the renewing of the mind through the receiving of God's words, our spiritual medicine. God truly understands how we feel, that is more the reason for Him to point out these felling so we can have the opportunity to train our minds away from them. It is true that sometimes, the medicine we use could irritate the wound before healing it. For this reason, I am stable in my hope for a positive result in the minds of my readers.

The complexities in performing my responsibility toward my readers are that this teaching should not be perceived as being punitive, reproachful, and provoking resentment. Conversely, the condition is to provide information that would build stability in faith, restore higher values in ministering and to bring order in the use of the given gift. Let me support this statement with a short story about how irritation could turn to a positive result. I had an accident where a glass jar broke in my hand and caused a serious injury in my left thumb. Being that the skin was totally removed, I could not stop the bleeding on my own. So, the opened wound was still bleeding until the next day. My husband, who was concerned about the bleeding, decided to take me to the emergency room at Metropolitan Hospital in New York City, where I worked.

The doctor prescribed some pain relief pills and put me off duty for a couple of days to alleviate the pain and stop the bleeding. After eight days of nursing and dressing the wound, I noticed no improvement in the healing process. I could no longer tolerate the slow process of healing, so I decided to do something about it. The first thing that crossed my mind was some ancient home remedy that my late Father normally used when I was wounded during my childhood. The terrifying experience about this remedy was that this it would irritate the wound. In this case, I had two choices. The first one was to take the risk of continuing to use what was prescribed to me by the doctor and slowly deal with the consequence of an infected wound. And the second one was to bypass fear and take a chance with the home remedy. Since the doctor's prescription was for pain relief only, there was no reason for me not to try something else for the healing.

I recalled the positive results of my experience and decided to face the irritation and tried the home remedy. I went home that night and added some sea salt to fully boiled water. While the water was still steaming, I dipped my thumb in it quickly several times. Let me tell you, it may sound like a crazy idea, but it worked. The salted hot water did irritate the wound and increased the excruciating pain for a short time. But with no exaggeration, the healing process went from level two to four immediately. I woke up the next day with the wound already shrunk, and within two weeks my thumb restored a new layer set of skin and healing was the result. That is my reason for saying that sometimes the pain may get worse before the wound gets healed.

When I thought about the nature of this teaching, it was difficult for me to express it in a way that it would not annoy people. Tough love could also be annoying. Also, using the home remedy of words of knowledge to bring about the truth for the given gift could pass as tough love. God does use toughness to correct us when it is necessary. Besides that, we do know what God says about chastising whom He loves. ***"Now no chastening seemeth to be joyous, but grievous: nevertheless, afterward it yieldeth the peaceable fruit of righteousness unto them which are exercised thereby" (Heb. 12:11).*** But, because I understood about what the consequence would be by not doing so, I had to make a wise decision to follow God's ancient remedy (the Bible). Though the word of God could be tough on the conscience, most importantly it will also quickly heal and restore. I had to comply with the ordinance of God, knowing that the misuse of the gift is not a dead-lock situation. I was not willing to take a risk of being indirect about my responsibility to reveal the truth about such important topics.

I am responsible to disclose the elements that injured my ministry from my experience and make useful what I had learned to those who sought knowledge. I no longer need to fear people's perceptions. There is no reason for me to feel discomfort about my obedience in handling my responsibilities or disguise any information because I am authorized by the Lord to do so. As God safeguarded me, I am comfortable in facing any objections or criticisms, if I fulfill this mission in the accomplishment of His destiny, which is to stop the spiritual bleeding in the use of the given gift and allow spiritual healing to take place.

The Master requires *that* **"Him that is taught in the word communicate unto him that teacheth in all good things" (Gal. 6:6).** I am fortunately blessed to have been given the opportunity to teach. Teaching, singing, and composing gospel songs are some of the passionate ways that I use to express my love for God. As I draw near to His goal in my service, I can see the glory of His presence in my work. My ministry is established by God, and it is in His will for me to use it triumphantly. **"Now thanks be unto God, which always causeth us to triumph in Christ, and maketh manifest the savor of His knowledge by us in every place" (II Cor. 2:14).**

To identify our responsibility for the given gifts, we must first acknowledge where we stand with this subject. There is no other way that we could understand our responsibility without acknowledging that we are gifted. One of my responsibilities is to teach people that those gifts are from God with purposes. Through self-awareness, I saw that it was wise to first present you with my personal responsibilities towards God for my given gifts. I would have a hard time explaining to you about my personal responsibility if I did not acknowledge that I was gifted in certain ministerial areas. Recognizing and understanding the purpose of my gifts makes it easier for me to function in them effectively and teach about them with accuracy.

Why is it necessary to apply my responsibility in teaching people about the given gift?

I believe that teaching is the solution under the deviation of the intent of the given gift (s). Everyone has been given a different and variety of gifts by God. It does not matter whether that you are Christians, spiritual or religious. In addition, the process of using the gift adequately has nothing to do with nationality, personality, or degree. But, operating in the gift in accordance with God's intent is important. One must know God and not about Him; because knowing God will help us discover His principles and operate in them accordingly. It is also authentic that any person who has been given a gift needs an adherent to inform them of their responsibility. If I should discuss the general view of gifts, my subject will be too broad. To be consistent about why it is necessary to know about the given gifts, I am only going to emphasize some of the spiritual gifts and ministerial positions such as:

Singing, Song Writing, Teaching, Producing, and Performing music, etc.

As you become familiar with the purpose of the given gifts, my aim is that you too will determine to perform your responsibility as ministers of the gospel. I can only hope that taking this step in fulfilling my responsibilities will be a win-win result for both me and my readers. The win-win result is for me to see that those who receive this teaching would take it as a spiritual medicine to rebuild a healthy relationship with Christ, heal their wounded hearts, establish a strong foundation in using their gifts, straighten their crooked paths and restore their broken ministries. Now, let the truth about what God wants us to know concerning the *principles and standards* for the fulfillment of the given gifts be revealed.

Talent vs. Gift

Following the traditional perception about *talent*, I had believed my ability to sing was just a hobby. In fact, I had always listed singing in my resumes as one of my hobbies. As an uneducated Christian, I was handicapped by low self-esteem, insecurity, and spiritual defeat. Using singing for so many years to elevate my low self-esteem, I faced many moments of humiliation and deception.

My voice was misused by many as a talent to compete with others. It did not matter to people whether I was saved if they satisfied their desires. I traveled long distances to sing here and there just for the sake of fame. Most people didn't even care to help me with carfare. Some had recorded my voice and sold my work without being compensated. I was not sure about their *motives,* but I allowed them to use me to fulfill their dreams. In addition, the inability to produce my own recordings created plenty of room for other artists to make a mockery of me. Someone called me "wasted money." These experiences are only a few of the dishonorable stages of my life's stories before my singing became a ministry. Today, I sincerely appreciate those memories because God has reversed the negatives into positives. In fact, thinking about these episodes boosts my appetite to share my progress in the Lord.

Talent and gift are two very common words that seem to mean the same thing, but the difference between the two was never explicit to me. Both talent and gift may be somewhat different from what we know. Not knowing the difference between those two could create conflict in our ministry. It is important to know how to differentiate them for these reasons. This will help changing our perspective about the use of our gifts and learn to appreciate and utilize our gifts in God's intents.

The New International Webster Pocket Dictionary refers to both talent and gift as "natural ability or something freely given." Further research outside the Biblical aspect stated that a talent is an inherited ability to perform under proper training to achieve something. If what we call talent or gift must be developed through training, could it mean that it is a genetic element? In Jesus' own prophecy of the word talent, was defined as "good." The root of the word talent is from the Greek "*talanton*" It could be anything valuable that could be traded, such as money, gold, or silver used in exchange for a debt.

Another definition of talent according to Christ's illustration is that it is given as a capital good, and this good is to be invested for profit. The objective of the Master for distributing the talent is for that person to work with it and increase it. Otherwise, it can be taken away and released to another who is willing to use it wisely. Therefore, if talent in this sense could be taken away, could it mean that it is a condition attached to it? After analyzing the difference between the Biblical terms of talent, and others, I realized that the traditional definition for the word doesn't fit in the category of gift. To avoid confusion, I will not elaborate on talent as "good;" rather let us talk a little about the inherited talent, or a person's inborn ability to do something well.

Sometimes, an inherited talent could be misrepresented, depending on the understanding of how it was taught to the one who possesses it. Another- words, if we should use the inherited talent, we will see that this kind of talent is often taken for granted. When it is taken for granted, it is misused as an interest to motivate materialistic visions, such as wealth, fame, and self-elevation. For example, talent is often displayed to compete. We are all familiar with the so-called "Talent Show." And some of us will probably relate to what I am about to share. I recalled how anxious I was when I was asked to take part in a talent show to compete with other talented singers. I felt fortunate to have been one of the chosen. Honestly, I did not see anything wrong with participating in a talent show because I understood it to have been something profitable, but I did not really know to what point. I just wanted to be one of the special chosen ones because I did not comprehend the purpose for my gift. My mind was set on four aspects: (1) to show off my voice (2), to prove to myself that I can win the contest (3), to become famous, and (4) to seek people's approval.

In addition, before I understood the difference between talent and gift, it was a normal thing to feel prideful about it. When I performed in concerts with other artists, my heart was not devoted to pleasing God, edifying the church, or preaching the gospel because I was never taught about it. I did not understand that the gift that God trusted me with was not for my own interest, but for His interest and the interest of others. My performances were about seeking vanity and glory to please myself rather than God. I failed to know that this gift was not to fulfill my own destiny, but it is God's resources to me for the ministry of soul winning. Now I praise God because He is faithful. He opened my eyes to see and know the differences. Knowing the differences gives me a new desire and a passion to please Him. And as I learn to please Him, I enter a fellowship with Him who gives me the gift. ***"God is faithful, by whom ye were called unto the fellowship of His son, Jesus Christ our Lord" (I Cor. 1:9).*** God desires that all would be in fellowship with Him. The only intervening variable that could stop you is change of mind. If you should let go of your own desires to promote yourself, all false presentations of the gift will be banished.

About the Gift:

On the other hand, the truth of the interpretation of the term gift has been changed from its original significance. We perceive a gift as something given or received such as a present for a special occasion. By changing the term to express our own ideas, we fail to understand its true value in our lives, thereby creating a conflict between what we know and its original term. The good thing is that our perception about the gift is not perpetual because we could still learn more about it.

The Greek word for gift is "*Charisma*" which also means **Grace.** If the term gift has been believed to be grace, then *how do we perceive grace?* According to humanity's view, the adjectives that describe the term grace are as follows: "elegance, polish, refinement, charm, goodwill, devotion, love, and beauty etc." But the term gift itself stands for: "mercy, pardon, blessing, giving thanks and to beautify, etc."

What is grace from the Biblical point of view? If we should focus on the Biblical definition of grace, we can clearly see that God's point of view of grace is different from our view. In God's point of view, grace is the **source** of: *"salvation, calling of God, faith, justification, forgiveness, and consolation." Grace* is the mercy of God to forgive our undeserved sins. When we get so caught up in trying to fulfill our own destiny, we are basically operating under *"the works of the flesh"* (sin). If we fail to operate under the authority of His spirit, most likely, we will fall short of His glorious promises. In addition, the description of grace stands for: *"All-abundant, all-sufficient, glorious, great and rich."* Therefore, we would say the term grace is not based on the terminology of talent. However, we are going to focus on the spiritual aspect of the gift.

What is the Biblical term of gift? Gift in the Biblical terms is *unmerited favor*. Though one could ask another for a favor, this type of favor is not selected or requested by anyone. So, let's concentrate on the term gift. A gift is *anything* assigned by God to anyone He pleases. We learn that **"Every good gift and every perfect gift is from above, and cometh down from the Father of lights, with whom is no variableness, neither shadow of turning" (James 1:17).** If it is assigned by God, then we cannot help but to agree with His term. The adjectives that describe this *gift or grace* are much deeper than that of man.

In contrast to inherent talent, **a spiritual gift** is given by God to one as a unique and natural ability or quality. It is unique because *spiritual gifts are assigned* to those who are called and ordained by God for service, and to anyone who will listen.

Sometimes, we might not even be aware that we possessed certain spiritual gifts. If we are not aware of them, we will not be able to use them or understand their complete purpose. That is when we need some type of spiritual guidance. Spiritual guidance starts with the introduction to the gospel of Jesus Christ. When I was a little girl, my dad was the first one to introduce me to the Protestant Church in St. Marc, Haiti. I was only six years old when I stood on the pulpit to sing. Although I did not fully understand why, the name of Jesus was often mentioned in the songs that I sang. I was not aware that my singing gift was related to the plan of redemption. Though I was predestined to use my gifts to serve God, it had to be revealed to me. So, allow me to take you to the path of your spiritual enlightenment in this teaching.

You see, no one really must earn a gift. To earn a salary, you must work hard for it. If it is given to you without having to work for it, then that's the value of *grace given gift.* Often, people would ask me; "Do you take voice lessons?" My answer was always no. However, I had to polish the gift to preserve its condition. No one could ever add the gift of singing into an individual's life. The person could only train you how to utilize it efficiently, only if you already possess it. Otherwise, everyone who desires to know how to sing will just go and purchase it. Taking voice lessons for improvement is costly. I could imagine how expensive it would be to purchase the actual quality of a voice. Therefore, only those who could afford it would have it. That is why it is essential for those of you who are gifted with any kind of gift to show gratitude to God who is the giver of all gifts.

This **core** concept describes the identity of the one who possesses the given gift. It lays in the designated grace of God, who gives us the knowledge to use the gift as obedient servants. How we use the knowledge will demonstrate our strengths and the quality of our gifts in how we perform them in the standard of our core values. While maintaining our *core values* in return, our attitude will lead and prepare others to appreciate their gifts and use them according to grace. Here are four components that we could consider as core values:

✓ What message do we want to convey when using the gift?

✓ Do our performances relay the message that God gives us to deliver?

✓ Do our performances display spiritual energy, and do they recognize Jesus in us?

✓ How serious do we think about using the gift in the building of God's kingdom?

I will elaborate more about the foundation of these core values later in Session Four when I teach the motive outside God's intent.

SESSION TWO

In this session you will learn about:

- *God's destiny for our lives, and how we should avoid temporary vain glory.*
- *The processing of confession in our lives, and how to keep it active.*
- *How our decisions could generate good and bad ideas.*
- *The road and phases to repentance that we should know.*
- *What exactly is man (the self)?*
- *The importance of active confession.*
- *The process of deliverance.*
- *The prerequisite to the ordinance of the principles as set by God.*

Crossing over the Bridge of a Fairy-Tale Destiny

What *is a temporary vain glory?* Trying to obtain one's desire by reaching out to what is available, even if it doesn't last, is my definition of a temporary vain glory. When temporary vain glory expands itself for a long period of time, it becomes a **fairy-tale destiny.** One of the most attractive bridges where Gospel Artists get stuck is at the bridge of a fairy-tale destiny. In other words, this pertains to Christians who consider the pleasure of the world as the way to reach their destiny. They become so obsessed with the craving of becoming popular with the world, which being pulled by the magnetic flame of becoming a celebrity. They forget about the promises of God and begin to depend on the determination of the world to fulfill their dreams.

Why settle for a temporary vain glory? It is a disgrace to see how people who are familiar with the gospel are so hooked up to a temporary vain glory. The result of its effect is the accumulation of stress and dismay. They force their way through the narrow space of disloyalty and get crushed by the crowded world of fame. To obtain temporary vain glory, they are vulnerable to being *deceived* by the adversary. He knows their weaknesses and what they crave for. So, he uses their own weaknesses as smoke to suffocate them at the narrow door of fame. Once they are pulled by the magnetic realm of temporary vain glory, they are now pushed over by the heat of anxiety waiting for the world to vote for them to reach their fairy-tale destiny. Besides that, they are trapped in following the paths of the few who survived the smoke and became rich, and gain nothing after; to the point of being victimized by mental illness even to the point of committing suicide. Some of them are reading the word of God, praying, and fasting for success, yet have no intention of keeping God's ways. God's ways for success are already fixed in His word. There is no other way around it. **"Now therefore hearken unto me, O ye children: for blessed are they that keep my ways" (Prov. 8: 32).** They are allowing this apparent success to take over their hearts. They think accepting worldly offers is the answer to their prayers. They are deceived by Satan because God cannot do anything else but to honor His word. They are also afraid of being disliked by the world. So instead of taking God's promises at full value, they rather settle for a temporary vain glory. **"Marvel not, my brethren, if the world hate you" (I John 3:13).** Apparent success will bring painful memories. We do not have to settle for stressful life. We ought to be encouraged by these words: **"Be not thou afraid when one is made rich, when the glory of his house is increased; for when he dieth, he shall carry nothing away: his glory shall not descend after him" (Ps. 49:16-17).**

What is a fairy-tale destiny? People who are passionate about reaching their desires will do anything, even if it means doing the wrong thing. *The imagination of possessing a royal position is my idea of a fairy-tale destiny.* The Rev. Dr. Alfonso Wyatt described it as "Blind Ambition. This person's intent is to rise to the top no matter what or who gets in the way. If people get hurt, the feeling is they "should build a bridge and get over it" (*Leadership by Number* p. 98). The more people rely on the world's capacity to elevate them, the deeper they fall into failure. It is very hard for them to see the reality of their choices. They are blinded by the world's point of view and trapped over the bridge of a fairy-tale destiny for a very long time. Every step they take is a slow-motion movement in getting them closer to disappointment rather than crossing over the bridge of their fairy-tale destiny.

The longer people remain in this state of blindness, the more deprived they are from reaching their fairy-tale destiny. They now must compete not only against each other, but also against the world who is watching in the mirror of the TV screens. They are hoping that the opinion of the world will "pump up the volume" of their dreams. But the fact of the matter is only a few will penetrate through the narrow door of fairy-tale destiny. Consequently, the result is the disappointment of not being selected. Once the world which they counted on failed them, they have a psychological break; they blame themselves, and become their own enemy. Now, the bridge that seemed to have been the true way of crossing over to meet their destiny becomes the darkest pathway that they are stuck in.

I found myself falling for the fairy-tale destiny numerous times; especially when I watched "The Grammy Awards." I was constantly exposed to my fairy-tale destiny because I desired to be counted among those celebrities. I even cried when they cried. My emotional state was heightened by the desire for fame. In addition, their attractive appearance penetrated my heart through the door of my eyes. I was caught up between the contestants' emotional state and my own. The more I watched, the more attached I was to my fairy-tale destiny. This attachment did nothing else but increase dissatisfaction in my heart. There were no signs of stability in my life.

By not giving much *attention* to God's word, I could not discover His plan for my destiny. I got caught up in the intensity of the moment, built up a fantasy in the projected mirror of the world, decided to visualize myself outside the will of God and then had the audacity to blame Him for my failures. Keeping God out of the equation was a foolish thing to do. ***"The foolishness of man perverteth his way: and his heart fretteth against the LORD" (Prov. 19:3).*** Because I *denied* my attachment to the fairy-tale destiny, it was difficult for me to identify and be content with who I was at the time. I was just an immature, rebellious and irresponsible Christian. Nonetheless, I came to understand that there is a *limitation* to temptation for Christians. This limitation is the application of resistance through the knowledge of God's precepts. When I began to apply God's precepts to my daily living, I was transferred from the bridge of a fairy-tale destiny to a higher place in faith. I left this world behind me, and it is no longer about fairy-tale destiny, but rather about whom God had designated me to be. I listened to Paul's saying to me: ***"If ye then be risen with Christ, seek those things which are above..." (Col. 3:1).***

I met a young lady who happened to have had the fairy-tale destiny experience. I was at a Laundromat, and she happened to be discussing the world of fame with another young lady who worked there. It so happened that I was close enough to take part in the conversation. In the conversation, she mentioned how God had drastically rescued her from the mentality of the fairy-tale destiny. She did not use this term, but I quickly identified her experience with that term basically from what she was saying. She said that she used to be very hungry for fame, but she did not feel this way anymore. I asked her what had happened to cause this change. She said that God saved her drastically from a near-death experience. She believed that a second chance was given to teach her a lesson and for a purpose.

In addition, she mentioned how God had rescued her from being tied up in a contract that would cause her to deviate from her Christian faith. Furthermore, she said in the artistic world, many young girls often got trapped in a contract which they did not expect, because they so badly wanted to make it there. They didn't realize what they had signed, until they found themselves too deep in performing inappropriate acts. The greatest thing about her testimony was that after being delivered from the fairy-tale destiny, she came to realize that her voice was given to her for a special purpose. She sings gospel opera. Although some people found her style to be boring, she is not concerned about what they think because she is very content with whom she is in Christ Jesus. And I said AMEN to that.

As I continued to think about the subject on my way home that night, I came to understand that in the world of fairy-tale experience it is not for those who want to become famous. In the secular music industry, those with high aspirations; "hope to make it big", often sign contracts that they don't understand, that benefit the promoters. In that process, the artists often forfeit their rights, dignities, and even, often, end-up holding the short end of the stick financially. God wants a Christian minister to understand that he or she is not anyone's product to be promoted on sale. That is why Christian artists must dissociate from the fairy-tale destiny trap before it gets too far. So, in order to dissociate with this idea, the Christian must cross over the bridge of the fairy-tale destiny. Let me add that some of us are still trapped in this bridge for a long period before we finally realize that it is a dead-end trap. It is hard to cross over that bridge without supernatural help. For this reason, we need to reach out to God, who will help us cross over.

Now, how do Christians cross over the bridge of a fairy-tale destiny?

The fairy-tale destiny is a spiritual illness; that illness is called *lust for fame.* To be healed completely from it, there are important phases to be taken into serious consideration:

- *Phase One:* We must *acknowledge* that we have a spiritual illness called *lust;* and it is curable in the clinic of God through the blood of Jesus. **"If we say that we have not sinned, we make Him a liar, and His word is not in us" (I John 1:10).**

- *Phase Two:* We need to *make an effort to give special attention* to the voice of the Holy Spirit and confess our sin. Further in this teaching, you will learn more about the importance of confession.

Trust the Holy Spirit. He will not hide the truth from you because He is there to show the truth to all God's children and not to judge them. The Holy Spirit will refer us to Dr. JESUS, the great physician for all types of illnesses. His prescribed word to us should be taken daily and not as needed. Doctor Jesus Christ will be prescribed to us the truth each time we see Him because He knows exactly what we need. ***"Even the Spirit of truth; whom the world cannot receive because it seeth him not, neither knoweth Him..." John 14:17).***

• *Phase Three:* We must *follow the direction* in obedience. Be open-minded and honest, and submissive when we pray, and follow God's instructions. The daily dose of the spiritual pills (God's word) should be carefully taken. ***"And whatsoever we ask, we receive of Him, because we keep His commandments, and do those things that are pleasing in His sight" (I John 3:22).***

• *Phase Four: We must have a prayerful life built on faith.* We also need to have a prayer partner, someone who will not judge us. We should not hesitate to disclose our weakness and ask others to pray for us. Keeping it secret will only delay the process of our healing. The result of prayer is not for treatment for the lustful disease. Treatment is for temporary relief only, so we should expect total healing and forgiveness for our sins. This healing is not instantaneous. We just must remain patient and wait in faith. ***"And the prayer of faith shall save the sick, and the Lord shall raise him up; and if he has committed sins, they shall be forgiven him" (James 5:15).***

• *Phase Five: We must make a sincere decision to quit the routine.* If we still have the symptoms of continuing to expose ourselves to temptation, I believe it would be beneficial to try to avoid exposing the eyes, ear, and mind to the environment. We should put a STOP sign next to the TV screen to remind us. Moving forward is the right thing to do. Looking back is not part of the requirements for those who want to cross over the fairy-tale destiny. ***"But whoso looketh into the perfect law of liberty and continueth therein, he being not a forgetful hearer, but a doer of the work, this one will be blessed in his deed" (James 1:25).***

•   *Phase Six: We should always* have a song of praise in our mouths for our healing. Our songs show that we have a grateful heart toward God. Our singing will help us fill the empty space for the addiction. Not only that, but it also helps with the dismissal of any sad thoughts in our minds. When our praises reach the ears of God, it changes our states of mind. It is guaranteed that our praise will boost our joy. ***"Serve the Lord with gladness: come before His presence with singing" (Ps. 100:2).*** My advice to those who have crossed over the fairy-tale destiny bridge is to stay focus on God's promises and never look back again to the artificial offers of the world.

Is Confession Necessary In Ministers' Lives?

Crossing over the bridge of a fairy-tale destiny is not the end of the struggle. The minister must hold on to determination; and confession plays a major role in that. Confession controls the fairy-tale thoughts, closes the door to unresolved sin and allows the Minister to contemplate the goodness of God's mercy. Not only that, others like Susan J. White *in Foundations of Christian Worship* adopted that 'Confession is good for the soul, the old saying goes.' "Once we have acknowledged who God is and what God has done, it is inevitable that we will turn our thoughts to the distance that exists between the goodness of God and our own worthiness to receive it" (p. 34).

Some of us assumed that confessing is uncanny. Others think of it as something tremendous. Nevertheless, it does not matter how we see it, just know that no ministers should be unrestrained when it comes to confession, because it is the act of taking upon oneself a conscious decision. A true confession is not based on secret thoughts, but it is the manifestation of *self-abasement* to obtain mercy from God, and to bring about a full elimination of an undesirable lifestyle. ***"He that covereth his sins shall not prosper but whoso confesseth and forsaketh his heart shall fall into mischief"*** **(Prov. 28:13).** To avoid unnecessary failure in our ministries, we need to learn more about what they are and why it is necessary to confess our sins.

With all that we know about the self, there are still greater things to discover about who we are. Some of us think of the self as a human being who possesses a heart and many organs that contain emotions, etc. Since spiritual discernment, knowing parts of the body is not sufficient. It is in God's will for us to know about who we are.

What exactly is man (the self)?

Man is a *spirit* created in God's image; and that spirit is connected to a *soul*. Both abide in the body. Knowing this much introduces us to our next question.

What is a spirit? The Ludwig Wittgenstein Dictionary describes the *spirit* as a "mysterious part of you which is not the body, the soul, or an eager state of mind." Now let's look at the definition of spirit according to the Bible. ***"For what man knoweth the things of a man, save the spirit of man which is in him? Even so the things of God knoweth no man, but the spirit of God"*** **(I Cor. 2:11).** That means, without the spirit we will never identify what is in our mind and the mind of God. Also, when God communicates to man, He is addressing man's spirit.

The Spirit of God was first introduced to us in the story of creation in Genesis chapter one, verse one. It was the Spirit that moved upon the face of the waters to bring every element into existence. When we read further, we discover that we were created in the likeness of God (*Spirit*). God then created man with dust of the ground (*man's exterior body*,) and breathed into him the breath of life, (*man's spirit*) and man become a living soul (*man's inner life*). Though the spirit uses the body to manifest itself, it is not as important as the spirit: ***"For as the body without the spirit is dead…"*** **(James 2:26).**

In addition, the body is very limited because it could quickly age and gives up on us at any moment. As God's Spirit is *everlasting*, so is the spirit of man. But the *soul,* who is the property of God, is subject to *die* because of sin *(Ez. 18:4).* But there is good news to those who incline their ears, and come to God, their soul shall live *(Isa. 55:3).*

Being created in the likeness of God might be an uncertain idea because it doesn't make sense to some of us since God does not possess a physical body like we do. At least we could identify with God the Father, the Son and the Sprit which defines the "Trinity" right? In this case, if the Bible declares that we are created in the likeness of God, then it is what it is. We should not be persuaded any other way. Trinity should be the alarm that notifies us of who we are. That means no one has the right to decrease any human being as being less than the image of God. Nevertheless, the misunderstanding about who we are is not irreparable. We just must believe God's word entirely.

What does Trinity mean?

Trinity means three in one (The Trion God). If we could agree on that, we could also identify that man's spirit; soul and body also reflect Trinity. Though we possess three parts, we are only *one being.* Not only have we had the Trinity in common with God, but we also possess His characteristics. God is good, loving, merciful, forgiving, kind, patient and jealous. In terms of jealousy, God expressed Himself very well about His legitimate right of worship saying: **"I the LORD thy God am a jealous God...." (Ex. 20:5).** I must say sin causes us to deviate from some of these characteristics. But thank God for His perfect love providing the plan of salvation, through His Son Jesus Christ to reinstate those characteristics in us. This explanation describes the complete nature of the self or man.

What is the soul? The *soul* is our inner being where sin is centered. In addition, the soul enables us to do both: *loving (obedience) and hating (disobedience).* To have *dominion* over sin is to: **"Love the Lord our God with all our hearts, and with all our souls, and**

with all our strengths, and with all our minds" (Luke 10:27). The soul contains two major components, the *conscience,* and the *will.* Our consciences reflect our *conceptions or ideas*. The nature of ideas is to bring about an opinion, making an impression or reaching a goal: traits that we all relate to. The unseen condition of man's characteristics: desires, decisions, and impulse.

These characiscticss aren't sinful in themselves however, when misguided; these traits may lead into sin. Our ability to hate, love, resent, suffer, obey, and sarve are the products of the soul. All the negative feelings of the heart, the process of thoughts, the decision of the consent of the will and the conduct of the body work together as one unit. As components that make up our soul, one can understand why thought and will must work together as one unit to convict the inmost soul. Once temptation becomes sin, and we are made aware of it, then the soul directs the will, and then sends an affirmative response to the intellectual conscience.

What is the will and what role does it play?

The *will* is God's given gift to us as our ability or freedom to *choose* between right and wrong. It serves as an *executive* that coordinates all the functions of the soul. It processes the messages that we think, feel, hear, or see, and sends it out to the conscience. Conscience is like a written law in our hearts. **"Which shew the work of the law written in their hearts, their conscience also bearing witness..." (Rom. 2:15).**

The *conscience* receives the message then generates a decision. This decision could be choosing to *yield or reject* a confession. Being able to think and make decisions is a *privilege* from God. But if we don't use them wisely, God will be displeased with our decisions because our decisions may lead to destructive. We can see how the will and the conscience communicate back and forth with each other to generate a decision. Though deciding may seem as quick as the twinkling of an eye, there are many incoming and outgoing messages involved. That is why when we are thinking about something we have done we can say that the will and the conscience are communicating.

Our decision is made of thoughts, the reasoning of the mind. Our thoughts could generate good and evil imaginations, or (good and bad news). The bad news is that there will be a day **"When God shall judge the secrets of men by Jesus Christ according to His gospel" (Rom. 2:16).** The *good news* is that God already provided a cure for those who confess their sins. The evil imaginations could be brought to obedience. *"Casting down imaginations, and every high thing that exalteth itself against the knowledge of God and bringing into captivity every thought to the obedience of Christ" (II Cor. 10:5).* Sometimes, our decisions could shift from bad to worse. When the will wants to take full control, a wall of defense is built in our thoughts against the principles of God. When this happens, the heart is hardened, creating a wider path for sin to grow, and weakening the path toward confession.

How does the process of confession take place?

This is how confession is processed. According to *(Proverbs 20:12). "Hearing ear, and Seeing eye, the LORD hath made even both of them."* Confession takes place when hearing and seeing are seen as gifts from God, who intended for us to use these gifts as blessings and not as curses. Since the soul receives information from what we think, hear, and see, we need to know how to align them with confession. Stay focused! You will soon understand why I give such a detailed account on confession.

We live in a world that contradicts the will of God. As a result, what we think, hear, and see can control our deep desires and actions. But thank God, it doesn't end there, because the power of God's grace is unbeatable greater than our deep desires and actions. Knowing that our spirit becomes knowledgeable of sin and holiness, what is sin and holiness?

Sin (transgression) is the act of breaking the law of God. Conversely, holiness is practicing righteousness. ***"Whosoever committeth sin transgressth also the law: for sin is the transgression of the law" (I John 3:4).*** Though we all inherited Adam's sin, God's love is powerful enough to penetrate our hearts if we confess our sins. ***"If we confess our sins, He is faithful and just to forgive us our sins, and to cleanse us from all unrighteousness" (I John 1:9).*** If we accept this truth, then we will also understand that God, in His perfect plan, has a destiny for His children. ***"He shall choose our inheritance for us..." (Ps. 46:3).***

Experiencing the *glory of God's promise* is to know Him at a deeper level. That experience compels us to remain in His perfect plan. It also arouses in us a deep interest to produce ***"The fruit of the spirit,"*** (righteousness).

What is righteousness?

Righteousness is to live and walk *(wholeheartedly and willingly)* in obedience to God. As Christians, we are mandated to leave the old man behind us and live our newness in Christ Jesus. ***"And ye put on the new man, which after God created righteousness and true holiness" (Eph. 4:24).*** When we deviate from the path of righteousness, the work of the flesh operates in us to do its will. Once the work of the flesh is diagnosed as sin, immediate attention calls for us to repent, confess and never turn back. Without *repentance,* there can be no *confession.*

What is *repentance?*

Repentance is allowing the Holy Spirit to take the wheel of our will in the soul. The soul desires to continue driving us to the road of sin (destruction). For our hearts to *turn* from the road of destruction, we must allow The Holy Spirit to take full control of the wheel. Once the Holy Spirit has control of the wheel, He will drive our conscience straight to the Road of Repentance. Please stay with me, we're almost there.

What is the road to repentance?

The road to repentance is when you allow the remorse or sorrow of your sin to penetrate your consciousness and bring to awareness of your wicked condition, which must be dealt with.

"Repent therefore of this thy wickedness, and pray God, if perhaps the thought of thine heart may be forgiven thee" Acts 8:22). Since repentance represents remorse or sorrow, you also need to know that there are two types of repentance. One is negative *and leads to destruction, and the other is positive and leads to forgiveness.* For instance, we could use the repentance of Judah and that of Peter to compare both the negative and positive repentance. Though Judah's repentance could have led him to ask for forgiveness, he did not exercise his sorrow in a positive way. He felt sorry and shameful for betraying Jesus, but by hanging himself his repentance was handed down (as if by a rope) from Satan to strangle himself to death.

We also know about Peter's repentance for denying Jesus. Was there any difference between the two concerning the betrayal of Christ? No, because both Peter and Judas' sins are equally balance in God's scale. Peter made the right choice of repentance by asking for forgiveness. In fact, Peter's forgiveness increased the anointing of God in his ministry. Until this day, God's power in Peter's ministry is one of the greatest legacies in Christian history because it was through his message that the church increased.

"Then they that gladly received his word were baptized: and the same day there were added unto them about three thousand souls" (Acts 2:41).

The stigma of our sin could be wiped away through the blood of Jesus but, there is one condition: confession. We must be convinced that God is faithful to his promises. The good news is that the cure is found in God's word. ***"If we confess our sins, He is faithful to***

forgive us our sins and to cleanse us from all unrighteousness" ***(I John I: 9).*** When we reach this point, our sins can no longer avoid the voice of conscience which manifests truthful confession through the gate, the mouth.

Next, we fall on our knees and cry out loud to God and expose our sin and ask for His forgiveness. This example is the reality of all the necessary steps that one must complete to reach the state of a *true confession.* When we surrender to the Holy Spirit, He is responsible for sending messages to our spirit. The benefits of surrendering include receiving the word of God, which is made possible by what has been heard through revelation. Sin is revealed because the Holy Spirit searches our inner thoughts. Many ministers never experience deliverance because they are not aware of their condition. Let me say this; until we experience complete deliverance from our strongholds, our ministry will be fragmented by the weight of sin.

What is deliverance?

Deliverance is the state of being rescued or set free from sin that keeps us bound. Being saved is not a magic potion that quickly rids sinful habits immediately. And example: After Jesus called Lazarus... (John1:43-44). This unique event brings us to conclusion that after the spirit comes forth; the soul still needs to be liberated (the unbinding). This is the only way the body (person) will be free to serve. Like Lazarus, God will often use individuals in the journey towards the unbinding of the soul.

What can we learn from that example?

I believe there is a great lesson to learn about a minister's participation and cooperation in the lives of those who are bound. This is not an assumption, but a reality. When our dead spirit is called from the grave of sin, there are *three steps* involved, and we minister, who are called to serve, are required to fulfill them. Being a minister is not simply a title or an appearance, but being called, gifted, and ordained by God to fulfill a purpose. Let's look at some of the requirements of a minister. See more about my personal view as a minister in Session Eight.

First: Hearing the call (The preaching of the gospel) ***"Go therefore and make disciples... "Behold, I stand at the door, and knock: If anyone hears my voice, and opens the door, I will come into him, and will sup with him, and he with Me" (Mark 28:19; Rev. 3:20).***

Second: Answering the call (accepting the invitation by making open confession through words) ***"That if thou shalt confess with thy mouth the Lord Jesus, and shalt believe in thine heart that God hath raised Him from the dead, thou shalt be saved" (Rom. 10:9).***

Third: Come forth (following the instruction of God) ***"Incline your ear and come unto me: hear and your soul shall live..." (Is. 55:3).***

Fourth: Deliver (Liberty to accomplish God's work) ***"Deliver us from evil."*** (Matt. 6:13).

Here is another example. In this case the manifestation of *hearing, answering, and delivering* are present.

In the book of **Acts chapter nine,** Paul, formerly named Saul, was personally called by Jesus Christ. *Act one*: ***"And he fell to the earth, and heard a voice saying to him, "Saul, Saul, why are you persecuting me?" (v. 4).*** After the call, Paul became blind because the glory of Christ's presence was there. *Act two:* He responded to the called and asked: ***"...Who are thou Lord" (v. 5)?*** *Act three:* Thereafter, he was told by Christ to go to Damascus to see a man named Ananias to lay hand on him, so that he may receive his sight back, and prepare him for the work of God's kingdom. ***"And Ananias went his way, and entered into the house; and putting his hands on him"... (v. 17).***

Agree or not, all who are called by God need to be delivered from some types of sinful habit or demonic curse. Each, answering and deliverance, carries a separate function. *Answering* to the call removes our names from the list of hell's candidates. *Deliverance, on the other hand,* places our names in the book of life. Your birth certificate signed by the blood of Jesus puts you in a position to have dominion over sinful habits. After we are called from the grave of sin, God uses those who are blessed with certain gifts to partake in our deliverance. God could use anyone, and in different ways, to deliver His people like he did use Moses; whether through teaching, praying, or the laying of hands. That is part of my mission. I pray that this Biblical teaching convinces your heart, triggers a voluntary response, and delivers you from the active sin that keeps you from serving God in full capacity.

The same privilege that was given to those who witnessed the resurrection of Lazarus, and Ananias who was given the privilege to lay hands on Paul, also applies to those who are called to use their gifts. Now that you know about your privilege, what is your next step? Will you continue to allow the work of the flesh to have a hold on you? Or will you make a healthy U-turn and use your gift to set someone free?

The Prerequisite to the Ordinance of the Principles:

Religion vs. Salvation

The scriptural ordinance was long established by God, who sought to instill His regulations in the hearts of His people. God does not want us to be ignorant and deceived. The meaning was to unfold the principles of spiritual gifts. And if anyone is influenced by this teaching, I testify they will be encouraged to stand firmly against the misuse of the gift. There are 2 prerequisites (reflective questions) needed to guide us on how to use our gifts effectively. Let's look at them together.

Answer to Question One: *THE PREREQUISITE*

Accepting God's blameless invitation to salvation is the number one prerequisite needed to becoming an accepted minister before God for three (3) reasons: (1) it is the only doorway by way we can have access to God's grace; (2) It is for those who by faith received the gift of Salvation and the benefit of His reward; (3) there can never be the gift of the Holy Spirit without (having first) the invitation into God's grace. This first engagement is encouraged by the apostle Paul, ***"That if "Thou shall confess with thy mouth the Lord Jesus, and shalt believe in thy heart that God hath raised Him from the dead, thou shalt be saved" (Rom. 10:9).*** Eliminating salvation will remove the cloud of darkness and transfer us into the light of God's perfect love so that, we might the fullness of his blessings.

Many of us write or sing gospel songs without accepting God's ultimate gift of salvation through Jesus Christ. Trying to operate in the spiritual gifts without receiving first the gift of salvation is a violation of the requirement and a stumbling block for evangelism. Why is that? The answer is simple. The message of the lyrics will be out of order and confusing. Being a song writer does not automatically make one a minister of the gospel of Jesus Christ. Some of them can tell a good story about their mother's salvation in the lyrics, but they are not saved. To bear light, one must be in the light. We ministers are the eyes that people see when looking for direction. Unless we let them see the light of the gospel in us, there is no chance of them knowing the difference between being religious and being saved. In sharing the gospel through our ministry, we take turns teaching people. In return, we expect them to learn and share their knowledge. Therefore, if one never accepts the gift of salvation, it will be impossible to relate to sharing it. Besides that: ***"God shall bring every work into judgment, with every secret thing, whether it be good, or whether it be evil" (Job 12:14).***

How can one deliver what he or she does not have? Myself as an example, although I attended church and sang gospel hymns since I was a child, my life did not reflect Christ until I accepted him in my twenties. My life did not reflect the character of Christ. The problem was my parents were unsaved and religious and I followed their example. I can empathize, how could they have taught me something they didn't themselves didn't know? Christianity was something ambiguous to me.

Though I enjoyed singing, I was very distant from God. I claimed to be a Christian, but my lifestyle as a so-called Gospel Singer was inappropriate because of my lack of knowledge. I needed someone to teach me about the truth so that what I sang could correspond with the guideline of God's principles. I was in the category of those who praise God with my words, but I never really thought about Him. ***"This people draweth nigh unto me with their mouth, and honor me with their lips; but their hearts is far from me, but in vain they do worship me, teaching for doctrines the commandments of God" (Matt. 15:8-9).*** This verse helps me to understand my worship was vain because I did not know that God wanted my worship to mean something to him.

Oh, what an experienced filled lesson. It is good to know that all the treasures of heaven are opened to those who accept the gift of salvation. Once we accept the precious gift of God's salvation, we discover the treasure of His divine grace toward us. At this point, we are assigned to a long-term ministry in the heavenly kingdom. This is what Gregory A. Barker said in Jesus in the *World's Faiths* that "It was true for the first disciples, women and men, by the Sea of Galilee:

Jesus brought the word of Eternal life *(John 6)* into a community that embodied the mystery of the Divine" (p.53).

But, if you are using your gift singing Gospel songs as gigs, and you haven't made Jesus your personal Savior, I advise you to STOP and accept the gift of salvation, at once. By operating outside of this prerequisite, you are making a mockery of God's intent, and that's a dangerous act against the Gospel of Christ. The main idea, in this portion of the teaching, is to encourage you to stop operating outside the circle of God's principles and allow Him to first redeem your soul. But for those of you who are already saved by Grace, you will notice as you begin to operate in these principles, that you are developing a closer relationship with your heavenly Father. Eventually, your ministry will be bountiful as you express the light of this truth in your gifts.

Accepting our gift because of God's love will allow us to discover His desires. Discovering God's desires will develop a passion to devote our gifts to serve Him faithfully. Some of us mix up *salvation* with *religion,* and we need to clarify this conflict. The word religious is a scientific terminology. The term according to research means "A person who manifests devotion to a deity." A deity is some form of idol god or goddess which could be a statue, or anything of nature. So, what does that have to do with acceptance? That is a very good question. It is simple. When one is not a born-again Christian, you automatically accept to be devoted to a deity. Anything we place above the Almighty God takes the first place (idolatry). If it is so, then our priority to serve God using our gifts in a ministry will not be possible because a ministry does not exist without devotion to God All-Mighty.

I suppose it is easier for some of us to be religious because it does not take much to be a religious person. All we must do is enjoy life as we please and go to a church occasionally ("live and let live"). Religion gives us the freedom to profess believing in something, doing what we wish and saying what we please. God's word tells us about the uselessness of religion. ***"If any man among you seem to be religious, and bridleth not his tongue, but deceiveth his own*** *heart, this man's religion is in vain" (James 1:26)*. As mentioned before, I was not excluded from the religious ones; this is why I shared my experience in participating in a talent show and competing with other artists. If we do not accept God's giving gift (Salvation), we are automatically practicing a worthless religion giving Satan easy access into our lives. The practice of religion without accepting Christ as Savior will lead you to a place the Bible calls hell, a place of eternal torment. "And these shall go away into everlasting punishment. This is a very serious matter. If you do not believe me, verify it yourself. *"And these shall go away into everlasting punishment, but the righteous into life eternal" (Matt. 25:46).*

Answer to Question Two

Now let us transition to talking about the word **"Salvation."** The Greek word for salvation is "SORO" which means redeeming or rescuing. You might ask, what is it that we need to be rescued from?" It's clearly outlined in Romans 3:23, ***"For all have sinned, and come short of God's glory" (Romans 3:23).*** We inherited the curse from Adam and Eve, this is why we need to be rescued from the curse of sin revealed (to us) through the perfect law of God. Conversely, Salvation is the water that removes the stain of sin through the precious blood of the Lamb. What would our world be like if Christ did not choose to redeem us from sin? What a humble and selfless thing He did for us.

Those who accept this gift will spend eternity in Heaven with God. The most important phase in God's salvation program is his sole ability to connect us in the chain of his unbiased love. His grace and mercy are extended to us without ceasing. The love of God led Him to offer His Son as the eternal sacrifice. Those who accept this gift will spend eternity with God in Heaven. The most important aspect about salvation is that it connects us to God's love. Grace then allows us to receive mercy. It was the love of God for us that caused Him to offer His son to the cross. Now that you understand the difference between religion and salvation, what will your next step be? Will you make this important decision in your life to receive God's abundant grace? You too can be an instrument of the Gospel. Later in Session Thirteen, you will see one that inspirations focus on this subject "I'll be There"(in heaven). Most of all, I would like to see you in heaven with me but know that religion will not secure a trip for you there; salvation is your valid passport, stamped by the blood of Jesus. Amen!

PART-II

SESSION THREE

In this Session, you will learn:

- *God's principles in the establishment of the spiritual gifts.*

- *The five acts of the principle in the operating of the gift.*

- *Why should we submit unto the Holy Spirit while using the gift.*

- *How should we express gratitude to God for the gift.*

- *The obstacles that could hinder our gift.*

- *How and why God uses music for different purposes.*

- *Godly wisdom VS natural wisdom.*

- *The moral danger in conforming into the likeness of the world.*

- *Patterns of good works that we should know and produce.*

The Establishment of the Principles:

As we continue with our study, my request to God is that we welcome this opportunity to understand the principles behind the gift(s). With the Holy Spirit as my guide, I will precisely break down this teaching in accordance with the *principles* that are attached to the gifts. In addition, as we become more familiar with their standards, I will show you in which category of these principles that each of my songs belongs, in accordance with each theme based on my audience. Now let me ask a strange question. Are you ready to go further?

If not, please, feel free to take a break, but remember to continue because the best is yet to come. If yes, then let's go.

Looking into the establishment of the principles, we must approach this session with an open mind. The establishment of these principles is simple to understand, such as: the means that shape our characters and take us to a higher place in our ministry. The principles are made of *acts,* and every act is determined by the word of God. The first act we need to know concerning the principles is that *God established them for: instruction, counsel, and encouragement.* Keeping these guidelines basically is for our own protection in the ministry. *In Journeys through Philosophy, A Classic,* Nicholas Capaldi and colleagues agreed "That principle is that the sole end for which mankind are warranted, individually or collectively, in interfering with the liberty of action of any of their number, is self-protection" (p. 39). A ministry is not effective without principles to follow. Principles are the building blocks of spiritual fruits. Good works will be evaluated and approved by the Master as to be unacceptable, acceptable, or excellent. Whenever the Bible mentions good works, it means *doing God's will.* It is through principles that we learn that we will not be starved spiritually, but rather nourishment for our souls. Jesus himself declares that **"My meat is to do the will of Him that sent me, and to finish His work" (John 4:34).** That too should be our goal. But we need to comply with that of Jesus. He followed His Father's principles.

How do we produce good works outside the Master's plan? It is not possible. The plan is in His word. In it, we find the resources that we need to be adequate and effective in our service to Him. In the word, we find all types of descriptions to what our assignment might be in terms of using our gifts. If we have no clue who gave us our assignment, then most likely we will do whatever we want. If it is so, who do we report to? God did not give us the gifts to operate in it however we want. He prepared a platform for us to operate on; that platform is found in the book of Hebrews. That is what He wants us to know in this teaching. Therefore, a great portion of this teaching will be focused on the acts of the principles, about how to use the gifts according to God's will.

Let me address something that is very important. The reason why God wants us to know about these principles it is because if we follow these simple methods, it will save us the trouble of having to answer to Him. God's law cannot be changed and altered. Taking a *righteous position* is to abide and function in accordance with God's perfect plans. It takes more than just knowing about the principles. They are to be applied as our honorable service to God. They are to be used as tools to influence the world as we are the light and salt of the earth. Most importantly, we are to use them without reproach as beneficial to our spiritual growth.

Before going deeper into the principles, I pray that God will open your heart to receive the truth and abide in it. How true these scriptures have proven the establishment of the principles. Now, without guessing, let's get the full description of these principles in the book of **Hebrews 5:12.** In this verse, God established the guidelines to the acts that help us to understand His principles. Most of you are acquainted with this verse but have not yet taken an approach to practice them. There is no doubt concerning these principles. The Bibles reveals that the Holy Spirit assigns certain gifts to Christians. *These gifts are the origin of the acts of the principles.* We are about to discover about the spiritual condition of each of them in accordance with God's purpose. Along the way, we will also discover the necessity of their manifestation in building faith in God and strengthening in our ministry. Perhaps, it would be well to take some notes.

The Five Gifts of the Acts of the Principles Are Presented As:

Apostles, Prophets, Evangelists, Pastors, and Teachers. These gifts carry the foundation of the acts of the *principles* that I understand to be *reasonable services or good work*. These acts will be fully developed in PART III, Session Six which covers "The Purpose of the Gift."

Besides other gifts, the prophetic word of God reveals that I have been blessed with two specific spiritual gifts, teaching, and healing. As I analyzed closely these gifts mentioned in the Bible, I did not see *singing and healing* listed. I wanted to know why those two are not listed on that list. My curiosity compelled me to seek the answer. I carefully searched God's word and the Holy Spirit directed me to the truth, and I would like to present them to all who might have questions about the gift of singing and healing ministry. To my surprise, the Holy Spirit led me to a new channel of spiritual gifts where I could see the connection between singing and healing.

Even though singing and healing are not listed in these titles, I have come to realize that they work closely together. Singing (worship) plays a powerful role in the healing ministry. Healing can sometimes occur in mysterious ways. When we sing under the anointing, the Holy Spirit releases faith, and faith is magnetic to healing. When we sing in faith, it pleases God. By pleasing Him, miracles take place. **"But without faith it is impossible to please Him..." (Heb. 11:6).** Now we can acknowledge that singing and healing work together through faith.

Where does writing fit in the title? Though writing is not included in this list, it is the cream of the crop, and we need to understand the power of this function. Songs are derived from inspiring written words and words express how we feel. We may not have realized it, but those of us who have been given both the gifts of singing and writing songs are fortunately blessed. For instance, David, one of the Psalmists, wrote more songs than anyone else in the Bible. In his expertise level, he wrote songs for every situation and every circumstance. He was also consistent in communicating with God through his songs. In fact, In Psalm fifty-one, he was very honest about his weakness when he wrote this song. He asked God to "restore the joy of his salvation so that he may teach transgressors God's ways." In his honest prayer, he had a purpose. I want you to know that the songs you write have valuable purpose to God.

The most interesting discovery is that the ministry of writing is so powerful that it contributes to all five categories of the gifts mentioned above. Through this concealed gift, one can clearly convey the message of the gospel as an apostle, an evangelist, a pastor, and a teacher. It is a great honor to know one who possesses these gifts can use them globally. See more about writing gospel songs later in *Session Seven.*

Identifying the Principles in the Use of the Gifts:

As you begin to identify these principles in the scriptures for the good use of the gift, I hope you develop a greater appreciation for what you have. However, I am looking forward to your undivided attention as I teach the essentials of these principles. To understand the nature or the purpose of our spiritual gifts, these *intrinsic* questions were selected by the Holy Spirit to guide us in how we should operate the gifts. However, it is important to save these questions into the hard drive of our minds.

1. Should we submit to the Holy Spirit? And how do they do *that?*

2. *How can we express gratitude to God for their gift(s)?*

3. *What could hinder our gifts?*

4. *Is it wise for Christians to conform to the likeness of the world?*

5. *Should Christians play pagan music in exchange for financial means?*

6. *Does God use music for different purpose?*

I am fully aware of both the complexity of this subject, and the questions that might arise in the mind of my readers during this teaching. Please consider that these questions must be properly answered in the boldness in which they were given to me by the Holy Spirit. ***"Nevertheless, brethren, I have written the more boldly unto you in some sort, as putting you in mind, because of the grace that is given to me of God" Rom. 15:15).*** With this scripture in mind, I am asking for your collaboration in the receiving of the answers as not from my own intellect, but from God our heavenly Father. Know also that these questions will cover a greater portion about God's intent for the given gift.

Principle to Question One:

Should We Submit to the Holy Spirit? And How Do They Do That?

How do we submit to the Holy Spirit? **Submitting** to the authority of the Holy Spirit is an essential requirement in God's principles. Submission is our loyalty to maintain a life of Godliness as ***"partakers of the divine nature" (II Pet 1:4).*** We submit to the Holy Spirit by exercising humble obedience to the will of God. Submission demonstrates our willingness to let go of what we desire in exchange for God's Grace. ***"...God resisteth the proud, but giveth grace unto the humble" (Jas. 4:6).*** Those who submit to the Holy Spirit are rewarded by having a perfect harmony with God, the Father. God will never require something from us that He Himself would not approve.

Being submissive also comes with a price. In **Luke chapter four,** the Bible opens a window where we could see the manifestation of submission in the life of Jesus. So let us look through that window for a moment. In *verse one (1)*, Jesus was *full* of the Holy Spirit and was *led* by the Holy Spirit into the wilderness. Verses *two (2)*, Jesus *suffered* long-term physical hunger and He was *tempted* by the devil. Verses *three (3)*, the devil tempted to inject doubt in Jesus' mind. In verse *seven (7),* Jesus was challenged to submit before the devil and worship him in exchange for wealth. *Verse eight (8),* Jesus instead submitted to the will of His Father, wherefore He overcame all temptations. Jesus won the devil over because He was Spirit-filled, led by the Holy Spirit, and submitted to the Holy Spirit. This is what I was able to see in that window. If Jesus Himself had to pay the price of suffering physical temptation, we as well will suffer physical temptations in whatever the cost it may be. Ministers cannot resist the devil without submitting first to God. Submitting to God is submitting to the Holy Spirit. There is no other substitute. Once submission is put in place, resistance automatically takes its position. ***"Submit yourselves therefore to God. Resist the devil and he will flee from you" (James. 4:7).***

We will also be faced with seasonal relapses. These relapses are due to the re-appearance of stubbornness which is weakness of the flesh. Stubbornness could only be subdued when ministers own their actions and exercise authority over it. God has given us power and authority over all powers of darkness, but the Holy Spirit oversees that power. We cannot afford to be disloyal to God by refusing to submit to the Holy Spirit, who can help us exercise our authority. Therefore, when the Holy Spirit brings the relapse of stubbornness to our attention, we must quickly attend to this emergency through fasting and prayers. It is the Holy Spirit who empowers us with boldness to face all contradictions.

Much more, stubbornness is transparent, and so is submission. If we are stubborn, people will recognize it through our behavior. I had a relapse using inappropriate behavior at church towards my husband. As I was about to exit the church, three sisters approached me and asked to have a meeting with me and my husband. We stayed a little while longer and talked about what had happened. They were not judgmental but concerned. The discussion was done in an elevated manner, which we appreciated very much. I did not try to cover up my stubborn attitude. Instead, I thanked them for their love and prayer. Immediately after the meeting, I presented my situation to my Heavenly Father in prayer; and the Holy Spirit led me to seven days and nights fasting, to combat the forces of stubbornness.

Being submissive is not a matter of weakness but of strength. This strength allows us to acknowledge our weakness and stand up for righteousness. God has created us volitionally—with a personal will. We can choose whether to submit. Nevertheless, we must keep in mind that the adversary is determined to hold us captive by our willingness to sin. But if we should allow the Holy Spirit to take charge of our will, He will rule over our volition, and give us strength to rule over our weaknesses.

I personally had to discover this type of strength for me to be able to teach it. Those who submit to the Holy Spirit are more likely to submit to the authority of those God place before them. One day I was strongly reprimanded at work by my supervisor in the presence of my co-workers to the point that I wanted to retaliate and yell back at her. But I thought about whom I represent as a Christ follower, I held my tongue and maintained my calm. A few days later, my supervisor found out that I was a pastor's wife. She came to my office and apologized to me in front of everyone. On another occasion she even told me that she was expecting more of me than my co-workers. Should I take credit for that? No. It was the Holy Spirit that subdued my will to stand in the truth of who I was at that moment. My co-workers may have found my reaction to the situation a weakness because they felt that I should have reported the incident to the union. I thought, can the union handle the situation better than the Holy Spirit? The positive outcome was the result of submitting to the voice of the Holy Spirit inside of me.

We live on this earth and our ministry is established by God in it. It is through our submission that ***"God's will be done on earth, as it is in heaven" (Matt. 6:10).*** That is what Jesus taught us in the Lord's Prayer. Being resistant to the Holy Spirit will make us weak vessels. Submission is our daily dose of vitamins to protect our spiritual immune system against evil bacteria on earth. We also need submission for the strength of our soul. A strengthened soul is a healthy soul. A healthy soul is a Spirit-filled soul. Ministers should be Spirit-filled. Spirit-filled ministers will stay in the will of God by obeying God rather than devils. ***"If we live in the Spirit, let us also walk in the Spirit" (Gal. 5:25).*** I realized being Spirit-filled was transparent. At that point, what my co-workers thought of me was not important.

The most important principle was to be conscious of what caused the incident, not blaming my supervisor for being aggressive towards me. Suffering the abusive remarks from my supervisor was the cost that I had to pay. ***"Servant, be subject to your masters with all fear; not only to the good and gentle, but also to the froward" (I Pet. 2:18).*** When the Holy Spirit led me to this scripture, it blew me away. This scripture was the plaque that God gave me as a token to higher degree in submitting to authority.

What does submission have to do with using your gift? Coming from someone who experienced the reward of submission, it is essential to be in perfect unity with the Holy Spirit when it comes to submission, because we need His help. Christianity is a lifestyle. If people know that we are ministers of the Gospel, we are automatically placed in the spotlight. Therefore, they are expecting more of us than the unsaved. The last thing we want to do is to shut the door to our ministry because of evil acts. Stubbornness is an evil act. This could become a stumbling block to our subordinates. Submission will block every access that the adversary has to our ministry, and the flame of the Gospel will sparkle wherever we go. ***"He is faithful, and shall establish us and keep us from evil" (II Thess. 3:3).*** Therefore, let submission become our final alternative when it comes to pleasing God. ***"We ought to obey God rather than men" (Acts 5:29b).*** Above all, the essence of submission is to be governed by the Holy Spirit.

Principle to Question Two:

How Can We Express Gratitude to God for Our Gifts?

Expressing our gratitude to God is our way to show Him our appreciation for the gift He has given us. Our Heavenly Father does not want us to be ignorant in that subject. We express our gratitude in the beauty of our obedience to following His precepts. Obedience is enmity with pride because when we obey, pride is dismissed and replaced with gratitude. It is less likely to disregard God's precepts under the influence of obedience. People who are ungrateful take all the credit and leave God out of the equation. It's all about "ME, MYSELF, AND I." We can only have what we desire from God when we take pleasure in elevating Him. ***"Delight thyself also in the LORD; and He shall give thee the desires of thine heart" (Ps. 37:4).*** It is impossible to please God through our gifts when we lose focus of His precepts. Following His precepts is operating the gift in truth and uprightness. That is the way to blossom gratefulness in our ministry. We cannot ignore God's precepts and expect our gifts to be fruitful. The use of our gifts is the works of the LORD through us. The word of God declares that ***"The works of his hands are verity and judgment; all his commandments are sure. They stand fast forever and ever and are done in truth and uprightness" (Ps. 111:7-8).*** Therefore, see that your work reflects gratefulness and uprightness.

Recognizing the gift as Gods' **grace:** not because we deserve it. It is through grace that we become partakers with Him. As partakers of the gospel of truth, we recognize that we were called to bring forth fruits. We need grace because it is our hope until our work is ended on this earth; and that is the truth. ***"For the hope, which is laid up for you in heaven, wherefore ye heard before in the word of the truth of the gospel, which is come unto you, as it doth also in you, since the day ye heard of it, and knew the grace of God in truth" (Col. 1:5-6).***

Presenting our gifts as a ***cup of blessing*** to God. Each time we could serve in the house of the Lord; it should be recognized as an honorable opportunity to bless Him. God values our blessings because it is a channel that serves for the outflow of our gifts. ***"BEHOLD, bless ye the Lord, all ye servants of which by night stand in the house of the LORD" (Ps. 134:1).***

Being thankful for the ***anointing*** of the Holy Spirit that comes with the gift. *The **anointing** of the Holy Spirit is the glory of our gifts.* We are ordained by God through the anointing. The anointing is to be possessed by the Holy Spirit who prepares and empowers us for service. The anointing brings the captives in liberty and draws people to the well of living water, (the blood of Jesus). Ministry without the anointing is risky because the flesh can fail us and jeopardize our gift. The anointing represses the adversary and enables us to cross over trials and tribulations. It is also the anointing that guides us into the journey of a glorious victory. ***"THE Spirit of the Lord God is upon me; because the Lord hath anointed me to preach good tidings unto the meek; he hath sent me to bind up the brokenhearted, to proclaim liberty to the captive, and the opening of the prison to them that are bound" (Is. 61:1).***

*Enriching our songs with **God's word** is empowerment for winning* souls. Without the word of God, our knowledge is limited, and limited knowledge could bring forth shameful words. God's word increases our knowledge, touches our hearts, and makes our services attractive to God in greater degree. God's word is our daily provision for the sustaining of our ministries. ***"Uphold me according unto thy word that I may live: and let me not be ashamed of my hope" (Ps. 119:116).***

➢ Walking in the **righteousness** of God *is to live what we preach* through our songs. It is not right to preach to others what we do not apply in our daily lives. We embrace righteousness by setting good examples. We must try to be blameless in our walk with God. It is the evidence that shows that we have peace with God. ***"And the fruit of righteousness is sown in peace of them that make peace." (James. 3:18).***

➢ *Seeing our voice as a **precious stone*** that God polishes and places in a special position for the building of His church. That stone is there to coordinate as a part for the harmony that carries forward the work of the kingdom. ***"To whom coming as a living stone, disallowed indeed of men, but chosen of God and precious" (I Pet. 2:4).*** Many of us resist our precious position because of the lack of knowledge. If we do not understand that our voice is a precious stone that contributes to the outcome of the work, consequently, that stone will fall out and lost its placed in the building of God's kingdom. Our voice is so important to God that it opens the golden gates of heaven so that He may hear us. God's amazing hands tune and polish our voices to bring honor and glory to Him. It is delightful to God when we lift our voices to worship Him, our KING of kings. ***"Now unto the King eternal, immortal, invisible, the only wise God, be honor and glory forever and ever A-men" (I Tim. 2:17).***

Principle to Question Three:

What Could Hinder Our Gifts?

God is very much aware of the struggles we face in our ministry. He gives us plenty of warning in the scriptures about hindrances. These aspects contain the necessary daily prescriptions for healthy ministry. As Paul said in (I Corinthians 4:14), *"I write not these things to shame you, but as my beloved sons I warn you."* Know this for sure. The notification of the LORD in these scriptures is not to judge us, but to keep us from drifting away from His principles. Therefore, for the sake of increasing our knowledge, we are advised by our MASTER to take note of them and store them in our hearts so we can have them ready when we need them the most.

"LORD, who shall abide in thy tabernacle? Who shall dwell in thy holy hill? He that walketh uprightly, and worketh righteousness, and speaketh the truth, in his heart. He that backbiteth not with his tongue, nor doeth evil to his neighbor, nor taketh up a reproach against his neighbor" (Ps. 15:1-5).

*Beware of longing for **praise.*** The adversary knows that we long for praise, and he is always waiting for an opportunity to trap us with flattering words. We do not need to seek flattery. God will lift us up in due season. *"But he that glorieth, let him glory in the Lord" (II cor. 10:17).*

➢ *Beware to **render** to God praise and glory that only He deserves. "For of Him, and through Him, and to Him, are all things: to whom be glory forever A-men" (Rom. 11:36).*

➢ *Beware of **pride** because pride will discredit your service. Remember what I said about the definition of good works in the establishment of the principles "Pride goeth before destruction and a haughty spirit before a fall" (Prv. 16:18).*

➢ *Beware of **jealousy** because jealousy against the success of other ministers could escalate to hatred. That is the work of the flesh. "Now the work of the flesh... Idolatry, witchcraft, hatred, variance, emulations..." (Gal. 5:20).*

➢ *Beware of **harmful lyrics**. It is not necessary to use offensive lyrics as rocks to hit the conscience of those you are trying to reach. We ought to preach the gospel in our lyrics in the purity of Christ's love and allow the Holy Spirit to do the rest. "That ye may be blameless and harmless...." (Phi. 2:15).*

➢ *Beware of **poor reputation.** Our lifestyles must reflect the message we sing. So, avoid dispute and conflict. "Therefore, as prisoners of the Lord, I beseech you to walk worthy of the vocation wherewith ye are called with which you were called, with all lowliness and gentleness" (Eph. 4:1).*

➢ *Beware of **unacceptable services** to God for our duties should be performed with a pure heart. Our services should illustrate tender mercy, kindness, and forgiveness. "Put on therefore, as elect of God, holy and beloved, bowels of mercies, kindness, humbleness of mind, meekness, long-suffering" (Col. 3:12).*

➢ *Beware of **self-pity over criticism** because it is a serious trap to keep us from enjoying our ministries. Accept criticisms as medicines for correction. "These things I have spoken unto you, that my joy might remain in you, and that your joy might be full" (John 15:11).*

➢ Beware of **foolishness** because our attitudes could spread negative vibes that would stop people from listening to us. *"Forsake the foolish, and live, and go in the way of understanding"* (Prov. 9:6).

➢ Beware of yielding to **corrupted influences** because it will remove our attentions from God's instructions. So, stay away from those who could direct you away from God. *"Have no fellowship with the unfruitful works of darkness, but rather reprove them* (Eph. 5:11).

➢ Beware of what produces **fear** in our lives. Remember fear is not a gift from God. We must not be intimidated by it. The promises of God are real, but fear is not because it is based on false imaginations. You can boldly release it with sincerity to the Lord. *"So, we may boldly say, the Lord is my helper, and I will not fear what man can do to me"* (Heb. 13:6).

➢ Beware of **neglecting the word of God,** for it is the foundation of our beliefs. In addition, the word of God is the light to the pathway of our ministry. Much more, the word of God is milk for our spiritual body. *"As newborn babes, desire the sincere milk of the word that ye may grow thereby"* (I Pet. 2:2).

➢ Beware of **neglecting prayer** because prayer is the strength of our ministry, and the security of our relationship to the heavenly Father. Prayer keeps us sober and vigilant. So, be quick to faithfully pray about everything because the adversary is quick to attack you faithfully. *Be sober, be vigilant; because your adversary the devil, as a roaring lion, walketh about, seeking whom he may devour"* (I Pet. 5:8).

➢ Beware of setting our minds on **worldly things**. Instead, expel all temptations that stand against our belief. *"Set your affection on things above, not on things on the earth"* (Col. 3:2).

➢ Beware of **Hatred** because resentment escalates to hatred and puts a barrier between you and God. Therefore, resist resentment through love, and embrace reconciliation. *"Hatred stirreth up strifes: but love covereth all sins."* (Prv. 10:12).

➢ *Beware of **boasting** about our work. Boasting is a foolish deadly trap. God does not approve it because it transfers God's credit to us. Instead, give God the credit in exchange to longevity. "But God said unto him, thou fool, this night thy soul shall be required of thee" (Luke 12:20).*

➢ *Beware of **Anger.** Anger gives entrance to Satan to manifest himself in keeping us bound. Here is the prescription. "Let all bitterness, and wrath, and anger, and clamor, and evil speaking, be put away from you" (Eph. 4:31).*

Principle to Question Four

Is it Wise for Ministers to Conform to the Likeness of the World?

I love the Bible because it is God's letter to us; and every question of truth and error are revealed in it. I struggled long to understand the effect of worldly conformation among Christians in the music industry, which is more the reason for me to consult the Bible. Never once did I think what the answer might be until this teaching. When the Holy Spirit brought it again to my attention, I could not resist the opportunity to learn the truth and teach about my discovery. I understand some of the gospel music composers may object to this subject. But conversely, some might be convicted of their ignorance and make a complete turn towards reformation.

Biblically revealed, the answer to this question is absolutely NO. It is *unwise for* ministers to be conforming to the likeness of the world because the essence of our conformity is already set by God. **"For whom He foreknew, He also did predestinate to be conformed to the image of His Son, that He might be the firstborn among many brethren" (Rom. 8:29).** There is no doubt concerning the subject of conformity. God has already made provision through Jesus Christ. The simplicity of this matter is we just need to reach out to what is already there. Understanding our predestination is to open our minds to be conforming to the image of Christ. Once we reach that dimension of transformation, the way we present the Gospel in our music will be transformed as well.

Primarily, God created us for His own pleasure. Being that we were created in His image for His own pleasure, nothing else should please Him better than us. ***"For the Lord taketh pleasure in his people: He will beautify the meek with salvation" (Ps. 149:4).*** However, we have concluded that music is God's masterpiece, and it is natural for us to love music because He loves music. Nevertheless, God allows us to use our creative gifts to compose and expose the harmony of instrumental sounds so we might praise Him with gladness.

What should be the setting when producing Gospel songs? The Psalmist experienced gladness when he composed songs using all sorts of instruments, but you can tell that the setting in his heart was a perfect harmony. That was his reason for declaring that we should: ***"Praise Him with the sound of the trumpet: praise Him with the psaltery and harp. Praise Him with the timbrel and dance: Praise Him with stringed instruments and organs. Praise Him upon the loud cymbals: Praise Him upon the high-sounding cymbals" (Ps. 150:3-5).***

There is absolutely nothing wrong with using any types of instruments to compose our gospel music, but the setting in our hearts must be pure. Too many gospel productions are in similarity to that of the world. There must be a difference between the two. Otherwise, people will not be able to identify the Gospel in its purity. There is one other contradiction that I know. I am sure I am not the only one who noticed that. Some so-called Gospel songs do not even mention the name of God or Jesus. They have been replaced with pronouns. Here is my personal advice to you. If you are a person to sing Gospel, you might want to think twice about the gift, because there is much more to it than just being a Gospel singer. You don't have to compromise your belief to some producer who wants to record your voice for profit. If he is ashamed to profess Jesus' name in the songs, then you should question his salvation and motive. Those who know God will not be ashamed to profess His name. So let God have what is due to Him and to devil what is due to devil.

What should be the setting when recording gospel songs? If you are recording Gospel music, let the setting you chose to work be a godly environment. If the setting is not aligned with your intention, the environment could spoil it. The result could be a mixed-up message. For example, my husband took me to a particular studio to record a song. During the recording, there were so many interruptions within the environment. The engineer was making loud jokes with others in the studio. Besides that, the walls were covered with witchcraft arts. This was not the setting that I had in mind. Consequently, I felt so uncomfortable that I lost my concentration, and I ended up leaving frustrated. Consequently, the result of my intention was spoiled. Therefore, don't be quick to just pick any studio. Pray that the Holy Spirit would be the pilot that leads the environment of your recording so your work could satisfy both, God, and you.

I believe there is a *standard* when composing music that's pertaining to God's kingdom. It is through this standard that we are granted permission by Him to enjoy what we do without improper conformity. If there is a standard in composing gospel music, then this leads us to two major questions:

(1) Why do Christians conform to the likeness of the world when composing music?

(2) How do Christians avoid conforming to that of the world?

When it comes to conformation, God's viewpoint is different from ours. He who is omniscient knows that we would be drifting away, creating a map to guide us to His standard. That standard is nothing else but God's way of doing things. The *way* of the Lord is that ***"Our works should be done in the meekness of wisdom" (James 3:13).*** I believe the reason why some Christians conform to the likeness of the world is because they lack *Godly wisdom*.

Why do we need Godly wisdom? It is a *foolish* perception to depend solely on our knowledge. ***"The way of a fool is right in his own eyes: but he that hearkeneth unto counsel is wise" (Prov. 12:15).*** Some of us are so envious in our thoughts about the use of the gift, and foolish enough to depend solely on our capacity to do the work of the Lord. If God Himself used wisdom to create the world, how much more we, who have been created in His image, should thirst for His wisdom. Some men like Boulton, Kennedy and Verhey agree "that wisdom has a position beside God, helping Him in His creation and then coming down into the hearts of man on the street." *(From Christ to the World p. 250).* The idea of writing Gospel music using our knowledge is all that we need, is not divine inspiration. Here is the truth; we are operating under demonic inspiration. The Bible says it better. ***"If ye have bitter envying and strife in your hearts, glory not, and lie not against the truth. This wisdom decendeth not from above, but is earthly, sensual, devilish" (James 3:14-15).***

How do we avoid operating under devilish inspiration? Inquiring about Godly wisdom will be the necessary *transition*. Godly wisdom is the nourishment to grow closer to *spiritual maturity*. The ability to discern the difference between Godly and devilish inspirations is spiritual maturity.

There are two types of **wisdom:** *The natural wisdom of man and Godly wisdom.* There is no similarity between the two. *Natural wisdom* is limited, and it involves the ideas of thinkers (philosophy). That is, a certain morality is used as a guideline to life. It is also about considering one's multiple experiences before he determines which one is best. After the thinkers take in the information they gain, they provide it to society. They are expecting that we should accept and apply these moral behaviors in our lives as a standard.

In addition, the natural wisdom of men must be developed through a great deal of study before discovering certain things. That is why we could only tap into the ingenuity of technology one step at a time. The existence of technology is beyond men's knowledge because it pre-existed by the Almighty before it could be discovered. The entire universe reflects the divine technology of God. For example: How do we understand God's magnificent wisdom and power? ***"To Him who alone doeth great wonders...." To Him that by wisdom made heaven. To Him that stretched out the earth above the waters. To Him that made great lights: the sun to rule by day, the moon, and stars to rule by night...." "Such knowledge is too wonderful for me; it is high, I cannot attain unto it" (Ps. 136:5-9; Ps. 139:6).*** Although God allows us to explore the world through natural wisdom, we are still limited in knowledge, and will never understand the capacity of His wonders. ***"There is no searching of His understanding" (Is. 40:28b).***

It is evident that God allows us to use our thoughts to evoke the world through philosophy. Philosophy endeavors to teach us many things that make sense but are still very far from God's divine revelation. Sense has absolutely nothing to do with Godly wisdom. That is why men are trying to make sense of their knowledge; they become slaves of their own philosophy. This puts them in a position to be confounded by God because they cannot comprehend the magnitude of His wisdom. That is why some prefer to be atheists because: ***"God hath chosen the foolish things of the world to confound the wise...." (I Cor. 1:27).***

Engaging in philosophy is one of the most deceiving devices that the prince of darkness uses as a deposit to deviate us from Godly wisdom. This device controls the minds of many, even among Christians. Philosophy is so powerful that it is very difficult for one to discern its effects to one's mind without having a relationship with

God; simply because: ***"In God are hid all the treasures of wisdom and knowledge" (Col. 2:3).*** Philosophers teach us that people are naturally good. But the Bible teaches us the opposite. The concept to the goodness of man was abolished after the fall of Adam. Therefore, we are all descendent and inherited of the deadly disease of his sin.

It is necessary for us to be aware of the power of men's philosophy. When I was first introduced to philosophy at Brooklyn College, I did not know what to expect, but I approached the subject with an open mind. This study was fascinating to me because I wanted to see how far men will use their thoughts trying to debate with God's magnificent wisdom. The lectures were so interesting that they filled my mind with wonders. When great thinkers express their philosophies to Christians, the Christians' faith must be unshakable, and they must be knowledgeable because the discovery of what apparently makes sense could cause lots of confusion.

I recalled a professor who, at the beginning of each class, would ask the students to take a certain position with closed eyes, leaving mind and body open for *meditation*. The entire class participated in this, except me. I considered this experience as an opportunity to use discernment to evaluate my faith in God. I took advantage of learning about philosophy based on my unshakable faith, without letting the idea take dominion over me. Therefore, I exercised Godly wisdom. During the meditation session instead of leaving my mind open, I used the time to pray.

Meditation has different meanings depending on the reasons and beliefs of the individual. It is an open mind interaction with a deity. Some people believe that meditation simply means relaxation for the body to release stress. For others, it is a mental exercise that is used to alter consciousness. And many think of meditation as focusing their attention and interrupting the typical flow of thoughts. Certain types of meditation give access to devilish encounters. I would rather excuse myself from the classroom, than to have left my mind open and to give access to devilish spirits.

As a Christian, I learned that meditation is *"the quiet contemplation of spiritual truths."* I didn't have to close my eyes and chant some foreign expression to meditate. I only meditate in the word of God. *"Mine eyes prevent the night watches that I might meditate on Thy word" (Ps. 119:148).* I thank God for the knowledge of His word. Instead of yielding to man's philosophy, it was a privilege for me to back up the answers to my homework with Biblical texts, when I had to prove certain points. I was hoping that the professor would have an open discussion about the way I answered my questions, but it never happened. Thank God for Godly wisdom. I was able to discern the difference between both spiritual and devilish meditation through the word of God that warned me to *"beware lest any man spoil me through philosophy and vain deceit, after the tradition of men, after the rudiments of the world, and not after Christ" (Col. 2:8).*

How do we gain godly wisdom? Godly wisdom must be sought to possess it. Godly wisdom is not based on philosophy, but it is a divulged by God, Almighty who brings all living things into existence. This type of wisdom helps us to view gospel music in God's perspective. Without Godly wisdom we will find ourselves falling short of His glory. *"If any of you lacks wisdom, let him ask of God, who giveth to all men liberally, and upbraideth not; and it shall be given him" (James 1: 5).*

You see, in the map of God's standard, Godly wisdom is one of the *establishing principles* for composing gospel music. Therefore, it is unwise of us to even think that we could use our gifts in good conduct without His wisdom. God is committed to our success, and we must know that His wisdom places us in a royal position. All we must do is *ask* for it and use it according to His fashion. Complying with God's standard (wisdom) is the proper way to show good conduct through our works. *"Who is a wise man and endued with knowledge among you understanding among you? Let him show out of a good conversation his works with meekness of wisdom"*

(James 3:13). If our music conforms to that of the world, then it is not done in the meekness of wisdom. This takes us to our next question.

Principle to Question Five

Should Christians Play Secular Music in Exchange for Financial Gain?

If I should ask this question in an open forum, people will probably have lots to say about this subject. I am sure that everyone would have different opinions. Trying to answer this question on our own might create chaos. Even though we volunteer to give our opinions, it is not for us to determine whether a Christian should play pagan music because of financial hardship. As for me, I am responsible for leading the weak to the light of hope in this teaching. **"We then that are strong ought to bear the infirmities of the weak and not to please ourselves" (Rom. 15:1).** This approach is an invitation to face our weaknesses and discipline ourselves in the operating of spiritual gifts. In this hope, it is better to let the Bible give us the answers to this question. **"For whatsoever things were written, aforetime were written for our learning, that we through patience and comfort of the scriptures might have hope" (Rom. 15:4).**

Greater are some of the most significant challenges that we face in the ministry is need, a major influence. Need is a common factor for everyone. We learned that a need is an "inner or outward lack or a compulsion to something." Some of those compulsions are necessities that arise from something. The placing of need otherwise as aim to achieve individual financial means, removes faith out of the equation. "The aim is not simply high peaks of individual achievement, but a community in which the pursuit of our goals also enables others to live a good life" stated Lovin (p. 31).

What does this say about your commitment to a mission-minded ministry?

Besides individual achievement, the aim of the minister should include **moral, spiritual, physical, and financial goals.** I would like to examine these needs, in accordance with God's words, to find the answer to this question. Here is my *first discovery*. It doesn't matter the condition of the need that we face as Christians, God's *promises* are connected to all of them. **"But my God shall supply all your need according to His riches in glory by Christ Jesus" (Phil.4:19)**. Capture the word *all* in your mind because it is the dominant factor that covers moral, spiritual, physical, and financial needs that God will fulfill. Being God's children connects us to His promises when we trust Him entirely.

Does the resolution of our financial problems depend on our level of trusting God? Having seen what, the scriptures said about supply for our need, I would say yes. Then if the answer is yes, we need to know why. The principle of moral need connects us to the lack of *maturity in trusting God* when Christians compromise their gifts to meet their needs. **"For everyone that useth milk is unskillful in the word of righteousness, for he is a babe." (Heb. 5:13).**

How does the Bible further connect need to spiritual maturity in trusting God? The following are some of the directions the Bible gives us regarding the conditions pertaining to this question. *The first condition*: morality is the principle of *right conduct*. *The second condition*: morality is based upon our *conscience. The third condition*: morality is based upon the new birth in Christ Jesus. **(Rom. 2:14, 15; II Cor. 5:17).** Let us look at these factors that support these conditions.

What does moral need have to do with the principle of trusting God's promises? Morality comes from the heart of God, and He also implants it in our hearts. God has already made a covenant with His children. He promised that **"He would put His laws in their mind and write them on their hearts; and He will be their God, and they will be His people" (Heb. 8:10).** Thereby, whatever we may think of our achievement or no matter what the circumstances may be, morality signifies right conduct. The laws of God should be always on our minds and in our hearts because it is His laws that govern our right conduct.

Not only so, but we should also know how to evaluate our achievement in the sight of those whom we have called to set an example for. "The moral evaluation turns on how the gift is used. Including our goals: we should have an eye not just to the easiest and most immediate results, but to those achievements that will make a lasting difference in our lives and in the lives of those around us" Lovin concluded (p. 30).

Since the time that God promised to be the provider to all our needs, nothing has changed. We can twist, turn, push, and pull away from God's promise by the waves of *Adultery*, but His promise remains. That is correct. Adultery does not base itself only on sexual misconduct. When we cheerfully exchange our gift with the world for money, we commit spiritual adultery which is the exercising of a spiritual misconduct. Many have joined this infidelity not knowing how it affects their relationships with God. In addition, making ourselves vulnerable to this type of infidelity by reasoning that God is not capable of providing or supplying for our needs provokes Him to jealousy. ***"Neither be ye idolaters as were some of them; as it is written..." (I Cor. 10:7).***

What does spiritual need have to do with the principle of trusting God's promises? Morality and spirituality are partners because morality is prompted by the Spirit. ***"If we live in the Spirit let us also walk in the Spirit" (Gal. 5: 25).*** The two Spirits in this verse are only connected to God's Spirit. In the case of spiritual need, we are looking at two categories of spirits. The lower-case spirit is referring to the spirit of man, and the upper-case Spirit is referring to God's Spirit. The ambition of man is connected to man's spirit, and the passion to love God is connected to God's Spirit because love is the fruit of God's Spirit (Gal. 5:22). When such differences occur one can easily detect the fruit of the Spirit.

This is how morality works in partnership with our spirit. Because of the relationship between our spirit and God's Spirit, our moral character is a bright light into the world. This light reveals who we are in every area of our lives. ***"We are the light of the world. A city that is set on a hill cannot be hid" (Matt. 5:14).*** So, when Christians compromise their spiritual gifts to sing secular music as to labor for an unbeliever, the light that was supposed to be used to pull the unbeliever from the darkness automatically loses its quality and becomes impaired. For this reason, the minister will be held accountable. ***"So, then every one of us shall give account of himself to God" (Rom. 14:12).*** However, it is not at an impasse, because the minister could always have a change of heart and repent from his or her sin.

What does Physical need have to do with the principle of trusting God's promises? The association between physical need and trusting God's promises is marked by our interaction with Him in our prayers because He is omniscient. ***"But when ye pray, use not vain repetitions as the heathen do... For your Father knoweth what things ye have needed of, before ye ask Him" (Matt. 6:7-8).*** Also, the logical concept of this interaction proves that we are in fellowship with Him. Fellowship is the act of sharing common interests. Jesus Christ shares the plan of salvation in common with His Father. Since God is a Spirit, He had to send His son Jesus Christ in the flesh, who also shared physical need in common with us.

In fact, when Jesus was hungry for food, He trusted His Father even more. Satan thought that he could use food to test Jesus' vulnerability to tempt Him, but He overcame his snare by rebuking him with God's words saying: ***"It is written; man shall not live by bread alone, but by every word that proceeded out of the mouth of God" (Matt. 4:4).*** So, what is that telling us? Even though we may be tempted by physical need, that is not an excuse to fail to trust God's promises. It is just a matter of choice. God offers more than a temporary joy in reaping. If you believe that the fulfillment of your commitment to God is more superior to making a quick buck, He will fulfill his commitment in allowing you to enjoy the fruit of your belief.

One other interest Jesus happened to share with us is *suffering.* Because of His fellowship with His Father, remembering that His Father had promised to glorify Him before man, Jesus therefore agreed to suffer just like we do physically for the sake of *love* to honor His Father. This is indeed the kind of fellowship that God desires for us to have with Him, so we too may show our love for Him in honoring our Father*. **"That which we have seen and heard declare we unto you, that ye also may have fellowship with us: and truly our fellowship is with the Father and with His Son Jesus Christ" (I John 1:3).** So, the principle in supplying physical need is to be in fellowship with God our Heavenly Father, who is our Jehovah Jireh, *God the provider* (*Gen. 22:14).* Here is the bottom line. If God is our Father, we will honor Him as our provider. **"A son honoreth his Father, and a servant his master: if then be a Father, where is mine honor? saith the LORD of hosts unto you...?" (Mal. 1:6).** We cannot have it both ways. It's either we are in fellowship with God or with Satan. Being in fellowship with God will help us to leave no place in our hearts to be in fellowship with Satan. Before allowing our physical need to make us pounce over materialistic concerns, we need to activate our love for God. **"Ye cannot drink the cup of the Lord, and the cup of devils; ye cannot be partakes of the Lord's Table, and of the table of devils. "Do we provoke the Lord to jealousy? Are we stronger than He?" (I Cor. 10: 21-22).**

Many times, we are alarmed by the Holy Spirit, but we tend to ignore the tenderness of His voice. Even if we pretend not to hear His voice; through the mirror of the Word, we could clearly see our physical faults. The purpose of looking into the mirror is to expose our sins, repent and confess. If we should confess, the Holy Spirit will connect us back to the vine of God's tender mercy. As I taught you before *in Session Two*, confession is very important. Failure to obtain mercy from God will result to the lack of fellowship with Him. And without fellowship with God, there is no fellowship with the Son. And if there is no fellowship with the Son, we also have no fellowship with the Spirit. ***"For they that are after the flesh do mind the things of the flesh; but they that are after the Spirit the things of the Spirit" (Rom. 8:5).*** Generally, we are missing out on all spiritual blessings. And consequently, we will plunge deeper into the physical snare. To build a wall between our gift and physical snare is to trust that God will take care of us if we should say no to paganism offers.

What does financial need have to do with the principle of trusting God's promises? I do not need to be reticent regarding this question. Honestly, most of our needs must be solved with money apart from salvation. In that sense, it is logical that everyone happens to be vulnerable to money.

The principle in trusting God's promises is *to remember that we belong to Him*. Knowing that we are His should also remind us that He is more than capable of taking care of His own. If God remembers to take good care of the sparrows, surely, He will not forget about us. ***"Are not five sparrows sold for two farthings, and not one of them is forgotten before God?" (Luke 12:6).*** Think about this question. Is a little child responsible for his or her needs? The logical response is no; because it is the parent's or guardian's responsibility to do so. Forasmuch, God also guarantees us the safety to cover for all our needs at His own cost. This guarantee encourages us to devote our trust in Him. Trust is supported by waiting patiently for the answer. If we wait patiently, eventually, He will attend to our needs. And that is a fact. ***"Now the just shall live by faith: but if any man draws back, my soul shall have no pleasure in him. But we are not of them who draw back unto perdition; but of them that believe to the saving of the soul" (Heb. 10:38, 39).***

As God's children, we have the privilege to present our need to Him knowing that He is a great provider. Nick Hennessey openly shares his purpose in the music ministry on national television. Hennessey, who is a Christian Evangelical Artist, said that: "What matters to him is the presence of God. He does not focus on money to feed his family. Nothing else is greater than giving time and talent to God; while He takes care of us." He added by saying that "through his teaching, about 600 students came to know the living Christ." This is the attitude that Christian Artists should have as ministers. I repeat, God is more than sufficient to take care of our needs if we develop an attitude of trust in Him.

How can we deal with financial need oppression? The matter of withstanding financial oppression must be followed by spiritual adjustment in our behavior as we are supposed to be the salt of the earth. **"Ye are the salt of the earth: but if the salt have lost his savor, wherewith shall it be salted?" (Matt. 5:13).** Don't we know that we are representatives of Christ? Don't we know that having to process worldly music causes us to lose our ministerial flavor, and puts us at risk of sharing the gospel with the non-Christian? When financial snares come our way, we must learn not to yield our minds to the control of money. Instead, we ought to augment our faith, and live by example to keep the purity of the gift. **"Let no man despise thy youth; but be thou an example of the believers, in word, in conversation, in charity, in spirit, in faith, in purity" (I Tim. 4:12).**

Being under the influence of the love of money could be burdensome. Sometimes, we need to be retrospective about God's faithfulness towards us. If we should take a moment to recognize His faithfulness, we will extract our minds from things that do not please Him and release ourselves from this type of oppression. Leon D. Pamphile, PH. D said, "When we rise up to assume control of our future with the mind of Christ, we become architects who use our God-given talents to design and build a better future for ourselves and humanity" *The Mind of Christ, Your Weapon of Victory* (p. 960). God does not condemn anyone for having or wanting to earn money because He understands that we all need money to buy what we want or need. However, He is concerned about how we allow money to control us. We must consider that money can control us.

The bigger problem is the *love of money* and not money itself. To reinforce this statement, some of us could testify that the love of money is a course of darkness that leads to the shadow of sorrow. **"For the love of money is the root of all evil: which while some coveted after they have erred from the faith and pierced themselves through with many sorrows" (I Tim. 6:10).** Let us think about this for a moment. What business does a Christian have making a pact with a non-Christian to create music for the amusement of the world just to make a few bucks?

Giving gifts is not to be operating as a type of amusement for money, but for ministering. Of course, God can use our gifts to supply money for the ministry; but not contradicted to His intent. The gift is not just a career because we do not earn it through a degree. I understand that some people make music their career. That is not what I am referring to. The difference is using the gift how we please and leave God out completely. By giving so much attention to money, we are piercing ourselves with many sorrows; and forgetting that **"we brought nothing into this world, and it is certain we can carry nothing out" (I Tim. 6:7).**

You might ask, what is the difference between having a non-Christian as an employer and producing music for the amusement of the world as a job? We could take this question further and see what the Bible has to say about it.

The matter of working for a non-believer is not a priority concern to God. Most people work for non-believers to earn a living. God's concern is rather on the *moral and spiritual danger* that Christians yield to when using their spiritual gifts as artists or ministers. As Christians, we have the support to set up boundaries through restricting ourselves from the types of jobs that would cause a moral or spiritual danger to our relationship with God. With that support, we do not depend solely on our own ability, but better in expose our vulnerability to God, who orders our steps in righteousness. ***"Order my steps in thy word: and let not any iniquity have dominion over me" (Ps. 119:133).***

What causes the moral danger? Remember, we are still focusing on the main idea. The main idea was *a Christian producing music for the amusement of the world, in other words, worldly music.* Here is how the Bible presents this type of work as both moral and spiritual danger.

"In all things, showing thyself a pattern of good works: in doctrine showing incorruptness, gravity, sincerity" (Titus 2:7). In this verse alone contains the general description of the full remedies of morality.

The basic moral: The vessel that holds the remedies is the Christian artist in accordance with the will of God. The analyzing of this verse will help us to determine where we stand in terms of moral and spiritual danger.

** First moral remedy:* PATTERN *of good works.* We could say that a pattern is an example of something physical. For example, anything used as a guide or model for making something. The word pattern carries both physical and spiritual aspects. In the physical aspect we can use a pattern to make a costume or a dress of choice. Some patterns are attractive, and others are not, depending on one's taste. Fortunately, this verse is about the spiritual aspect of the pattern, which is based on Christians works; and that's exactly where we ought to be. The spiritual pattern of an acceptable work in terms of Christians' works has been mentioned throughout the entire manual. We learned according to Titus 3:14, that good work is to meet *urgent needs, and to be fruitful* in God's service. Keep these words active in your mind: **urgent needs and fruitful.**

What is so urgent about the work? The urgency of the work is the *primary need to be fruitful in winning souls to Christ.* Remember, this person who claims to be a Christian artist or a minister is not doing this work to win souls, but rather for amusement and salary.

What is wrong with that? Here, we discern a contradiction in committing to the doctrine of the spiritual pattern of good work that we have learned so far. If it is in God's will, He will approve it; if not, it will be rejected. I will emphasize further about God's disapproval in my own ministry in Session Four. The rejecting of our work will result in the withdrawal of God's protection over our lives. We ought to be very careful of that because God's protection is our umbrella over the rain of temptations. This is an illustration of why God would approve that which is in His will: ***"That ye may walk honestly toward them that are without, and that ye may lack of nothing" (I Thes. 4:12).*** Therefore, if our walk with God is dishonest, it creates lacking in our needs. This means one might work longer hours in order to make ends meet, yet still lacking the need. If so, it is better for the Christian musician to resist the approval of man in exchange for a recovery of recompense.

* *The second moral remedy:* Showing INTEGRITY. To show integrity, one has to act in the uprightness of the pattern of the characteristic of a Christian. Some of the characteristics give clear manifestation as part of the work effort in **serving, performing, honesty and behavior.** These characteristics should be addressed first to God, and second, they are also evident to those around us. If the Christian artist or musician is serving God in Spirit and in truth, his or her performance should be *honest in heart and in behavior*. In this case, the heart of the artist or musician was not on God neither was his nor her service. Therefore, the behavior of the artist does not correspond with honesty. Again, we see another contradiction against integrity. So, this takes us to our next discovery.

* *The third moral remedy:* REVERENCE. As we have learned before, reverence is a feeling of deep respect to God. ***"God is greatly to be feared in the assembly of the saints and to be had in reverences of all them that are about Him" (Ps. 89:7).*** The word saints are equal to Christians. If a Christian chooses to produce

non-Christian music, then there is a lack of respect towards God according to what goes on in his or her work. In terms of what goes on, we could see how the Christian left the assembly of the saints and ended up trespassing into the assembly of the unrighteous. This type of behavior is unacceptable to God because it provokes Him to jealousy. ***"Do we provoke the Lord to jealousy? Are we stronger than He?" (I Cor. 10:22).*** The work of the Lord is delegated to us for the profit of others, not for our own profit. Our personal goal should be to accomplish the work unselfishly. This is what the apostle Paul teaches us: ***"Even as I please all men in all things, not seeking mine own profit, but the profit of many, that they may be saved" (I Cor. 10:33).*** If we place other's spiritual needs first, at the end God will evaluate the result, and it becomes profitable to us as well.

** The fourth moral remedy:* INCORRUPTIBLE. Incorruptible is the seed of our new spiritual birth in Christ Jesus. This moral is the evidence that we are *trustworthy* of the gift through the incorruptible nature of Jesus Christ. If Christian artists are trustworthy of the gift, it will be evident and effective to all around them. That means they will not jeopardize their faith by compromising their gifts for corrupted rewards. ***"Hearing of thy love and faith, which thou hast toward the Lord Jesus, and toward all the saints; that the communication of thy faith may become effectual by the acknowledgement of every good thing which is in you in Christ Jesus" (Phim. 1:5, 6).*** These verses bring us to this conclusion. Our testimony must align with what we profess in terms of the moral and spiritual values of Christianity.

We could plan our lives and or do whatever we want to do, but, fundamentally, not all things are profitable in God's eyes. The assumption that earning money with the gift is profitable to our need, but that assumption is little in comparison to God's promises to us as ministers of the Gospel. Although God could allow us to use our gift to raise funds for our ministry, this does not license us to sell it to the world using Christianity as a cover-up. ***"For bodily exercise profiteth little: but Godliness is profitable unto all things, having promise of the life that now is and of that which is to come" (I Tim. 4:8).*** I believe the Bible is clear concerning this matter. Now, if you are one of those people, will you trust God and let Him lead you to becoming an incorruptible Christian? If you should make that decision today, only then you will be able to set your boundaries concerning the heavenly kingdom's work. In general, these remedies do not pertain solely to those who produce worldly songs for money, but to all who trespass the assembly of the unrighteous. Some of you might be performing worldly songs in a club or other places for a salary. Others might also struggle with playing worldly music with a non-Christian band. Nevertheless, whatever the case may be; I recommend that you take a pause and think about what you learned so far in this teaching. Trust God to supply all your needs like you never did before. You cannot continue to dine at both tables: God's and Satan's. That dangerous corruptible practice must be put to an end. ***"Awake to righteousness, and sin not: for some have not yet the knowledge of God" (I Cor. 15:34).*** As I mentioned in Session One about my responsibilities, I must present this teaching shamelessly without reproach from God. You have the knowledge of God, and you must make a choice between the two.

"Be not deceived: evil communications corrupt good manners" (I Cor. 15:34). Teaching about the area of corruption is not a blame game in this teaching. Its practice is extremely contaminated. This is a call to surrender to God. You, the reader, also have your own responsibilities. According to James chapter three verse one: ***"Those who know will receive the greater condemnation."*** If you would please listen to God's warning as I did, it will save your life and the lives of those that you are hindering through the misuse of the gift. Let no one no longer deceive you in continuing to practice what you know to be against the will of God. ***"For therein is righteousness of God revealed from faith to faith: as it is written, "The just shall live by faith." "Who knowing the judgment of God, they which***

commit such things are worthy of death, not only do the same, but have pleasure in them that do them" (Rom. 1:17; 32).

Principle to Question Six

Does God Use Music for Different Purposes?

We experience music through a diversity of instrumental sound. This instrumental sound is based on the *sacred law of music.* The use of each instrument that determines the purpose or the occasion is the *sacred law of music.* Each instrument produces a specific sound to accomplish a specific purpose. Because instruments contribute to God's purpose for music, we are authorized by Him to use them according to the sacred law of music. Understanding the sacred law of music could change the way we perceive its purpose.

How could music be perceived? Music is like a *tree with many branches*: The roots of the tree represent *God as the foundation.* The trunk of the tree represents the *purpose* or the significant occasion. The branches represent the selective *instruments,* and the leaves represent the *harmonious sounds.* Just as leaves cannot produce sound without the wind, music cannot be heard without a musician. So, you see, being a musician or a composer is a peculiar gift because without these special gifts, instruments will have no value. As God who established the ornaments of music — the trunk, the branches, the leaves, and the wind that carries the sound — the contribution of a musician or a composer is required to bring out the harmonious sound of instrumental attraction. Therefore, the musician's or a composer's gift is very valuable to both God and mankind. Having to understand the importance of your gifts, please do not take them for granted.

As listed in the Bible, some of the branches (instruments) are: "cornet, cymbal, dulcimer, flute, harp, organ, pipe, psaltery, sackbut, tabret, timbrel, trumpet, and violin, which completes an orchestra (the leaves)." Some of them are foreign to us, but we are familiar to most of them. We all are aware that certain instruments are used for specific occasions such as services, farewells, weddings, funerals, processions, celebrations, and victories. The music or the instrument must correspond to the occasion it serves. For example, through common sense, we know that the style of music that one selects for a funeral service would be different from that of a wedding ceremony.

It is interesting how the history of music in the ancient days revealed God's ownership of music. Let's look at how God used some of these instruments according to the Bible. *Trumpet* in the ancient days was made of *ram's horn,* which is a male sheep. But today we use the modern type of man-made traditional trumpet. The ram's horn trumpet was used by seven priests as a *signal of God's presence* to assure victory to the people during the battle of "JERICHO" (Jos. 6:13). God had given specific instructions of what type of instrument to use. The people were instructed to shout out for victory only after they heard the long blast with the *ram's horn, which* was the sound of the trumpet (Jos. 6:5). It was also used for *marching, calling assemblies, as an announcement to gather the nation, and as alert against the enemy, etc.* All these events indicated a significant occasion.

Here is another example of how God uses an instrument. That instrument was the *harp.* This instrument was used to deliver a man who had come short of the presence of God. Keep in mind that when the Bible mentions the Spirit with the capital (S), the reference is God's presence. The story tells us that the Spirit of the Lord had departed from Saul, and an evil spirit from God troubled him. Understand this, when God's Spirit is departed from someone, automatically evil spirit is given the access to enter. For Saul to find relief from that evil spirit, someone had to play the harp. ***"And it came to pass, when the evil spirit from God was upon Saul, that David took a harp, and played with his hand: so, Saul was refreshed, and was well, and the evil spirit departed from him" (I Sam. 16: 23).*** To my understanding, this example is that God can also use a simple instrument through people to demonstrate and release His power.

It is evident that music holds a special place in our lives. In the primitive days, only few were selected by God to take part of a musical setting that complemented the voice for those who worshiped

Him. But today, because the door of Grace is opened, this privilege is equally given to all believers. If only we understand that special privilege, we would be more attentive to how we use music in the ministry. I believe that the Lord has chosen these examples to show us that He designed music and could use it however He pleases. That alone reveals God's ownership of music.

Does this mean we as well could do the same? I don't think that was God's intention. However, because of the liberty of our free will, He allows us that choice. If God did not create music, we would not miss it at all because it is impossible to miss something that doesn't exist. Since music exists, it is important for us to know what roles it plays in our lives, and how valuable it is to God.

Because music is valuable to God, Satan also mimics God in its value. God used David and his instrument as empowerment to relieve Saul from the evil spirit. Satan also used the similarity as empowerment to intimidate people. In Daniel chapter three, the king at his own choice displayed a golden image and commanded the people to worship it. In this case, the king represents a type of Satan. If one refused to worship this golden image, that person would be punished to death. We don't need to guess what he used for this specific event.

At the king's command, he uses an orchestra as a sign to accomplish his evil mission. He declared: ***"That at what time ye hear the sound of the cornet (horn), flute, harp, sackbut, psaltery, dulcimer, and all kinds of music; ye fall down and worship the golden image..." (Dan. 3:5).*** We need to know that Satan is very much aware of the capacity of the influence of music in people's lives. It is no secret that he is envious to possess God's belongings. In addition, he is very aggressive in imitating everything that compliments God. We know already that God created all for His own purpose, but don't ignore that Satan also uses them for his own purpose. That is why we need to be informed about some of the different ways that God uses instruments; and how Satan duplicates God's pattern to captivate and intimidate people.

PART-III

SESSION FOUR

The Motive Outside God's Intent

*W*hat *should be the motive behind our singing?* There are many reasons for one to sing gospel songs, but the motive most likely is the primary one. I don't think we truly understand how fast and how wide this operation spreads, but we do know that the Holy Spirit separates the gifts according to God's intents. One of God's intents is that "we should only use our gift in the capacity in which it was given." We know that we have the gift when we can operate in it fluently and efficiently. One other way to find out whether we have the gift is when people can acknowledge it through our performances.

Singing is an extraordinary gift, and everyone enjoys listening to those who possess the gift. However, when one does not possess the gift of singing, it is clearly obvious. The gift was not given to us because we are Christians, but rather because God has a purpose. Everyone can sing worship songs in the congregation of the LORD regardless of the quality of their vocals. But in the secular world, the gift must be proven through competition. If Satan, who did not give the gift, requires the best, how much more rightful is it for God who has given it, to get the best of our worship through the beauty of our voices? It is a disgrace when one who does not possess the gift has the audacity to use singing for profit, while using the name of Jesus. Clearly, that person is deceived by Satan. Recording a song and quoting the name of Jesus does not mean that you own the gift, because the devil himself acknowledges the name of Jesus. That action is unacceptable to God because it does not, please Him.

Those who possess the gift of singing are ordained by God for the advancement of the gospel. Too many people who are not ordained try to take the back door, thus creating scandals against those who are faithful in working for the advancement of the gospel. Every one of God's children has a gift. Instead of using something that we are not called for, we should allow God to reveal to us our gifted areas. That way our gift could bring satisfaction to God, not disappointment. Allow me to share a story so we can have a better understanding of *the motive outside God's intent*.

In 2009, Bethel Christian Church had their annual revival in Brooklyn, New York. To promote the revival, we had prepared some flyers for distribution. My husband, who is the pastor and founder of the church, got a phone call from a woman who had received one of the flyers. This woman came to Brooklyn from Florida and claimed to have been a recording gospel artist. I, as an Evangelist Artist, gave her the benefit of the doubt to have been one. Guess what? I must admit that I was wrong. She said that she desired to take part in our revival while she was in New York. So, my husband discussed it with me, and we scheduled to meet with her for an assessment. During our meeting, she mentioned that she was staying temporarily with someone and needed to have a place to stay a little bit longer. Being blessed with the gift of hospitality, I agreed with my husband to have her stay in our guest room at no cost.

In the excitement of her emotional state, she offered to start a Saturday morning prayer at the church. Since our church was young and we were in need for volunteer missionaries, we welcomed that offer with open hearts. In addition, she had told us that she needed help selling her CD's, so she could meet her responsibilities in Florida. Since we have a broadcasting ministry, we decided to listen to the CD before it could be exposed to our audience. There are four things that are valuable to me when I listen to a new CD: the voice, the anointing, the theme, and the lyrics. Unfortunately, only some of the lyrics were attractive to my ears because they were hymns that I like. None of the others were present. Even though the lyrics were inspired hymns, the way she presented them faded the flavor from the message. I believe the reason the CD did not edify me was because of the motive behind the recording. Not being aware of her motive, we purchased twenty of her CDs to support her so-called ministry. Evidently, she did not possess the gift of singing and should have no business using these inspired hymns outside of God's purpose.

Once she suspected that we may have discovered her motive, the offer that she made to start the prayer meeting vanished. She had no intention of taking part in the growth of the church. She used our hospitality to her own advantage. We barely saw her during weekdays because of our work schedules. She scheduled herself to visit other churches so she could sell her CDs. To my surprise, one day I went to the guest room to change the linens on the bed, and I found out that she was using our guest room as personal storage for retailing other items for her business. She basically invaded our privacy and conducted an illegal business in our home creating a conflict of interests.

One day, I happened to ask her about how she was doing with selling her CDs. This question opened a can of worms. She furiously displayed her anger towards the churches that forbade her from promoting her CDs. She claimed that she was sick and tired of the attitude of the people for not giving her the chance to sing. She was constantly using witchcraft lyrics to curse those who she claimed to have been "loogaroos" which means "witches." In addition to that attitude, she openly revealed her hatred towards one of our well-known gospel artists in the Haitian Community. She claimed that she would never forgive him for not supporting her, after he had promised to help her with the promotion of her CDs.

My point is when the motive is wrong, eventually people will hear it. Nancy T. Ammerman and colleagues in the "*Studying Congregations*" *advised the leaders about* "those whose skill, longevity and influence put them at the heart of your congregation's life will have a special role in the theological work you do" (p. 29). One of the roles of pastors is to ensure that they do not hinder the congregation by giving access to people who create confusions. I agree. They must be prudent; otherwise, they will be responsible for not providing the safety of their flocks. It will affect their work. Furthermore, if they should neglect such responsibility, they would have to face the consequences. Therefore, one should not be offended for not being allowed the chance to be placed at the heart of the congregation if one does not qualify. Those who have been granted the privilege to influence the congregation in a positive way should be able to use their gifts with excellence.

When I heard these claims from her, I began to analyze her motive for making this recording. I realized that this was an unusual case for me, and I had to handle it very carefully with God's guidance. I tried to reason with her several times using the word of God as my references, but it was a waste of time. She just was not willing to submit, even to the word of God. Her behavior and attitude did not fit the characteristics of an evangelistic Christian. I did not want to be in the company of one who took upon herself to blaspheme the gospel of Jesus Christ. For the sake of preserving my reputation, I could not tolerate such blasphemy.

I needed to be honest to the Lord about my feelings. So, I put on the whole armor of God and He began to show me who this woman really was. While I was fasting and seeking direction, I had a dream. In that dream, the Lord clearly showed me that this woman was on a satanic mission. I took authority over the spirits behind her motive. I released the power of God through His words to cast out this evil spirit out of our home. When she could no longer resist, she confessed to me that I was the anointed one. As a matter of fact, when she first heard me sing, she said that I could be making so much money with my voice and wished that she could sing like me. When she could not convince me with flattering words, she attacked the anointing in me by sarcastically stating that I was a millionaire on vacation, and I was wasting my time with this treasure. No matter what she said, I did not allow her insulting comments to stand against my relationship with my heavenly Father, because my motive for singing was different.

I submitted my will to God. I was able to resist, and she had no other choice but to flee back to Florida. She claimed that she "was going for a doctor's visit" and "would be back in one week." Well, she never returned. We packed up her belongings and sent them back to her in Florida. When the motive is not corresponding to the will of God, He will reveal it to us and make a way out, for His name's sake. It is not for my own interest that I share this experience. I found this episode to have been a perfect example to illustrate the concept of a motive outside God's intent. We will face many obstacles in our ministries that we need to share with others because Jesus said, **"Whatever I say to you in the dark, you must tell in the light. And you must announce from the housetops whatever I have whispered to you" (Matt. 10:27).** My exhortation to you in that sense is to take heed to this example. Do not allow yourself to fall into the trap of supporting those who perform outside of God's intent.

Using the gift in the capacity in which it was given simply means that if you do not possess a gift, it is not wise to create an artificial one for retailing purposes. God knows the gift he installed in each of us. As the Word exhort us to learn to minister according to our gift: ***"As every man hath received the gift, even so minister the same one to another, as good stewards of the manifold grace of God" (I Pet.4:10).*** If you should fit in that category, take this advice, repent and be forgiven. The Holy Spirit is there to help you discern your inner gift and will allow you to operate it in the manifold of God's Grace.

Another area where people have the tendency of operating outside God's intent is in the joining of *any type of functions,* just for the sake of being counted as one of the participants, but not as a minister. Many join the youth or the adult choir, and some join the praise dance group, etc. Since our gift is to be used as an opportunity to serve God, He wants you to know your given gift and the motive for your participation. We have already learned that the proper motive is to focus on what is pleasing to God. Now, I want to give you a broader view about using the gift within the wrong motive. Do you ever think about why you are in the choir, etc.? If not, this question should help you determine your reasons.

When you joined the gospel group, the choir, or the praise dance in your church, what was your intention? I do not need to know your answer; I just want you to think about it for a moment. Just in case you don't know the answer, I want to inform you that God has the answer, and He intended for you to know why you decided to join one of those functions. I did not take any pride in excluding myself among those who once sang outside of God's intent. So, there is no need to feel uncomfortable if you are using your gift outside of God's intent. Perhaps you and I have that offense in common. Now that I know the truth, and can identify my intent, I would like to help you in this sense. Being that you have reached this far in the reading of this manual, you might as well take that information into consideration. To help you out, I am going to share another example with you about using the gift outside God's intent. Hopefully, this will help to remove any doubt or confusion.

I had a conversation with one of my co-workers without knowing how useful this will be to my teaching. She shared a scenario with me concerning the subject of using the gift in the wrong motive. That day, she was dressed nicely in black. I gave her a compliment and she said, "Thank you." She continued by saying that she had joined the church's choir, and the choir would be performing that night. So, she was dressed accordingly for the revival service. Then she invited me to her office, opened her bag and showed me a beautiful scarf that she had put together to match the choir's uniform.

Having this conversation meant so much to me. I was thinking, "Look what God had done!" I said to myself. "This Sister had been saved and delivered from the confusion of religion." At one time, she was a confused Muslim who did not believe the Bible entirely as the words of God, but rather believed the Bible as partially contains God's word. Sharing the gospel of Jesus Christ was annoying to her. Once, she had strongly reprimanded me for leaving Bible scriptures on her desk. Glory to God! Today, she is saved, baptized, and using her gift of singing to worship the Lord much more. What a marvelous turn that is. This conversation about the choir was so interesting that I could not hold myself from using it as my next example about using the gift outside of God's intent.

She told me that recently she had joined this mega Church choir in Brooklyn. She pointed out that the church had several choirs. She willingly chose one of them to participate in. I listened to her carefully about her desire and passion to sing for the glory of God; but she was also being confronted with some serious issues at her church. These issues were about the attitudes and the behaviors of some of the choir members, and even one of the Assistant Ministers.

My co-worker had some questions that needed to be addressed. She wanted to understand: "Why do people who claim to be Christians act so inappropriately towards others who want to use their gifts to worship God?" I allowed her to express herself openly without interruption. I listened to what she had to say. "When I joined the choir, I had so many confrontations. It's unbelievable to see how people take time to inquire about unnecessary things. Three of the choir members approached me at different times and wanted to know *how I got into this choir*. Others wanted to discuss *the cost of the choir robe* because they are so caught up in competing. And one of the Assistant Ministers approached me and demanded an explanation about *why I chose to join this choir* instead of her choir?" I thought that was essential because these questions stuck with me. I did not provide the answers to her, but I pray that this manual will answer her questions.

Some people know about their intents for joining an activity, but others might not know why. Particularly, those who understand their purpose for using the gifts might pick up on their intents faster than others who do not understand the purpose. This is not a misinterpretation, but rather a reality. In fact, I made mention of how sometimes I could discern some people's intent based on my conversation with them in my introduction. Some people's intent is pre-calculated, but some just happened to follow the crowd, and others are driven by curiosity. No matter which one it may be, these intents will be addressed appropriately in this session.

Let me make a short comparison between those who have the wrong intent to those who have the right intent. When the focus on God is lacking, automatically, the intent is wrong, and that is when people have the tendency to misuse their gifts. Those who understand God's intent would not have to focus on these questions quoted above. Instead, they would be focusing on God's intent for the giving gift which is to *worship (putting God first), evangelism (bringing people to the knowledge of salvation) and edifying the church (teaching encouraging, supporting, and loving.)* Now, let's analyze these questions so you can see whether these questions reflect these characteristics.

First question: How did you get into this choir?

We could say that there is nothing wrong with asking someone this simple question. I could understand that, but the matter is not the question itself, but rather the motive of the person who asked the question. You probably want to know about the motive, right? Well, don't rely on my opinion. All we need to do is to see whether these questions reflect one of the characteristics of God's intent. Shall we answer these questions together?

What is most important? Is it to know how someone joins the choir or to be satisfied that he or she joins the choir? How do we know if she got to the choir because of *worship, evangelism, or edification?* So far, we can see that her motive does not fit in any of them. Therefore, we could say that the question does not reflect any of God's intents. For example, focusing on God's intent would be: "welcome to our choir. We are pleased to have you join us. I believe that together we will praise the Lord and bless the congregation." I think that approach would better fit the category of *worshiping and edifying.* If so, we could use this example as God's intent.

Second question: *How much did you pay for the choir robe?*

It's okay to ask someone about the cost of a robe. But if the intent turns out to be competition, which it was, according to my co-worker's comments, then this would be the opposite of encouragement to a new member who is trying to invest in God's kingdom. Perhaps if she was interested in evangelism, she would have encouraged the newcomer to be comfortable in investing in the work of the ministry instead of wondering about the cost. Don't you think? A *supporter* will give some words of knowledge and wisdom to a newcomer, not discouraging one from investing in the work of his or her ministry.

Third question: *Why did you choose this choir instead of my choir?*

If God intended for her to be in that choir, then I don't think it's any body's concern. Can you identify the characteristics of edification or love in this question? I can only identify preference. I am pretty sure now you have an idea where I am leading you. Perhaps if the person's intent in joining the choir was to allow God to use him or her to edify the church, then he or she would have not given access to the spirit of jealousy because jealousy is the opposite of love.

If you happened to be a leader or director in your ministry, that is a privilege. You must understand the participants are not your personal property. They are part of the body of Christ's church, and so are you. In whatever you are doing, let your intention focus on these functions: *worshiping God, evangelism to lost souls and edifying the church.* The word of God encourages us to work with each other: **"For the gospel's sake, that we might be partakers of it" (I Cor. 9:23).** Your intention is the passport to take you around the world as God's partner. Stay away from the magnet of political biases in the church. It is unfortunate to know that political biases are very a common corruption in the church. All of us will be held accountable for what we do. So, in whatsoever you do, let God's love reign among you. That is one of God's intents for the given gift. Look forward to learning more about Performing vs. Ministering in Session Eight.

Now, let me share with you some insights that the Holy Spirit revealed to me about Jesus' concern for the given gift. I believe that insight contains the spiritual base of our **CORE VALUE** for the given gift from Christ point of view. When Jesus lifted His eyes to heaven to pray for those that God had given to Him and those to come, He was preparing the platform for our ministries. You will find this prayer in *John chapter seventeen.* I encourage you to read the entire chapter, but for this teaching I will only emphasize verses. "I have <u>glorified</u> *You* on the earth. I have <u>finished</u> the work which You have given Me to do" (v. 4). The work that Jesus has accomplished is found in verse three. "And this is *eternal life, that they may know You, the only true God, and Jesus Christ whom You have sent."* "I have <u>given</u> them the <u>words </u>which You have given Me... (v. 8). *"Sanctify them in Your truth"* (v. 17). "And all <u>Mine are Yours</u>, and Yours are Mine, and I am <u>glorified in them</u>" (v. 10). I underlined these specific words so you may fully grasp the importance of this prayer.

There was nothing exaggerated in Jesus' prayer for us. He was extremely exclusive about whom this prayer was for. Such a claim is found in verse *nine.* "I pray for them. I do not pray for the world." Now, shall we analyze the underlined words?

- ✓ Jesus *glorified* His Father on earth. We also ought to glorify God in our works.

- ✓ Jesus has well *finished* His assignment, and our assignments must finish well with God's Grace.

- ✓ Jesus has *given* us His *word* to overcome evil and help us accomplish the task accurately. That is, to attract many through our ministries, which they too may come to know God as we know Him.

- ✓ If we *belong* to both God and Jesus, then let them stop acting as though they own themselves, and not taking any pride in the accomplishment of their works.

- ✓ Jesus is to be *glorified* in our lives.

You must know that joining the kingdom of God is not a coincidence because Jesus prayed for you too. "Sanctify yourselves by the truth."—This is the word of God (v. 17). These are the possessive characteristics that qualify you as a minister. Jesus said: "As the Father sent Him into the world, He also sent us into the world" (v. 18). Take these words seriously and apply them daily in your life, that the joy that Jesus offered in verse *thirteen* might be fulfilled in your lives and in your ministries.

(1) You ought to be **Faithful** because when you give priority to things which pertain to God, you are glorifying Jesus Christ for the accomplishment of the work you do. (Rom. 15:17-19).

(2) **Diligent:** Be diligent because as a diligent minister, your work will be abundantly covered by God's Grace (I Cor. 15:10).

(3) **Meek:** *Be meek* because the humility in you will be like

pleasant fragrance to draw people to God's love in you (II Tim. 2:25).

(4)   ***Impartial:*** Be Impartial because it is part of your responsibilities to be fair to one another, and not prejudiced (I Tim. 5:21).

(5)   ***Obedient:*** Be obedient to attend God's order as a minister because God delights in those who obey His voice for rebellion is as the sin of witchcraft. (I Sam. 15:22, 23).

(6)   ***Spirit-filled:*** Be Spirit-filled because you need the power of the Holy Spirit to witness with boldness (Act. 1:8).

(7)   ***Compassionate:*** Be compassionate to those who are ignorant of the word because you too once were in their positions (Heb. 5:2).

(8)   ***Prayerful:*** Be prayerful because prayer will sustain your ministry and preserve your steps from falling (Acts 6:4).

(9)   ***Sincere:*** Be sincere because to walk in the light of ministry, you must renounce all hidden things of the past, to handle the word without deceit (II Cor. 4:1-2).

In conclusion to this session, I want to emphasize that our given gifts should not be perceived as a competitive collection of stimuli to impress the self or others, but rather to be used as spiritual weapons to unshackle those who are bound in sin. When God allows us to experience freedom in some ways, it is necessary to take advantage in releasing our testimonies through our songs. There are many souls out there just waiting to be unshackled by a message in a song that can be used as a doorway to escape. One perfect word from a testimonial song alone is worth more and can break the curse of death in one's life, than ten thousand imperfect words. For instance, the mystery for which God had allowed this conversation to take place between me and my co-worker was yet to be revealed, one year after our first meeting.

In continuation, the same co-worker and I had an unexpected conversation, wherewith, I felt compelled to ask her about her conversion to Christianity. In response to my curiosity, she downloaded a gospel song by Le' Andria Johnson, entitled, "The awakening of Le' Andria Johnson's single, Jesus." According to my co-worker's testimony, it was the message in that song that unshackled her from the curse of death. Having experienced the scars and emptiness that life left behind, she had taken thirty pills of Advil pm, trying to put an end to her misery. After taking these pills, she went into a three-day coma. During those three days, no one bothered to reach out to her while she was home alone. Being given a second chance by God, she found herself awake, staring at the ceiling, and wondered, "Why am I still alive?" One day she was listening to Le' Andria's testimony in her new single, she was digesting every word as though it was her own story because the lyrics took her back to where she had been, and then she realized that God has a purpose for not letting her die.

She said to God: "If you allowed me to live, I am surrendering my life to You as Andria." Fortunately, that was one of her reasons for joining the choir. She just wanted to serve and worship God, as a way of showing gratitude to Him. This example serves as an example to both, those who join a ministry with a motive that satisfies and those who join a ministry with a motive that dissatisfy God.

If you are not sure about your motive and cannot yet define your ministry,take an inventory to see whether you possess those qualifications. If you should find that you are missing some of them, you may ask God to help you fill the blanks in your ministry. If you do not possess any at all, then you are in error. Your next option is to surrender your heart to God. If you have already made that confession but lacking in your commitment, you still have time to make it right with God while you are still breathing. Why am I teaching you this? It is because I am mandated by God to: **"Love my neighbor as I love myself." (Mat. 19:19)** You are my neighbor, and I love you. I would want my neighbor to warn me as well. We learned from the Bible that the judgment of God will start with us, who know the truth. **"For the time is come that judgment must begin at the house of God..." (I Pet. 4:17).** This judgment will not be based on salvation but rather on stewardship.

Does God Approve or Disapprove Our Works?

To see both sides of this question, I am going to break the answer down by using three major substructures: **ownership, love and obedience.** Let us consider how the work together.

Ownership: First, we need to understand that God's approval is based on two claims: *He claims us as His by giving His son to save us from sin. And we claim Him as our Father by giving Him our love.* Let's see if we could understand that statement from God's point of view by analyzing this verse. **"BEHOLD, what manner of love the Father hath bestowed upon us, that we should be called children of God: Therefore, the world knoweth us not, because it knew Him not" (I John 3:1).** This scripture sealed the strength of God's love for us to be called His children **(ownership)**. There we see that God's claim placed us in a different position than those of the world. Those who love God should not be ignorant about the type of love that God has bestowed on them, and the type of love that we should bestow on God.

What manner of love has God bestowed on us? **"In this the children of God are manifest, and the children of the devil: whosoever doeth not righteousness is not of God..." (I John 3:10).** This verse categorizes both those who belong to God and those who belong to the devil. In other terms, the word *righteousness* covers love in its fullness. Why? Because righteousness is equal to both: *love and obedience*. If love and obedience are equal to righteousness, then there is no other way that those who are God's children to demonstrate their love but through righteousness.

Love: *How do we show God that we love Him?* Let us go to **John chapter fourteen** for this question. The matter of our love for God caught my attention in this chapter at least six times. To my understanding, these repetitions are a constant reminder to us of what loving represents.

In verses fifteen, Jesus stated "If ye love me, keep my commandments." Again, in verses twenty-one, Jesus said "He that hath my commandments, and keepeth them, he it is that loveth me: and he that loveth me shall be loved of my Father, and I will love him, and will manifest myself to him." In verses twenty-three, "If a man loves me, he will keep my words: and my Father will love him…" In verses twenty-four, "He that loveth me not keepeth not my sayings: and the word which ye hear is not mine, but the Father's which sent me."

Loving God is the life of our relationship with Him. Love is so strong that it can only be proven through actions. We learn about the strength of loving God through Jesus Christ when He said: **"But that the world may know that I love the Father; and as the Father gave me commandment, even so I do…" (John 14:1).** The condition of our hearts will determine who to love most. Jesus emphasized fluently on how love should be proven. Love sits on a very powerful pole called **keeping**. This foundation is the establishment of grounded righteousness. As God's children, it is important that we should beware of who we are working for in terms of ministry. How do we meet the requirement of love? Of course, it is by discipline in how we keep on operating in what is pleasing to God. To be clear, listening to God's instructions and complying with them are counted for love. This discipline disconnects us from selfish acts and connects us to the act of love. What is this act?

Obedience: When it comes to obedience, there is no tolerance or favoritism in God's sight. It's either we obey and get His approval or disobey and get His disapproval. Going back to what Jesus promised: "The Father's love will be manifesting to those who proved their love though obedience." There is no excuse for using our pattern of disobedience in trying to impress God. The manifestation of our Father's love is the approval of what represents the work of His kingdom. A work that is not considered to be done in obedience is not sufficient to demonstrate or to gain God's approval. Beth Moore said *in Giving Christ First Place to* "Take away our excuses and we're forced to assume personal responsibility for our actions" (p. 48).

Basically, the failure to obey God's instruction and remain in disobedience is to face the consequence of its result, which is disapproval. But when we obey God, there is no doubt that we will earn His approval. Obedience is always followed by a fair compensation because obeying God turns on the force of the manifestation of His blessings. By any case, if you as a child of God should experience a suspension by the Holy Spirit during the work, it is in your best interest to stop and listen to His instructions; if you wish to gain His approval and be compensated by Him. At least, you have the privilege to ask your Father in which areas you fail to love Him. I will emphasize my personal experience with disobedience in Session Twelve.

How do I demonstrate my love for God? Some time ago, I met a young lady named Perla Arias whose parents are from Santo Domingo. She was one of the Gospel artists that performed at one of my concerts that took place at La Hermosa Christian Church in Manhattan. At that time, I believe she was only fifteen years old. From the first time I heard Perla sing, she shook the ground of the church with the power of the anointing of God. I mean, she really edified me through the way she expressed her love for God. It was such love that immediately connected us. We exchanged numbers and continued to communicate. Our conversation was basically always about how desperate she is to please God with her singing gift and to deeply know Him. Because we share the same love for God and the same interests in pleasing Him, I invited her to participate in my work for God during the recording.

I met with Perla's parents in the Bronx when we gathered for rehearsal prior to the recording. Shortly after, I scheduled for a recording session that was to take place in Pennsylvania. We picked up both Perla and her mother and we headed to Pennsylvania for that weekend as planned. The most attractive think about Perla is that she was really focused in keeping her identity as one of God's children. During our traveling time, all she talked about was strengthening her relationship with God. As a teenager, she understood about the type of love that God has bestowed in her. She shared with me about how she took time out to nourish her relationship with her heavenly Father in fasting and praying. She knew that it would be difficult for her to make a difference without walking in righteousness. So, her priority was to build up a strong foundation by seeking God's face to please Him. Besides her own responsibilities as a young artist and minister, she was willing to invest time helping me build my ministry. And that is how she displayed her love to both God and me.

The recording did not go according to our plan, because God suspended and changed our plan. When we got there, it seemed that there was no preparation made for the recording though it was scheduled ahead of time. To prevent me from getting upset, I assembled everyone who travelled with me for that purpose and used the time for rehearsal and prayer. Finally, we were told that the set up was concluded and we were ready to record. The session began with the backup singers. Suddenly something bizarre happened right in the middle of the recording session. Perla stopped singing and asked if she could have a word, and I said "Yes." I ask everyone to give attention to what she had to say. "I am sorry Sister Myrtha, but I must be obedient to the voice of the Holy Spirit. The Lord is telling me that this is not how He wants the work to be done. He requires more than that." Reader, listen. That's all I needed to hear. With no questions asked, I discontinued the recording session, asked everyone to pack up and we left for New York the same day.

How did I know that this message was from God? I have two answers for this question. First, God knew what happened before the recording had distracted me emotionally, physically, and spiritually. I needed to get back on track with the Holy Spirit. Second, Jesus who is righteous gives me discernment in His word saying: "Little children, let no one deceive you: he that doeth righteousness is righteous, even as He is righteous" (I John 3: 7). This is my answer. I witnessed the righteousness of God manifested through Perla's love for God. She is a perfect example of what a real Christian should look like. Perla did not use her singing gift to compete with me. She is the type of person who is happy for other's success. She helped me to understand that I did not have to force my way through pressure to use the gift. She simply positioned herself to be used by God at any place. Now, do you understand why I had no doubt that God was using her to communicate with me? Even though we spent money and time to get there, I did not dare to question the reason for this disruption because I knew as God's child, I had to perform His work according to His righteousness. The most important thing was not having the work done, but to do it right. To my surprise, even my husband did not bother to discuss the disruption of the work. Now, what can we learn from this episode?

Investing my time and money towards the recording could not replace the act of love; neither could it impress God if I did not meet His higher standard of love. Continuing this recording would have been just a waste of time, trying to impress God with something that He did not approve of. Therefore, having to obey God by allowing Him to stop this mediocrity was an opportunity for me to show my love for both God and Perla. I respect God because He owns me, and I respect Perla because she had made herself available to show her love for God through the act of obedience.

SESSION FIVE

The Dispersion of Worship and Praise:

What is the dispersion of worship? It is commanded by Jesus, that **"God the Father is looking for true worshipers to worship Him in spirit and in truth" (John 4:23).** The distribution of your gift, by sharing what is due to God with other deities *is the dispersion of worship (idol worship).* This is despicable to God.

We learned that *worship* is the act of "reverence rendered to God." *Praise* is the "act of exalting (elevating) God." We should take these acts very seriously because it is a direct command from God saying: Please note that the word *due* is an absolute possession, which means Satan is not due of our worship or praise, that ardent devotion pertaining to God only.

The attitude of a true worshiper is displayed through knowing that "God is LORD of all." The essence of such attitude is giving to God what is due solely to Him. **"Give unto the LORD the glory due unto His name" (I Chr. 16:29).** In the absence of such attitude, we are worshiping other gods, and that is displaying hatred towards God rather than love. Those who hate God would have to deal with the consequences. Here is what God says about worship: ***"Thou shalt not bow down thyself to them, nor serve them: For I the LORD thy God am a jealous God, visiting the iniquity of the Fathers upon the children unto the third and fourth generation of them that hate me" (Ex. 20:5).*** Only Jesus, who is one with His Father, shares that equal reverence. That is why the Wise Men from the East were led by a star to go and worship Jesus ***(Matt 2:10-11).***

What is the dispersion of Praise? The second honorable way to worship God with our gifts is to give acceptable praise in gratitude for our existence and His marvelous works. Taking interest in exalting the self or having pleasure in receiving praise from others for our works is dispersing God's honorable praise.

Praising God by acknowledging who we are and showing gratitude for installing gifts in us should not be a complicated attribution. The simplicity of the expression of praise is explicit in the Bible. Listen to the declaration of the Psalmist while expressing gratitude to praise God: ***"For thou hast possesses my reins; thou hast covered me in my mother's womb. I will praise thee; for I am fearfully and wonderfully made: marvelous are thy works; and that my soul knoweth right well" (Ps. 139:13-14).*** In this case, the Psalmist knows very well that his life is a gift from God. He has a responsibility to honor His requirements and commands. It does not matter what portion of the gift that God has given unto us. He gave specific gifts for a specific purpose, but all are equally important when it comes to worship. Whether it is singing, writing, teaching, or composing, acknowledging them as God-given abilities to use according to His taste is more reasonable. "The appropriate way to regard one's abilities and opportunities, as Paul argues in Romans, is to see them as gifts," said Robin W. Lovin in *Christian Ethics an Essential Guide (p. 30).*

What does it mean to NOT worship God in spirit? This illustration provides us with the understanding of one that does not worship God in Spirit. The Bible tells us that while Jesus was in Capernaum, they uncovered the roof where He was, and let down a sick man. When Jesus saw their faith, He said unto the sick of the palsy lay, (paralysis) "Son, your sins are forgiven." But there were certain of the scribes sitting there, and *reasoning in their hearts*. And immediately when *Jesus perceived in His spirit* that they so reasoned within themselves, He said unto them: "why are you reasoning these things in your hearts" *(Mark 2:8; John 4:24)?*

In this event, unknowingly, the spirits of the scribes were communicating to the spirit of Jesus Christ. As we learned, He and the Father are one. When the scribes rejected His authority, they also rejected the Father's authority. The scribes did not give reverence to Christ for His good deeds. Instead, they were reluctant in accepting His power to forgive sin. This point represents that the spirit of man displays what is in the heart. Though they appeared to be on God's side, but they did not worship Him in spirit. Whatsoever is in our hearts, the spirit will report them to God. Since nothing is hidden from God, we ought to be careful of what's in our hearts, so we would not reject God's authority in our spirits towards Him.

What is worship in truth? People could take any direction in believing what they perceive as to be true worship. For many, worship is traditional. In the context of this teaching, *the truth is the bowing of our hearts, mind, body, spirit, and soul while giving reverence to God.* Notice, it is not the bowing of our heads and bodies only. One could bow the head and body as a form of worship without having to bow the heart, mind, spirit, and soul. Overall, the truth is to accept that God knows whether we are worshiping Him in spirit and in truth.

Let us go a little further with the subject of worship and praise in terms of music. At this point in this teaching, we should know by now that the subject of worship in Spirit and in truth is well pleasing unto God and should be. If the focus of worship and praise is *dispersed* among other deities, this leads us to another question.

Who is responsible for that dispersion? The horrible result, which would inevitably lead to the dispersion of worship and praise did not start in the Garden of Eden, but rather in heaven. "Instrumental in the form of humanity, Satan has acquired a very vast experience in opposing mankind. Having tempted the highest and the lowest, he knows exceedingly well what the strings of human action are and how to play upon them" said Charles Spurgeon in *Spiritual Warfare in a Believer's life (p.63).* Some of us are aware of Satan's rebellion in heaven concerning his envious desire and jealousy to counterfeit what is due to God; and that was worship and praise. Satan, whose prior name was "Lucifer", had a natural rebellion against God's law because he had always desired what is due to God. Satan was dismissed and cast away from his heavenly position due to his desire to dominate and steal God's worship and praise. ***"How art thou fallen from heaven, O Lucifer, son of the morning…? For thou hast said in thine heart, I will ascend into heaven; I will exalt my throne above the stars of God… I will be like the Highest…" (Is. 14:12-14).*** The dismissal of Satan in his position in heaven did not change his desire.

On the contrary, that desire continues to increase even more. In fact, Satan is very much responsible for the dispersion of worship and praise in the church of Jesus Christ. Using his Satanic and deceitful tactics, he manages to pull away many gospel artists, and use them for his pleasure. He uses physical and emotional desire to convince many into trading their gifts for pleasure and temporary happiness. We also know that Satan is very wise and has a very distinguished taste in music. When it comes to imitating God, he has no problem to exercise his wisdom to inspire many to compose music outside God's intent. In fact, music is Satan's greatest device to dictate to people how to worship him. He then blocks their consciousness by creating a momentum through various types of entertainment to distract them from worshiping and praising God, so that he might have his way in our midst.

How do we invite Satan in our midst unknowingly? By misunderstanding the concept of God's worthiness in our music, we automatically invite Satan to take position in our midst. Clever as he is, Satan inspired those who are vulnerable to welcome him even in the church through music. He twisted their minds making them to believe that paganism worship is normal in God's church. Therefore, being deceived by his masquerade movement, true worship is being replaced by paganism worship to modify God's standard of worship. He also compounds music by making it funny, enjoyable, sensational, emotional, sexy, and confusing. That is why, without discernment, it is not easy for many of us to acknowledge his concealed motives in the congregational services.

Satanic music in our congregations is not a suspicious matter, but rather a movement. This movement of street music is like a deadly disease gradually demoralizing and demolishing our desire for Godly worship. Ed Rainer Sainvill stated in *Tambours Frappés Haitïens Campés* (At the sound of Tambour, Haitians stand up) that "Haitian's music "raras" has always been manifested in diverse manifestations in the street" (p. 228). As a matter of fact, I know a gospel musician who used to play bass guitar for one of the well-known Haitian Gospel bands in Brooklyn, New York. He also composed jazz instrumental music. He was playing one of his jazz pieces when I walked to my friend's studio one night. He asked me "Can you recognize this sound?" and I said "No." He then told me "That is raras." Raras is one of the Haitian's traditional street voodooist music. To my surprise, he mixed the music so well with other instruments to hide its identity. It is critical to see how fast this street music is spreading in churches all around the world. It has already been accepted, adopted, and claimed to have been used to get people to come to Christ or to stay in church, especially young people. Is that really the true way to win souls? Or is it a tragic deception by the adversary? Through this teaching, God wants to remind us again that music is simply an instrument to enhance worship and praise. It is not meant to be used as a way of attracting people to Him. There is no mention of such gospel in the Bible. That is a false concept. God doesn't need anyone to modify the gospel to win souls to Him. For this, I testify, that the command of Jesus will never be diffused when it comes to those that His Father predestinated to be His followers. ***"For whom he did foreknow, he also did predestinate to be conformed to the image of his Son, that he might be the first –born among many brethren" (Rom 8:29).*** Amen to that!

Just as the holiness of music opens the door of our hearts to welcome God in our midst, using music the improper way opens the door and allows evil Satan in our midst. For example, as a Haitian, I know that music in the Haitian culture is one of the ways to welcome demonic spirit. I recall when I was about eleven years old; my mother who lived in Grand Bahamas, and was a pagan at the time, she would go to Haiti each year, and to faithfully honor Satan through some ritual ceremony called "gombo." In this ceremony, there were specific instruments that were used with certain beats or rhythms, especially the tambourine. They used this ritual rhythm to welcome the manifestation of demonic spirits in a person's body. Sadly, to say, those similar rhythms and beats are also adopted by our congregations in the church of Jesus Christ. "Haitians in New York City feel their loss of access of Saut D'eau and to the annual pilgrimage for Ezili Danto. They compensate in various ways…" *God of the City Robert* A. Orsi (p. 90).

People think using certain music will keep members in the church, but conversely, these types of music are keys that open the door to the minds and souls of those who have not yet been delivered from them. Personally, for this reason, when I became a Christian, I tried to avoid listening or affiliating to any types of music that would attract demonic spirits in my home or life. Even my children could testify to that statement.

It came to pass that while I was in a worship service at a certain Pentecostal Church in Brooklyn, New York, there was an amusing, so-called praise going on using the similar paganism cultural rhythms of Haiti. Somehow that rhythm gave legal access to demonic possessions to manifest through people right in the worship service. They lost control of themselves, distracted people and disturbed the worship service. I do not want to focus on the details of those experiences too much at this moment because I might want to elaborate more about them in further teachings. But I just wanted to use this episode as an example to share about how we could invite Satan to our worship service through music unknowingly.

Some people are so accustomed to this worldly conformation to the point that they claim that the worship service is monotone without pagan music. Others hold that culture has something to do with it, as though culture should be used to justify their conformity. "How much of a role does an ongoing memory of our religious tradition play in our identity as a congregation today?" asked Ammerman and colleagues in *Studying Congregations A New Handbook (p. 29)*. The work of the minister should reflect his Christ-like identify. If not so, ongoing religious tradition will have a negative impact on the congregation. The negative impact is the deviation or dispersion of true worship and how the gospel should be presented.

They also said to: "give the people what they want." That means, if the people want to mix satanic ritual in the church, let it be, if we keep them coming and happy. Could you be a witness to what I am saying? The Gospel of Jesus Christ is not set to give people what they want, but what they need. The nature of men naturally desires sin, but what we really need is to be rescued from sin. The most dangerous part of this belief is that if we do not educate our children and the church about this type of contaminated conformation, it will continue to pollute our belief system.

Because of the strength of this false belief, one must be bold to even mention its effect even to people in the church. I have not heard anyone preach or teach about such an epidemic deception. If we do not pay attention to this revelation, there will be greater consequences to face. ***"For the wrath of God is revealed from heaven against all ungodliness and unrighteousness of men who hold the truth in unrighteousness: Because that which may be known of God is manifest in them; for God hath shewed it unto them" (Rom.***

_1:18, 19)._ No consequence is greater than having to face God's judgment for what we know. If you are one to agree and receive this message as it is from God, then be bold. I invite you to play your part in the spreading of this teaching. Take a stand with me today. Some of those you know might be affected by this illness. Help them achieve their breakthrough. Let the ministers arise from their comfort zones of pagan worship. Learn more about its influence and teach each other about how to take back our possession of Godly worship in our services. Let us triumph in this battle together.

The Fruit of an Acceptable Worship:

The monotheism that pertains to all is to believe that there is only one God, the Almighty God worthy of our worship, which we learned through this entire teaching. When we truly believe that God is the only one that is worthy of our worship, our love automatically sends an invitation to Him. From this point on, the Holy Spirit connects us to the library of God's word where we could find a variety of ways to express our worship. Most importantly, it is through the sincerity of true worship that we experience God's power because true worship separates us from the world and unites us with the Holy Spirit. As we are becoming one with the Holy Spirit, God releases His power in the atmosphere to deliver and heal His people. In the presence of God, Satan could never resist but just flee from the environment.

Talking about keeping Satan out of the environment, here is one episode that I consider to be acceptable worship. In the process of this work, the Lord set me up in a sudden interview with a servant of God. I met Pastor Jean Harry at Metropolitan Hospital where I had worked for over two decades. I never thought that meeting him could have become something so important to this teaching. Truly, we never fully know what is in God's plan.

It was my lunch hour, and I was going to stop at the Hospital Chapel to pray, and to minister to a lady friend of mine that I hadn't seen in a while. That was my desire, but I never made it to either one that day. I got in the elevator from the fourteenth floor and pressed the button to take me down to the second floor. For some reason, the elevator stopped at the thirteenth floor, but no one was there. As the door opened, a Haitian man who worked in the Human Resources Department was pointing a finger backward, indicating something that he wanted me to see, and that's when I saw Pastor Harry. He said to me: "I just got back from Haiti." Since I wanted to get the current news about Haiti's situation, I asked him about the progress there. Instead of answering the question directly, he said: "I took part in an adoration service in Haiti, and the people put me to shame." He continued and said, "I thought that I knew what worship was until I saw true worshipers in action." I thought what a coincidence.

My question was very precise. But why didn't he answer my question, and switched the answer to worship instead? I sensed that there was something that God might want me to learn about Pastor Harry's trip to Haiti. Earlier I shared with you about voodoo worship in Haiti. Nevertheless, there are some Haitians that do worship God in truth. I told him that I was writing a manual about spiritual gifts, and I asked him if I could stop by his office for an interview. Since time was not in my favor, I immediately followed him, and he shared twenty minutes of his time discussing his experience with worship.

Pastor Harry worked in partnership with Pastor Prosper Dorméus who is the shepherd of "Vivifiante Church of God" in Queens, New York. He happens to have a church extension located at Croix des Bouquets in the suburban part of Haiti. The church was in great need of musical instruments because the people for many years have been conducting services without music. Pastor Dorméus shared the need of the church with Pastor Harry, and he was compelled to help. So, he collected a love offering and used the funds to purchase instruments and donated them to the church in Croix des Bouquets. The time had come for them to go to Haiti, to establish the instruments. Pastor Harry was the guest preacher for the occasion, and that was his mission to Haiti.

This was how he described the worship service there that day. "I have never experienced such worship. Despite the poor condition of the people, they worship with open hearts. Their minds were focused on God rather than their needs. They worshiped until the glory of God ascended in their midst. At the end of the worship, Pastor Harry was given the microphone to preach. Instead of preaching, he was led by the Holy Spirit to continue with the worship.

"In the assembly was a certain Pastor named Frank Mesidor," he said. He had been paralyzed due to a stroke and was unable to walk. As the glory of God spread in their midst, Pastor Harry grabbed Pastor Mesidor by both hands, and asked him: "Do you believe that God could do it?" Pastor Mésidor answered: "Yes." Then Pastor Harry let go of his hand and commanded him to get up and walk. In the meantime, the people were singing: "Leve kampe pou'w mache frè mwen!" meaning ("Get up and walk my brother!"). Pastor Mesidor tried to stand but was about to fall. Pastor Harry forbade the people from helping him. He said: "If anyone helps you, then Jesus is not here." So, they left him alone. Pastor Harry declared that: "It is the same God and the same power that healed in the old days, and there is no limitation." Upon the receiving of these words, Pastor Mesidor began to walk and ran around the church.

In addition to that, there was a ninety-four-year-old lady who had been suffering with bone marrow disease for many years. Pastor Harry looked at her and said: "If you believe, you will see the glory of God. Age has nothing to do with the gift. Do you agree?" Pastor Harry asked. The elderly lady too got up and started to run around the church. "Discovering the gift is the power of evangelism." It did not stop there. Immediately God changed the theme of Pastor Harry's message to "Fok sa changé" meaning (This must change). This acceptable adoration brought forth the fruit of healing. When God is pleased, He manifests His presence through wonders.

I have enough experience to testify about acceptable worship because God allowed me to use worship as an empowerment to deliver people from demonic possessions. One thing that I always desire of God is that He uses my gift of singing as a key to free the captives. I am not asking you to be my followers. If you are not led by the Holy Spirit to use your singing in that sense, then don't do it. But if you are, just follow the voice of the Holy Spirit and allow Him to use you.

Coming from work one evening, at about 6:15 pm, I walked out from the subway station in Flatbush Avenue, Brooklyn. I was carrying my bookbag in one hand and in the other a bag full of groceries. I was tired and rushing to get home to cook. I walked one block, and a thought came to me saying "Don't go straight home. Instead, go see this sister in Christ who lives on East 31st Street." I thought that was very strange because I had never been there before. I kept walking and passed the building that I was led to. The thought came back to me again, and then I stopped, put the bags down, and called the sister to see if she was home. Fortunately, she was because God had set it that way.

I told her that I was nearby, and I wanted to stop by her place. She quickly responded, "Please come." As soon as she said that the thought directed me to go there and just worship in songs. When I got there, I realized why the Lord had led me to this sister. He led me there to intercede in songs. Just as God used David to play the flute in the situation of Saul, he also used my worship as an instrument to do His work. In the bedroom was one of the sister's daughters who had been tormented for several years by demonic possession. For this mission, my worship was empowered for her deliverance. I greeted the sister with a kiss and said nothing else. I put my bags down and began the battle through songs. As I sang, the demonic spirits began to rage on the young lady, using all sorts of profanity trying to get me to stop. From the time I obeyed and accepted the mission, I was constituted under the umbrella of the Holy Spirit to overcome this warfare.

Worshiping God using His word was the ultimate bullet that was used to combat these demons. I sang, I sang, and I sang until there was total silence within the environment. I never got to see the young-lady's face, but I prayed with the mother and left. After few weeks passed, I received an invitation from that sister to attend a thanksgiving service that she was offering to the Lord. Without hesitation, I went, and I was glad that I did. It was in that service that I first met the young lady for whom I was interceding in worship. Glory to God! There she was totally free. Not only did the Lord set her free, but she was also anointed to be a worship leader for the church which her Father is the pastor. She was praising God with such a passion. To confirm the deliverance, the mother testified to the Church about how God had used me as an instrument to unshackle her daughter. It so happened that the Lord did grant me what my heart desired the most.

My reward was that this young lady later was one of those who God had anointed as a true worshiper. This is the kind of fruit that I am talking about. There was nothing mysterious about this deliverance. All it took was a willingness to obey the Holy Spirit. Like I mentioned before, using the gift is not about me, but about God. I had to share this episode with you, so that you may know that I experienced the fruit of an acceptable worship. This worship was not acceptable to God by favoritism; anyone who is willing could experience it. Furthermore, it is not about preference, perfection, or professionalism; it's all about faith and submission. So, be sensitive to use faith and be submissive to God's voice; and you will see how gloriously God will move with you while using the gift through worship and praise.

PART-IV

SESSION SIX

The Acts of the Purpose of the Gift:

The Five Acts of the Ministerial Gifts:

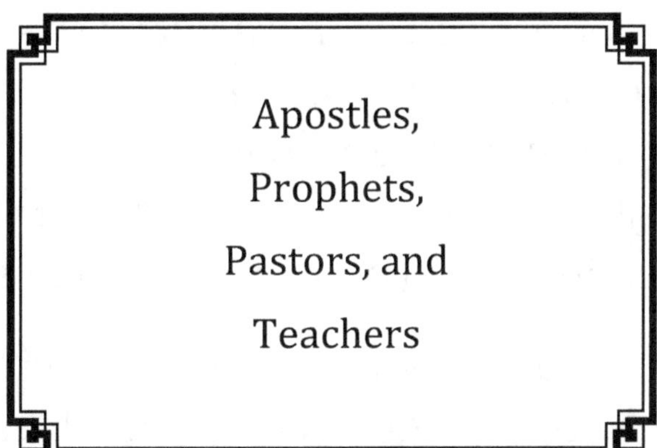

A gift can be used for multiple reasons, but those who are ministers of the Gospel should have a clear understanding of the purpose of their gifts. When the purpose of the gift is clear, spiritual vision will be the result rather than materialistic vision. Besides the spiritual vision, the minister's expectation becomes greater as their wisdom increases.

As we continue with this teaching, I want to share with you two words that I discovered in the word of God that applies to all these titles, *NEGLECT and EQUIP*. The first required principle is that the minister should not neglect the gift, ***"Neglect not the gift that is in thee which was given thee..." (I Tim. 4:14).*** I must admit that I was one of those who neglected my gifts. I could have had many recordings and written many books, but I was insecure with the feeling that my voice and writing might not be good enough to compete with those who sing or write better than me. I was racing with my own negative thoughts, telling me that I have enunciation issues. My gifts were unseen and unheard. For this reason, my blessings from God were held in captivity. Some of my friends are disappointed in me for not having my songs out there blessing people. I always tried to avoid answering their questions. I struggled with the answers to those questions; "What good is it to have unseen and unheard gifts? Where do I begin? Can I honor God with these gifts after all? And how can I make my life a vessel for God's kingdom?" I finally have the answers to these questions by just realizing that I was neglecting these gifts. God's intent was not for me to compete with others who can sing and write better than I do, but to use the gift in the capacity it was given to me, for His glory. To meet the requirements, I had to admit that I should no longer neglect my gifts because they were assigned to me for ministry. God is waiting for you too. So, what are you waiting for?

Another area where people tend to neglect the gift is to think that they can use it without being equipped. I have seen it happen too many times, where Gospel singers attempted to do the work of ministry without praying first. Lacking prayer is a huge way in the neglecting of the gift. The Holy Spirit assigned these titles based on God's order accordingly. For this reason, *whosoever carries any of these titles should be fully equipped.* It is imperative that the minister should know that God put together a special uniform called "THE

WHOLE ARMOR" just for that purpose. This is not just a regular armor but of GOD. ***"Put on the whole armor of God, that ye may be able to stand against the wiles of the devil" (Eph. 6:11-18).***

God intended that we use the full armor, not some of them. There is a valuable reason for God to require that the minister should wear these six *pieces* of garment which represents a perfectly clothed minister. Each has its place in our spiritual bodies. In verses eighteen, the minister must have *a prayerful* life because prayer is the pole that holds perseverance in the work. Besides that, prayer as bonus and the fuel to sustains our ministry

I wonder what other pieces of spiritual garment they have missed from the armor.

Also, I noticed in the seventeen verses that the *helmet of Salvation* and the *Sword of the Spirit work together*. This is crucial because the minister must be saved to have access to exercise the power of God using His word. Next in verses fourteen, I see the *loins girt about with truth and the breastplate of righteousness* work together. I could understand this because if the minister's life is not aligning with the truth of the Gospel, then he or she will not be able to exercise the gifts in righteousness.

To continue, in verses fifteen, the minister's feet must be shod with the *preparation of the Gospel of peace* because this is one of the qualifications to those who have ministerial titles. They must be able to bring the Gospel of Jesus Christ to the unsaved. Most importantly in verses sixteen, the *shield of faith* is placed alone and above all things. I believe the Bible makes it clear that the minister cannot please God without faith. ***"But without faith, it is impossible to please Him, for he that cometh to God must believe that He is..." (Heb. 11:6).*** Listen, if God finds it necessary to put together the armor for us, I think we should pay attention to wear it as required. This might save us from falling apart when Satan, the enemy comes to destroy us. So, now that we know how God perceived a well-armed minister, it is in our best interest to be fully equipped for our assignment. See more detail about the importance of having to wear the Gospel armor in Session Twelve

What is the priority purpose of our gifts? The priority **purpose** of our gifts is giving back to God what is due to Him. Giving back to God what is due to Him is to recognize that our gifs are seeds to sow in God's kingdom. It is essential that we should recognize the *purpose* of our gifts because it helps us to understand the importance of rendering our services to God faithfully. The result of a faithful service will be followed by great spiritual harvests. Now let the Bible give us the answers. The book of Ephesians helps us to understand the purpose of the gifts. We discern that all gifts were given by God **"For the perfecting of the saints, for the work of the ministry, and for the edifying of the body of Christ" (Eph. 4:12).**

Gift- 1: Apostle

The Purpose of the Gift is Presented as Apostolic Role:

What is an apostle? An *Apostle* according to study, is one who is sent forth by God Himself. From the Greek word "APOSTOLOS" means "one sent forth." When we are given the gift of singing, God has great expectations from us. We have received Jesus Christ as the first gift, who gives us grace to accomplish the work in obedience to God's expectations. **"By whom we have received grace and apostleship for obedience to the faith among all nations, for His name" (Rom. 1:5).** We are called to take forth the message of the gospel through our voices and lyrics, and God is expecting us to win souls. The title of apostle is not frequently used in this era, but it does not mean that it is inactive. From the example set by our Master Jesus Christ, there is no difference whether His followers are called disciples, messengers, or apostles. **"And when it was day, He called unto him His disciples: and of them He chose twelve**

whom He named apostles" (Luke 6:13). Bearing witness is the work of an apostle. One of the most supernatural ways to send forth the Gospel to the world is to bear witness through recorded words, and singing is included.

The primary mission of an apostle is one who is divinely sent to accomplish a mission. That mission is to testify of what Jesus did on the cross. For this reason, the apostle should perform his tasks zealously as an advocate of the gospel, through the power of the Holy Spirit. That was the role of the Apostle Paul. **"But when the Comforter is come, whom I will send unto you from the Father, even the Spirit of truth, which proceedeth from the Father, he shall testify of me" (John 15:26).**

When we answer to the calling of God, we become partners with the Father, the Son and the Holy Spirit. Just as Jesus Christ and His Father were partners in the creation of the world, an Apostle is one who is ready to fulfill his assignment in partnership with all three. This means in performing the task of singing as an apostle, we should be very careful not to attempt to do it independently. Therefore, since we are sent forth to accomplish a special mission, each recorded song should be inspired seeds for a soul harvest. When the seeds are planted in good ground, it will bring forth a good harvest. A farmer plants the crops to get a harvest in return. Good harvest is what our Master is expecting from us as an Apostle.

Gift- 2: Prophet

The Purpose of the Gift is Presented as Prophetic Role:

What is a prophet? A *Prophet* is one who speaks "by direct divine inspiration and revelation from God." The Greek word for Prophet is "PROPHETES," which means an inspired messenger. Jesus, the messenger of His Father, who came to set captives free, used His prophetic authority over demons. Obery M. Hendricks Jr. agreed that "Jesus speaks as a prophet should speak boldly and on point, identifying the demon in no uncertain terms." *The Politics of Jesus* (p. 148). The ability to write gospel songs is not based on our philosophic capacity. The beginning process when writing gospel songs is to be spiritually connected with God as His messenger. The Holy Spirit gives divine revelations to the prophet. That means our thoughts as prophets should be directed by the Holy Spirit when writing the lyrics. If the Holy Spirit is not directing our thoughts while we write, the self will take the lead or even worse, Satan. When the self takes the lead, we are most likely to deviate from the truth and mingle in vain messages. When Satan takes the lead, evil spirits become the ministers. What the Lord requires is that we stay in harmony with the Holy Spirit who is our direct inspiration when writing Gospel songs.

The primary responsibility of the prophet is to deliver the message of the gospel of Jesus Christ for the remission of sins. ***"To Him give all the prophets witness that, through His name, whosoever believeth in Him shall receive remission of sins" (Acts 10:43).*** If we profess to be true prophets, the light of the truth should be the vital power of our songs. Therefore, we should not think about writing songs outside the direction of the Holy Spirit and expect to be successful in our ministries. When we are not directed by The Holy Spirit, the gift is used as weapons to diminish others to elevate ourselves. That is the pattern of the world, and we should not limit the power of prophecy by hiding our identity as a prophet. That title should always be worn.

True Prophet vs. False Prophet

What is a true prophet? A true prophet is one who pronounces God's message as it is without adding or taking away from it. We know the difference between the two when God honors His words. If the message is not from God, then that prophet is false. One who carries the title of a prophet should be prudent because there is a warning from God for such a title. ***"But the prophet, which shall presume to speak a word in my name, which I have not commanded him to speak, ... shall die" (Deut. 18:20).***

In the days of old, God gave good and bad warnings to His people through a prophet, but that was done under the moral "Law of Moses." This law is conditional because those who disobeyed God will miss out on His blessings. ***"And all these blessings shall come on thee, and overtake thee, if thou shalt hearken unto the voice of the Lord thy God" (Deut. 28:2).*** In this verse, God's principle is supported by the condition of being obedient to be blessed. But in this present time, the condition of the principle is based on what Jesus did on the cross, to be saved. When the prophet does not rely on "GRACE" in his lyrics, then the message will create confusion. ***"For God is not the author of confusion, but of peace, as in all churches of the saints" (I Cor. 14:33).*** The prophet must also avoid writing wordless songs.

What is a wordless song? A wordless song according to my revelation is a song made up of one or two sentences. In other words, it is the repetition of the same sentence throughout the entire song. There are two aspects to a wordless song. It could be either a complete or an incomplete song. One: If it is use as a direct reference to worship the ALMIGHTY GOD, then it is complete because this is the heavenly pattern. ***"...And they rest not day and night, saying, Holy, holy, holy, Lord God Almighty" (Rev.4:8.*** Two: if the wordless song is addressed to a different audience as a message, then the prophet's message is incomplete. For instance, "I am a friend of God" is the chorus of a song. If the writer had left out the details that explain what makes him a friend of God in this song, then the song would have been a wordless song. This song is presented as a full Gospel song because it describes the love of God. When a song is properly detailed, it better serves the spiritual well-being of the listeners. The worst-case scenario about this matter is that many get caught in this repetition accepting as though it is the right way to transport the

Gospel. Others might even find it amusing dancing to the beat, but there should be more to it than that. The prophet must also avoid adding too much to the lyrics.

How do prophets add too much to the lyrics? Adding too much is when the prophet brings inappropriate words that have nothing to do with the Gospel of Jesus Christ. Such as "Come to Jesus and your problems will be over." That is not true Gospel. Unknowingly, this is a false statement. The true Gospel is where Jesus says to ***"Come unto me, all ye that labor and are heavy laden, and I will give you rest" (Matt. 11:28).*** Note that the verse did not mention the word "problem," but heavy laden. I believe that "heavy laden" refers to our sin, and rest refers to the peace that we have in Christ Jesus. So, when we declare that Christianity is problem free, we are not telling the truth. Honestly, as one of the Haitian artists, I find this to be very common among them. Therefore, to avoid transgressing the Gospel, the prophet is responsible to seek Biblical knowledge before transmitting the message to the public.

Is it right for the prophet to use his or her gift to bring judgment? When we prophets boldly declare direct condemnation over sinners, we are taking God's judgment upon ourselves. We, too, were sinners saved by God's grace. Using the authority that comes with the gift does not place us in a position to judge or condemn anyone because we don't know what God might do in the next second to one's soul. On the contrary, the prophet should use the authority to deliver them. This does not mean that the prophet cannot warn sinners about hell. The difference is the prophet has no right to send anybody to hell. That final judgment belongs only to Jesus Christ, the judge of all judges.

A true prophet will profess and voice out only what he hears from the Holy Spirit. If the Holy Spirit is the Spirit of Grace, then He will teach us how to arrange our lyrics in the truth of God's Grace. If we should understand that principle and are convinced by the Holy Spirit during this teaching about being judgmental through our lyrics, we should: ***"Come boldly unto the throne of grace, that we may obtain mercy, and find grace to help in time of need" (Heb. 4:16).*** This is a critical time of need. It takes boldness for the prophet to turn to God for mercy because now, he or she is on the other side. It is guaranteed that God will grant mercy to a false prophet who repents. By this, the prophet will be careful not to taking away or adding to God's message in the lyrics. Let the lyrics be solid facts that are based on Biblical knowledge, so that those we touch through the prophetic words of our songs could be able to identify us as true prophets. Thank you for your attention to God's warning through this teaching.

Gift-3: Evangelist

The Purpose of the Gift is Presented as Evangelistic Role:

An *Evangelist (Preacher)* is one "who proclaims the good news of the gospel." The Greek word of Evangelist is "EVANGELION" which means good news. Evangelizing is a distinct way to share the gospel through songs because it gives us the opportunity to step out of the four walls of the church and attend to the needs of the lost world-wide.

There are many avenues available for evangelism. For example, some of us singers are not outspoken, but at the same time could be powerful preachers through songs. Another avenue that engages us with powerful evangelism is direct and indirect contact through broadcasts whether through television or radio. Another avenue is that evangelism can reach any class or nation regardless of which title we use through social media. Much more, no specific style is required to reach souls. In general, we just must be ready to use any God-given gift. That way there are no limitations as to how many souls we might reach.

As evangelists, we need to stand firm in the fulfillment of our work. Our strength should be like that of Jesus. That is to be able to do the work courageously. The work of the ministry is marked by endurance. Endurance will safeguard the minister against the arrow of rejection. ***"But you be watchful in all things, endure afflictions, do the work of an evangelist, fulfill your ministry" (II Tim. 4:5).*** No matter what, salvation is preached. Evangelism in songs should be one of the ways to win souls. We need to recognize how privileged we are to be able to use our gifts as instruments to preach effectively. Effective preaching is when the light of your songs shines so bright that people can see where they are and surrender their lives to Christ.

Much more, an Evangelist is: ***"The salt of the earth" (Matt. 5:13).*** Our songs ought to be used as salt to influence people. One can use many ingredients to create a specific flavor, but without salt, the flavor will be less attractive. My question is: why God uses salt as example besides all other flavors. I believe it is because salt does not only give flavor but also preserved. In order words, preserving is to keep safe from spoiling. We could see that salt is most definitely important in the menu of the Evangelist.

What can we say salt represents? Salt literally is to preserve and keep safe an item. So spiritually, salt is mercy and truth (grace). ***"...O prepare mercy and truth, which may preserve him" (Ps. 61:7).*** To add flavor to our songs, salt must be added to our ingredients. The ingredients could be health, wealth, love, forgiveness, joy, peace and more, but if it does not contain grace something tremendous is missing. The evangelist must share the gospel in a way that it would attract sinners to God's mercy and truth. The truth is ***"For God so loved the world, that He gave His only begotten Son, that whosoever believeth in Him should not perish, but have everlasting life" (John 3:16).*** When an evangelist composes a song that contains grace, the lyrics must clearly display the love of God that saves us from damnation.

What is a flavored song? A flavored song should reflect God's grace, love, and forgiveness. A flavored song brings satisfaction to the Holy Spirit. A flavored song will bring glory to God, and a flavored song will meet the needs of the body of Christ. An Evangelist is an agent of the Gospel. When Christ dwells in the heart of the agent, he or she will be subjected to Him. Being subjected is the power of obedience. The Holy Spirit will enlighten the vision of the agent when writing the songs.Subjection is achieved through the discipline of devoting quality time in praying, seeking God through His word, and listening to His command. When we listen closely to the voice of the Holy Spirit, we can better evangelize and meet the needs of people.

Evangelism through songs has nothing to do with mental biases or opinions. This mentality can contaminate the purpose of evangelism. Traditional biases are when we write songs that express our opinions or other's rather than love. Some of the biases that I often heard in what they refer to as gospel song is *gossiping*. The Bible says that we ought to exhort our brothers and sisters with love. **"Exhorting one another: and so much the more, as ye see the day approaching" (Heb. 10:25)** Gossiping is not exhortation. Gossiping is using your gift to point out others' weaknesses, such as songs that tell people about their dress code, make up and so on. Exhortation is to exercise our responsibilities and point them to the light of the word and allow the Holy Spirit to do His work.

Most importantly, the Evangelist should be humble and ready to resist traditional *biases*. This has to do with using spiritual wisdom. Resistance could apply in both positive and negative aspects. The positive aspect is to apply our God given wisdom and the ability to discern what we are doing wrong, and then repent from it.

The negative resistance is when we are aware of what we are doing wrong, and we have been given the opportunity to discern it but resist changing our ways or styles. By resisting the truth, we are saying that God is unable to transform us. Consequently, we are holding hostage both our deliverances and the deliverance of those we are trying to reach. God is kind enough to reveal to us our rebellious conditions through His words, which is the mirror of our lives, but it is totally up to us to take advantage of His kindness. If we should let go of negative resistance, and yield towards God's instructions, our gifts will bring glory to God.

This is an example of what a spiritually flavored song can do. Several years ago, I was singing at a church in Manhattan, New York where I was a member for over two decades. The song that I sang reached the heart of a lady named Marie Joseph who was struggling with forgiveness issues. Several weeks after, Marie approached me to give me feedback about my singing ministry. She told me that she visited our church one day, and she was sitting in the back when they called me to minister in song. She even remembered the title of the song, which was "Friend of a Wounded Heart." I want you to understand that song ministered to her heart, helping her to see that Jesus was the friend that she needed now. My heart humbly rejoiced when she told me that it was that song that brought her to repentance. The word declares that **"If we should lift up the Lord, He will draw men unto Him" (John 12: 32).** So, we Evangelists must lift God in the way we evangelized.

Immediately after this testimony, I followed up with spiritual nourishment. A new believer is a fragile soul that needs to be handled with care. With that in mind, every morning at six am I would call to instruct Marie with the word of God and pray with her. This went on for at least two years. I was able to witness her life transform, and the fruit of my labor was to see her growing in grace. Sister Marie was my prayer partner for many years. Thank God until this day we are still connected.

I used to think that evangelism pertained to the people of the street only, but that experience gave me a new perception. There are unsaved people among the congregation too. We can lead them to Christ wherever they are. The bottom line is evangelism through songs is powerful, and it should not be diminished by the way it is presented. The good news is, if we set our minds to follow the principles that come with the gift, is that our songs will bring forth great soul harvest. God has already provided us with all that we need to help us fulfill the work with confidence.

Gift-4: Pastor

The Purpose of the Gift is Presented as Pastoral Role:

A *Pastor* is one who shepherds the flocks. The word "Pastor" comes from the Latin "Pastor" which means "shepherd." Pastors' role wouldn't have much meaning without the flock. Likewise, the role of those who minister in songs would be incomplete without an audience. Jesus our Good Shepherd was appointed by God the Father to sets very good examples of what pastors should be like. The role and the characteristics of Jesus our shepherd is what minister should focus on in this portion of the teaching.

God places both ministers and pastors in the front line for a purpose. They share the same space. That space is leadership. It is easier to spot someone in the front line than those in the rear. Those who are placed in front have special qualifications. They are trained and prepared to meet the Lord's requirements. I do not know about you, but when I have the privilege to stand in the front line, that is my time to put into action what I have been trained for. That is to meet the need of my flock which is whatever audience that I am ministering to.

Jesus, our Good Shepherded was always prepared to meet the need of the people. Jesus met their social need when He mingled with them so He could express His Father's unconditional love. In fact, Jesus' performed His first miracle at a social gathering. At the wedding, Jesus turned water to wine, which was the best wine the people ever tasted. Jesus met physical need when he fed five thousand men, all at once. Jesus met physiological need when He transformed Zacchaeus' life by a home visitation. Jesus met spiritual need when He taught His disciples about God's kingdom. Jesus met sinful need when he healed the woman with the bleeding issue. Jesus said to her "go and sin no more." Jesus met the need of those who were bound by Satan's chain. All these performances were done using His power and authority.

Ministers are not placed at the front line alone. Jesus had promised to send us the Holy Spirit to help us, and He did. Ministers' hearts ought to be filled with the words of God to meet the need of the flock (audience) as needed. Jesus never neglected the need of the people; ministers too should not neglect the need of their audience. Ministers should use the word of God in their lyrics. Jesus made himself available to always hear from His Father; He did nothing without the Father's approval. Ministers also are to be available to hear from God at any time. That is the pattern that all ministers should follow.

The characteristic of a pastor is what ministers should possess. One of Pastors' responsibilities is to show concern for one lost sheep. Jesus never tired of caring for us, He is constantly watching out for the lion that is after to devour God's church. As well ministers are responsible for making sure that their flock (audience) minds are protected by what they teach in their songs. Jesus speaks words of peace during our storms. We minister to bring peace to the soul of a troubled sheep. Jesus blesses us with all sorts of blessings by ensuring us with the benefit of stability, which is more reason to trust Him. Pastors or ministers are to stabilize a strong relationship with their flock to gain their trust.

Furthermore, Jesus uses His words as rod of correction because He loves us, and not to destroy us. Pastors should not tolerate the practice of sin but should correct the flock with precaution through love. Jesus' feeling towards us is not bitter, but sweet in kindness. Pastors should also express kindness towards their flock. Jesus guards our hearts from filthy thoughts and foolishness, and always creates an opportunity for us to repent without doubt. Pastors should always try to create an atmosphere that would lead the flock towards repentance.

Once ministers possess these characteristics, they could never starve their audiences, and feed them the wrong spiritual food through their lyrics. We must know that our lyrics are nourishment to God's people. ***"... We are His people and the sheep of his pasture" (Ps. 100:3b).*** If the flock belongs to God, then ministers would have to answer to Him for their negligence's. The Lord made it very clear when He declared ***"For thus saith the Lord God; Behold, I, even I will both search my sheep, and seek them out"*** (Ezk. 34:11). Ministers or pastors should know by this declaration what God is expecting from them as shepherds.

The kingdom of heaven is a wide field in which all types of opportunities are given to pastors or ministers to exercise the love of God through their gifts. For this reason, each time the door of an opportunity is opened, they should always take advantage to reach a higher standard, especially through singing. Singing gospel songs is the highest opportunity that one can have because it covers so many areas such as to feed the flock with spiritual nourishment, preach the world of God to sinners, teach the word of God for spiritual growth, praise and worship the name of the Lord and heal and set the captives free. These benefits are ministers' higher standard. This higher standard is abundant care for the flock in God's pasture. David, the psalmist made that declaration in *Psalms twenty-three.* They flock should never feel neglected for any reason. ***"The Lord is my shepherd; I shall not want" (Ps. 23:1).*** One who is gifted to minister in song needs to nourish the flock with abundant inspirations. Remember, our flock is our audience. Look forward to learning more about the type of audiences that we minister to in Session Seven.

Gift-5: Teacher

The Purpose of the Gift is Presented as Teaching Role:

The church has always been the center of the Gospel of Jesus Christ. God does not want any of His children to be ignorant of the benefits of serving Him. Therefore, He designated and appointed teachers for this reason. A ministerial teacher's aim is to focus on educating the body of Christ through the gift of teaching. If knowledge is the fruit of Edification, then a fulfilling lyric should be used as seed for *good teaching.*

Lyrics have great influence on the listener's belief, attitude, and emotion. The teacher has to be conscious of how to clearly unfold the teaching. If the structure of the song is to teach on God's love, then the song should be supported by scriptures that focus on that aspect.

A good Teacher of the word is one who is faithful in learning from God. This is a serious scholar because the church was established through teaching. As we learn from God, we make it easier for the church to learn from us. It is not easy to understand the Gospel of Jesus Christ without divine instructions. Having the gift does not exclude us from learning how to use it more effectively. Although there are many channels that could be used to promote the Gospel, teaching is the most successful above all. We can also use good teaching in our lyrics to bring knowledge to those who are enslaved by sin.

A good *teacher will meet the requirement of his Master.* **"The LORD requires of us to do justly, and to love mercy, and to talk humbly with Him" (Mic. 6:8).** Our passions to please our Master are the keys to fulfilling our commitment to Him. When teaching is justified by love, mercy, and humility, it will lead to perfect understanding. Perfect understanding is a chain of blessings that brings the church to order, spiritual maturity, and reconciliation.

A good teacher will know that Judging is not part of the requirement of the principles. The teacher should not be angry with his or her students. The gift is not to be used as a hammer to nail others, but to instruct them and pick them up when they fall. Jesus has already been nailed for the sins.

A good teacher will know that using teaching as a weapon to discredit the church is a direct offense against God. Teaching should not be used as a tool for revenge. That is satanic motivation. Satan's pattern should be avoided in our songs. Using this pattern is not showing love but hatred. For example, a *satanic motivation* is to write lyrics to let someone know indirectly that we know about their sinful habits instead of teaching them how to get out of them.

A good teacher will know that incorrect teaching could also intoxicate the spiritual health of the church, and even cause members to retaliate against the teacher and abandon their assemblies. **"But if ye bite and devour one another, take heed..."**

A good teacher will know how to capture the congregation's attention in the teaching. Capturing people's attention is capturing their hearts, and it should not be taken for granted. Taking for granted is to come unprepared while they are expecting something special from the teacher. What we prepare to teach in our songs could either draw people to God or push them away. When people are down, there is a need that must be fulfilled. It is not necessary to overwhelm someone's mind with negative lyrics that complicate the situation while they are looking for a solution. We may not be the solution, but our songs can lead them to God who is the solution. Also, they need to listen to something that is related to their situation. If the teacher comes prepared to meet them where they are, I am sure the outcome will be a blessing. In general, the teacher's lyrics must be blameless. **"Giving no offense in anything, that our ministry may not be blamed" (II Cor. 6:3).**

A good teacher will be honest in his or her teaching. Dishonesty is marked by envy and strife. Be careful with those two. Be happy with your gift, stay in your position, and be satisfied with what you do. Remember, you will be judged based on your assignment. **"Some indeed preach Christ even of envy and strife; and some also of good will" Phl. 1:15).** Keep in mind, when we stand before the audience, we are the leader and people tend to follow the leader. We are to teach by example. For example, sometimes I observed how quickly the teacher's dishonest lyrics can attract the weaker, those who support their dishonesty. They are quickly motivated to use this moment as an opportunity to display strife against other members. Perhaps, they might know something personal about that individual's life. They automatically joined the leader's remarks in the lyrics as they shouted "Amen!" sarcastically. Therefore, let our teaching bring excellent results to the church.

The Beneficial Attributes of Teaching to the Congregation:

"Let the word of Christ dwell in us richly in all wisdom, teaching and admonishing one another in psalms and hymns and spiritual songs, singing with grace in our hearts to the Lord" (Col. 3:16).

Even though no congregations are alike, it should be clear that edification remains the sole center of the church and that is done through teaching. Some teachers perceive that their teaching pertaining only to those they teach. Conversely, the teacher should be convinced first by what he or she learns from the Holy Spirit before teaching into others. And that is a fact. Here are some of the important fruits of teaching. Those who teach should have an idea about how to extend the Bible's views in their teaching. The enthralled approach of the Bible about these attributes increases both the teacher's (the minister) and the congregation's (church) knowledge, in learning to appreciate God's word. The teacher's responsibility is to first receive the principles of God in the word, and hand them down to the church in accordance with these attributes in faith. The church on the other hand is responsible for accepting the principles from the teacher and enriching their lives with these attributes.

The Benefit Attributes:

• **Teaching is a direct command with a promise from our Lord and Savior Jesus Christ.** *"Teaching them to observe all things whatsoever I have commanded you; and, lo, I am with you always, even unto the end of the world" (Matt. 28:20).*

• **Teaching is God's way for the church to grow.** *"Teach me thy way, O LORD, and lead me in the plain path, because of mine enemies" (Ps. 27:11).*

• **Teaching shows us God's path.** *"Show me Thy ways, O LORD;*

teach me thy paths. Lead me in Thy truth and teach me: for Thou art the God of my salvation; on Thee do I wait all the day" (Ps. 25:4-5).

- **Teaching is Gods' will for the church to prosper.** *"And he shall be like a tree planted by the rivers of water, that bringeth forth fruit in his season; his leaf also shall not wither, and whatsoever he doeth shall prosper"* (Ps. 1: 3).

- **Teaching empowered God's people with knowledge.** *"But the comforter, which is the Holy Ghost, whom the Father will send in my name, he shall teach you all things, and bring all things to your remembrance, whatsoever I have said unto you"* (John 14:26).

- **Teaching brought forth spiritual truth to the church.** *"For all shall know me, from the least to the greatest..."* (Heb. 8:11).

- **Teaching helps the church to live a holy life.** *"Teaching us that, denying ungodliness and worldly lusts, we should live soberly, righteously, and godly, in this present world"* (Titus 2:12).

- **Teaching gives good life to the people of God.** *"For thou, Lord, wilt bless the righteous; with favor wilt thou compass him as with a shield"* (Ps. 5:12).

- **Teaching gives encouragement to believers.** *"And let us not be weary in well doing: for in due season we shall reap, if we faint not"* (Gal. 6:9).

- **Teaching reinforces hope to the people of God.** *"In hope of eternal life, which God, that cannot lie, promised before the world began"* (Tit. 1:2).

- **Teaching makes us successful Christians** *"But seek ye first the kingdom of God, and His righteousness; and all these things shall be added unto you"* (Matt. 6:33).

- **Teaching comforts the church.** *"Wherefore comfort together and edify one another, even as also ye do"* (I Thess. 5:11).

- **Teaching keeps the church in the light of fellowship.** *"But* *if we walk in the light, as He is in the light, we have fellowship one with another..." (I John 1:7).*

• **Teaching gives peace to the people of God.** *"Now the Lord of peace Himself give you peace always by all means" (II Thess. 3:16).*

• **Teaching helps the church to walk in love.** *"Let brotherly love continue" (Heb. 13:1).*

• **Teaching encourages the church to walk in the goodness of God.** *"Let us not be weary in well doing: for in due season we shall reap, if we faint not" (Gal. 6:9).*

• **Teaching keeps the church focused on Christ.** *"Let this mind be in you, which was in Christ Jesus" (Phil. 2:5).*

• **Teaching reinforces faith.** *"For we walk by faith, not by sight" (II Cor. 5:7).*

• **Teaching helps the church to be steadfast.** *"Therefore, my beloved brethren, be ye steadfast, unmovable, always abounding in the work of the Lord, forasmuch as ye know that your labor is not in vain in the Lord" (I Cor. 15:58).*

SESSION SEVEN

Identifying Our Audiences:

In this session, you will learn about:

- *Specific audiences in the ministry and how do we meet their spiritual needs.*
- *How to focus on the theme while writing the lyrics for Gospel song.*
- *To differentiate and detached audiences.*
- *The roles of Gospel music in our lives.*
- *Some examples of my inspiration to reinforce the teaching.*

The purpose of this session is to focus on the title or the subject matter "AUDIENCE." As we go along, you will be able to identify with the three most powerful aspects about the use of the gift. Knowing that I have my being in Jesus, left me with a craving to leave my heart and my ears open to wisdom. This was when the Holy Spirit revealed *three* important aspects that must be present when writing gospel song: *(1) God must be glorified through the song, (2) the Gospel of Jesus Christ must be preached, and (3) the church must be edified by the song.* All these aspects are dependent on the type of testimony, and the direction in which the author is heading, while writing the song. Having these aspects in mind, writing gospel songs should not be a difficult task.

I had a conversation with a co-worker and told her that I wrote songs. She asked me "What kind of songs do you write?" I told her that I only write Gospel songs. She then said, "I write songs too, but I found it very hard to write Gospel songs no matter how hard I try." I did not elaborate further in the conversation because it was not the appropriate time or place for me to talk about such a subject. But I knew right away why she could not write Gospel songs. Writing Gospel songs is not an art, but rather a Godly inspiration. People who write songs most have something in mind. Some write to express their love, others write as a career to improve romance, and some write because they are trying to reach a goal or a dream. But when it comes to writing gospel songs, this is a different approach because the inspiration is divine.

One might be saved, have many testimonies, and even could write gospel songs, but the lack of a personal relationship with God blocks the ability to release his or her testimonies. That led me back to what I have been teaching in this manual. There should be a spiritual connection between the individual and the author who gave the gift (GOD).

What kind of attitude does the author need to have? We can follow the Psalms of David. Look at his attitude towards God. David declares that ***"His soul, wait silently for God alone, for his expectation is from Him. He only is his rock and salvation" (Ps. 62:5).*** For instance, for every circumstance in his life, he wrote a song to the Lord. I believe it was because David's heart and mind were always open to God's love for him. We too have similar testimonies. If we should allow our minds to focus on the amazing grace of God, we will always have a new song like David.

There are various groups of audiences. Among all others, we will focus on the three that we most tend to minister to: (1) primarily God, the ultimate audience, which could be either "individual" or "incorporate" (2) the unsaved audience which is "targeted" and (3) the congregational audience which is "selected." I thought it would be a good idea to add some of my inspirations to this session as references. Also, included, you will see some inspired photos along with Bible verses projecting the images which expressed the message that I desire to convey to my audiences.

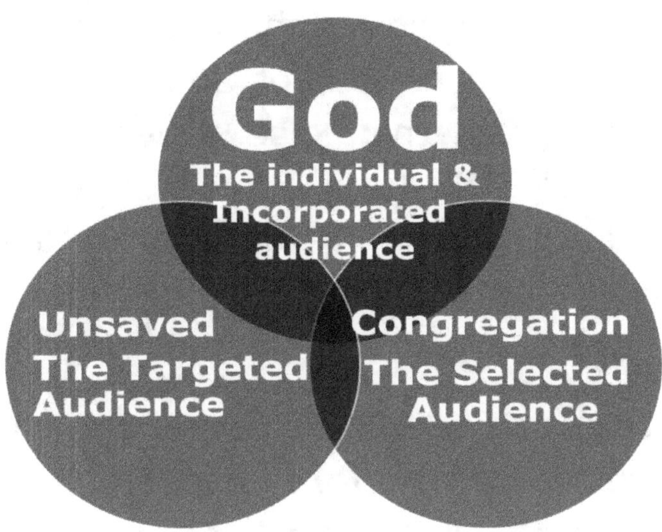

GOD, The Individual Audience:

When *God* is our *individual* audience, our focus is on Him and Him alone, for He alone is worthy of our praise and worship. Focusing on God is giving Him priority. At that point, our song is dedicated to Him.

The conditioning of the focus comes with humility and reverence. Reverence is giving respect, love and esteem to God. Humility permits the fragrance of our praise and worship to welcome God in our midst. There are no limitations when it comes to freely express our love to God. We express ourselves not to the degree of feelings or sensation, but through the acknowledgement of the magnitude of who is to us. We also have the choice to either magnify or diminish our love for God. It all depends on what is on our mind. If our mind is on God, then He will be magnifying. If not, conversely, He will be diminished. Before presenting our praise and worship to God, we ought to condition our hearts to highly minister to Him in Spirit and in truth. ***"God is greatly to be feared in the assembly of the saints and to be had in reverence of all of them that are about Him" (Ps. 89:7).***

How do we condition our hearts before ministering to God? The first thing we need to do is to get the self out of the way by taking time out to meditate on His goodness. When our hearts are filled with His goodness, we are automatically charged and ready to pour our love on Him. If we are not conscious of God's goodness towards us, then the focus will be on something else. I love the way the Psalmist identifies his relationship with the goodness of God. The Psalms are songs written by ordinary people like us. We can use their patterns. Let us analyze how the author expresses his admiration to God in these words to his song.

"I will love thee, O LORD, my strength. The Lord is my rock and my fortress, and my deliverer; My God, my strength, in whom I will trust; My shield and the horn of my salvation, my high tower. I will call upon the Lord, who is worthy to be praised" (Ps. 18:1-3).

Notice how the Psalmist freely expresses his thoughts. He did not say "I will praise or worship you." Rather, he says *"I will love you."* That means the word love is so strong that it covers both praise and worship. Then he follows up with his reasons for loving God. It is clear how he magnified God for His goodness. Notice that he is ministering directly to Him as a possessive pronoun: *"my."* He is telling Him that He is his **strength, rock, fortress, deliverer, shield, horn, salvation and high tower.** His focus is showing gratitude for the blessings of who God is to him. That to me, my friend, is an excellent way to love our God. I hope this example is helpful to help you magnify the LORD in a new perspective.

Our worship and praise put God in His rightful place, "ALPHA AND OMEGA" That is why our attention should be addressed to Him as a personal expression and not as a testimony or exhortation to others. The hymn of the writer focused on God from the beginning to the end. So, when we mix our praise and worship with testimony and so on it may sound good, but we are addressing a different type of audience rather than God directly who should have been the audience. We might not be aware of it, but switching from telling God to telling the people removes our direct focus from Him; and that is very common. Beware not to lose focus on God, the audience, and deviate to another audience.

Michael W. Smith one of the gospel Ministers freely expressed himself directly to God as his audience. I believe that "The Heart of Worship" was inspired during his meditation of God's sovereignty. Listening to such a song brings my heart to join with him at the feet of the Lord. As in the days when Solomon expressed his love to God, Michael did not depend on music to worship God. His affection was very transparent in the lyrics.

> "When the music fades, I'll bring you more than a song; for a song is not what you have required. You search deeper within the way things are viewed; You're looking into my heart. I am going back to heart of worship, and it's all about You Jesus. King of endless worth, no one could express how much You deserve. Though I am weak and poor; all I have is Yours, every single breath. ..."

Even though the song was custom made for God, those who are relating to God in that sense could join with Michael in worship. Therefore, when a song that is addressing God touches God's heart, it makes a double impact, because the church also is edified by it.

The Holy Spirit dwells in the heart of the believer and nothing can change that. When our hearts are conditioned to honor God, our bodies have no other choice but to follow. It should not be a scary thing to free our hearts and bodies when we worship the Lord. At that moment, we become dead to the self so that the Holy Spirit might manifest in us. Paul supports this statement by saying that ***"Always bearing about in the body the dying of the Lord Jesus, that the life also of Jesus might be made manifest in our body"*** **(II Cor. 4:10).** Once the Holy Spirit takes control of our spirits, minds, bodies, and souls, we are free to worship in spirit and in truth.

Nothing else matters because it is not about us. The Holy Spirit is the one who convinces our hearts to devote our attention to God. When that happens, He has complete control of the atmosphere. His glory reflects in our attitudes, and our hands are positioned to uplift God, All-Mighty! We began to praise God in the fear of His presence. We praise Him because we acknowledge that we were ***"wonderfully made by Him" (Ps. 139:14).***

Inspiration One

The Intent of this Song is to Address God, My Individual Audience:

The original subject of *"Jesus, I need You!"* is the **Prayer of a Troubled Servant.** It fits in the category of **God, my individual audience** because it is a direct supplication.

Acknowledging the intensity of frequent temptations that I face daily as a Christian, demonstrates that my only way of overcoming these obstacles is to depend completely on God's strength. As God's child, I have legal access to go to Him and express my troubled heart. Claiming that I am strong without the might of God is denying my weakness. I acknowledge that facing the challenges of self-inflation, pride, hypocrisy, jealousy, and many more are stronger than my will to serve God. Since nothing is hidden from Him, therefore, there should not be any reason why I should not be honest with Him about my daily struggles.

My Lord and Savior Jesus Christ had faced all sorts of temptations. He never delayed presenting His causes to His heavenly Father through prayer and fasting. Nothing should stop me from reaching out to God in my distress. There are no rules in the Bible that prevent me from revealing my weaknesses to God. That is why in this song I tell God how much I need Him every day in my life. If I do not confess my weaknesses to my heavenly Father, the adversary will use them to destroy my relationship with Him. I could never be a loser by presenting my cases to God. I yield in prayer to bring vulnerability into the open. By doing so, the adversary cannot accuse me of something that is already confessed.

When I wrote this song, I was struggling with rebellion, loneliness, and depression. The adversary makes it his business to cause me to debate with my faith in God daily. Prayer was and is the strength of my relationship with God. Instead of giving into Satan's constant accusations, I ran and presented my case to my Heavenly Father. It is Satan's job to bring discontent to the hearts of the ministers. The reversal of discontent is to believe in the promises of Christ. "He will never leave nor forsake me." There is no need to pretend that I can carry my burdens alone. It is in prayer that I release my burdens to the Lord. I could not make it this far on my own. That is why I do not hesitate to openly ask my Heavenly Father to help me to stay on the straight and narrow way in this song.

The Holy Spirit governs my will and directs me to be honest with myself and to God in my prayers. Prayer is my only way of communicating with my Father. Prayer preserves me from falling. My prayer was a consistent deposit in God's heavenly bank. With prayer, I could catch one who is falling out of faith. An honest prayer brings maturity in faith. It is through maturity that I can pray for the healing and deliverance of many. Prayer permits me to reach beyond my weaknesses and worries in exchange for perfect strength. Besides that, experiencing the results of a prayer is rewarding. When I could see my past sins behind me and I am remaining in the straight and narrow way, which is the evidence of God's mighty protections over me.

My continuous prayer is that you, too, could stop trying to make it by yourself, but by truthfully reaching out to God's unfailing hands.

Inspiration One Expression to:
GOD, The Individual Audience

* Give ear, O LORD, unto my prayer; and

   Attend to the voice of my supplication.

   In the day of my trouble, I will call upon Thee;

   For Thou wilt answer me.

* I sought the LORD, and he heard me, and

   Delivered me from all my fears.

* Cast thy burden upon the LORD,

   and He shall sustain thee; He shall never

   suffer the righteousness to be moved.

* Thou art my hiding place;

   Thou shalt preserve me from trouble;

   Thou shalt compass me about with songs of deliverance

   (Ps. 86:6-7; 34:4; 55:22;   32:7).

JESUS *I need You*

a) Jesus, I need You each and every day. In this world of darkness, You are the light that shines my way. Day by day, I want to be obedient to Your will. Reach out and hold my hand and lead me through this troubled way.

b) Step by step I will follow wherever Your Spirit leads. Let not my heart be troubled when the waves of life are raging. Though I cannot find my way, allow me to see the light. Reach out, hold my hand, and lead me through this troubled way.

c) There are two ways LORD: One is straight and narrow, the other is wide and confusing; that's why I need Your help. Keep me on the straight and narrow way. My destination is in Your hand. Cover me with Your grace Lord, that my life may glorify Your name.

d) For You alone I want to live, in joy, in sorrow and in pain. My heart and soul belong to You. Only in You I place my trust. This narrow way is sometimes high. I cannot make it without Your help. Your word of peace is in my heart. My journey is in Your hands.

Yes! I really, really need You. No! I cannot make it with You.... I need You. …

e) I am surrounded by evil! And You are my strength. Elohim, Elohim! Cover me! You are my Shepherd; only You can guide my feet in this troubled life.

You are my loins girt, my breast plate, my salvation, and the sword of the Spirit. You are my refuge, hear my prayer! I really, really need You

God "The Incorporated Audience"

When God is my *incorporated* audience, I praise Him for His marvelous works, for His wonders and power and for His mercy and grace. My love for God is displayed by praising and worshipping Him. Praise and worship are priorities in pleasing my Master. If praise and worship are not included in my offerings, the purpose of my gift is diffused, and I will become the priority rather than God. ***"Give to the LORD the glory due unto His name: bring an offering, and come into His courts" (Ps. 96:8).*** Giving to the Lord what is due to Him is the proper way to devote myself to Him because when I minister to the Lord, I hear from Him.

I want my songs to be filled with *words that satisfy God.* Praise and worship attract the holiness of God's presence, and the aromas of my worship become the intimate romance like the blossom of a rose in my heart. I found myself relating to the Psalmist's praise when he said: ***"It shall blossom abundantly, and rejoice even with joy and singing..." (Is. 35:2).*** At the presence of the Lord, I just cannot help it. Tears of joy always stream down my face. My heart beats and melts in the contentment of His holiness. The more I acknowledge His presence, the more I surrender to Him. As I fellowship with God, I am also in communion and becoming one with Him. I shout aloud the sound of Hallelujahs and tremble before His presence. When I submit myself to His holiness, the devils have no choice but to vanish away.

My late friend Brother Duval Destin had an extraordinary experience with the glory of God at "The Calvary Campground" in Ashland, Virginia. The Calvary Campground was designed for people who desire to draw closer to the Lord. This is where Christians meet and interact with people of many nations and different cultures. At the temple, people have the freedom to express their love for God as a whole. Anyone who gives ear to the Holy Spirit, and seeks God whole-heartedly, would be blessed. Somehow, Brother Destin was one of these people. He knew about my longing for the Lord, and he was eager to share this experience with me. As soon as he returned to New York, he called me and insisted that I should go and face the glory of God. As he described the moment of his life to me, I began to feel the need to go.

Shortly after, I called the Camp office and made a reservation to attend the next conference. It is not necessary to share all the details of what I experienced during my visit there. Before I went there, I thought that this special place would be something out of the ordinary, but it was just the opposite. I was stunned by the simplicity of the sanctuary. It did not have expensive ornaments and furniture. In the sanctuary there was a plain carpet, some chairs, and baskets full of flags of many colors. Anyone was free to use the flags as they worshipped and danced before the Lord. In addition, the background of the pulpit was made with a white satin drape on which was inscribed "THE WAVE OF GLORY." Everyone had one thing in common (their love for God). They united their hearts and voices to worship Him and expecting a word or a miracle from Him.

The point that I am making is that my obedience to accept Brother Destin's invitation to the campground changed my worship routine forever. It was there that I experienced the power of incorporated worship because our sincere worship opened the door that leads to the knowledge of the glory of God in our midst.

What is the door that leads me to God's glory? The glory of God was a mystery to me until it was revealed in the book of *Romans chapter 5: 1-2.* This familiar verse changed my perception about the glory of God.

Let's allow the Holy Spirit to simplify the explanations. **"Therefore, being justified by _faith_, we have peace with God through our _Lord Jesus Christ_"(V. 1). "By whom also we have access by _faith_ into this grace wherein we stand and rejoice in hope of the glory of God" (v. 2).**

So far, there are *two visible aspects* about what I know: (1) I *know* for sure that I am *justified* by putting my *faith* in God; and (2)

I also *know* that I *have peace* with God; not through my good deeds, but through Jesus Christ, who died in my place.

(V. 2) simplifies what I have as a Christian. Again, through Jesus Christ I *have access* by having *faith* to enter God's *Grace* and stand and *rejoice* in the *hope* of God's *glory*.

Whenever a word is emphasized repeatedly that word is the principal *subject.* Evidently, we could see that the subject is the underlined word "FAIT," and JESUS CHRIST is the ultimate Author.

In summary, *justification, peace, access, grace, rejoice and hope* are the spiritual blessings given unto me as bonuses to enrich of my faith in God. When I approached God at the sanctuary, I did it with faith and hope. The result of putting my faith and hope in God led me to the discovery of these spiritual blessings listed above. What a wonderful discovery that was.

Understand this, when I draw near to God's presence in faith, the Holy Spirit dresses me with the garment of blessings. Blessings that only He can provide such as *grace, justification, peace, and hope.* Most of all, *faith* is the key that gives me access into the glory of God.

Basically, the glory of God is based on two powerful words: **KNOW and HAVE.** (1) I know that I have faith, the key that gives me access to enter the glory; and (2) I know that my faith in Jesus Christ is the door that leads me to the Father.

I would say it was not the Calvary Campground that drew me to the glory of God. Rather it was my faith in meeting God there. When I entered God's glory, I was comfortable in His presence. At this point, even my voice changed to an angelic one. When I sang with the congregation my voice stood out as if I was the only one in the temple. I was so marveled by the presence of the Holy Spirit. After the service, a sister brought to my attention how she was blessed with my singing, and she wished that I wouldn't stop singing. Although my singing edified the church, I had to remove the focus from me and give credit to the Holy Spirit. Whence can such blessing come but the Holy Spirit? I learned that when my audience is God, I should not allow anything else to come between me and Him. My beautiful voices alone cannot render my worship acceptable to God. But because I give God the priority in my heart, I experience the glory of His presence. ***"What we do is not to please men, but to please God which trieth our hearts" (I Thess. 2:4).***

Inspiration Two

The Intent of this Song is to Address God, the Incorporated Audience

The original subject of *"Give Praise to the Mighty King"* is my invitation to the people of all races to join me in praising God. My aim is to make one voice with the people of God and take the anointing praise to a higher level while proclaiming **God** as my **incorporate audience**. It fits in the category of **Praise**.

My lips are filled with praise when it comes to the outpouring of my devotion to God. Heaven is a holy place and contains no defects because it is the dwelling place of a Holy God. I am also convinced that when we come together and praise God in unity, His presence in our bodies as His temple becomes the Holy of Holies. When God is present, He removes every defective trait and infirmity. The harmony of praise attracts divine touch. Healing and deliverance contain the seal of the evidence of God's presence in our midst. The Holy Spirit is touched by our worship; and as a result, brings healing and deliverance into the atmosphere. The imperfect becomes perfect, the weak becomes strong and peace reigns in my heart. When God is my ultimate audience, I let Him be magnified in my song and at the same time invite people to Welcome Him in our midst.

It is part of my duty to encourage the people of God to declare praise to Him. What I bring into the atmosphere was already conceived in my spirit even before I entered the congregation of the saints. I imagine experiencing the joy of God's presence in heaven while I am still here on earth. The intent of this song is not just to sing the melody and lyrics. It is rather an invitation to experience the glory of God's Holy presence when we praise together, in unity.

Please understand that experiencing God's Holy presence is not an ordinary feeling, but it is a connection that begins with an intimate relationship with Him that lasts throughout one's lifetime. Without such a relationship, there is no way I could bring any one into fellowship with God just by inviting them to sing a song repeatedly. The individual must have some type of interest in practicing personal intimacy with God in his or her dedicated time. That way when we come together, our minds will already be set in the same direction. One also must have a hunger for experiencing the glory of God. It is my daily intimacy with God that inspired me to write this song. Even when I am sometimes distracted, the Holy Spirit always leads my mind back to where it should be.

This song is just to remind God's people that we could declare His glory in the congregations as well as it is in heaven. The significance of expressing our songs by using our whole beings through the clapping of hands, our holy dances, our joys and our shouts of praise is to carry out our devotions to the "Mighty King." As a result of God's unconditional love for us, we, as one family, come together in discipline and formality showing gladness, inclining, and imploring His presence.

Expressions to God:
the Incorporated Audience

* O praise the LORD, all ye nations: praise Him, all ye people.
  For His merciful kindness is great toward us:
  and the truth of the LORD endureth forever. Praise ye the LORD.

* Because thy loving kindness is better than life, my lips shall praise
  thee.

* Declare His glory among the
  heathen, His wonders among all people.
  For the LORD is great, and greatly to be praised:
  He is to be feared above all gods.

* And again, Praise the LORD, all ye Gentiles; and
  laud Him all ye people.

 (Ps. 117; Ps. 63:3;   Ps. 96:3; Rom. 15:11

GIVE PRAISE *to the Mighty King!*

As the glory of God covers heaven, let His glory cover up this place. Let the Church feel the joy of His presence; fill our hearts with the light of His word.

Chorus

Come together in the presence of the Lord. Let's praise His name. Come together in the presence of the Lord, proclaim His name. Come together in the presence of the Lord, all ye people. Give praise to the Mighty-King! (2) God of all nations.

Chorus

Stand together... (3x) All ye people.
Praise Him, Praise Him, Praise ye the Lord!
Sing together...(3x) all ye people.
Clap your hands... (3x) all ye people.

Rejoice; rejoice in the ... (3x) all ye people. Give praise to the Mighty King. Give praise to the Mighty-King! (2x) God of all nations.

The Unsaved Targeted Audience:

When the unsaved is my audience, my passion is focused on spiritual welfare to win the heart of the unsaved. To fulfill this passion, I must have a vision for them to be saved. Therefore, my vision will be clear in the lyrics, where Jesus Christ is presented as the ultimate Savior. This is when I have the privilege to visualize the brilliant light of transformation in the lives of the unsaved. They must understand that Jesus is the only light that can reach the darkening hearts of men. I need to be mindful that I am not at war with the person that I am trying to reach. It is not my place to use my lyrics against the unsaved, but I am responsible to let them know that **"The wages of sin is death; but the gift of God is eternal life through Christ Jesus our Lord" (Rom. 6:23).**

I am accustoming of hearing inappropriate lyrics amongst some of the Haitian Gospel Artists. For example, telling people to change their way of living in a song will not help them to understand their need for salvation. Religious people follow certain principles which they believe to be the truth. People can change their ways without conversion. One can also be converted to any religion other than Christianity. Knowing that makes me more careful with how I present the Gospel. I am aware that the nature of man is to avoid God, but the nature of God is to love them as they are. In fact, the message in one of my songs *"The lost Sheep"* covers that subject. I will give more details about that song as you continue to read this manual.

How do I present the Gospel in my song? To honor my teaching, I need to respect the requirements by following the principle to **"Study to show myself approved unto God, a workman that needeth not to be ashamed, rightly dividing the word of truth" (II Tim. 2:15).** What I profess in my songs must be supported by scriptures. This means that I spend quality time searching spiritual knowledge; otherwise, it will be obvious in my ministry. I can easily lose sight and misrepresent the Gospel through my songs. To avoid being a false prophet, I must be competent and ready to defend my faith. Sincerity is a very important factor in reaching my unsaved audience. I approached the intent of my theme wholeheartedly and displayed the truth using my own testimony. That will serve as a support to convey hope to my unsaved audience, something that would lead to repentance. Repentance is always followed by reconciliation, and reconciliation is rewarded by salvation. Therefore, if I could accomplish these three steps through my lyrics, then my mission is complete.

Inspiration Three

The Intent of this Song is to address the Targeted Audience:

The subject matter of *"The Man from Galilee"* is sharing **"Evangelism"** in which I am addressing **the Unsaved as my targeted audience**. Covered by the shadow of religious beliefs, some people have their own perception of who Christ is. This question was raised by Jesus, the Man from Galilee to His disciples*. **"What do people say about the Son of Man?" "Some people say you are John the Baptist or maybe Elijah or Jeremiah or some other prophet"* *(Matthew 16:13-b; 14).* Since people's opinions about Christ still matters, it is the responsibility of His disciples to reveal to the world His identity.

Note that Jesus Christ expected that the disciples should give an accurate answer to this specific question. We need to be certain about the identity of our Lord. He did not ask the unbelievers because they would not know who He is. Christ identity had to be revealed by the Heavenly Father. It was revealed to the selected ones so they could let the world know about this precious man. This commission also applied to me. That was my inspiration for writing "The Man from Galilee."

John the Baptist refers to Jesus Christ as "The Lamb of God to take away our sins." His righteousness should be recognized in the darkened hearts of man. That means every song should proclaim His marvelous works. Throughout history the Bible has been proclaiming the coming of the Son of Man. This is something that cannot be avoided. Christ may be a mysterious being to those who neglected the foretold prophecies, but He has revealed Himself to those who received Him. His existence among us is the source of life. His infinite wisdom is powerful to those he taught. He carried the responsibility for our transgressions and confirmed the certainty of salvation through the shedding of His blood. One word from His mouth transformed the life of the woman He met by Jacob's well. He fully manifested His perfect love to all, and it was by faith that I met the "Man from Galilee."

In the hours of great distraction, Jesus has always been the answer for the world. The greatest gift that we could offer to someone is to introduce him or her to "The man from Galilee." Jesus calls upon both men and women to deliver this gift. The essence of this gift is the package that contains salvation, healing, and deliverance. They need to know that following idols could never lead to this package. The worshipping of idols will only lead to destruction. That is why as a Christian, I need to make popular the identity of Christ. To bear witness to Christ's identity is make known His miracles, especially the miracles of our lives. And the greatest miracle of all is to be born again.

Some people are brutalized by old wounds that only Jesus can heal. Others are not even conscious of their states of mind. They are misled by the world and confused about who they are. In addition, they are seeking happiness and peace in all the wrong places. Misery continuously binds them. They need to know about the "Man from Galilee," He who gave His life in exchange for their lives. Without this man's touch, their lives will be counted as worthless. That is why I am leading them to accept Christ's marvelous touch in this song. One look in Jesus' eyes is a sign of deliverance. And one word from Him is enough to make things right. I want them to know that nothing else matters when it comes to the saving of one's soul. Therefore, I pledge to testify about this Man everywhere I go as long as I live.

Inspiration Expression to the Unsaved,
the Targeted Audience

* He was in the world, and the world was made by Him, and the world knew Him not. He came unto His own, and His own received Him not. But as many as received Him, to them gave He the power to become the sons of God. …

* Behold! The Lamb of God, which taketh away The sin of the world!

* And He came and touched the bier: and they that bore him stood still. And He said, "Young man, I say unto thee, arise." And he that was dead sat up and, began to speak. And He delivered him to his mother.

(John 1: 10-12; John 1:29; Luke 7:14-15)

1- Have you heard about the man from Galilee? His name is Jesus of Nazareth, the promised one. He changed water to wine, healed the sick and even raised the dead. With a few loaves of bread and two small fish, He fed five thousand and more. John testified about him, the man from Galilee. He said, "Behold the Lamb of God to take away our sin. I baptize you with water, but He with Holy Ghost and fire. No, I am not even worthy to untie His shoes."

Chorus

One word from His mouth could change your life around. One touch from His hands could heal your broken heart. One look from His eyes could set your spirit free. Once you open your heart, you'll never be the same.

2- "O Nazareth" Nathanael asked. "Can anything good come from you?" When Jesus entered Jerusalem, they called Him King. In Samaria near Jacob's well, was a sinful woman. She drank the living water and ran to testify. There was a man of the Pharisees named Nicodemus. He came to Jesus with questions pertaining to salvation. Jesus replied and said to him, "Verily, and verily. Except a man is born again, he cannot see the Kingdom of God."

The Intent of this Song is to Address, the Selected Audience:

The subject matter of *"I am glad I know"* is **Edification** which I am addressing to the children of **the Congregation.** Children are the harvest of the church, and they too need to know that they are saved by God's grace. Tracing my experience as a child, I would say that salvation was not something that I clearly understood. Although I did not fully understand the perfect plan of salvation, I was fortunate to be one of those children to attend Sunday school regularly. Planting the seed of the gospel in the heart of a child is a lifetime gift that cannot be compared with any other.

When a child is exposed to the gospel at an early age, that child is more likely one to be eager to learn about God. My personal interest in sharing the Gospel with children is the result of my late Father's decision to have me attend Sunday-school, thereby exposing me to Godly teaching. I was influenced by teachers who understood the importance of the seed of salvation in a child's mind. That seed began to grow gradually many years after it was planted.

When the seed of the Gospel was planted in my mind, it was just in the form of Bible stories. I recalled that my Sunday school teachers would demonstrate the stories on the board using magnetic pictures. The way they presented the stories to the class was very effective. For each story that was told, I had to memorize a Bible verse. In fact, I earned my first Bible as a competitive prize for memorizing the most Bible scriptures. More importantly, the verses that I had learned have become the foundation of my salvation. It was during my teens that I recognized that I was influenced positively by what I learned in Sunday school.

I will never neglect the importance of these Bible verses in my life. That is my legitimate reason for sharing my story in this song *"I am glad I know"* with the children. This song came to my thoughts one day while I was coming down to my living room one early morning.

I thought about my children, and I wondered if they understood the plan of salvation. I sat in front of the piano and the memories of my childhood began to flow through my mind vividly. The episodic flashbacks of sitting in Sunday school class became the lyric while the Holy Spirit inspired me with the melody. Meanwhile, my younger daughter, Justine, who was at the time five years old, came and joined me, and we began to sing the song instantly. It was as though this song already existed in our spirits. Justine did not really understand what was going through my mind, but it was a joyful moment for both of us. Her participation in the writing of the song influenced me to have the desire to someday record the song with both of my daughters. In due time, I did invite them to take part in the recording of the song. Since my biological daughters are now grown, I had the privilege to gladly invite my spiritual children to join me in the publicity of this song.

God has granted me the opportunity to reach out and share my stories as well as His word with the children, and I take that assignment seriously. The souls of children are very dear to Jesus Christ. And I believe that there is a special blessing reserved to those who take the time to instruct them about salvation. Leading children's souls to Jesus is equal to that of adults. That is why I must make attractive to them how honorable it is to know God and to work for Him at a very early age. Today, I truly have the assurance that my work with these lovely children will not be in vain, even if I don't live long enough to see the results on Earth.

Inspiration Four

Inspiration Expression to the Congregation, the Selected Audience:

** And all the ends of the world shall remember and turn unto the LORD: and all the kindreds of the nations shall worship before Thee....*

** Train up a child in the way he should go: and when he is old, he will not depart from it.*

** Lo, children are a heritage of the LORD: and the fruit of the womb is his reward.*

** Suffer the little children to come unto me, and forbid them not: for of such is the Kingdom of God.*

* All thy children shall be taught by the LORD, and great shall be the peace of thy children.

* All your children shall be taught by the LORD, and great shall be the peace of your children.

(Ps. 22:27, 28; Prv. 22:6; Ps. 127: 3a; Mark 10:14; Isa. 54:13)

I'M Glad I Know

1. If I could have my way to change the day of my salvation, I would have asked Jesus to come into my heart the very first day I was born. I would go to Sunday school, give attention to the teachers. I would have treasured in my heart the Bible verses I had learned.

Chorus

I didn't know what Jesus did for me. I didn't know such love He has for me. If I had known it was for me He died, I would have surrendered my life to Him before.

2. I am so glad I know the Lord at a very early age. I could not think of anything better than the sweet love of Jesus. When I go to Sunday-school I love to hear the stories. I will treasure in my heart the Bible verses I have learned.

Chorus

I am glad I know what Jesus did for me. I am glad I know such love He has for me. Oh yes, I know! It was for me He died. Because I know, I surrender my life to Him.

SESSION EIGHT

In this session, you will learn about:

- *The role of Gospel music in our lives.*
- *The influence of Gospel music in our lives.*
- *The improper and the proper motive of music.*
- *The language of music.*
- *How does music communicate to us?*
- *Performing vs. ministering.*
- *How do we experience our ability?*

What Roles Does Gospel Music Plays in Our Lives?

The subject of the influence of music should be imperative to all Christians who could produce music. The reason being is because music in its own language plays a major role in people's lives. The creativity of Gospel music is a very special gift, and we should not allow anything to destroy what it represents. I believe God has His specialty when it comes to music. That is why there are many types of music. Therefore, Gospel music should be properly presented and interpreted as God intended it to be because music could be used for both *improper and proper motives.*

What is the improper motive? An improper motive is based on false pretends. False pretends is to say or do one thing, but it is just a masquerade. If the minister's motive focus on what makes people feels good, and what is in it for him or her, and then the motive is improper. Using music in the improper motive, clearly, is abominable to God because He knows the secret behind the motive. When the motive is rejected by God, it did not *move* His heart. This means, the motive moves Satan's heart. If the motive moves Satan's heart, then he gets the attention and the praise that was due to God in the music. What about that? This is something to think about. I had to think about producing my music.

What is the proper motive? Yes, moving God's heart should be a priority in the minister's production. This can come about only because of having a proper motive. God only takes pleasure in music that blesses Him. He should have that right of blessing from us because He gave us the gift in the first place. To bless God, He must be first in the mind of the producer. A song that moves God's heart blesses Him, which means that the writer has a unique passion that fulfills His purpose. This is not an emotional passion, but a spiritual passion. An emotional passion is based on self-satisfaction. Conversely, a spiritual passion is based on a long-term relationship with God. This spiritual passion will go further and further until it meets every area of God's intent in the use of the gift.

If music has a language, how does it communicate to us? I believe music has its own language. Everyone is connected to that language, one way or another; but some of us are more familiar with that language than others. The language of music is the *thought* that produces the sound behind the motive. That language is not silent, because it can be heard by those who possess the sense of hearing.

Music communicates to us on a *three-way channel.* The *first* channel in which music communicates to people is through *sound.* Sound is powerful, and our ears are sensitive to its motion. Once we hear the sound, it quickly stimulates a sensation to our entire beings. When music penetrates to our ears, it communicates to our minds, hearts, bodies, and souls. I have witnessed people who stand in service trying not to physically participate in certain styles of music. But the next thing I noticed was that their heads and feet began to respond to the beat through voluntary movement.

Frequently, part of the motive of the composer in designing the music is to have some type of control over the listener's emotion. The design includes *spiritual and physical attraction, expression of love, hatred, and fear.* The motive of the sender (composer) is to captivate the receiver's attention and taste. The writer or sender sends the information captivating our attention, and our ears pass the information to the body which triggers some type of reaction. Regardless of the message it may convey, it has a different interpretation to the receiver. That is the reason why a certain sound is purposely put together to create an emotional reaction to fit the purpose or the occasion in response to these emotional sentiments. We learned already that music is used for different purposes depending on the motive or occasion.

Now, let me give you one of the very familiar examples about how music communicates to the people of my own culture as a Haitian. One of the occasions upon which I experienced the language of music was the attendance of a Haitian funeral service. Based on my personal observation, people are more likely to show extreme emotional outpouring when hearing a certain sound of music. The result of the music impacts their vulnerable states and enables them to push out the loudest scream. Why is that? It is because the sound of certain instruments stimulates movement that turns on the force of emotional sensation. So, when people are facing the loss of a loved one, the music they play in the funeral service very much contributes to their reactions.

Nevertheless, I who sometimes sang at funeral services would use this moment as a channel to connect the unsaved to the reality of death without salvation. For this reason, I would sing a song that would lead them to know that God promised all who repent eternal life through Jesus-Christ. Concerning this matter, White, S J, stated in *The foundation of Christian Worship* that "Those who argue that a funeral is primarily an evangelistic opportunity, a chance to warn unrepentant sinners about the judgment day that awaits them, will not find any real support in the most recent generations of Christian burial rites" (p.149).Despite these challenges, what should be our concern to the listeners? When it comes to sharing the good news, the ministers' priority should be about winning the soul of the living, since it is too late to minister to the dead. If this would spare one from hell damnation, then the minister's work is fully supported by God rather than man.

The *second* channel in which communication functions is through lyrics. Lyrics are written words (poems) converted to melody. The purpose of communicating through words is to develop an idea and to send a message. Communication takes place when people hear the lyrics, connect to it, and input it in the hard drive of their memory bank. The *hearing* of the words and the melody is how the receiver *participates* in the communication. The sender or the writer then gets feedback from the receiver alerting them that the message is being saved. Then the sender responds to the receiver by developing more attractive ideas to accomplish more. What I understand so far is that what we created in our lyrics communicate something to the mind and the heart of people in different ways. We know that by the impact the lyrics produce by the society's response.

The *third* channel in which music communicates through us is *harmony.* A good harmony quickly catches the attention. The coordinating of harmony is the beauty that sustains communication. A series of sounds put together organizes the sweet harmony that penetrates the heart. If the harmony is strong enough to convince the receiver, most likely, it will be appreciated. Once it is appreciated, it will be selected and stored in a safe place called a "repertoire." The memory saves the melody in the repertoire of the brain and preserves it for the appropriate occasion whatever it may be.

Exposing ourselves to the influence of music introduces us to the role of gospel music in our lives. I already gave an example of how music activates sadness and so on. In the gospel world, we need something supernatural from God to make a difference. Now I want to give you two other demonstrations. To verify the *positive roles* that music plays in our lives, let us look at two outlets: *the anointing and the spiritual.*

How does anointed Gospel music influence Christians spiritually? I will answer this question based on my own experience. The ministry of Gospel music is one of the most effective ways to communicate to Christians. The spirituality of the anointing in gospel music is like oil to moisten our minds, bodies' spirits and souls. When I was tested and hindered by the trials of my life, music contributed very much to my recovery. I learned to use gospel music as a powerful resource to support me. There were times when I had listened to gospel music to eliminate worries. I preferred to listen to music than to have turned on the TV. I used music as a refreshment to restore my broken heart and to chase away negative thoughts. I felt sheltered and surrounded by God's love just by listening to hymns and worship songs. Gospel music boosted my belief and increased my hope in God. That is why I have great interest in using my music to minister to others.

My other personal experience with the anointing came about when I had some difficulty singing normally. I was the lead singer for a mass choir, and I suffered with allergies. This abnormality went on for several years. Each time I was ready to perform, my voice would clog up. I did all I could, but the problem persisted. But what I want you to capture is this. The anointing of God was so strong upon me, that people could not even identify that I had issues with my voice. You see, beautiful voices do not attract the anointing of the Holy Spirit. What attracted the Holy Spirit were my vulnerability and my dependency on Him while I minister to both God and the church.

How does Gospel music bless us spiritually? In general, Gospel music covers many aspects in the lives of a Christians. Everyone has a natural tendency to be attractive to the *joy* that Gospel music provides. The accomplishment of effective Gospel music is greater than a relationship. Gospel music helps meet the spiritual needs of many. Each song carries a particular message depending on the person who is receiving it. The possibility for someone to overcome a situation sometimes is just one sentence that the person could relate to. Not only does Gospel music enrich our lives with gladness, but it also enriches us with peace within. When the message penetrates our hearts, it injects the oil of peace which ventrally renews our hope and we become exceedingly joyful. There is much more, Gospel music is a forced for the outflow of evangelism. It is so powerful that no one really knows how many souls they reached through Gospel music until they reach to heaven. What more can I say?

Performing vs. Ministering

When we accepted the calling of God who welcomes us into His kingdom, we were automatically authorized by Him to become ministers of the Gospel. A minister is nothing less than a representative of the gospel of Jesus Christ. Regardless of the title or the position, as ministers, we obtain certain abilities. These abilities give us the security to carry out our assignments adequately. But before we can experience the abilities, we must first reach some type of spiritual enlightenment about the true meaning of a ministerial position.

Honestly, it took me over twenty years to identify myself as a minister called to serve. Before I reached my personal enlightenments about this subject, I have always accepted what others portrayed me to be. I was called a singing bird, an artist, but never a minister. There is a great misunderstanding in the church regarding the minister title. Based on other information about a minister, it was stated that "a minister is one who is authorized by a certain organization to perform certain tasks under such titles as Pastor, Clergy, Bishop, Chaplains and Elder."

That statement implicitly denies God's divine ordination because it does not apply in the world of Christianity. If we should accept that only those who are authorized by an organization to be ministers, then we have failed to understand the discernment of God about ministerial work. There are many who either are placed or place themselves in positions in which they are not called for. Whether or not we are authorized by an organization, we are first authorized by our Lord and Savior Jesus Christ who passed His authority to us. He assigned us to "THE GREAT COMMISSION" saying ***"All power is given unto me in heaven and in earth. Go ye therefore, and teach all nations, baptize them in the name of the Father, and of the Son, and of the Holy Ghost: teach them to observe all things and whatsoever I have command you..." (Matt. 28:18- 20).***

When we hear the word ***"performer"*** or the word ***"minister"***, do we really think to stop and identify the difference between the two? I know I did not. *Is there really a difference between both a performer and a minister?* The answer is yes. Let us talk about the difference between a performer and a minister. The word performance according to Dictionary research signifies some type of public presentation. The function of the performer is to entertain and satisfy the audience with some type of desirable presentation, such as a musical or dramatic act, etc. In addition, a performer is one who fulfills some type of requirement based on a promise. Furthermore, a performer could use his or her skill to demonstrate a role to an audience. Much more, a performer can execute a role to accomplish something.

Conversely, a minister is one who serves from the Greek word "DIAKONEO" which means "to serve." Since serving could be displayed in many ways, then what type of service are we talking about in terms of ministry? As I analyzed the functions of both performer and minister, I could see that they have some similarities. But there are distinguishing characteristics as well. I would say both take some type of discipline. One of the disciplines in common is that it does not matter whether we are performing or ministering; we must have some type of commitment in perfecting what we want to present. As performers, we spend time learning and rehearsing. As ministers, we spend time learning and practicing. As performers, we want to satisfy our audiences. And as ministers, we first want to satisfy our Lord. The overall concept about both is that we desire to be good performers and good ministers, but the contents of the performers are different than those of the ministers.

During the time of my ministry, some would ask me "How come you do not seem to be nervous while you are performing?" I believe that she used the word performance because she did not know the difference. I could not properly respond to this question because if I were to answer it, I would have to feed her in every detail of the reasons that I minister the way I do. But today I could truly say that it is because God had rescued me from being a performer to being a minister. As I was led to include this session in this manual, I feel privileged because I finally can share the secret behind the success in edifying people in my ministry, even though I was not counted as one of the recorded artists.

One who performs has a different mission statement than one who ministers. Why do I make such a statement? I am not sure if we all have experienced both, but I have. When I considered myself to have been a *performer,* I depended on the capacity of the time that I invested in rehearsing so I could prepare myself to entertain my audience. As a performer, I was not concerned about Godly image; rather I was concerned about worldly appearance. As a performer, I did not think to touch God with my songs. Instead, I wanted to please people. As a performer, I did not think about praying before my performance. Instead, I feared people rejecting me. As a performer, I did not care to use my voice as an instrument to honor God. As a performer, if they offered me fame and false hope, I was satisfied. As a performer, I had no hope for a heavenly reward. As a performer, I did not have a vision for the ministry. As a performer, I did not have a passion for lost souls because I was self-centered. As a performer, I did not communicate with God that often; therefore, my performance was empty and did not bear fruit. These attributes stood in the way, blinded my vision and captivated my passion to be a minister of the Gospel.

How do I experience my abilities as a minister? I began to experience my abilities when I yielded to the calling of God. As a minister of the Word, my mission statement has changed. As a minister, I recognized that my ability to write and sing is a gift from God. As a minister, I challenge myself to be submissive to God. As a minister, I acknowledge that it is by grace that I was chosen by God, not by my own effort. As a minister, I know that I represent Jesus Christ. As a minister, I depend on the Holy Spirit to prepare me and use me. As a minister, I reverence God with my voice and not people. As a minister, I acknowledge God's sovereignty in my life and place Him above all. As a minister, I no longer use my voice to compete. Instead, I manifest my love for God through my songs. As a minister, I established a relationship with my heavenly Father and His Holy Spirit. And as Minister, I don't mind suffering for the sake of the Gospel of Jesus Christ.

As a minister, my body is the tabernacle of God. As a minister, I accept my responsibility to serve in both good times and bad times. As a minister, my intent for singing is different. As a minister, I bring my prayer and supplication to God with hope. As a minister, I am partnering with God in soul harvest. As a minister, I have the discernment of my Father's will. As a minister, I condition myself to seek for God before I minister. As a minister, I flee temptation because I depend on God's strength. As a minister, I serve God because I love Him and not because of self-interest. As a minister, I do not focus of the reward, but on the service. As a minister, I lay up for myself the treasures in heaven. As a minister, I submit my will to God and allow Him to have His way in my life. As I minister, I look forward to influencing people in a positive way.

As a minister, I struggle with sin, but I am not defeated. As a minister, I learn to be sincere and honest with God and people. As a minister, I am conscious of my sin, and live a life of repentance. As a minister, I take pleasure in serving rather than being served. As a minister, I present my body as a sacrifice to God. As a minister, I am a channel for the outflow of the blessings of God. As a minister, I put all worldly desires behind me. As a minister, I look forward to sharing my knowledge in Christ. As a minister, the Gospel of Jesus Christ will be preached in my life as long as I live. AMEN!

If you did not know the difference between a performer and a minister, now you know. The question is "What is the next step about your discovery?" As a Christian, if you are a performer, God wants me to let you know that He desires for you to be much more than that. You are to be a minister of the gospel of Christ. If you fail to preserve your identity as a minister, you still have a chance to reverse that by accepting this truth. God is ready to lead you to make a giant move in becoming a minister of the Gospel.

PART-V

SESSION NINE

In this session, you will find various details on:

- *How inspiration takes form about the aim of the theme*

- *Preparation before the writer begins to write.*

- *What tools does the writer need to bring out the strength about the theme?*

- *Certain applications in writing gospel songs.*

- *Specific settings in terms of writing gospel songs.*

- *I will also include some inspirational lyrics in this session. This will serve as a pattern about focusing on the theme, and how to structure the message that we want to convey and why.*

Principles for Writing the Lyrics as it Corresponds to the Aim and the Theme:

What about rhymes? Songs can be used to express anything, but anything is not God's intention or the remedy for the heart. God's intention is for us to follow His guidelines (Principles). The remedy for the heart is to have a *vision* behind our **theme;** a theme that would strongly influence people in a positive way. The strengths of the theme are the appropriate details that support it, not *rhymes*. The details must be consistent with the theme when writing the lyrics. Sometimes, we write songs just for the sake of writing songs. When we focus too much in the rhyming of the song, we leave no room for the Holy Spirit to participate in the creation of the song. The most important technique about writing the lyrics is for our hearts and minds to relate to where the Holy Spirit is leading.

During an honest conversation with one of my daughters (Justine), a question came up about writing the lyrics. She asked me: "Why don't you rhyme your songs?" My answer was short and straight. I told her when I write songs, most of the time the priority focus of my inspiration is not on the rhyming; rather, I concentrate on the details that support the *theme* because the song must make sense.

So, she replied: "Are you saying that a song that rhymes does not make any sense?" Then I said: "That is not what I am saying. What I am saying is that getting the message to reach a heart according to the guidelines of God is my priority. Even when the words of my songs happen to rhyme, it happens naturally." This is to say, that even if a song makes sense to the listener, it doesn't mean that it is spiritually rich. Sometimes writers focus more on the rhyming of the lyrics than on the spirituality of the song. The positive impact of the theme is very important; and that's if they have one. A writer could have so much to say without having a theme in mind. Let me make this a little bit clearer. Do not confuse a title with a theme. There is a big difference between the two. The title is just a name tag. Conversely, a theme is a subject for discussion. One cannot discuss something leaving out the details.

Is there a specific intellectual confidence in writing Gospel songs? There is no intellectual confidence in writing Gospel songs because one does not have to be an intellectual to be gifted and used by God. Nevertheless, there is an act of dependency. This dependency is to be quick to listen to what the Holy Spirit is leading us to write about. Writing gospel songs is not a magical interpretation or a religious feeling. One does not write good lyrics just because he or she is a Catholic, Protestant or Baptist. The nature of writing an uplifting

Gospel song is supported by the openness and willingness of the expression of the heart in relationship with God.

I was flipping the TV channel one day, and I came across a very interesting interview. This was a live interview in 710 AM Radio, but also live on TV with Mike McDuffie, one of the Catholic artists who wrote a successful worship album entitled "Hiding Place." Nancy T. Ammerman and colleagues agreed that "People standing in a different social location within the congregation will understand and act in different ways" *Studying Congregations* A New Handbook (p. 32). Even though I was not in a church setting, I was really blessed and edified by the lyrics of the song he performed. That is my reason for sharing my blessings. These were some of the words that caught my attention. "Holy Spirit, come let me fly on your wings into the Father's heart where I would never thirst again." Basically, the song was about his thirst to be in God's presence. As he invited the Holy Spirit to come and lead him to his heavenly Father so that he may find rest in His presence. He was sure about the message that he wanted to convey to his audience.

Questions for the Development of the Principles of Writing a Meaningful Song:

1. How does writing the lyrics come about?

2. Is there any preparation before the artist begins to write?

3. How do we bring out the strength of the theme?

4. Is there a specific application in writing gospel songs?

5. Are there specific steps to follow in terms of writing gospel songs?

6. What is the importance of including personal stories in our songs?

7. Is there a specific place or time to write a gospel song?

How does writing the lyrics come about? Writing the lyrics is like designing a painting. The Artist should at least have in mind a vision of his or her painting. If the vision is to create a vase or a tree, then the artist's ideas will lead his or her hands to create such a picture. Just as we use certain colors that would display the beauty of our artistic work, writing our songs should also be designed with certain scriptures to match the vision of the theme. Once the artist or the minister has a theme that is based on the aspects of the principles, the Holy Spirit takes the idea and inspires the artist through the song.

Inspiration for the Development of the Aim for the Theme:

The original theme is *"Can I be the One?"* is based on **Availability for "Stewardship."** As I pray to the Lord to send workers to work for Him, why not ask Him that I should be one of them? Therefore, stewardship will be fully developed in "Can I be the One?" which is the theme.

Overflowing with the grace and the favor of God in my life, I long to be partners with Him in the great work of redemption. My heart yields in compassion for the lost when I see the conditions of humanity. I submit my will to God by asking Him; "Can I be the one that He can use to help the lost find their way?" I have the assurance that heaven will be faithful to those who are faithful in the work of redeeming souls; and I want to be one of those faithful ones. The Holy Spirit convinces my heart that God's amazing grace must be presented to the world, and I dedicated my life to be one of God's representatives. As my body becomes the tabernacle of His gospel, I tend to profess the Gospel of Jesus Christ. Thinking about how the days are passing me by so quickly, I needed to bring some satisfaction to God for his kindness.

I was in my kitchen one day cooking and listening to a Gospel song, when my reflections took me back to the goodness and faithfulness of God towards me when I was in the desert of afflictions. I recall having flashbacks to some tragic episodes of my life from which God had rescued me. The title of "Can I be the One?" flowed through my mind instantly along with the melody. Usually when God gives me a song, I would use a tape recorder to save it and then finish it later. But the melody of this song stayed with me throughout the day. Therefore, I did not see the need to record it because God had already saved it in the disk of my heart.

In the details of the song, I mentioned in the second verse *"When I saw the mountains I have climbed, the long valleys I have walked, and the waters that I have crossed. You were the only one that saw me through. My soul cries, in Jesus' name. Allow me to go for You."* While I was counting my blessings, I noticed that I could have been worthless without Christ. There are many that are depending on someone's testimonies like me to lead them to Christ. Yet, I was so into self-inflation and laziness, that my eyes could not see the needs of the needy. My relationship with God was unstable, and I needed to bestow my place in Christ. Though I valued Christianity more than anything else, I was still short on God's presence in my life. Day after day, I longed to be a faithful servant but failed to reveal what He is to me. My conscience started to tap into my unfaithfulness toward God, and I began to weep before His presence. The truth is, in my conversation with God, I needed to be honest. Serving God faithfully was not the center of my life. I confessed to God about my unreliable service and asked Him to forgive me. Creating that space in my heart was the beginning of my relationship with God. Sharing my weaknesses with the Lord took me to the comfort of His presence. I was listening to my heart while building a way to honor Him through my songs. God's affection surpassed my weaknesses, and I finally gained the courage to ask Him "Can I be the One to be a vessel for His Kingdom?" I began to focus on the necessity of reaching souls with greater devotion. In the chorus of the song, I expressed my longing to be like that woman that the Bible refers to as the virtuous one to her Lord. ***"She stretcheth out her hand to the poor, yea; she reacheth forth her hands to the needy"*** *(Prv. 31:20).*

My inspiration in this song is the renewing of my commitment for stewardship. I took the focus off me and placed it on the needy. I wanted to contribute to the growth of God's kingdom, a task that would give meaning to the existence of my gifts as a minister of the Gospel. But first, I had to be in communion with Christ before I could share my inheritance with those who are oppressed, wounded, crippled and helpless. My gifts would be meaningless without stewardship. I gladly conquer selfishness in exchange for one's soul. I hope to continuously use my gifts to communicate and bring significant change to the world. I also pray that my songs shall be included in the list of the honorable Gospel songs from generation to generation. I will not neglect to spread the gospel through my lyrics. I am expecting that God will continue to use me in a greater dimension as I commit to be a good steward in His kingdom.

Inspiration Five

"And He hath put a new song in my mouth, even praise unto our God: many shall see it, and fear, and shall trust in the LORD" (Psalm 40:3).

** Ye have not chosen me, but I have chosen you, and ordained you, that ye should go and bear fruit, and that your fruit should remain: that whatsoever ye shall ask the Father in my name, He may give it you.*

** The harvest truly is plenteous, but the laborers are Few; pray ye therefore the Lord of the harvest, that He will send forth laborers into His harvest.*

** Defend the poor and Fatherless: do justice to the afflicted and needy. Deliver the poor and needy; Do justice to the afflicted and needy: rid them out from the hand of the wicked.*

** And your feet shod with the preparation of the gospel of peace*

(John 15:16; Mat. 9: 37-38; Psalm 82:3-4; Ep. 6:15).

CAN I BE the One?

Is there any preparation before the artist begins to write? Yes. Let's take, for instance, an artist that designs a painting to bring about a friction message. That means the artist wants to present his painting as an opinion, to make a point. Before beginning to work, the artist had to first make some *planning* such as: *the characteristics, to bring out the idea, and the expectation* of the outcome of the work.

The same discipline applies when we are writing the lyrics, but the perception is different. Ministers do not write friction messages to present our opinion about the Gospel. We prepare by first making our hearts available to the Holy Spirit, second, we visualize our work to be acceptable to God. And third, we pray for our songs to bring a bountiful harvest outcome in the lives of the listeners. Notice, I did not say planning, but preparation. For example, we might be grateful unto God for His faithfulness. Let's say the theme may be our *vision* of **gratitude towards God**. The elements we need to address are what we *desire* to say to God about gratitude. For this, we become partners with the Holy Spirit who reveals to us all the necessary hidden tools from our hearts to express that theme.

Inspiration for the Development of the Aim for the Theme:

The original theme is *"This is my Reason"* which is my **Tribute** to the LORD. It fits in the category of **Worship and Praise**. Therefore, my tribute will be fully developed in "This is my reason" which is the theme. The divine beauty of God's faithfulness will always be expressed in my songs. God should be praised for His marvelous works, from the least to greatest things.

I wrote this song because I am very impressed with the faithfulness and the goodness of God towards me. Giving reverence to the Almighty, my King is what I live for. His love for me inspired me to reverence Him in the beauty of this lyric. This song is my personal love song to the one who loves me beyond measure. Not once in my life did I ever think of writing any other songs but Gospel. I give special attention to God alone who gives me this gift. Sometimes I hear people expressing what they feel towards one another in songs. For me, there is nothing like expressing my love to the One who shows me what love is. Like the attractive fragrance of the balsam tree of Myrrh, I desire that the fragrance of this song would be attractive to the nostrils of the Love of my life. I use Myrrh because it's a distinct quality that causes me to appreciate the first part of the syllable of my name, Myrtha. I don't think my mother had any idea how precious my name is.

The development of this song started with the influence of God in my life. My thoughts are always on Him. My relationship with my heavenly Father began by understanding that no one else would have exchanged the life of their only son for a gift for my life. I want to be intimate with Him all the days of my life. In fact, I was commuting by train when I thought of my reasons for serving, worshiping, and praising God. I was born under the curse of the law of sin and bound by generational curses. When I was a child, even children my age were prejudiced against me, and made me feel inferior because I was poor. I grew up in misery with low self-esteem as my shadow. Tradition was my enemy, and provoking me to retain religion, rather than having a relationship with the Lord. I was in a state of rebellion and contaminated by my own will. Gradually, the Lord delivered me from all. Praise His holy name! This song represents my logical inventory of the kindness and tenderness of God towards me. It also reflects my deepest appreciation, adoration and impression to my King and Redeemer.

My soul could never fully be satisfied without God in my life. He is always with me. As long as I live, I will always give God what is due. And that is to give reverence, honor, and gratitude. Nothing impresses God more than a grateful heart. The dead ones cannot show gratitude. That privilege pertains only to the living; and I am a living being. ***"I will sing unto the LORD as long as I live: I will sing praise to my God while I have my being" (Ps. 104:33).***

Tracing back my difficult times, I am convinced that I could not have reached where I am today without God's love and direction. I understand that my fellowship with God should be initiated with actions do not phrase. Not only had I watched for special opportunities to tell my stories to all who thirst to know Him, I also demonstrated my love for Him through my lifestyle. I cannot keep in secret my interests in praising God in this song. I want this song to help people recognize that they too should have special interests in praising Him. Overall "This is my Reason" reflects how I rejoice over the works of the Lord with a grateful heart.

Inspiration Six

* Love the LORD your God with all Your heart, soul, and mind. This is the first and most crucial commandment.

* I will love You, O LORD, my strength.

* The LORD is my rock and my fortress And my deliverer.

* While I live I will praise the Lord; I will sing praises to my God while I Have my being. Before I was afflicted I went astray, but now have I kept Thy word.

* Thou hast also given me the shield of Thy salvation: and Thy right hand hath made me great. Your gentleness has made me great.

(Mat. 22:37-38; Ps. 18:1; 146:2; 119:67-68; 18:35)

THIS IS My Reason

I love to serve You, I love to worship You. This is the reason that I love to praise You.

1- Often I think about Your marvelous love; I pour my heart like perfume and cover You with my praise. My shame and pain You bore at the cross of Cavalry, and exchanged Your life for mine, so that I might be set free.

Chorus

This is the reason that I love to praise You. This is the reason that I worship You. I exalt You, and I magnify Your Holy name. Let my life be a living sacrifice and acceptable to You.

2- Your love, I find to be so amazing to me. Such infinite and perfect love is priceless above all things. And often, I wonder why You love me in such a way. If I could understand, then I can love like You.

3- Since You've saved my life; All I want is more of You. I surrender all that I am, just to serve You my King. You are the source in which I find fullness of joy. Nothing else in this world could satisfy my soul.

This is my reason; my personal reason that I love to praise You.

How do We Bring Out the Strength of the Theme?

The strength of the theme does not depend on our knowledge, capacity, or ability to produce a good song. Allowing the Holy Spirit in helping us to stay in line with the theme of the song essentially is the base and the strength of the message we want to send. For example, sometimes I listen to songs that start with a particular theme, but the author then loses track of the theme and mingles with other subjects that have no relationship to the theme. If the message is about an invitation to **salvation,** then stick to salvation. Be careful not to mix salvation with worship because it sends a mixed message to the listeners; and they have no idea where you want to take them.

It is not to criticize that I make mention of this problem, but to bring awareness to its effect because those who find themselves in this category might not be conscious of what they are doing. In writing Gospel songs, there is a straight path to follow. This path is to apply the structure that carries the fulfillment of the theme (the principles). For instance, I sing songs of other authors, but it takes me time to select a soundtrack. The reason why is because I am attracted to songs that minister to me in a way that makes me feel blessed rather than feeling good. Once a song touches my heart, I know that it will do the same for others that I minister to. So, beware not to depend solely on your own understanding to accomplish a Spirit-filled song.

Inspiration for the Development of the Aim for the Theme:

The original theme is *"The Lost Sheep."* It fits in the category of **"Evangelism."** Therefore, evangelism will be fully developed in "The lost Sheep" which is the theme.

The Bible makes it clear that *"All have sinned and come short of the glory of God" (Roman 3:23).* All have discarded the way of life. In addition, because people are contaminated by worldliness, they turn against the truth. Satan inspired them with richest and self-righteousness. They are lost and confused by Satan's ways. Their hearts are inflated with pride, jealousy, insincerity, and apostasy.

They need to know that despite their malicious hearts and ways God still loves them.

Because man disobeyed God, justice had to be made. This justice was eternal death. Satan, the prince of evil, celebrated the falling of man. But God defeated his celebration with His perfect plan of salvation. God's unconditional love did not permit Him to bring early judgment upon man. Therefore, God offered His blameless and harmless son as a substitute to man's death. Jesus Christ is the foundation of our reconciliation to God the Father. When our sins reached up to heaven, instead of bringing judgment upon man, He reversed man's chastisement upon Jesus Christ. It is not in the Good Shepherd's nature to neglect a lost sheep. But it is in His nature to go and look for the one that is lost. I am so grateful to have been one among them that was found.

Those who assumed that they could be saved through their own works need to know the truth. Many are standing in false beliefs and are in the greatest need to be rescued from their false beliefs. In the setting of Jesus Christ as the ultimate sacrifice, the correction was made, and the solution has already been provided. Since God took it upon Himself to solve the problem of sin, there shall be no excuses for those who denied His unconditional love. There is an appointed place called hell for those who worship themselves or idols.

Some of you profess to have received Jesus as your Lord and Savior, but then turned away from Him. The helmet of salvation is your belief to protect you against false doctrines. When you allow that helmet to be removed, you are deviating from the Gospel of Jesus Christ, which is the act of backsliding. Maybe because of insecurity in faith, or the fear of facing critical judgment by the church, you are trapped in the coat of self-pity and not quite sure how to turn back on your own. Well, I've got good news for you. When Jesus brings you back to His pasture, heaven and earth will rejoice for your return. God wants all to experience that joy. The lost sheep that is found will inherit God's kingdom because he or she had become the righteousness of God through Jesus Christ. Truly God's mission to save you from sin was not in vain.

Inspiration Seven

* Fear not, little flock; for it is your Father's Good pleasure to give you the kingdom.

* All we like sheep have gone astray. We have turned, everyone, to his own way.

* I say unto you, likewise joy shall be in Heaven over one sinner that repenteth, more than over ninety and nine just persons, which need no repentance.

* I will seek that which was lost, and bring Again that which was driven away, and will bind up that which was broken, and strengthen that which was Sick…

* They profess that they know God; but in works they deny Him, being abominable, and disobedient, and unto every good work reprobate.

(Luke 12: 32; Is. 53:6 a; Luke 15:7; Ezek. 34:16; Titus 1:16 a)

THE *Lost Sheep*

No one is seeking after God, but He is reaching out to all. They all have gone out of the way of life. Many choose to be atheist, and some lust after riches. Instead of light, they choose the way of darkness. Only God through His mercy; could offer man His salvation. Despite all, He sent his son to die.

Chorus

Joy, joy, o joy! Over one lost sheep returned.

Joy shall be in heaven over one lost sheep returned. His mission was not in vain when Christ came to seek for you.

2- Many profess to know God, yet reject Jesus His son, and think self-righteousness is salvation. If only they knew who God is, they had given Him the highest praise, and they would have grabbed the abundant grace He gives. Though they think they found the truth but are deceived by the devil's schemes. But Love is still reaching to rescue man.

Joy shall be in heaven...

3- You may have gone astray from God. I want you to know He still loves you. He wants to redeem you from your sin. And your burdened soul He wants to free. Joy shall be in heaven for you, precious sheep. Joy shall be in heaven for you, for your return. Joy shall be in heaven.

Inspiration for the Development of the Aim for the Theme:

The original theme is *"It's an Honor."* It fits in the category of **"teaching."** Therefore, teaching will be fully developed in "It's an Honor" which is the theme.

Our children need to know that they too are called to serve the Lord. How would they understand their calling if the church did not teach them about the importance of stewardship?

It is in the best interest of the church to get the children involved in sharing the gospel with their friends. I say this because children interact with each other regularly, either at school, by commuting, playing in the park or even during family outdoor picnics. One thing that I notice about children is that they are anxious to learn and are quick to deliver what they learn. I believe, sometimes, we adults are undermining our children's ability to serve. We might perceive that they are too young to deliver the gospel of Jesus Christ. We need to repent such perception and give the children a chance to serve. It is the church's responsibility to convey the message of stewardship to the children.

When I was a child growing up in Haiti, I don't remember that anyone in the church ever explained to me about sharing the gospel with other children. I just did not know how to honor God that way. In fact, I was ashamed to carry the Bible that I had won in the Sunday school contest. Christianity was never part of my conversation with other children. I needed to be taught that sharing the gospel was something honorable and not a shameful thing. A home with no biblical teaching is like a ship without a sail. Children tend to imitate what they see. If we lead and raise them in the light of the Bible, we will impact their lives in a positive way. They will follow the clear pathway of our heredity and carry other children with them.

I had a conversation with my older daughter, who is now a mother, in regard to this subject. She shared with me something that I was not aware of. She said to me that her younger sister was not exposed enough to Bible stories. Somehow, during one of their conversations she realized that her younger sister was short in knowledge in what she should have known already about the Bible. I sensed that she held me responsible for not having saturated my younger daughter with Bible stories. I did teach her some Bible verses, but because of the lack of practice she failed to remember them. Raising children while both working and attending college full time, tremendously reduced my time to read Bible stories to them. Giving them animated Bible story books did not spare me the guilt that I felt. I blamed myself for not putting time in reading them to her as often as I should. And that was a new awakening for me.

As I tried to deal with such defeat, a scenario came to my mind. When I was a young girl in Haiti, I liked planting corn in our backyard. I remember putting only four seeds of corn into the ground. But during harvest time, my four seeds had become four whole corns. So, what is this saying to me? Telling a few Bible stories to a child does not seem to be enough. But, in due time the harvest of understanding the gospel of Jesus Christ from these few verses that I taught her will become far much greater than the few stories that were planted in my daughter's mind. All it takes is one precious seed of the gospel to own a soul harvest. There was no need for me to feel guilty for not reading Bible stories to my children as often as I could. I had already planted the seed in their minds. Now I continue to pray and allow the Lord of the harvest to increase their knowledge in due season. And sure enough, I will live to witness and rejoice when we share together about their discoveries in the words. Greater harvest was yet to come because now, both of my daughters become my inspiration in terms of winning souls for Christ.

It is a moral danger to our society when heresy and false teaching gets into our children's minds because of the lack of Bible teaching in the home. Our younger generations are challenged daily with dreadful technology. Their minds are polluted with the corruption of radio, television, games and the sinful acts of man. Expecting that our children will draw boundaries between them and the world, without the proper teaching, is desolation. We often promise them, but do not deliver. ***"Ye therefore, beloved, seeing ye know these things before, beware lest ye also, being led away with the error of the wicked, fall from your own steadfastness" (II Pet.3:17).*** How could they be obedient to God if they do not know how? We parents are there to define what they do not understand and explain the doctrine of Jesus Christ. That is why God is constantly raising godly men and women by giving them His written word, the Bible, to teach and guide the children to the truth. The process of helping them escape false doctrine is to teach them how to be on guard while they are yet young.

"It's an Honor" not only serves as an encouragement to children to share the gospel, but it is also to remind the church of her responsibilities in leading, training, teaching, and preparing the children to be vessels of honor for the Lord. For the children to be involved in the sharing of the gospel, they must be confident about their own salvation. Also, they need to understand that it is required by God that their lives should bear fruits. That way they will treasure the opportunity to share their stories with other children. This is the message that I want to convey to the adults. In the celebration of their secured salvation in Christ, I encourage them in joining me in committing some time towards the spreading of the gospel.

Giving this special attention to the children will increase their knowledge. When a child gradually experiences the knowledge of serving God, he or she will not easily deviate from the truth. That is why it is important that the church should develop a relationship with them. I am very comfortable working with children. I am attracted to the beauty of their enthusiasm to learn. I thank God for inspiring me to encourage the children to draw near Him. I give great respect to teachers who give their priority in volunteering their valuable time to ministering to children. I envision that someday the children that we inspire to serve God will replace those who have completed their works. But the training and preparation starts today.

Inspiration Eight

* And Jesus said unto them, Come ye after me, and I will make you to become fishers of men.

* I have taught thee in the way of wisdom; I have led thee in right paths.

* Even a child is known by his doings, whether his work be pure, and whether it be right.

* Train up a child in the way he should go: and when he is old, he will not depart from it.

(Mark 1:17; Prv. 4:11; 20:11; Prv. 22:6)

IT'S an *Honor*

1- Jesus says to follow Him, wherever He leads, I'll go. Fishers of men I will be, working for God's kingdom. I am His workmanship, Created for good work.

Chorus

It's an honor to be a vessel for God's kingdom; following His footsteps, spreading out the good news. Now I am working for Gods' kingdom, walking side by side with Him. It's an honor to be a vessel for Him.

2- Jesus says if I love Him, I must go and feed the sheep. They are wounded, weak and lost, waiting for a shepherd to guide them to safe path. He is depending on me.

(Solo) It's an honor to be working for the King….

Chorus

It's an honor; it's an honor, working for God's kingdom: Following His footstep, spreading out the good news, working side by side with Him.

Are there specific steps to follow in terms of writing gospel songs? Yes. There are *three* important steps that we need to follow when writing gospel songs: *(1) the theme, which is the frame that holds the structure of the lyrics, (2) the structure, which are the appearing details, and (3) the audience to whom you are addressing the song.* The message that we intend to bring in our songs must be supported by lyrics that support the theme. Since we are called to **witness the truth**, we should match our songs with evidence from the word of God. We do not need to apply skills to be good writers, but we need to be filled and led by the Spirit. That is, to have a steady relationship with God and learn to think Biblically while writing our lyrics in correspondence to the theme.

What is the importance of including personal stories in our songs? As gospel artists, we are obligated to promote *spiritual maturity* through our songs. We promote spiritual maturity by telling our stories truthfully. Jesus teaches through many stories to express the kingdom of God. The reason why Jesus' stories have touched many lives was because he disciplined Himself to stay in contact with His heavenly Father. So, He told only of what He heard from the Father. ***"It is the spirit that quickeneth; the flesh profiteth nothing: the words that I speak unto you, they are spirit, and they are life" (John 6:63).*** For instance, in the book of Matthew alone we find different types of stories. Although each has its own character, they all are based on *salvation.* For example, ***"The Rich Young man story" (Matt. 19:16-23), the story about "The Three servants, (Matt. 25: 14-28), and the story about "The Great Banquet" (Matt. 22:15-21).*** We, too, must follow His example. If we intend our stories to transform lives, then it is in our best interest to be generous in sharing them. God will inspire us which story to share at a particular time.

Our **stories** are based on experiencing the miracles of God in our lives. Our stories revealed the love of God towards us. Our stories also become our testimonies. And our testimonies bring encouragement and comfort to the body of Christ. The strength of our testimony is the rebuilding of one's relationship with God. What good is it to keep in secret the marvelous works of God, when we can share them for the purpose of setting captives free, and increasing the faith? Faith is the stream that stimulates healing and deliverance. There is nothing shameful about sharing our stories. In fact, our stories display the beauty of the supernatural power of God. The knowledge of the secrets of the kingdom of God has been revealed to us through stories*. **"And He said, unto you it is given to know the mystery of the kingdom of God: but to others in parables" (Luke 8:10).***

When the unsearchable love of God is revealed to the affected ones, it awakens the hearts and the minds, and brings them to a level of gratitude. Something I often experience is that I cannot remain still when I am edified by someone else's testimonies. I express my gratitude freely. I stand boldly with my hand uplifted in reverence to God who has done marvelous things in their lives. My hope is renewed, and my spirit fills with joy and contentment of their victory. Most of all, it boosts my faith to look forward to my own victory.

Inspiration for the Development of the Aim for the Theme:

The original theme is *"From Tears to Laughter."* It fits in the category of **Testimony**. Therefore, testimony will be fully developed in "From Tears to Laughter."

Being caught in the realm of life's hardships, we sometimes ask, "Why me?" or "When will it be over?" Most Christians relate to these questions because we are accustomed to facing hardships, trials and tribulations. When facing such experiences, we tend to be very hard on ourselves. We try to find out where we failed. Was there something we could have done to prevent the situation from happening? When we cannot figure it out, we come up with all sorts of doubts. Therefore, we search for answers from many directions instead of first confiding in God. We wait for changes to take place, but the solution seems longer than we expected. Since the adversary sought to break our faith, he leads us to doubt. That is when we give ground to sadness and lose the joy of our salvation. I have been there. That is how I know.

When I wrote "From Tears to Laughter" I was going through a very hard time. Satan had destroyed my family. My first and only son was sent to prison for ten years. My house was in foreclosure, and I was in debt. Depression opened wide to swallow my faith. I was worried about losing everything that I had worked so hard for. I spent most of my time nourishing self-pity. The anxiety of fear oppressed me, and I was afraid of losing my mind. I was longing to understand why I was going through so much. I confronted my fears in prayers. In the process, I took inventory of what I needed to do, to overcome these situations. *(1) I needed to stand firm in the promises of God. (2) I needed to allow God to take charge of the situations instead of trying to solve my own problems. (3) I needed to be conscious of who were my enemies. (4) I needed to seek the Lord with my entire heart. And (5) I needed to persevere. Are you related to these strongholds?*

As I mentioned before in this teaching, a minister must be equipped. This was a good occasion for me to put on the whole armor of God. Wearing the whole armor of God helped me to put into subjection all that could hinder my faith, such as fear, doubts, worries, self-pity, remorse, and bitterness. Cleansing my soul from these obstacles brought significant change to my life. My joy has been restored. That is why I can write about it. This song is my testimony. I want everyone to know that God was there to change my tears to laughter. Every time the adversary tries to remind me of my past, I sing from tears to laughter. I want to encourage you through these lyrics. Hold on to your faith, and don't ever let it go. God is good to all of us. And He will always keep His promises to you.

Whatever bridge you are stuck on, don't you look down. Look up instead. God's unconditional love will cross you over. Stop complaining about your situation. It will not save you time. Be encouraged, get up, shake up, stand your ground and shout for joy. Your victory is certified by your heavenly Father. Declare your gladness with dance, praises, and thanksgiving. You can defeat the devil with your sacrifices of praise. Stay in touch with your Heavenly Father for He desires to hear from you. Guard your heart from filthiness and keep on believing. Your faith is in the treasure of your heart; safeguard it in faith patiently. And most of all, your testimonies will be remedies for many troubled souls, like my testimonies to you. I pray that you receive this message deep down within you and allow God to take you from glory to glory in your ministry.

Inspiration Nine

** To appoint unto them that Mourn in Zion, to give unto them beauty for ashes, the Oil of joy for mourning, the Garment of praise for the spirit Of heaviness; that they might Be called trees of righteousness, The planting of the Lord, that He might be glory.*

** They that sow in tears shall Reap in joy*

** Come to Me, all you who Labor and are heavy laden and I will give you rest.*

(Is. 61:3; Ps. 126:5; Matt11:28)

FROM *Tears to Laughter*

From tears to laughter (2) God has wiped all my tears away in exchange for songs of joy.

2- I was shackled by life's trials, and the tears streamed down my face. God has changed those tears to laughter, and peace and joy filled my soul. For the Lord's yoke is easy. And His burden is light. I took my cares up on my master's feet, left them there and walked away.

Chorus

From tears to laughter! (2)

My tears are gone; I'm rejoicing with songs of joy. They that sow in tears shall reap with songs of joy.

From tears laughter, God has wiped my tears away and filled my soul with joy. They that sow in tears shall reap with songs joy.

2-There is no need to fear or worry; your Father knows your daily need. He will help you in your struggles and will lead you to the end. There is no need to doubt His promise. He will do just what he says. He is the greatest source of joy I know; seek for Him and He will be Found.

From tears to laughter God will wipe your tears away and fill your soul with peace. They that sow in tears shall reap with songs of joy.

Lift your head and be encouraged;

He hears your cry. I testify that God has been good to me. They that sow in tears shall reap with song of joy.

Is there a Specific Place or Time to Write a Gospel Song?

If I should answer this question truthfully, I would say NO. The most important thing to know is that the beginning of the process of writing gospel songs is to be *heavenly connected.* Heavenly connection to me is to have our hearts and minds always on the kingdom's work. Having my mind on the kingdom's work stirred up a sense of openness in my mind. In fact, some of my songs were written while commuting in the subway. I could be either waiting for the train or riding in it. My point is that it does not matter where we are. We can make ourselves available and contact the inspirations of God.

It is a marvelous experience to stay always connected. When that moment of inspiration comes, we can block any distractions and give undivided attention to the voice that speaks to our inner being. I discovered that making room for the Holy Spirit to use our minds and hearts happens to be one of most effective ways to meditate on God's intent while writing songs. Otherwise, the song could be an empty song. *What is an empty song?* The teaching in Session Nine clearly explained the principles of writing the lyrics. Our songs will never be empty if we follow these principles. An *empty* song is a song in which the writer has no *theme,* no *vision,* no *structure*, and no *expectation.*

An empty song could be very attractive to the ear, but it does not mean much to the writer nor the listener. It's like mixing all spices to get an unusual taste. We are eating, but we have no idea what's in it nor do we know how our bodies will react to it. But a professional chef can easily taste all the ingredients included in the mix and even could tell their purpose. Similarly, one who is spiritually grounded in the word of God will easily detect that the Holy Spirit had no part in the creation of the empty song. It is important that the minister should feed the spiritual bodies of the audience with healthy lyrics, lyrics that are meaningful and Spirit-filled. Eventually people's hearts will be subdued by the message in a positive way.

Some of you possess the gift but are accustomed to writing empty songs due to the lack of knowledge. This teaching is not to discredit your gift but to instruct you. God understands that, and He wants you to learn how it should be done. That is why He is using me to provide you with this teaching. Therefore, I encourage you to take advantage of this and change your attitude about your way of writing. Beware that the adversary could easily transform himself to deceiving you behind the lyrics by just inspiring you to mention the word *hallelujah* in it. You should be able to discern that **"Satan himself is transformed into an angel of light" (II Cor. 11:14).** To avoid writing empty songs, you must be active in those areas:

- **Beware of the devil's schemes**
- **Be vigilant and sober.**
- **Be open-minded to the word of God.**
- **Be vulnerable to the Holy Spirit.**
- **Be careful of self-interest.**
- **Be a faithful agent of the gospel of Jesus Christ.**

Inspiration for the Development of the Aim for the Theme:

The original theme is *"Let Freedom Reign."* It fits in the category of **exhortation.** Therefore, exhortation will be fully developed in "Let Freedom Reign", which is the theme.

It is essential that we Christians understand the **principles** of freedom. Many times, we find ourselves in situations that are withholding our freedom. We all know that the opposite of freedom is bondage. This bondage that I am referring to is not only physical, but also mental and spiritual. One of the most contaminated bondages is *resentment*. This contaminated bondage has a stronghold and if we don't let it go, it will drown us and destroy our relationship with our Heavenly Father.

Keeping secret our struggles to forgive one another is not profitable to us in several ways; (1) we are transgressing the law of God; (2) we are blocking our own forgiveness since we too are not perfect; (3) we are hindering our relationship with our Heavenly Father; (4) when resentment corrupts our hearts, it creates room for depression, sicknesses and diseases; (5) the overall aspect of resentment is destructive to the mind, body, and soul. And all these things are equal to **bondage.**

What exactly is freedom to some Christians? This question asks you to know your position. I could only say what freedom is to me because I have experienced both bondage and freedom. Freedom to me is obeying God's principles. These principles are based simply on two words, *submit* and *resist.* Submitting is obedience. Obedience is to apply ourselves to what God asks us to do. If I do not walk in obedience, the result will be failure. *Resisting* is the application of righteousness. The application of righteousness is resisting our wills. If we are not resisting our wills, then we are not walking in righteousness. Freedom to me is to be conscious of my sins. I could only confess my sins if I am aware of them. Freedom is my strength to wait on God for justice. Freedom to me is confiding in God about what is of concern to my relationship with Him. God will always take charge of what could hinder his children. Freedom to me is to walk in love. Walking in love is power, and power is maintaining my freedom.

Jesus Christ has already set the platform for our freedom when He exchanged His life and forgave our sins. Therefore, there should not be any reason why we cannot do the same for others. When we claim that we are unable to forgive, we are contradicting the word of God. That is ***"The God of all grace, who hath called us unto his eternal glory by Christ Jesus, after that ye have suffered a while, make you perfect, stable, strengthen, settle you" (I Pt. 5:10).**** If we seek the Lord with all our hearts when we approach Him, we will find that forgiving those who hurt us is giving a precious gift to ourselves. That gift is freedom. We can eliminate all those negative aspects mentioned above, if we only follow the principles of submitting and resisting. When these negative aspects are eliminated, only then we can declare that we are free in Christ Jesus.

Imparting the knowledge of spiritual freedom is the understanding and the practicing of the word of God. That is my reason for quoting these Bible verses. Forgiveness is God's nature: ***"For Thou, LORD, art good, and ready to forgive; and plenteous in mercy unto all them that call upon Thee" (Ps. 86:5).*** We Christians should not give credit to Satan for diminishing our capability to love. That is exactly what we are doing when claiming that we are unable to forgive. I learned that a long time ago when I asked the Lord to teach me how to forgive those who had broken my heart several times. How many times has Jesus Christ forgiven me for breaking His heart with my transgressions?

If I should answer this question truthfully, my answer would be countless. But Jesus answered it better. ***"Therefore, all things whatsoever ye would that men should do to you, do ye even so to them: for this is the law and the Prophets" (Matt. 7:12).*** The remedies for my freedom are based on only three principles: *submit, resist, and love.* Jesus submits to His Father's will for me. Then He resists all types of temptations for me. He did both because He loves me. The reason why we fail to forgive others is because we ignore these basic principles. I had to understand that forgiveness is not a performance, but an act of power over the self. Once I understood that, it was easy for me to snatch back my freedom from Satan. He will not have the audacity to accuse me of such a thing because I exchanged my bondage for freedom when I entered the light of true forgiveness. That is my perfect aim for writing *"Let Freedom Reigns."*

The key to my freedom is my determination to walk, live, sleep, and breathe in submission and in resisting the devil. What about you? If you should understand the importance of your freedom as a Christian, please join David's declaration when he asked God to *"Create in him a clean heart."* Be open and truthful about your sins to God. Honestly, that is the only ultimate choice that we Christians have in keeping our freedom. Keep in mind that resentment is our enemy, but conversely, freedom is our friend.

* For, brethren, ye have been called unto liberty; only use not liberty for an occasion to the flesh, but by love, serve one another (Gal. 5:13).

* Stand fast therefore in the liberty where Christ hath made us free and not be entangled again with a yoke of bondage (Gal. 5:1).

LET *Freedom Reign!*

1- If you want to be free, you may have to let go and let God be. Just submit yourself to Him, to resist Satan. You should not have to be bound because Jesus has died to set you free. Put on the armor of God. You have been equipped and sealed by faith. When you feel, you can't let go, confess your sin, and He'll hear your prayer. Let obedience be your freedom.

Chorus

Here is freedom; it is in the Word. Take your freedom and hold onto it. Freedom is to let go and forgive. Walk in your freedom, live your freedom, and breathe your freedom. Freedom is the will of God. Open your heart, and allow freedom to come in. You must let freedom reign.

2- You must understand freedom, in order to love as Jesus loves. Freedom is your wisdom you should never let it go. You must learn to forgive; that is not something that you can ever buy. Love will never fail you. Your freedom is a reality. Just as Jesus forgives you, and you too must, forgive as well. If you obey, then you will be free. Hereis your freedom; just love your enemies. Bless those who despised you and pray for them. Freedom is forgiving yourself. Freedom is your strength, freedom is your light, freedom is your power and freedom is the will of God. Open your heart, allow freedom to come in. You must let freedom reign. Let go! Let freedom reign!

Inspiration for the Development of the Aim for the Theme:

The original theme is *"For His Glory."* It fits in the category of **Praise.** Therefore, praise will be fully developed in "For His Glory."

My heart earnestly praises God for who He is. It is a mystery to some that God illustrates His presence in all living things. Acknowledging the existence of God is not scientific research. All we must do is to look, see, and feel His presence around the universe. We don't need to go far to understand the sovereignty of God. *The* Psalmist, even in his distress expressed the wholeness of His sovereignty***. "Then the earth shook and trembled; the foundations also of the hills moved and were shaken, because He was wroth. He bowed the heavens also and came down: and darkness was under His feet. The LORD also thundered in the heavens, and in the Highest gave His voice; hail stones and coals of fire..." (Ps. 18:7, 9, 13).***

Furthermore, the attraction of the existence of God is shown through each cell in our organs. Nature in whole shows the presence of God through the life of every living thing. The loveliness and beauty of the lilies attract the eyes of humanity and causes the heart to smile. The brightness of God's presence makes His nature perfect. The ocean waves reflect the authority of God. The wind shakes the foundation of the ground and manifests God's magnificent power. Every creature praise God in its own way. And the evidence of God's love for humanity which He created in His image is revealed through His son, Jesus Christ. What more can I say to convince you of the sovereignty of God? My own words and efforts are insufficient to explain the magnitude of who God is. Therefore, if nature in whole worships the Almighty, how much more that He who created us in His own image should be crowned with our worship, praised and honored for He alone is perfect and worthy of all?

The sovereignty of God caught my attention after a premature death experience. This experience produced in me fear for Him. God's unfailing love brought me back to life when I was dead in my sins. I professed to know God but rejected the presence of His sovereignty. I also had to face physical death to acknowledge that God created me and everything else for His own glory.

I recall when death approached me in the form of a Caesarean surgery. I was in my mid-twenties and pregnant with my second child. I received the shocking news about my older sister who had died at the age of thirty-one from a long-term illness. This news shook the ground of my life because I had seen the condition of my sister's lifestyle, and I knew that she did not make it to heaven. Fear covered my soul to the point that my body could not resist withholding the baby for another month. I was hastened to Metropolitan Hospital in New York City, where I am living, for a Caesarean section. Because I faced the surgery under stress, I could no longer sustain the distress, so my spirit left my body. That was when my spirit went to the rocky road of darkness. I saw my soul traveling alone trying to find my way through a dark tunnel with a signal light. I sensed that the entrance of that road was the way that leads to destruction.

Climbing the pathway of death, I remember staring at a string of lights in the middle of the valley of darkness and screaming the name of Jesus. I was crying "Give me a second chance!" I had no strength to race death, but I recognized that the name of Jesus was my only way out. God, in His compassion, had mercy on my dying soul and sent my spirit back to my body. When I awoke, I was in excruciating pain. The pain was so unbearable that they gave me a high dose of medication to put me to rest. The next day I felt a strange spirit haunting me at the hospital bed, trying to take possession of my body. I needed help. My marriage was drowning. I was emotionally disturbed, spiritually confused, and mentally distracted with the fear of death. I realized the reason for my fear was because I had followed a religious pattern of life, rather than having a relationship with God. I did not have the assurance that I was saved.

I felt that the same spirit that killed my sister was out to get me too. I had two options: surrender my life to God or remain bound by the spirit of fear. Before I left the hospital, I chose the first option and made a pledge to the Lord. I re-dedicated my life to Him and determined to stay on track. When I made that decision, the light of the gospel of Jesus Christ illuminated my path. I could no longer be inconsistent with serving God. The Lord preserved me from eternal death, and I was permitted a second chance. I fought my ugly past and insecurity, then embraced my relationship with Christ. Reaching out to the word of God and prayers, the Holy Spirit convinced me of the forgiving grace of God. I began to increase in knowledge of the heavenly vision. I understood that keeping in touch with the Lord would put a barrier between me and evil spirits. As I opened the door of my heart to the Lord, many things were revealed to me about His marvelous sovereignty.

Opening the door of my heart was exactly what God was waiting for. Soon after, God gave me a vision that I would never forget. I saw on the screen of heaven a young lady dressed in a long-pleated cream dress with a bow tied in the back. She was wearing a straw hat that also contained a bow. I stood there staring at the screen as though I was watching a movie. I observed the young lady walking with her head steadily straight forward, and she never once looked to the left nor right. I watched her walk until she disappeared from the screen. I turned around, and I saw a man preaching in the dark and a spotlight was on him. I began to follow the man, and suddenly I heard the children singing and playing behind me. In an instance I removed my eyes from the preacher-man and looked over to see the children. When I turned back to follow the preacher-man he had disappeared from the scene.

For several weeks I prayed to God to reveal to me the meaning of this vision, and He did. I came to understand that this message was precisely to show me the way that I should walk with the Lord. Practically, the young lady represented the way that I should walk with the Lord without looking left or right. The preacher-man, on the other hand, represented the word of God that I needed to follow faithfully. And the children represented the distractions of the world.

I gladly received this message as a warning to remain focused on God, and to receive more revelation from Him. Each time I would think in a worldly manner, the Holy Spirit brought this vision back to my memory.

One day, I was sitting at the piano to worship God, and He began to speak to me about the title of this song "For His Glory." In an instant, He gave me both the lyrics and the melody, even the musical arrangement. Although I have been singing gospel songs all my life, this revelation was different from anything else that I had heard in my spirit. In 1999, I recorded this song with Joy Records as a solo, without the choir background. I was never satisfied with the incomplete work of the song. It was not due to the quality of the work but rather because I did not wait on the Lord. I recorded the song without the choir background. It was important that I waited for the season. Consequently, they did not compensate me for my labor nor reimbursed me for the cost of the musical arrangement. In addition, the distribution of the album stopped shortly after it was released.

A few years passed. Then suddenly the Lord completed the order of the song by allowing the choir background to be heard. One early morning the sweetest harmonies awakened me with the vocal arrangement of how the background should be. The sound filled my bedroom, manifesting the glory of God's presence. Today, it is with great joy that I share this harmonious sound with all who have the privilege to participate in "For His Glory." I want my readers to know what I liked the most about these episodes of my life is that: God gives us more than a second chance. If He was a God of second chance only, then I would not have made it this far to share my testimonies. He gives me another, another, and another opportunity—until I recognized that all about me should reflect His glory. Praise God for his patience and mercy!

Inspiration Eleven

** Holy, holy, holy, is the LORD of hosts; The whole earth is full of His glory!*

** For thus says the LORD, who created the Heaven; God himself that formed the earth andmade it; He hath established it, He create it not in vain, He formed it to be inhabited: I am the LORD; and there is none else.*

** All thy works shall praise thee, O LORD; and thy Saints shall bless Thee. They shall speak of the glorious majesty of Thy kingdom. Thy kingdom is an everlasting kingdom and Thy dominion endureth throughout all generations.*

(Is. 6:3B; 45:18) (Ps. 45:10-13; 145:10-13)

FOR His Glory

1-

In the beginning, God created Heaven and Earth. He made the sun to rule by day; the moon unfolded its light by night, and the stars sparkling in the sky; *for His glory*. Created Adam with His hands, breathed in him a living soul, and from his ribs created Eve; *All for His glory.*

2-

God's magnificent power displays throughout the world. How great is He, the Most-High God. His dominion endures forever. He even provides for the birds, *still for His glory.* We all are creations of God, but He desires to be our Father. Through the gospel we understand; *It was all for His glory.*

Chorus

Let all creations sing Hallelujah!

Let all God's children sing Hallelujah!

Everything that has breath sings Hallelujah!

For all the praise to God alone deserved.

Let all creations sing *Hallelujah!*

Let all God's children sing *Hallelujah!*

Everything that has breath sings *Hallelujah!*

PART-VI

SESSION TEN

Ministers' Contribution to the Development of the Given Gift:

Do you sing? I asked a fourteen-year-old boy who had just started to come to our church. The answer was "No." "Do you know about your given gift?" The answer was still "No." "What instrument would you like to play if you should have a chance?" "The drum," he replied. Now what interest do I have in asking these questions to a child that is not mine? We can identify with someone's inner gift by finding out about their interest in such an area. If the gift is already there, the idea will be constantly in their minds. For example, I knew that one of my daughters had the gift of singing, through my observation. When she was a little girl, she would wake up in the morning singing while she was getting ready to go to school. From that point, I trained and encouraged her to use her voice for the Lord. And today, she is one of my backup singers in the recording of "Can I be the One." I believe that it is a privilege for us to help someone to identify with their given gift. Our experience could be used to empower those to come and those who are left behind.

So far, we have learned many aspects about both the purpose and God's intent for the given gift. What remains?

As for us ministers who recognize the importance of the given gift, we have a genuine responsibility toward our new generation in helping them recognize their gifts. Selfishness should be excluded from the list. The trend to focus solely on our ministry must shift from solely ourselves and give our attention to others. If we are perfectly trained by Christ our teacher, we will be more like Him. He did not focus on Himself, but rather on teaching us about God's kingdom. ***"The disciple is not above his master: but everyone that is perfect shall be as his master" (Luke 6:40).*** The condition in teaching people to identify their gifts is an opportunity to manifest good work as a Godly pattern that they can follow.

What pattern does our work represent? There are a few guidelines that can be used as highlight patterns. The *first pattern* on the list would be **CARING.** Many times, one could be gifted in certain areas, but we just don't care to take the time to help them to recognize it or help them develop their potential. When we take it upon ourselves to help someone discover or develop their gifts, we are rolling over our gift. We all know that as we are getting older, our gift is also fading away. When we employ our time to work with others in their gifts, we are also investing in the kingdom of God by rolling it over to those who will replace us. In this way whether we are still alive or not, our informative contribution continues to magnify God in their lives. ***"According to my earnest expectation and hope, that in nothing I shall be ashamed, but with all boldness, as always so now also Christ will be magnified in my body, whether it be life or by death" (Phl. 1:20).***

Our contribution is a major investment, because it covers all the areas of God's intent for the given gift; that is, to glorify God, preach the gospel and edify the church. When our time is ended on this Earth, and our work is no longer available, those we help will carry over the legacy that we left behind. It was for this reason that I asked the young man about his given gift. Proceeding with my conversation with him, I did not stop with my inquiring about his wanting to play the drum. I worked my way to the next step. What we do today will determine the type of legacy that we will live behind for others to lean on.

The *second pattern* on the list would be **INTEREST.** *How do we show interest in the development of the gift?* Showing interest is to follow up in our caring through actions. Like I said, I personally believe that helping someone identify their gift is a privilege from God. As the Lord led me, I spoke to his parents about my interest in helping him develop his gift, and we concluded in a mutual agreement. Next, I called the music director at our church and asked him if he could arrange to have drum lessons for this young man. One week passed, I didn't hear from him. I pursued my interest with a follow-up call, but this time to another talented young man, whose gift is well-appreciated in the church. I told him that I was willing to compensate him, if he would help this other young man with the development of his gift. Right away, we scheduled his first drum lesson for the following weekend. Watch how God moved smoothly with my interest to invest in this young man's life.

It was a Saturday morning, and the lesson was scheduled for 10:30 am. I called the young man, and he was very excited about getting his first lesson. Unfortunately, he was confronted with transportation issues. His mother had already left for work; he had no metro card or change to get him on his way. Since I could not pick him up at the time, I was thinking, now what should I do? So, I decided to call the instructor. I explained to him the situation and he was more than willing to pick him up. They finally made it to the church by 11:30 am. Instead of two, there were three of them. One of them was an eight-year-old girl, who also played the drums very well. I sat them down and thanked them for their willingness. I especially thanked the instructor for his generosity and stewardship. I opened in prayer and gave them a short introduction about the importance of the development of the gift. It was fun watching them learn from each other. The young instructor sat at the keyboard, the young man sat on the drum kit; and the girl held the microphone, singing a worship song. After the first lesson, the young instructor and the girl left, but the young man stayed to practice for at least one more hour.

The *third pattern* on the list would be **EXCHANGE.** We ought to exchange our future incapability—due to the infirmity of old age—for the capability of those who are younger. We also know what we can do today; we might not be able to accomplish it tomorrow. In other words, it is best to take the little bit of strength that we have left and invest it in the lives of those who are more able to carry on the work. I am saying that we should review carefully and see what resources we've used to get to where we are in our ministry and pass them on to the younger generation. Eventually, they too will be successful in using their gifts, and duplicate themselves likewise. One of the greatest resources that we have is the word of knowledge. Since we are considered as righteous leaders before God that qualifies us to speak words of wisdom to them and help them follow the pathway of righteousness. ***"The mouth of righteous speaketh wisdom and his tongue talketh of judgment" (Ps. 37:30).*** It is critical to not let a gift go to waste while we are able to dictate to those who need our supervision.

The *fourth pattern* on the list is **SHARING.** When I saw the young man, I could discern his desire for service. The first move that I made was to help him take drum lessons opened a flexible relationship between me and him. One day after practice, I felt the need to ask him a simple Bible question. This was my question to him: *Do you know the story about Adam and Eve?* He put his head down and said,

"No." I was somewhat not feeling at ease with his answer because from what I knew, he was from a Christian family, and I thought that he should have at least known a little about the story of the creation. I asked him if he would like to hear it, and he said, "Yes." I looked at other options that I had, and I decided to encourage him to read the story of creation with me instead of telling him about it. To me it was nothing, but to him this was his first advanced discovery. This transition took us to a different level in the development of his gift for God.

I took time from my busy schedule to share something that was valuable to God, and to me and the young man. I taught him how to read the Bible slowly so that he might understand what he was reading. I considered that I had to eliminate *five possible obstacles.* (1) He was reading the story for the first time, and I needed to be patient. (2) He needed my guidance along the way to understand it. (3) I was careful not to go too far or too fast, so that he might not be discouraged. (4) I was respectful and sensitive to his weakness, and I tried my best not to embarrass him. (5) I realized if I was not being careful, I could push him away instead of drawing nearer to God. My primary concern at this point was to lead him to Christ. I was sure if he understood clearly about God's love for him, he could use the gift in accordance with God's intent.

Together, we concluded the first two chapters of Genesis. After reading the first chapter, I stopped and evaluated his knowledge. I asked him to share with me what he remembered, and to explain them to me in his own way. I was so proud and impressed by his devotion to learn about God his creator. Now, not only had he started to develop his gift, he also was privileged to develop his knowledge about God. The result of sharing is exactly what I was expecting, and that was to duplicate my discipleship in him.

Our objectives as advance ministers are established in our work-patterns for others to use. Our patterns could be structured in so many ways. Here are *twelve (12)* of those patterns that we should seriously take in consideration.

(1)	Don't *neglect* their salvations because we will not be able to escape such command. ***"How shall we escape, if we neglect so great a salvation; which at the first began to be spoken by the Lord, and was confirmed unto us by them that hear Him"*** *(Heb. 2:3).*

(2)	When God places someone before us to teach, we should never think of them as *burdens*. Rather, this is a heart movement to motivate them as their pilot. As good pilots, we ought to try our best to assure the safety of those who depend on us. ***"Laying up in store for themselves a good foundation against the time to come, that they may lay hold on eternal life"*** *(I Tim. 6:19).*

(3)	In communicating with them, have *no tolerance* for laziness. Encourage intensity for building skills and maintain control over laid-back attitudes. Their doubts could be seen through discernment. Take time to teach them how to advance in faith through Bible study. ***"This witness is true. Wherefore rebuke them sharply, that they may be sound in the faith"*** *(Titus 1:13).*

(4)	Use the opportunity with *confidence* to see a positive result. Positive results are the fruits of your patterns. This pattern must be used with a passion for eliminating doubts; and that they may continue in confidence ***"But continue thou in the things which thou hast learned and hast been assured of, knowing of whom they have learned them"*** *(II Tm. 3: 14).*

(5)	Learn how to approach them with *love* in a *non-threatening way.* Take them from the lowest level and walk them slowly to the pathway of a successful ministry; that they may ***"In all things showing pattern of good work: in doctrine showing corruptness, gravity, sincerity"*** *(Titus. 2:7).*

(6)	Build up their potentiality by *disclosing* our own weaknesses to them when necessary. That way, they will develop their own strengths through our experiences. ***"That the communication of thy faith*** *may become effectual by the acknowledgement of every good thing which is in you in Christ Jesus" (Philem. 1:6).*

(7)   Teach them that the gift *is about stewardship for the kingdom of God* and not about personal gain. That will help them to examine their motives. ***"And let ours also learn to maintain good work, for necessary uses, that they be not unfruitful" (Titus 3:14).***

(8)   Show them that their *weaknesses are part of their growth process*. Track their progress and speak words of encouragement for their achievements. In this way, we will be preparing to forward to them the love of God with dignity. Secure your contribution with *honest prayer.* In like manner, they too will learn to resist their weaknesses in praying for one another. ***"And this I pray, that your love may abound yet more and more in knowledge and in all discernment" (Phil. 1:9).***

(9)   Proclaim the *fear* of the Lord to them in the early stage of their new birth in Christ. They will not automatically know how to reverence God if they have not been taught. ***"The Lord gave the word: great was the company of those that published it" (Ps. 68:11).***

(10) Try to win their trust by making them comfortable and maintain confidentiality to their disclosures. Keep your comments simple so they will not be ashamed and frustrated. ***"But avoid foolish questions, and genealogies, and contentions, and strivings about the law; for they are unprofitable and vain" (Titus 3:9).***

(11) Allow them the opportunity to discuss what they have learned openly. Employ Godly techniques to teach them about the essentials. ***"All things are lawful for me, but not all things are not expedient; all things are lawful for me, but not all things edify not" (I Cor. 10:23).***

Can the Gift Become Ineffective?

As the Holy Spirit subdivided the gifts, it was not based on the subjectivity of the one who received it. Rather, it was based according to God's generosity in sharing the goodness of His kingdom for a purpose. That means, the one who received simply identifies the gift and operates in it progressively in God's purpose. Therefore, when there is a variation in the performance, perhaps, an invader came and interfered with the progressive use of the gift. If there should be a variation in the progressive use of the gift, then it becomes ineffective. As I thought about the cause of the ineffectiveness of the gift, I was led to one of Jesus Christ's parables about the kingdom of heaven *in **Matthew chapter 13.*** Remember, the kingdom of heaven is where we live at this present time.

(V. 24) The kingdom of heaven is likened unto a man which sowed good seed in his field. (V. 25) But while men slept, his enemy came and sowed tares among the wheat, and went his way. (V: 26) But when the blade was sprung up, and brought forth fruit, then appeared the tares also. (V. 27) So the servants of the householder came and said unto him, Sir, didst not thou sow good seed in thy field? From whence then hath it tares? (V. 28) He said unto them, an enemy hath done this, the servants said unto him, wilt thou then that we go and gather them up? (V. 29) But he said Nay; lest while ye gather up the tares, ye not root up also the wheat with them. (V. 30) Let both grow together until the harvest: and in the time of harvest, I will say to the reapers, gather ye together first the tares, and bind them in bundles to burn them: but gather the wheat into my barn.

What lesson can we learn about the ineffectiveness of the gift in this parable? With the help of the Holy Spirit, together, we will discover the truth. Are you ready? This parable is related to the planting of the seed of the Gospel, but also could even be used as an example of the effectiveness and the ineffectiveness of the gift. Since we are talking about the use of the gift, we will use it in that sense.

- *The first lesson* we discover is found in verse (24). Any given gift is *a good seed* planted by the Master of the universe in our lives; and we are the field in which He plants it. The seed is to produce a harvest in the universe while we are still living in it, so all could see its result. In other words, before we leave the kingdom of heaven (earth) to go to the kingdom of God (heaven), the effectiveness or ineffectiveness of the gift will be seen.

- *The second lesson* we learn is in verse (25). Something happened after the good seed was planted. "*While everybody was asleep; an enemy came and sowed weeds among the wheat, and then went away.* So, *who is everybody?* Everybody could be replaced by those who possess the gift, the church and those around us, etc. We all know that when a seed is planted, it does not grow instantly. It takes some time before anyone can see the crop. The growth of the seed does not depend on whether we are awake, but this verse simplifies it by indicating that anything could happen when we are sleeping. One, the seed could continue to grow, and two, something terrible could happen that can destroy the root of the crop. For example, one of the elements that could interfere with the effectiveness of the gift is when the church becomes so preoccupied in entertaining and neglects its responsibilities of the proper use of the gifts for the edification of the church. Instead, it loses its vision about the intent of their service to God. Consequently, the church becomes a social gathering rather than a house of edification. **"Wherefore comfort yourselves together, and edify one another, even as also ye do" (I Tim. 5:11).** Therefore, everyone got caught up in their interrelationships with each other, representing the sleepiness that we acknowledge.

- *The third lesson* is in verse (26) "*So when the plants came up and bore grain, then the weed appeared as well.*" The church, for pumping up her reputation, started to invite unsaved artists who use the gospel as cover-up for gaining fame. As a result, they left behind their worldly tracks for younger artists in the church to follow. Now the younger artists are trying to gain the same applause from the audience, mimicking them and acting the same way. They did not acknowledge that the adversary had come and sowed weeds among the wheat. The idea of edification (wheat) is now shifted to socialization (weeds).

For instance, one night I attended a revival service in one of the most famous churches in our Haitian community. When I heard that a preacher man, for whom I have great deal of appreciation, was preaching that night, I decided to attend the last night of the revival to edify my soul. Unfortunately, I was disappointed instead of being edified. It so happened that they had invited some artists to stir up the emotions of the people. I felt embarrassed by these false performers who, without reservation utilized the rapping style, screaming out their lyrics and mimicking the posturing of worldly performers. I was so turned off by their performance that I left even before the preacher came forth.

- *The fourth lesson* is in verse (27). "*And the slaves of the householder came and said to him, 'Master, did you not sow good seed in your field? Where, then, did these weeds come from?"* You see, among the people who are gifted, there are some who are using their gift according to God's intent. Those are the ones who give respect to God and honor Him (the grain). Then, there are also those who are showing off their gift and mimicking the worldly styles (the weeds).

- *The fifth lesson is in verse (28.) He answered, 'An enemy has done this.' The slaves said to him, 'Then do you want us to go and gather them?'* It is not because there was anything wrong with the seed of the gift that was planted in them, but because a critical attack from the enemy spoils the crops with weeds of the world trying to counterfeit and confuse the believers. *The slaves said to him, 'Then do you want us to go and gather them?'* Visualize yourself in the position of the slave for a moment. When the weeds clearly show in our congregation, we are anxious to get rid of them, but Jesus the Master of the church is telling us not to act irrationally against those who are like weeds and pretending to be wheat. It is not for us to take judgment upon ourselves to chase or remove them from the Church before God's time.

- *The sixth lesson* is in verse *(29). But he replied, 'No; for in gathering the weeds you would uproot the wheat along with them.* What exactly the master is telling us in His answer? Now, is it necessarily our responsibility to pluck weeds out of the church? Not at all. There are three reasons why God does not want us to take judgment in our own hands. (1) We did not die on the cross for their sins; therefore, we are disqualified. (2) We truly don't know the plan of God for their lives. And (3) we do not know what is in their hearts, only God does. By trying to pluck those who are not truly serving God out of the church, we could end up damaging the faith of those who are young in Christ. All we could do as ministers of the Gospel is to pray that God will give us discernment to avoid giving access to the adversary to come and sowed weeds in the church. For in due time, all we must give an account to the Master.

- *The seventh lesson is in verse (30). "Let both grow together until the harvest, and at the harvest time. I will tell the reapers, collect the weeds first and bind them in bundles to be burned, but gather the wheat into my barn."* When the time of harvest comes, the reapers will be given the opportunity to collect the wheat, which is those who produced good works with their gifts, and then of course the weeds (bad works) will be set aside for destruction. I had to learn about not getting involved with matters that pertain to God, to maintain my good works as a Sower of the Gospel. For those of you who are preoccupied by other obstacles and come short of the gift that God has given you, He wants you to know that those obstacles are the weeds that interfere with the growth of your ministry.

Some of the considerable sectors (weeds) that need to be recognized are:

Criticism, insecurity, discouragement, fear, scar, and secession.

Can criticism make our gift ineffective? Yes, it can. Sometimes, criticism is used as an urgent utterance to promote insecurity in using the gift effectively. It is a fact that *insecurity attracts physical and emotional instability*. Those who used to sneer against ministers have no way of knowing its effect on the lives of others, but the enemy who puts the thought in their minds does know how far he wants to go. His plan is to get us discouraged and stop us from producing good crops. *When discouragement finds its place in the heart of the minister, it creates plenty of room for fear.* When fear abides in the heart, we become very sensitive about what people think or say about us.

Can fear cause our gift to be ineffective? The answer is yes. *Fear is a dark shadow over our ministry because it brings variations in the way we minister.* One of the variations is query. A *queried mind* is a double minded person; one who doubts God. When Satan demonstrated against God's authority, he simply removed the word (seed) of His command and replaced it with weeds (doubt) in the mind of Eve. **"And the serpent said unto the woman, ye shall not surely die" (Gen. 3:4).** Eve fell into the shadow of fear since the time she yielded to Satan's offer. As a result, fear had become the planted weed in the life of Adam, and it was transmitted to every human being as a sinful scar. **"And he said, I heard thy voice in the garden, and I was afraid, because I was naked; and I hid myself" (Gen. 3: 10).**

Likewise, when we *yield to the slur of others, it leaves scars in our hearts*. And to move forward in our ministry effectively, *these scars must be completely healed.* Just as it takes the blood of Jesus to remove the scars of sin, it will take a serious stability in commitment to vanquish fear. This type of commitment must be engraved in our hearts as workmen of the gospel. ***"...The LORD hath put wisdom, even everyone whose heart stirred him up to come unto the work to do it" (Ex. 36:2).*** That means when we are chosen by God to work for Him, he also gifted us with skills and wisdom. If there is no stability in committing to use the gift in wisdom, the gift becomes rusty and ineffective. Consequently, the snare of secession will slowly take its place in our hearts as a deadly weed.

Can secession make our gift ineffective? The answer is still yes. When the spirit of *secession finds* its place in our hearts, we tend to *withdraw* from using the gift. We use the gift sometimes according to how we feel for the moment, or according to what we want to offer to God's people. We are made to know that God is not interested in scrap work, but rather in first fruit work. Scrap work is giving God the leftovers; conversely first fruit work is giving God our very best. The most important element in rendering a good service to God is not found in the quantity of our gifts, but rather in the quality of our devotion to God when using the gifts.

This is no foolishness. Let me share with you a story about my inclination about this subject. I know a young man who was very active in the church, singing as a lead soloist in a youth choir. I remember how blessed and edified I was each time I heard him sing. He was filled with passion for the Gospel, and very enthusiastic in using his gift to edify the church. In the process of my recording, he happened to cross my mind. I gave him a call and asked him if he would like to be part of the project as a backup singer. Our conversation went very smoothly, and he was very excited to be one of my participants. I emailed him one of the songs so that he could get familiar with it. Meanwhile I was so involved in the completion of the manual that it gave him plenty of time to learn the song. Several weeks after, I kept calling him to let him know that we needed to meet for rehearsal, but I had a very hard time reaching him. I prayed for him and hoped to find out what had happened since our last conversation.

After several weeks of trying to reach him, he finally responded to me and let me know that his schedule had kept him too busy; therefore, he withdrew from the acceptance of my offer. Though I really wanted him to be part of this project, I responded to his email, and told him that I was sorry to hear that, and that I hoped he would change his mind and be part of the second recording. It had been a while after my email, and I still did not hear from him. He often crossed my mind, so I just continued to pray. One Sunday evening, I was compelled to call him. Thank God, he did answer. We conversed for a while, and he shared with me that one of his reasons for withdrawing was because he had stopped singing for a while and didn't feel right singing at this time. The Lord put it in my heart to counsel him about the importance of the given gift, and I did. With an open heart he listened and was very grateful for my encouragement to him. Before closing our conversation, I asked if it was alright that I prayed with him, and the answer was "Yes."

The most important aspect of the moment of sharing the truth with him was the result of God's wisdom in me in performing the work with valor. I utterly believe that the message penetrated his heart. The lesson that I learned in this episode is that, when God opens a door at a particular time, we ought to take full advantage of the moment. We are God's utensils, and He has the right to use us at any given time. We should not use common sense to combat weeds among our wheat because it is spiritual warfare not physical. God has a greater way to use us in combating weeds in our midst.

He can use our encouragements as a shield to protect someone's heart. He can use our words of wisdom as strength to replenish those who are empty of hope. In addition, He can also use us as a flashlight to bring light into the hearts of those who fall in the dark shadow of insecurity. Furthermore, He can use us to prevent someone from falling off the track of using the gift. Much more, He can use us as predominance to overthrow the plan of the adversary who is determined to spoil our crops.

How do we reverse an ineffective gift to an effective one? Thank God for the positive answers regarding this question. There are significant principles to turn an ineffective gift into an effective one. I encourage the strongest to help the weakest by giving them a hand. Do not hesitate to reach out to them. Some of you like to discriminate against those who fall off track. For this, I urge you to renounce this selfishness and remain in a position to help them when they need you by continuing to exercise the following: rectify them and don't destroy them with hurtful words by trying to please your ego; do not force them to vacate the church with a selfish attitude; quench their thirst with the word of God, overtake them with love and compassion and teach them how to remain watchful over their hearts. I hope these definitions are clear in understanding the mission assigned to all ministers. Use them actively in your daily lives. Wait patiently and experience the reversal of an ineffective gift to an effective one.

Is it Right for Christians to Hire Non-Christians to Produce Gospel Music?

To summarize the previous sessions, I will answer this question based on what we have already learned about the principles that are attached to the gift. Hiring a non-Christian producer has hindered the ministry of many. The grand principle to the great commission remains in terms of disciples making disciples. This subject seems to be sensitive to many gospel artists, but I present my argument with great earnestness without discrimination and further hindrance to shed some light on this matter.

I know a servant who is gifted around writing gospel songs. She loves the Lord and desires to enrich the church with her gift. She shared with me that some of the people said to her that they "don't like the output of the production of her songs." Being that my husband and I were in the radio broadcasting ministry, we try to support the gospel artists by using their songs to help promote the gospel. So, without discrimination, I bought the CD from her. She allowed me to read some of her lyrics, and I could relate very much to them because she knew the word of God. Though she was not gifted around singing, there is no doubt that she is gifted in writing congregational praise. I sensed that she had a passion for writing gospel songs, but a major factor was lacking.

During one of my conversations with that artist, I happened to ask her this question: "Is the person producing your music a Christian?" The answer was "no." She did not see anything wrong by having a non-Christian producing her songs, but I automatically saw what the problem was. The missing factor was the lack of discernment. The producing of a gospel song should be viewed as an opportunity to better coordinate the message that it carries, which is the Gospel. The spirituality of a disciple is to be able to discern right from wrong. **"But ye that is spiritual judgeth all things, yet he himself is judged of no man" (I Cor. 2:15).** You see, the main problem in the use of her gift was neither the voice nor the motive, but she needs to ask God for spiritual discernment. If she had possessed spiritual discernment, her songs could have reached many souls for Christ. **"Give therefore thy servant an understanding heart...that I may discern between good and bad..." (I Kings 3:9).**

What can reinforce spiritual discernment? There should be a *commitment* when using spiritual discernment. That commitment is to operate the gift in accordance with God's standard that we learned in these sessions. The Bible is explicit about God's objective for those who are saved to minister to the world. If we want to maintain the quality of our discipleship in our singing ministry, we cannot go by what is available, even if it is free of charge. Making a commitment to use the gift according to God's principles is important because this will help us monitor our pledge to Him.

Making a commitment to work for God is pledging to Christ's command as we take responsibility to do what is right before Him. ***"And He commanded us to preach unto the people, and to testify that it is He was ordained of God to be the judge of quick and dead" (Acts 10:42).*** When we make a commitment to *worship God, preach the gospel, and edify the church* in our ministry, our performances should be steadfast as a testimony in the spirituality of these aspects. Thereby, if we have yet established such a commitment, we should take heed not to continue without making this very important decision. Once we make a commitment to follow God's principles, our approach to the work should be different than that of a non-Christian.

Hiring non-Christians to produce our songs means that we are willingly participating with their worldly expression. Instead of putting on Jesus, we join in partnership with the world by putting on the devil's coat, sharing similar ideas and feelings. We should be telling them how the music should be arranged; they are now leading us away from the inspiration we had in mind. ***"But put ye on the Lord Jesus Christ, and make not provision for the flesh, to fulfill the lusts thereof" (Rom. 13:14).*** With this partnership, we are disregarding God's principles left us only with the idea of entertainment. The non-Christian's motive is different than that of a Christian. Entertainment has no place in God's principles. Remember not every inspiration comes from God. Non-Christians do not have the Holy Spirit to inspire them. They can only imitate Satanic sensation.

"Be ye not unequally yoked together with unbelievers: for what fellowship hath righteousness? And what communion hath light with darkness?" (2 Cor. 6:14). Looking closer into this scripture, I found greater discernment. To understand my point, we first need to understand its context. Prior to this teaching, I misunderstood this scripture because I only viewed it from a matrimony perspective. I discovered that there is more to it than that.

What is a yoke? And what is it used for? Based on Biblical interpretation, a yoke is a frame uniting animal for work. In addition, a yoke also represents a type for slavery, oppression, bondage to sin, submission, and legalistic ordinances, etc. As you can see, the list is lengthy. But I am going to reduce it to one. I believe *"Slavery"* is more appropriate for this teaching. ***"Let as many servants as are under the yoke of count their own masters worthy of all honor, that the name of God and His doctrine be not blasphemed" (I Tim. 6:1).*** Wait a minute! I see a different revelation in this scripture. As servants of Jesus Christ, our Master, we are yoked or enslaved to honor Him in what we do so we would not blaspheme His doctrine. Is that right? That means, we could only be under the yoke by only one master. That master will be the one to control us. If so, when we partnership with an unbeliever in the use of the gift, we are no longer controlled by God, our master. Understand this, God's yoke is His command. So, when we are no longer under His command, we become vulnerable to being oppressed by another master. Wherefore, if the minister is yoked to God, his Master, he will count to honor Him in all productions. Otherwise, the production could become blasphemy to God's doctrine.

What is the difference between entertainment and edification? There are two distinct approaches when it comes to entertainment and edification. One does not need to have a relationship with Christ to be an entertainer. Entertainment is for the *pleasure of the soul and body*. There is no solidarity in it because it doesn't last. This means you must repeatedly refill the buckets of the soul and body with entertainment just for a temporary boost.

On the contrary, *edification* is the teaching that feeds the soul and spirit. In terms of edification, one must have a relationship with Christ and be filled with the Holy Spirit to fulfill the need for a spiritual thirst. The solidarity of an edifying ministry is to present our songs in the fullness and purity of the gospel of Jesus Christ. Trying any other way, our ministry will collapse. The establishment of the gift is to instill people with the knowledge of how to have a permanent relationship with God the Father, the Son, and the Holy Spirit. Therefore, when we mingle our ministry with other inspiration, we are building on shaky ground. We could do much better if we are rooted in our commitments to God. ***"Rooted and built up in Him and establish in the faith, as ye have been taught; abounding in it with thanksgiving"*** ***(Col. 2:7).***

Once more, we are sanctified by God to serve as laborers to produce soul's harvest. If we fail to do so, the result of reaching out to lost souls will be poor. The non-Christian is depending on you as the light that would lead them to Christ, not you are following them. ***"I have set you as a light to the Gentiles that thou shouldest be for salvation unto the ends of the earth" (Acts 13:47b).*** For example, I was having a conversation regarding my recording to one of the gospel artists in Brooklyn, New York; he advised me that "I should give the Haitian people what they want in terms of style." When I asked him what he meant by that, He told me that he performs *"konpa"* because that is what the people want to buy. By the way, konpa is the Haitian's worldly traditional beat or rhythm. Some of us reject its practice in the church, but many adopt it as acceptable. It does not matter to some people because this apostasy will permit them to make more money. But it does matter to God because He called us out to be a light of the Gospel of Jesus Christ; and it is our choice to refuse to join this apostasy. Some of us might say that "we have no choice." That is a lie from hell because there is always a choice. I am going to tell it like it is. We simply chose mammon rather than God.

What does konpa has to do with the fulfillment of spreading the gospel? Konpa originated from a non-Christian perspective. I use konpa as an example, but it could be any worldly style of music. Non-Christians neither have any desire to please God, nor care about the spreading of the gospel. In this case, being part of our music production is simply a job to them. What could they possibly contribute to our ministry, but entertainment? Let me tell you something, my friend, if your focus is to sell your gift as products to the world instead of evangelism, then you miss the point about God's intent or purpose for the given gift. Rather than committing to a ministry, you are committing to the operation of a retail business.

Look at it this way: there are two sides to this issue. The bad news is this: if you are taking a risky approach to display your gift in the context of a non-believer, then most likely you have been working without God's approval. Your work could only be approved when it is done according to His intents. Here is the good news: it is not too late to produce your music differently. All you need to do is to commit yourself to God's work by applying what you have learned in this teaching.

You have already learned about the three aspects of audiences that you should minister to while operating according to the acts of the principles. So, before engaging a non-Christian in your recording, you have *three* important steps to take: *first,* think about God's intent. *Second*, select an audience according to your theme. *Third,* allow the Holy Spirit to lead you to someone who shares the same faith and vision. Suppose your audience is non-Christians. Then your focus should be on evangelism, to draw them to Christ, not sending them the wrong signal about Christianity.

Dealing with conviction could be very painful. But it could be even worse to remain in this condition while procrastinating. Trust God, He will get rid of the pain sooner than you think. The first question pertaining to your inquisition should be initiated by asking *How can this recording be pleasing unto God to teach, preach the gospel and edify the church?* The second question you should ask is *How could you commit your soul to God in His will concerning your ministry?* **"Wherefore let them that suffer according to the will of God commit the keeping of their souls to Him in well doing, as unto a faithful Creator" (I Pet. 4:19).** Do not worry about your past mistakes. If you acknowledge your fault and ask for forgiveness, God has already taken care of them. Just deal with the present by taking your commitment one step at a time. God will guide you and provide the persons who will be in partnership with you in your recording project. I pray that this session will lead your mind and heart to a Goodly perspective in continuing your singing or music ministry.

The Expectations that Follow the Ministerial Work

What should we expect in the ministry of music? People could have certain expectations, but they sometimes reach a point where they get tired of waiting and give up. Sometimes, we are expecting only to see the easy side of the ministry but fail to wait on God because we encounter some difficulties along the way. Well, the type of expectation that I am about to discuss in this session is to help you boldly face both the negative and positive expectations of our ministry. Most likely, it is not easy to accept the negative expectations. Surely in the ministerial road we will encounter both. When God sent His precious son Jesus into this world, He had some expectations for Jesus' work. I could think of at least *fifteen (15)* expectations, but I am pretty sure there are more.

(1) God expected that Jesus would **fulfill the Father's will.** *"The Spirit of the Lord is upon Me, because He hath anointed Me to preach the gospel to the poor; He hath sent Me to heal the broken-hearted, to preach deliverance to the captives and recovery of sight to the blind, to set at liberty them that are bruised, to preach the acceptable year of the LORD" (Luke 4:18).*

(2) God expected that Jesus would **teach and preach about His kingdom** to everyone. *"I must preach the kingdom of God to the other cities also, for therefore am I sent" (Luke 4:43).*

(3) God expected that Jesus would **have many followers**. *"(And when the day began to wear away, then came the twelve, and said to Him, "Send the multitude away..." (Luke 9:12).*

(4) God expected that Jesus' message **would awaken the hearts of men**. *"When Simon Peter, saw it, he fell down at Jesus'*

feet knees, saying, "...Depart from me, for I am a sinful man, O Lord" (Luke 5:8)!

(5) God expected that Jesus would **teach His disciples** how to be true servants. *"For weather is greater, he that sitteth at meat, or he that serveth? Is not he that sitteth at meat? But I am among you as he that serveth" (Luke 22:27).*

(6) God expected that Jesus' works **would bring healing** to those who are ill. *"When he heard that Jesus was come out of Judea into Galilee, he went unto him, and besought him that he would come down, and heal his son: for he was at the point of death" (John 5:47).*

(7) God expected that his son would have ***many enemies.*** *"And they were filled with madness and communed with one with another what they might do to Jesus" (Luke 6:11).*

(8) God expected that people would **acknowledge the work of Jesus** and praise the Father in return."*...The whole multitude of the disciples began to rejoice and praise God with a loud voice for all the mighty works they had seen" (Luke 19:37).*

(9) God expected that Jesus' disciples to **tell the truth about Him**. *"If I bear witness of myself, my witness is true. There is another that beareth witness of me; and I know that the witness which he witnesseth of me is true" (John 5:31-32).*

(10) God expected that Jesus would **pray for His disciples** that they may stand firm against temptations."*...Satan hath desired to have you, that he may sift you as wheat. But I have prayed for thee, that thy faith should not fail..." (Luke 22: 31-32).*

(11) God expected that His son would be **denied even among His followers.** "And he denied Him, saying, "Woman, I do not know Him" (Luke 22:57).

(12) God expected that Jesus would **testify** about the doctrine of His kingdom. *Jesus answered them and said, "My doctrine is not*

mine, but His that sent Me" (John 7:16)

(13) God expected that Jesus would be **betrayed by one man.** *"And truly the Son of man goeth, as it was been determined: but woe to that man by whom He is betrayed" (Luke 22:22).*

(14) God expected that Jesus would **face many challenges,** even the death of the cross. *"But they cried, saying, "Crucify Him, crucify Him!" (Luke 23:21).*

(15) Above all, the work of Jesus continues in us. God sets these examples so we should know what is expected from whosoever possessed any types of spiritual gift. Especially from those who have a greater portion of the gift. ***"...For unto whomsoever much is given, of him much shall much required: and to whom much has been committed much, of him they will ask the more" (Luke 12:48).*** *Going over this list of expectations, we could see both positive and negative expectations.* As well, when we are sent by God to preach the gospel, we, too, can expect to face both *challenges and rewards.* Those of us who minister in songs might not even realize it, but each time we sing the truth of the gospel, we are challenging Satan and his kingdom. When Satan feels frightened, he will rage against us and will try his very best to distract us from our assignments. Like I mentioned before in Session Six about being equipped, remember to dress up with the whole armor of God for these occasions.

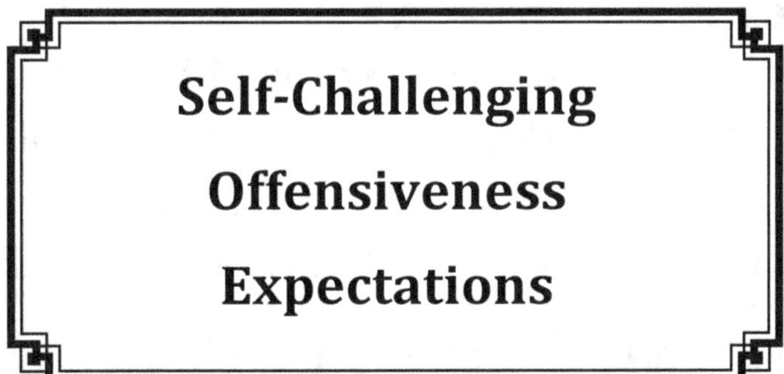

Self-challenge is a stumbling block in the singing ministry. To overcome the self, we must be steadfast in our humility. Our Master Jesus Christ faced the self-challenge of **offensiveness.** One of the famous examples in the Bible about humility was when Jesus volunteered himself to be the servant. Peter innocently offended Jesus in front of all the disciples and said **"...Thou shalt never wash my feet" (John 13: 8).** Jesus dealt with this offense at Peter's level. He knew that Peter had no idea of what he was saying. Jesus gave Peter an option to either accept or reject his position as one of His. After Peter realized that He could be excluded from the heavenly list, he made a very wise decision and accepted the offer by saying **"Lord, not my feet only, but also my hands and my head" (John 13:9).**

Peter did not offend Jesus just once, but twice. Satan new about Peter's love for Jesus, because of that, he injected the wrong idea in his mind. Peter was quick to always have something to say to Jesus, not knowing that he would offend his Master. He even debated with Jesus when He announced His upcoming suffering. Jesus rebuked him by saying: **"Get thee behind Me, Satan! Thou art an offense unto: for thou savorest not the things that be of God, but those that be of men" (Matt. 16:23).**

Sometimes, people are not aware that they are being offensive to others. That is when spiritual strength plays an important role in our ministry. Spiritual strength is the shield that covers our hearts from being offended. Jesus was shielded with spiritual strength and wisdom. If we are not willing to follow the perfect example of Jesus while facing offensive acts, then Satan will have his way in our ministry. I have never been in a position where I had to wash anyone's feet, except for washing my children's feet, but I have been put in positions where I had to face offensive acts. Having to face offensiveness made me discover my strength as a servant. Beside this, it is important for us to know how Jesus felt and dealt with such a situation.

Being a gospel artist in New York City for over three decades has exposed me to different types of churches. I was a member of the Wadsworth Avenue Baptist church in Manhattan for over twenty years and people never had to worry about dress code. Everyone was free to come to church wearing casual or formal clothes. As for me, modesty was my lifestyle because of my late Father who planted the seed in me since I was a little girl. I strongly believe in the modesty of a dress code that Paul instructed in *I Timothy 2:9.* I thought I could pass on that tradition to my daughters, but my approach was challenging to them. The dress code principle is so dominant in some churches that it takes the place of preaching about the gospel of salvation. Instead, they invested plenty of time trying to convince people about how they should not dress, the makeup and ornaments that they should not wear. Through my observation of the Haitian Gospel artists, those types of lyrics make more sale than any other lyrics. Though modesty is an important factor in the churches, too much emphasis on this subject could chase new converts out of the church. I believe that we should just concentrate on lyrics that build up confidence in faith and allow the Holy Spirit to do the conviction.

It was never a problem for me to comply with a dress code because I was introduced to it at an early age. Nevertheless, there were two forces that I often struggled with. One was the covering of the head. The other was the wearing of jewelry. Of course, we all know that some churches could exaggerate these subject matters. They might even misjudge and declare condemnation over those who have not yet met their traditional standard. I was invited to sing in a church in Brooklyn New York, and I went there to minister in song with my head uncovered. I noticed that, while I was singing, the members of the church were discriminating against me. The worst audience one could minister to is a cold one. I could not understand why the church was not edified by the anointing of God in me. I did not talk to anyone about it, but God knows I was offended by that. The reason for my offense was because self was in the way. After the service, a brother approached me and asked if he could have a word with me. And I said "Yes." He opened his Bible in the book of first Corinthians chapter eleven and read to me about the covering my head.

I was not supposed to be offended because the day before I went there, the Holy Spirit had led me to the very same chapter, and

I read it. I totally ignored it and did not care to follow God's warning. In the middle of the discussion, I asked the brother if he had read the whole chapter. He said, "he hadn't." Then I asked him to read verse fifteen. Verse fifteen states that *a woman's long hair is given her for a covering.*" He shook his head and left me alone. I am not sure if he was convinced, but I believe that I gave him something to think about. That night I learned not to ignore the voice of the Holy Spirit. If I had not done that, I would have avoided this offensive act and I would have prepared myself to edify the church. When we are challenged by cultural beliefs, we must be spiritually flexible if we want to edify the church. Flexibility means we must inquire about everything including dress code. That way we could step over the blocks of self-offensiveness by learning from our mistakes and prepare ourselves for the next challenge.

This episode remains so vivid in my mind. I visited another Haitian church in Montreal where I had to face a similar problem, but in a more visible way. I had the privilege to meet the pastor of that church through my relationship with another Baptist church in Brooklyn, New York. He had heard me perform as a lead soloist and was blessed by my ministry. I reached out to him while I was in Montreal visiting my friend, and he used that opportunity to invite me to minister in song to his church. It was a Sunday morning service, and it was my first time visiting this church without the choir. Normally, when the choir performed, everyone's head was uncovered, but it never occurred to me that the people in this church would be so concerned about the covering of the head. This offense was so obvious that it nearly distracted me from edifying the church. When they told me to come up to the pulpit to sing, a sister who was sitting way in the back took a piece of cloth and passed it from hand to hand until it reached up to my hand. I humbled myself and put it over my head. To me, I received it as a sign of mockery because if I wanted to cover my head, I would rather have worn a hat or completely veiled my head.

I stood there silently for a moment before I greeted the

congregation. My silence was my connection in prayer. The minute I prayed, the Holy Spirit immediately removed the feeling of embarrassment, and I was covered with the anointing. When I began to sing, I had the attention of the entire church. They acknowledged my strength in the Lord and gladly received my ministry. My ultimate choice was to place myself among the poor in spirit. I exchanged my embarrassment for the strength of the Lord. And you, what would you have done? Humiliation is a painful feeling, but the feeling of Humility is also rewarding. My reward was to overcome the self.

Another struggle that I encountered in the singing ministry was **inferiority** in the congregation. Inferiority is very common in the church, especially among the poor in Haiti. After my experiences in New York, whenever I am invited to a church to sing, I make sure to do an assessment of the type of congregation that I will be ministering to. And that is very important.

Again, I was sent by the Lord as a missionary to preach the gospel, this time in Haiti. It was a Friday evening, and I was sitting in the front porch of my Father's house in St. Marc. Suddenly, I heard voices like a multitude singing. I asked my sister-in-law about the singing, and she told me that there was a church "back there somewhere." I felt compelled to go and look for this church, and I immediately left to seek it. On my way there, I felt the need to take off my chain. I noticed that the skirt that I was wearing had no pocket. It did not matter to me because I knew what the Lord wanted me to do. I listened to my spirit, took off the little chain I had around my neck, and tied it to the hem of my long skirt. Before I entered the church, I looked around and saw that none of the women were wearing jewelry. It was not because they were Seven-Day Adventists, but because it was part of the principles of the church. I am glad that I was obedient this time. The people were comfortable with me because I understood and complied with their principles. I met them at their levels, and I did not appear superior to them. They were blessed by my humbled attitude.

My point for using these examples is to let you know that

ministering in song is powerful but could also be powerless when we don't follow the example of humility. At times, self could be a stumbling block in our singing ministry, but if we diminish self with humility and listen to the voice of the Holy Spirit, we could overcome all. Our profitable reward in the ministry is to be concerned about the needs of others and not our own. Paul supported that statement by saying that ***"Even as I please men in all things, not seeking mine own profit, but the profit of many that they may be saved" (I Cor. 10:33).***

Besides the negative aspects of expectations, we should also look forward to a positive harvest for the accomplishment of our work. Being able to operate in partnership with the Holy Spirit enables us to recognize that the gift is not the fruit of our prideful efforts. Nevertheless, we can also expect that God, in return, will allow us to see the fruits of our labor. Depending on God to bring forth our expectations is efficient to our ministry because to meet our expectations, we must believe that God will fulfill them through His promises.

- Expect that *God will increase knowledge and wisdom for the work.* The more we know God, the more our wisdom will increase.

- Expect that God *will use our gifts to have a direct and positive impact on people's lives*. So, use your gifts as much as you can because you never know what God might do.

- We can also *expect contact that maintains the harmony of a spiritual relationship with those we minister to.* That relationship will help us to identify with their needs.

- We should *expect that our songs will generate faith, repentance, and encouragement*. In return God will bless us because He desires to grant us our requests.

- We should *expect to operate in the gift as the poor in spirit.* The poor in spirit relies on the Holy Spirit rather than his or her strength *(Matt. 5:2-3).* For example, when I write a song, I depend on the Holy Spirit to clarify the message that my audience could relate to. I continuously seek His help from day to day. The more I depend on the Lord, the more insight I received for the theme of the song. What amazes me most is the fact that the Holy Spirit even enhances the message while I am in the recording process at the studio. *"He shall come down like rain upon the mown grass: as showers that water the earth" (Ps. 72:6).*

- There is a perfect expectation that applies to those who accept to humble themselves. *That is to take the cross of obedience and follow Jesus.* God will reward us for our faithful service. *An earnest worker should expect an earnest harvest.* Our faithful service creates room even for earthly rewards. Humility is the key to the fulfillment of the reward. *"Blessed are the meek: for they shall inherit the earth" (Matt. 5:5).* As we humble ourselves before God as ministers of the word, God will give us a good sense of both spiritual and material rewards. God's glory will fall like rain in our ministries because *"Many will receive the words as from God and not from men" (I Thess. 2:13).* When we humble ourselves in honoring God, *we can expect to be honored by Him.*

- It is approved by God to *expect that our works would be acceptable to those we serve.* They, too, will share our heavenly rewards. We must teach them about the rewards that are awaiting them when they welcome us. *"He that receiveth you receiveth me, and he that receiveth me receiveth Him that sent me. He that receiveth a prophet in the name of a prophet shall receive a prophet's reward" (Matt. 10:40-41).* God's promises are beyond sufficiency. Sufficiency is to have just enough to survive. God promises us abundant blessings and nothing less.

PART-VII

SESSION ELEVEN

In this session, you will learn:

- *How to defeat Satanic challenges in the ministry.*
- *The guidelines to overcome fear.*
- *True episodes about how I overcame Satanic challenges.*
- *Biblical instructions in how to win the hungry mind game.*
- *Ministerial experience about trust and obedience.*
- *God's promises with the operating of the gift.*
- *The contest between Satan and the minister.*
- *How to remain sober during the contest.*
- *A glimpse behind my personal victory over opposition and persecutions.*

Defeating Satanic Challenges

When people hear about Satanic challenges, they automatically have their personal definition of what it is or what it should be. Some think of it as being generational curses or witchcraft. Others think of it as demonic possession or as committing a crime. Many thinks of it as some type of myth or illusion. We never really stop to think about some of these challenges that I am about to discuss as being Satanic challenges. This subject could not be excluded in this teaching because I have faced them in my ministry. Truly, there are no exceptions in these challenges, and they can affect our ministries. And I believe it is necessary for ministers to know that there is nothing unfamiliar about-facing Satanic challenges while using their gifts. These challenges do not come to the front door of our hearts but sneak their way in through the back door because they come as thieves to rob our ministry. ***"Verily, verily, I say unto you, he that entereth not by the door into the sheepfold, but climbeth up some other way, the same is a thief and a robber" (John 10:1).***

Satanic challenges interfere with our ministry more often than we realize. The smaller we think these challenges are, the greater are the damages of their effects. Take for instance a mouse trap; it may be small and flat but powerful enough to trap down a mouse and a rat. And if they get trapped in the glue, the more they try to untangle themselves from it, the deeper they get into the glue. They will need a human force to pull them out before dying in the trap. Likewise, if ministers are caught in these Satanic traps, they will need a supernatural force or power to pull them out from them. That supernatural power is the truth, which is the word of God.

Do you ever think besides all other creatures; why would Satan disguise himself as a serpent to mess around with Eve's mind in the Garden of Eden? I believe it is because a serpent is very soft in nature and flexible to fit in any small area. All he needs is a very small hole to make his way into our eyes and minds. Once he makes his way into our minds, the negative thoughts begin to spread quickly like water in the surface. So quick that we don't even realize it effects in our ministry until it is too late. When that happens, whatever challenge it may be, holds a greater portion of our ministry. Now we are faced with stronghold that we were not even aware of. Praise God! There is much power and hope in this teaching to help us face them courageously. No matter the magnitude of Satanic challenges, God in us is more powerful to overthrow them in a second. But we must first acknowledge that these challenges are our enemies. Prevention against the worst is always far better than curing its effect. ***"Having therefore these promises, dearly beloved, let us cleanse ourselves from all filthiness of the flesh and spirit, perfecting holiness in the fear of God" (2 Cor. 7:1).***

My goal for this portion of the teaching is that the ministers will be fully aware of these hidden challenges persuaded by this teaching and be prepared to defeat these challenges. Also, ministers need to know that Satan is a brilliant deceiver. If we are not ready to meet these challenges, it will be very difficult to detect his tactics. We need discernment to understand how he operates to overcome demonic challenges. The reason being is that his strategies vary from time to time. He will use things that appear to be the norm to cover up his tactics. Ministers, here is the fundamental key to defeating these Satanic challenges. As you look into the mirror of the word of God, you must be able to see them as they are. ***"For if any be a hearer to the word, and not a doer, he is like unto a man beholding his natural face in a glass: For he beholdeth himself, and goeth his way, and straightway forgetteth what manner of man he was" (James 1: 23, 24).*** God should always have the last word in the challenges we see in the mirror. This is our obligation.

The urgency is to give God our full attention, and forget not the man in the mirror, if we are expecting the Holy Spirit to defend our case. This will save us from lots of chaos, pain, deception, and anguish. Keep in mind that Satan does not want us to know about these variations because he is terrified by our knowledge. Our knowledge is power over him. Conversely, in the absence of knowledge ignorance prevails. Why should we be ignorant and defeated when God already provided all the necessary instructions to educate us? So, it is essential that ministers should take full advantage of this teaching. God requires that we should not only know, but to do something about those variations that I am about to share. The list includes:

> **RESENTMENT,**
>
> **ACCUSATION,**
>
> **FEAR, HYPOCRISY AND**
>
> **DEFENSIVENESS.**

Defeating unforgiveness *(merciless)*: Resentment can easily become unforgiveness, and cause us to misrepresent God, as ministers. God is a forgiving God, and His children ought to be more like Him. I want to remind the ministers that God's forgiveness is our ticket to heaven. If our sins are not forgiven by God, we will not be able to confirm our reservation to be in His presence. From my personal experience, ***resentment*** is first on the list when it comes to Satanic challenges because I had to overcome it in my own personal life. Jesus Himself set that example on the cross for us when he said: ***"Father, forgive them; for they know not what they do" Luke 23:34).*** If we do not follow Jesus' example, we are hindering both ourselves and our ministries. One other thing minister need to know is that we do not forgive people for sinning against us because they can only sin against God; and only God can forgive sins. However, we can forgive them for their wrongdoing against us. Let ministers be quick to discern resentment when it comes to unforgiveness.

We are challenged by our own sins when we say to God in our prayers to ***"forgive our sins; for we also forgive everyone that is indebted to us. ..." (Luke 11:4).*** There is no truth in our statements because we are still holding on to that hurtful resentment. Standing before the congregation and preaching through our songs about forgiveness, yet we ourselves failed to forgive, we will face Satanic challenges. We are trying to free others while we ourselves are still bound. For example, are we being truthful singing a song saying, "thank you Lord for making us whole?" To be made whole is to be forgiven. But if we are still bound by our sins, this song will serve as a stronghold because God will not honor a lying tong.

Yes! Those who do not forgive others are bound by their own chains. Can a bound man release another? We should first take the responsibility for our faults by humbling ourselves and forgive others. By doing this we should be able to escape from Satan, the hunter. ***"Deliver thyself from as a roe from the hand of the hunter. ..." (Prv. 6:5).*** That is correct. One must first be free from his own bondage to free others. Jesus' mission on earth was centered on forgiveness. He was challenged by resentment and suffered for our sin. He did not have to do it; but He did it anyway through the power of love. And love became forgiveness, so He might free us from our sins. Why suffer resentment when we can be free from it? It is okay to suffer for a good cause, but to suffer for the cause of something that Jesus already suffered for is unnecessary. It is useless because resentment is self-destructive and can be avoided. That means we could overcome the spirit of resentment.

Here are three basic good reasons why we should defeat resentment. Once forgiveness is released, (1) the wound is healed, and the hurtful resentment vanished away instantaneously. (2) Now we can freely bring our petitions to the Lord, and Satan can no longer hinder our prayers. (3) Much more, we can stand firmly against evil, be a faithful witness and win souls to the Lord. Surely our decision to forgive others can exceed this satanic challenge through the strength of love. Finally, we can maintain our freedom, using the remaining prayer and ask God to **"lead us not into temptation; but deliver us from evil" (Luke 11:4b).**

Defeating Accusation: We ministers need to know that: Satan can eliminate our ministry by smiting it down using a fabricated accusation. He knows very well how to use scandals to promote his motive. I faced many accusations during my ministry. All of them were from people that are in the church and from those who were close to me. I remember many conspiring meetings that were conducted against me, to stop me from singing. At one point, I was even accused of practicing witchcraft, simply because I lived a prayerful life.

Some even think that I lived a wildlife because sometimes I would be coming home from choir rehearsal late at night. I overcame my accusers by not paying attention to their gossiping remarks. I am fully aware that Jesus, who is the Lord of my life, was accused of many things. **"The disciple is not above his master, nor the servant above his Lord" (Mat. 10:24).** Jesus was even accused by those

He served and healed. But all He did was tell the truth, whether they believed Him or not. Who am I that I, too, should not be accused by my neighbors? I defeated these accusations by wearing my breastplate of righteousness. I was determined to continue my Christian walk-in peace daily while I faced my accusers. Mark this. I did not depend on my own strength. I removed myself from foolish talkers. ***"The Lord is faithful, who shall establish me and keep me from evil" (II Thess. 3:3).*** I did not waste time trying to conquer accusations with my own words. Instead, I leaned on the word of faith by saying: ***"Nay in all these things I am more than conquerors though Him that loved me" (Rom. 8:37).*** As you continue learning in this teaching, implant these strategies in your mind and never let them go.

Defeating fear: Being fearful is a dreadful experience. The Bible often emphasizes fear. Fear apparently has its way in the lives of many Ministers, and it should not be. Fear is always based on something that does not exist. Jesus often warns us *not* to be fearful of anything ***(Mat. 10:26).*** What was His reason for emphasizing fear? He wanted us to know that Satan uses fear, a satanic tactic, to limit us from relying on God. When we fear evil, we switch to the unreal and making it a reality. This Satanic deception stops us from reaching out to God's unfailing hands. ***"But whoso hearkeneth unto me shall dwell safely and shall be quiet from fear of evil" (Prv. 1:33).*** The illusion of fear cheats us from the reality of recognizing its dominion over us. To clarify this illusion, I am going to use three (3) components that further connect us to defeating fear.

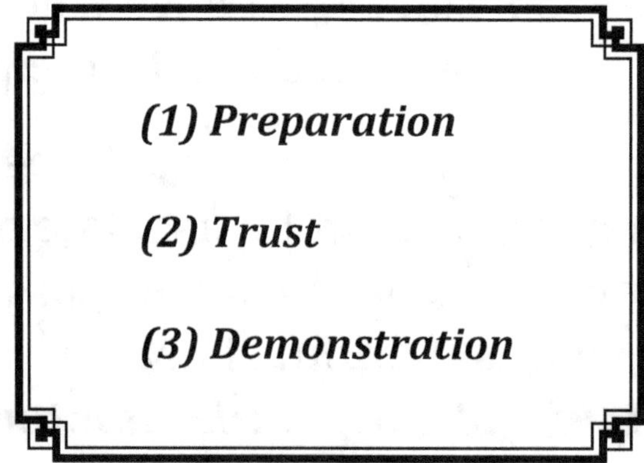

Preparation: There are always significant reasons behind one's fear. When a student faces fear before taking a test, most likely, it is due to a lack of confidence. Confidence does not easily come; it must be built by dedicating time, effort, and hard work. Having a desire to pass the test is not sufficient. What is sufficient is the determination to work hard toward success. To achieve that success, the student has to do some types of preparations. We could think of several things that could lead to success:

The student can start by paying attention to the teacher: Paying attention shows that the student recognizes his or her responsibility in keeping anything that could bring distraction out of the way.

Taking good notes: Taking good notes is essential because if the notes are not in an order that could be clearly understood, then the student will have a hard time comprehending the main ideas of the topic.

Asking questions: Asking questions that relate to the subject will eliminate any ambiguous thoughts, and eliminate anxiety.

Studying the notes is necessary: The purpose for taking notes is to have a record of what has been taught, and to emphasize what should be learned. Therefore, if the student just takes the notes without making any effort to study them, then the student is wasting paper, ink, and time. In addition, the student will not be able to deliver efficient answers without studying the notes.

Revising the notes before the test is a very good idea: the academic achievement of a good student depends on the amount of time spent on revising the notes. Revising the notes will condition the brain to get more familiar with the subject and allows the student to retain and deliver more during a test. These attributes contribute to the qualities of a good student who prepares for a course.

How can the disciples use this illustration to overcome fear? Followers of Christ are called disciples (students). They need to know that overcoming fear does not happen instantaneously. There should be some types of preparation to be successful in defeating it. The first thing they need to do when preparing to defeat fear is to give *undivided attention to the Holy Spirit, our teacher.* **"But the comforter, which is the Holy Ghost, who the Father will send in my name, he shall teach you all things" (John 14:26).** As the disciples learn from the Holy Spirit, they are responsible to take notes of what is being said about fear. If the disciples do not understand, they should be able to clarify their confusion by asking God in prayer to guide them through revelations. The disciples should then study these scriptures by memorizing them. Last, but not least, the disciples should continuously revise these scriptures. That way, when they face the test of fear, they could always go back and refer to their notes and use them as a constant reminder.

Should we not fear God? Absolutely, but Godly fear is different than the illusion of Satanic fear. This fear is caused by anxiety when approaching some types of danger; a danger that does not exist. It is not in God's nature to make us feel *threatened* to *trust* Him. I want you to keep the word (trust) open in your mind because I am going to connect it to the second part of the specimens that I mentioned above. We learn that fearing the unreal is not from God. **"...Fear not: for God is come to prove you, and that His fear may be before your faces, that ye sin not" (Exd. 20:20).** We must not mix these two characters. Note in this verse. The word *fear* appears twice; that is because each has its own significance. The first fear, the *circumstantial* one is negative. The second fear, the *loved* one is pertaining to giving respect to God by loving Him. At this point, we should understand the difference between those two fears. In general, fearing God is about what we know to be truthful, and what we receive from the truth we know.

What do we know and own as disciples? First and foremost, we know those who fear God are blessed. (Ps. 112:1). These blessings include power, love, and a sound mind. **"For God hath not given us** *a spirit of fear; but of power, and of love, an of sound mind"* **(II Tim.1: 7).** The answers to the questions come from the book of **Proverbs chapter five verses one to twenty-one**. They are to be noted.

These are what we know so far: We know that God commanded us to attend to His wisdom so we could obtain *understanding*. We know that we have *discernment*; that is to know hidden secrets about satanic challenges. We know that we have *freedom* to decide. If we decide to use Godly wisdom, we will defeat satanic fear. We have the *power to use wisdom* to discern the difference between both Godly fear and satanic fear. We know that we should not allow strangers to take away our wealth. Our *wealth* is our faith in God, and the stranger is Satan, the adversary. We know that God does not want us to be destroyed by our fear. We know that having "perfect love can cast out all Satanic fears" (1 John 4:18). We also know that fear is being defeated when we take our notes seriously and apply what we study. Now we are moving forward to our next step, which is trust.

Trust: *Will God fail those who trust Him?* God could never fail one who trusts Him. However, He might use adversities to test our trust, but eventually rewarding. We know we trust God when we believe that He will never break His promise. **"Let us hold fast the profession of our faith without wavering, for He is faithful that promised" (Heb. 10:23).** Trusting God is the soul of our faith. The only way we could know if we trust God is when we face satanic fear. In this case, whatever decision we take could impact us either positively or negatively. Satan knows whether we trust God. He could easily find out by his reporters, demonic spirits. They catch on to what we declare in the atmosphere and use them to fear us. The negative impact is the result of our very own words. Conversely, the positive impact is to declare the word of faith. For instance: Declare that God is our *peace* during the storms. "Declare that the *joy of the Lord is* our strength. Declare that *no weapons* formed against us shall prosper. Declare that God is our help in times of troubles", and so on.

We don't need to hold back our feelings and emotions. It is quite alright with God to be emotional in our prayers. We cry out to Him for He is our refuge. The voice of a child that cries from the heart catches God's attention. ***"I cried with my whole heart; hear me, O LORD: I will keep Thy statutes" (Ps. 119:145).*** Crying unto God because we desire to trust Him more is not murmuring, but rather, a heart that desperately needs help, and most of all a sign of dependency. There is no true relationship with God without dependency. The flesh is always at war with dependency because we deny that we need God to overcome our troubles. Consequently, we live constantly in despair. Personally, I would rather cry out to the Lord than to have the adversary keep me bound in despair. A life of despair is a hopeless life. It is okay to cry out to God when we feel hopeless. The Psalmist did it. ***"In my distress I called upon the LORD and cried unto my God: He heard my voice out of his temple, and my cry came before Him, even into His ears" (Ps. 18:6).***

The characteristics of a person in despair are marked by the following: heavy burdens, disobedience, disappointment, rejection, rebellion, etc. Trusting God wholeheartedly is the answer to all. The guidelines for defeating fear are as follow:

1. **We must believe always in God's promises:** *"There hath no temptation taken you but such as is common to man: but God is faithful, who will not suffer you to be tempted above that ye are able; but will with the temptation also make a way to escape, that ye may be able to bear it"* (I Cor. 10:13).

2. **We must trust always in God:** *"Why art thou cast down, O my soul? And why art thou disquieted in me? Hope thou in God: for I shall praise Him for the help of His countenance"* (Ps. 42:5).

3. **We must accept God's chastisement:** *"Now no chastening for the present seemeth to be joyous, but grievous: nevertheless, afterward it yieldeth the peaceable fruit of righteousness unto them which are exercised thereby"* (Heb. 12:11).

4. We must cast our burdens upon the Lord: *"Casting all your care upon Him for He careth for you" (I Pet. 5:7).* Let's continue with the guidelines to defeating fear.

Demonstration: Demonstration plays an important role in keeping Satanic fear out of ministers' minds. Our minds have a lot to do with the projection of fear. We just learned that we may fear the unknown. If our fear is based on what we don't know, then we need to demonstrate curiosity so we can better understand what we fear. For example, the ancient disciples demonstrated curiosity by asking Jesus many questions. They did because they were afraid. As well, we can question God pertaining to things we don't know. Asking questions demonstrates that we are eager to learn how to overcome Satanic challenges.

The disciples were very prompt in asking Jesus many questions. They asked Him questions about things pertaining to the kingdom. They wanted to know **"...Who is greatest in the kingdom of heaven" (Mat. 18:1).** They asked Jesus about the scribes' discussion concerning Elijah. **"...Why say the scribes that Elijah must first come" (Mark. 9:11)?** And they even asked about their failures. **"Why could not we cast him out" (Mark 9:28)?** Some people feel that, because of the Sovereignty of God, we should not question Him. However, the scriptures prove the opposite. It is not disrespectful to expose our ignorance to God, but rather an act of interest in knowledge. Above all, defeating fear is to take what we know and use it to take control over it. Therefore, I encourage the ministers to use this teaching as extended knowledge to discard ignorance, remove all doubts, and establish greater trust in God.

Defeating hypocrisy: As ministers of the gospel, defeating hypocrisy is not an easy battle to win because we fail to see it in our own lives. It is easier to recognize hypocrisy in others than in us. The influence of hypocrisy is very deceiving. Those who are influenced by hypocrisy are more likely to be susceptible to *projection.* Projection, according to man's perspective, is "an unconscious process that people used as protection by seeing their own feelings and shortcomings or unacceptable behaviors of themselves on others" (Dennis Coon, 2000). But Jesus Christ did not have other terms for hypocrisy. He calls it just what it is without reservation. ***"Thou hypocrite, First cast out the beam out of thine eye; and then shalt thou see clearly to cast the mote from out of thine brother's eye" (Matt. 7:5).***

It is hard to see our condition if we are falling short in sincerity. When we fall short of sincerity, it shakes the foundation of our ministry. If we wish to defeat hypocrisy, sincerity is an essential factor. Suppose we look in the spiritual mirror which is the word of God, and the Holy Spirit points out to us some nasty spots in our lives. What can we do about them? We have at least three options. *(1) We can pretend that they do not exist. (2) We can project them into someone else's life. (3) We can accept what we see and do something about these nasty spots.* The *third* option is the ultimate one, the virtuous one. That is, to do something about the nasty spots in our lives. Defeating hypocrisy is to *eliminate denial and pretense*.

How can ministers disconnect from these two flaws? By seeing ourselves as we really are and getting rid of the wicked ways. Keeping hypocrisy in our lives nourishes wickedness; and wickedness is filthiness before God. ***"Wherefore lay apart all filthiness and superfluity of naughtiness, and receive with meekness the engrafted word, which is able to save your souls" (James 1:21).*** We have the power of God in us to restrict ourselves from pretending not to see our conditions. The result is to see our wickedness in the mirror of the word of God and use it to set our lives in order. If it is not attractive to the Holy Spirit, then we need to remove the makeup.

Listing, beloved ministers, hypocrisy should be treated like a *contaminating disease* because that is exactly what it is. To prevent hypocrisy from spreading quickly, we need to know what precautions must be taken. I promised that I would be blunt and honest in this teaching, and I am. Some of us Haitian artists love exposing the term of hypocrisy in our lyrics. We sing about it as though we are excluded from it. Are we conscious about our own judgmental behaviors? Do we think this is pleasurable to God bringing each other down? Is there any self-satisfaction in the way we present the Gospel? I believe the Bible says it better.

Ministers are chosen by God to make a difference. The difference is for those who are strong to help those who are weak. **"We then that are strong ought to bear the infirmities of the weak and not to please ourselves" (Rom. 15:1).** Are we strong enough to admit our fault and repent from it? The gift is not to be used to agitate people; rather it should be used for edification. **"Let everyone of us please his neighbor for his good to edification" (Rom. 15:2).** It will take a great deal of courage to get rid of hypocrisy if we resist acknowledging it in our lives. It could be done if we are willing to let it go. If we take this teaching for what it is, we have a better chance to change our mind and let it go. God wants us to have the same mind which is the mind of Christ. Why is that? It is because the mind of Christ is one with the mind of the Father. That is the pattern that we ought to follow. **"That we may be in one mind and one mouth glorifying God, even the Father of our LORD Jesus Christ" (Rom. 15:6).**

How do we reduce the spreading of hypocrisy? Since hypocrisy is a satanic attack, this is how I dealt with it in my life. To avoid self-deception, we must **"Be doers of the word, and not hearers only, deceiving your own selves" (James 1:22).** I never knew that my lips were a doorway to hypocrisy until I discovered this truth. I prayed to God to show me how to overcome hypocrisy and the Holy Spirit revealed to me that the door of my lips was my mind. I wrote this verse and attached it next to the mirror in my bedroom where I could see it and memorize it. **"Set a watch, O LORD, before my mouth; and keep the door of my lips" (Ps. 141:3).** I prayed this prayer until the doorway to hypocrisy was shut down. Ministers, I know what I am talking about. I bid you to Keep alert and watch out for hypocrisy. It is worth trying to overcome this satanic attack.

I have been in the singing ministry for many years and, at the same time, struggled with the disease of hypocrisy in my own life. There was a time when I felt unworthy to minister to the people of God. I was deeply hurt by our new Pastor who denied me from ministering to the church due to gender discrimination. I sat on the pew every Sunday with a heavy heart. I was singing as loud as I could to cover up my hidden pain for over two years. One Sunday morning before service, something happened that agitated the situation. I was instigated by the Pastor's comments. He met me by the lady's room and without sympathy asked me "to decrease the volume of my voice when I sang with the congregation."

I was so vexed by that request that tears streamed down my cheeks like an open faucet throughout the entire service. I dropped down on my knees with my face on the bench. My pain haunted me even more when the people that are blessed by my singing ministry would ask me, "Why don't you sing anymore?" I told them to ask the Pastor. Confiding in God about my feelings, the Holy Spirit assigned me to investigate the word of God. In the mirror of the Word, I saw inside my heart a reflection of hypocrisy. I detected resentment, pride, worries, and anxiety. I invested valuable time in serving in many areas at that church before the arrival of this Pastor. I served as a Sunday school teacher; I conducted the Bible study to the women and children of this congregation. I also contributed to the worship service, and even helped with the music ministry. Now, these functions were all taken away from me with no explanation or confrontation.

I resented the fact that my ministry was rejected. That feeling decreased in me the desire to worship. Pride sat over me like a heavy coat and covered me with the spirit of rejection. Self-pity trapped me with worries each time I thought about people's perceptions of me. And being impatient about God's answer in the situation almost chased me out of the church.

The process of defeating hypocrisy was very slow, but I took the first step by being aware of its influence over my life. The Holy Spirit gave me precise instructions, and they were very straightforward. *First,* I was convinced to understand that my warfare was not with the Pastor. When I admitted that, the spirit of pride left me like a fast wind. *Second,* I had to forgive both myself and the Pastor for diminishing the purpose of God in my ministry. When I forgave myself and the Pastor, I dropped the coat of rejection, and embraced God's mercy. *Third,* I had to confront the Pastor, and relieve my conscience. Besides all that, there was still the one thing that I needed to deal with. I was very anxious to be taken out of the situation. I prayed about leaving the church quietly, but the LORD did not approve of my motives. I thought if I could not leave the church, I might as well confront the Pastor. I listened to my spirit and prepared myself for the meeting. I fasted for seven days and seven nights. After my fasting, I challenged hypocrisy and scheduled a meeting with the Pastor.

My expectation about the meeting was unstable because I did not know what the outcome would be. The Pastor had prepared himself. With the Bible on hand, the Pastor took me through the journey of the silence of women in the church (I Tim. 2:11-15). I listened to all his resentments about the ministry of women in the church. Though I did not approve of his misinterpretations of the word of God, I paid him great respect and listened carefully. He told me of how he resented the fact that the church applauded when I ministered in song. I did not feel eager to argue with him because the spirit of jealousy was clearly displayed. Before we adjourned, he told me that I should not expect to minister in the church again. I shook my head and began to weep. I wept because it grieved my heart to see that he was taking away one of the most edifying vessels of the church. I left the office sadly. What the Pastor did not know was that while he was rejecting my ministry, God was preparing me for a spiritual promotion. He could no longer wound my heart because I released the burden of my hypocrisy to the LORD while I was fasting.

The Holy Spirit advocated for me, and I exchanged my hypocrisy for agape love. I went home that day heavy-hearted. The Lord had stopped me from discussing the outcome of the meeting with any members of the church. During that time, the Pastor too, was facing some serious opposition from those who did not approve of his ways of administrating the church. The members were furious and wounded from prior scandals about our former Pastor. Therefore, it was a very difficult time for all of us. Many had left the church and the remnants were trying to recover. The church was desperately in need of a shepherd. Though we welcomed the new Pastor, the wounds were still open. Before my removal in serving at the church, The Lord had put it in my heart to teach about forgiveness. I spent months teaching about spiritual warfare to my Sunday school class.

My contribution to the church that I loved so much was to humble myself and stay in communion with the body of Christ. It was a necessity for me to intercede for both the Pastor and the church while I waited on God. I became more and more acquainted with the Lord's voice. He began to reveal things to me about the Pastor's struggles. The spirit of criticism and rebellion had overwhelmed him. In obedience to God's voice, I removed myself from the equation and focused on praying for him. Compassion filled my heart towards him. I often spoke words of encouragement to him.

On a Sunday night, several weeks after my meeting with the Pastor, I was quietly sitting on my couch in my living room, when I was suddenly overcome with renewed faith and divine strength; and I knew right then and there that I was about to conquer my oppression. In my spirit I knew expectantly that great things were about to happen, but I did not know what it was. I strongly felt that things were spiritually changing and shifting for my own good. I couldn't pinpoint exactly what the Lord was up to, but I sensed that His Spirit was actively working to fix and repair things and putting the broken pieces of my life back together. With this newfound energy and excitement, still seated on my couch, I began to anticipate the prospect of a beautiful future. Little did I know that seconds later I was about to receive a phone call that was in essence, figurative of the beginning of a fresh and new season of my life: a season of divine restoration, breakthrough, and victory. Sure, enough the phone rang, I hesitantly picked it up as I presumed that it was not a "typical" phone call. It was, to my surprise, the Pastor on the line reaching out to me and pleading with a heart of repentance to forgive him for misjudging me. In no time, and without any reservation whatsoever, I forgave him. We began to pray together, thanking the Lord for redeeming us from this satanic attack, and restoring unity between us once again. My spirit rejoiced enormously as I knew that greater and mightier things were about to happen.

Moving on forward I began to take all my disappointments, and my pains and the deep hurts to my heavenly Father. I learned of the virtue of forgiveness and closing the door to my disappointments and creating an entrance for His blessing to flow into my ministry. I promptly began to experience the releasing of a well of blessing that God had in store for me. Four months later, my ministry was re-established. My husband was called and ordained by God for pastoral leadership; and soon after, I was instituted as the church administrator of Bethel Christian Church located in Brooklyn, New York. The Lord left the door of that Baptist Church open for me. Furthermore, I was invited by the Pastor to go back and freely minister in songs, at the very same church I was previously "forbidden" to sing. When we shield our spiritual body with love and faith, we are defeating hypocrisy. ***"Above all, taking the shield of faith, wherewith ye shall be able to quench all the fiery darts of the wicked" (Eph. 6:16).***

Defeating the Spirit of Defensiveness: People generally tend to believe that being defensive around others shields and protects them from hurt and disappointments. Ironically, instead of getting protected, they end up getting deeper, so to speak, into a *graveyard situation*, where there seems to be no way out. Throughout many years in ministry, I have learned to recognize that the work of the spirit of defensiveness is very subtle amongst the saints, and very tricky to discern. The reason being it seems as if it is normal human behavior to always be on the defensive. Whenever people say things to us in a way that offends us, we mechanically find a swift answer to strike back and quickly get out of the hurtful feeling; all the while being unmindful of the consequences of our words and actions.

Being raised in an environment that did little to nurture my self-esteem, I suffered greatly from poor self-perception. For many years I acted defensively around friends and family. I hurt greatly from the effect of defensiveness, which I can only describe as a migraine that won't go away; it is rather a spiritual migraine that stems out of the fear of being hurt, which causes one to be hypersensitive to every word being launched at him. This weighs heavily on the mind, eventually, to the point where it becomes mentally painful. I have suffered with migraines of defensiveness for a very long time. The pressure on the brain to constantly seek ways of defending myself even without cause was great. It got to the point that sometimes, I would even find myself in the brink of a mental meltdown, as I was constantly overly protective of myself. Defensiveness is a dangerous thing; it is detrimental to oneself and to others; it destroys the quality of our relationships with fellow brothers and sisters and even our Father in heaven; the only remedy is forgiveness.

How do we discern the tricks of the spirit of defensiveness? Humans are obviously social beings who are designed with the need to socialize and fellowship with others. However, through our interactions with one another, our personality flaws get in the way of our conversations in which words are misarticulated by one, and regrettably misinterpreted by the other. The one is viewed as the offender, and the other the defender. The offender is looked at as the one who is trying to satisfy an uncontrollable need to belittle, and the other instinctively takes a defensive position in order to prove the offender wrong; and then the futile arguments perpetuate. What happens generally is the following scenario: when the defender runs out of strength to justify his case, he becomes angry and frustrated against the one who is perceived as the offender. The arguing perhaps escalates into an unpleasant and hurtful exchange of words, in which case both are left with deep hurt.

Perhaps It was, never the offender's intent to hurt anybody, he was probably just trying to express his thoughts which he believes to be fair and true. The other, who perceives himself as the victim, fails to avoid the need to justify himself, and quickly strikes back. This scenario proves that the more we use defensiveness, the more painful it becomes. This obviously may perpetuate as a vicious cycle, a hungry mind-game, I call it. A hungry mind-game is a mental place in which negative thoughts are incessantly repeated. The mind is bombarded with a barrage of unrealistic ideas about the possibility of being put down by the very people, friends and family members that may in fact care for you; however, your ego plays tricks on the mind and clouds your perception of the truth. This is a dangerous mind game that causes you to act irrationally, in fruitless attempts to satisfy this emotional hunger which does not exist. It is a perilous game that nonetheless, we can win; if we are willing to kick some spiritual bad habits.

How do we win this hungry mind-game? The decision to kick a bad habit starts with taking full responsibility for our actions. For instance, the habit of entertaining obsessive ideas about being put down and being perpetually on the defensive, can be kicked out if we decisively put in some work by following the steps below:

- The *first* step we need to take against this hungry mind-game is to be sure that our conscience is clear. If we have the confidence of having a good conscience, then we won't waste our time or energy trying to defend ourselves. ***"Pray for us: for we trust we have that we have a good conscience, in all things willing to live honestly" (Heb. 13:18).*** Clearly, we see the evidence offered to us by this scripture that *prayer* is most definitely a powerful weapon that must be utilized to essentially win this hungry-mind game.
- The *second* step we need to take against this hungry mind-game is to *deny the demands of* our ego. A wounded ego can easily

distort reality and alter our thinking. We need, however, to be watchful so as to not allow our ego to obscure our understanding and influence the choices we make. Moreover, as Christians, it is our responsibility to disconnect ourselves from corrupt thinking and sinful habits or anything that can potentially be harmful to ourselves or our ministry. The Christian should choose to do what is *good* and well-pleasing unto God, knowing that He is our defender and protector. ***"And who is he who will harm you if you, if ye be followers of that which is good" (I Pet. 3:13)?***

- The *third* step we need to take to win over this hungry mind-game is to completely *starve* some bad habits. We starve a bad habit by not "feeding" it, by being *serious, consistent, and watchful* in prayer. Being *serious* is to know that our responsibility to overcome this bad habit is a continuing process that requires determination and willpower. Being *consistent* is to commit ourselves to this new path of self-improvement no matter what obstacles or adversities may stand in our way. Being *watchful* in prayer essentially means to pray fervently, with all sincerity of heart, and to watch for all sorts of spiritual distractions that may hinder our relationship with God. ***"...Be ye therefore sober and watch unto prayer" (I Pet. 4:7).***

Knowing what is pleasing unto God is one of the requirements of being a minister of the Gospel. We all know that it is easier to preach than to practice what we preach. It is consequently of utmost importance to understand that being true to God in our service and ministry to Him requires a great deal of sacrifice and self-discipline. Our life as Christians and ministers of the Gospel becomes most impactful and life-transforming to others around us when we sacrificially surrender our thoughts and our purpose to God. We must decrease ourselves, so the magnitude of His presence can increase in us. Personally, I had to go though many episodes in my life in which I had to absolutely surrender to God and do what was right. I'd like to recount one of these episodes with you.

Living in New York City where everyone must be on his toes, makes my husband over-protective of me. Although I appreciate him for this quality, this over-protectiveness can sometimes be intoxicating. It so happened, after a long day of work, my commute back home was significantly delayed on the train. I was exhausted and totally drained out, and then suddenly a barrage of negative ideas began to flood my mind. I began to anticipate a potential argument with my over-protective husband who is probably waiting for me by the door, to greet me with a myriad of questions as to my whereabouts and why I came home so late. That is when I began to experience the effect of the hungry mind-game, the pressure to defend myself. I began to imagine the scene already: I predetermined that he was going to ask me why I came home later than usual, and as a result I prepared my reply in advance. "I was not the only one coming home late that night, why should I have to justify myself for something that I had no control over?" Clearly, I was preparing for some harsh answers to defend myself against what I thought I would face when I arrived home. The thought of this quickly rushed feelings of bitterness in me. I was by then, very upset about an event that never took place at all; it was all being played out in my mind, but it created much emotional disturbance in me. This is almost equivalent to insanity; it's almost like arguing with yourself and being angry at yourself, for no apparent reason.

However, during this emotional avalanche I was going through, the Holy Spirit rushed in and interrupted these filthy thoughts that were obstructing the flow of his presence in me. He reminded me of a scripture which I began to voice out loudly ***"Casting down imaginations and every high thing that exalts itself against the knowledge of God and bringing into captivity every thought to the obedience of Christ, and having in a readiness to revenge all disobedience, when your obedience is fulfilled" (II Cor. 10:5-6).***

I won the game, the hungry mind-game, by applying scripture to my situation. First, I *cast down* this imagined scene with all its emotional effects by *throwing* it out of my mind, in exchange for doing what was *right* according to the Word of God. Second, I liberated myself from the consequence of self-inflicted pain by rejecting and binding the evil thoughts concerning my dear husband. Thirdly, I *armed* my mind with the mind of Christ believing that he too suffered for doing the right thing (I Pet. 4:1). Finally, Using the *Sword of the Spirit,* which is the word of God, I *cut* myself from the spirit of disobedience and *treaded it down*. As my obedience to God was made complete, I walked home *fearlessly* into a peaceful atmosphere. In the end, I was a winner who victoriously cast down imaginations and vain ideas that exalted themselves above the knowledge of the Word of God. Most importantly I allowed the Holy Spirit to fill my soul with *peace, joy, and forgiveness.* My prayer is for everyone reading this book to experience this divine peace and serenity. If I overcame it, so can you because you too **"are filled with the fruits of righteousness, which are by Jesus Christ, unto the glory and praise of God"** **(Phil. 2:11).**

People often believe that the reason why they get into certain situations is because they have no choice. Sometimes in the past, I too, used to believe that was the case. This is a misunderstanding that has perpetuated for too long, amongst the people of God, and caused much damage in the life of many. The truth of the matter is that we do have a choice. It is crucial that we understand the decisions we make today - wise or foolish, positive, or negative - have eternal consequences. **"For what glory is it, if, when ye be buffeted for your faults...? But if when ye do well, and suffer for it, ye take it patiently, this is acceptable with God"** (I Pet.2:20). Although sometimes we might suffer for the cause of righteousness, it is however, rewarding to patiently wait on God in prayer, as we continuously make wise decisions to serve Him and be true to Him regardless of what may be occurring all around us.

Ministerial Experiences About Trust and Obedience:

On an early September morning of 1998, the Lord woke me up at three o'clock, he spoke to me, and assigned me to go to Haiti to preach the Gospel. He then led me to the scriptures from which He wanted me to proclaim his Word. However, I was somewhat hesitant and find going to Haiti would be challenging because of its unsafe condition. I began to cry and asked Him why I should be the one to go. As I was on my knees praying and weeping, the Holy Spirit brought back to my memory a request that I made to Him back ten years ago. I had asked Him to use me in whichever way He pleases (*"Can I be the One?"*). Convinced by my own past request, I replied affirmatively.

Although I said yes, a torrent of questions, however began to flood my mind: What part of Haiti is the Lord sending me to? Will I travel alone or will anybody else accompany me? Where will I get money to pay for all the expenses involved in this mission trip? Where will I stay? I shared my concerns with my Pastor about going to Haiti and he instantly asked, "Who are you going with?" "The Lord has not yet told me" I replied, and I asked him to pray for me.

Strangely, about a week later I was asked the same question by my friend Sylvia. As we were sitting near each other at a Choir rehearsal, at Beraca Baptist Church, I felt compelled to share with her that the Lord has been directing me to go on a mission trip to Haiti: "who you are travelling with?" She swiftly inquired. I reiterated the same answer I gave the Pastor earlier: "The Lord did not tell me yet with whom I will be travelling."

I prayed, trusting God, and waiting for His instructions. Finally, the Lord worked things out on my behalf, and I was able to arrange my travel date; however even then, the Lord still had not revealed to me what part of Haiti He was sending me to, and whom I would be traveling with. Moreover, I needed money. I took a portion of my saving and planted it as a seed of faith. I bought the plane ticket and decided with a Pastor friend of mine living in Port-au-Prince, Haiti to pick me up at the airport. The following Saturday, during our weekly Choir rehearsal my friend Sylvia handed me a letter, which she trusted me to deliver to her sister living in Haiti as soon as I get there. As the departure date was fast approaching, I called my younger brother, and my Pastor friend living in Haiti to advise them of my coming.

It was three o'clock in the afternoon when I arrived at the airport. The Pastor and his wife picked me up and drove me to their residence; they kindly offered me to spend the night with them. However, I was rather concerned about the letter Sylvia had entrusted me to deliver to her sister, and I wanted to promptly honor her request. I therefore declined the offer to spend the night at their place. Instead, I asked the Pastor if he could help me find someone to drive me around to deliver the letter.

I, then realized that my friend sister to whom the letter was addressed, was living in the same city, Cayes, Haiti, as an old friend and ministry partner of mine, Evangelist Laucita. Coincidently, Laucita happened to be in Haiti, at the time, attending to an orphanage she founded many years ago. We have partnered up for many years, even laboring and fervently praying together for the cause and needs of the orphanage. Over many years, I was particularly blessed to have had the opportunity to help organize several fundraising activities on behalf of the children. So, then I thought to myself that meeting those beautiful children and seeing them face to face would make this whole mission trip so much more fulfilling.

The Pastor told me that the trip to Cayes was after all very much feasible; however, I would have to get on the road and leave immediately, since it would take several hours to get there before dark. He introduced me to a man who was willing to take me there; however, his car had a series of mechanical issues, and tire problems that he demanded that I give him money to fix all the issues and buy him new tires before he can take me there. I was obviously short of cash, and therefore unable to afford to give him much. However, I reluctantly decided to go along with his plan to take the car to the nearest mechanic shop. But my brother and a friend of his, surprisingly showed up, arriving from the city of St. Marc. They reassured me that they would take care of all my transportation needs. In fact, my brother had borrowed a friend's car for the very purpose of taking me anywhere I wished to go. We filled up the tank and joyfully departed towards our destination. It was so reassuring to know that God was right there with me, making provision for the mission.

Cayes, a city located in the southern part of Haiti, is in fact, not considerably far from Port-Au-Prince, however it took us a long time to get there, due to the roads being extremely rough and bumpy. Nonetheless, I spent the entire trip, sharing the Gospel of Jesus Christ with both my brother and his friend. As we were about to reach our journey's end, my brother's friend burst out crying; he was convicted by the Word of God, and willingly accepted Jesus as his Lord and Savior. Glory to God!

Finally, we got to our destination where I was to deliver the letter, which I handed to Sylvia's sister minutes after I arrived. She immediately read it; and then turned towards me and told me that the Lord had already confirmed to her my coming, and that she was to assist me in preparing myself spiritually for the mission. She sent a girl to call in four prayer warriors: three sisters and one brother in the Lord. When they got there, I related to them the reason for my coming to Haiti. We all began to pray fervently, against all powers of darkness and spiritual hindrances that were standing against the mission. As prompted by the Holy Spirit, they circled around me, and prayed ardently that the Lord anoint me for the assignment ahead. The presence of God filled up the place and empowered me from head to toe.

After the prayer session we sat and fellowship together, and we began to plan out our first evangelical outing in a region of the city called Cite Lumière. It was rather a spiritually loaded area, so I was warned; I therefore braced myself for whatever demonic forces I was about to confront. Thankfully, Rose Myrtha and the four prayer warriors offered to go together with me. The next day, they arranged for some local church musicians to accompany me as well. God was on my side, confirming that it was He who sent me, and that He was faithful and just, to miraculously provide all that I needed: prayer partners, musicians, a sound engineer, and even electrical generators.

We prayed up, armed and ready to launch our first open door crusade. I knew, however, what I was up against spiritually; one could even feel a spiritual heaviness in the atmosphere. But I was set and ready to proclaim the powerful message of the Gospel of Jesus of Nazareth boldly and fearlessly. On the first day we set up our revival tent right across an open-air market at Cite Lumière, and I began to minister in songs. The sound of the music filled up the area and quickly drew a large crowd. The anointing of God filled my voice with strength, and I sang my heart out. Then, I began to stand in intercessory prayer attacking Satan's territory; the next thing I knew, I was surrounded by voodoo priests. There was one of them that particularly caught my attention. From the angry look on his face to his multicolored mystical costume, it was obvious that he was there to oppose what was happening. The voodoo priest was fiercely staring at me to intimidate me, but I stood there boldly, secured under the blood of Jesus, delivering the message that God had given me. I invited the people to repent and give their life to Jesus. However, what I saw was great fear in their eyes, and a reluctance to come forward. They were obviously intimidated by the voodoo priests all around them. I knew ahead of time that this was not going to be easy, so I trusted God, and I invited the people to come back later to a night of revival at a Church where I was scheduled to minister.

Once again, the Holy Spirit used me mightily to bring forth His Word at the Church revival. However, the battle continued all through the night. Even in my sleep I was under demonic attack, but I stood up wide awake, in the middle of the dark, declaring the Word of God boldly against the spiritual forces that were attacking me. With the power of God in me, I defeated the enemy, and by faith in the name of Jesus, I cancelled out Satan's attempt to disturb me in my sleep.

From that experience I knew more than ever before that faith in God avails greatly, as it is a weapon of choice against the plans and attacks of the enemy. Some may think of faith as a vague or abstract phenomenon; however, faith is the substance of things hoped for **(Heb. 11:1)**. Some must see "it" to believe "it", but that's not faith. Faith is having the assurance that the very God who calls us to serve, is the supplier of all our needs, and believing that **"all things are possible with Him" (Matt. 19:26).** All we must do is trust Him. **"Trust in Him at all times, ye people; pour out your heart before Him; God is a refuge for us" (Ps. 62:8).** Faith is our ultimate standing ground in ministry; it makes us unbreakable, and untouchable.

I compare faith to a chain, the components of which consist of trust and obedience. The clasps are larger than the chain links, and have the major function, to secure the chain. One end must be hooked onto the other, for the chain to be securely held together. In order words, faith is the substance of both *trusting and obeying.* Trusting is one end of the master clasp and obeying is on the other end. When trust and obedience are linked up together, then the promises of God on our behalf become secured and fulfilled by faith. God uses our acts of obedience as ground to manifest his blessings upon our life.

The Lord assigned me to go to Haiti, without giving many instructions as to whom I would be travelling with, and where I would stay; yet I trusted and obeyed Him. However, when I look back, I can see clearly now that God's hand was perfectly at work on my behalf, as if He were writing a perfect script to a great adventure of faith, trust and obedience. I will live to, forever testify, and praise Him for His faithfulness towards me. **"The salvation of the righteous is of the LORD; He is their strength in the time of trouble. And the LORD shall help them from the wicked, and save them, because they trust in Him" (Ps. 37:39-40).**

SESSION TWELVE

God's Promises with the Gift:

"Behold, I give unto you the power to tread on serpents and scorpions, and over <u>all</u> the power of the enemy: and nothing shall by any means hurt you" (Luke 10:19).

Power and authority were delegated to Adam by God since the beginning of human existence, in the Garden of Eden. He was to dominate over everything on earth. ***"And God said, let Us make man in our image after our likeness: and let them have dominion over the fish, of the sea, and over the cattle, and over all the earth, and over every creeping thing that creepeth upon the earth" (Gn. 1:26).*** Man had the highest authority, and power to rule over everything here on Earth. However, God clearly drew the one and only boundary for Adam and Eve to not ever cross, as He set the condition before them, in plain and simple terms. ***"But the fruit of***

the tree which is in the midst of the garden, God hath said, ye shall not eat of it, neither shall ye touch it, lest ye <u>died</u>" (Gn. 2:17). Yet they chose to listen to the voice of the devil; sin then entered the world. Ever since, there has been a shift in the spiritual order of things on the planet. Adam was stripped of his power and authority, which by principle was transferred over to Satan the devil. When man died spiritually, his power and authority, consequently transferred over to Satan. It is evident based on the condition the Lord had set in Genesis 2:17, that man's authority was conditional upon his obedience to God. It is therefore critical to understand that the Lord being the source of all authority, has the sovereign power to delegate to, or take away from whomever he pleases; it all comes down to his principles being reverently adhered to.

Throughout the course of history, even after the adamic fall, God selectively appointed and anointed special leaders, kings, and priests to lead over his people. While many had humbly answered the call of duty, and rightfully exercised their God given authority, many others, however abused their position of power, and mistreated God's people. ***"When the righteous are in authority the people rejoice: but when the wicked beareth rule, the people mourn" (Prv. 29:2).*** Such abuse of power is evident even more so today; men no longer wait to be instituted by God's positions of authority, as they create their own systems of government. Their failed ideologies, obviously, prove the point that God knows what's best for mankind.

Through the sharing of the message of the redeeming power of the blood of Jesus Christ, we have been given another chance to recover our power and authority. Satan can no longer rule over us. But we can now reclaim our authority and take back the power that was stolen from us. ***"For as much then as the children are partakers of flesh and blood, he also himself likewise took part of the same: that through death he might destroy him that had the power of death, that is, the devil" (Heb. 2:14).*** This verse serves as a seal that our rightful power has been restored, and that we now can uproot the stem of wickedness and sin from our heart. We, the people of God, have absolutely nothing to fear; Satan is already defeated. The power of the name of Jesus is the ground upon which our authority stands, giving us the right and entitlement to overcome all demonic forces in our life. We are no longer slaves to sin, we are free to conquer, free to live justly and righteously; free to love and forgive. Don't we see how powerful this is? We possess the power, through the shed blood of Christ, to greatly impact the world, setting the captives and the oppressed free in the mighty of Name of Jesus. ***"These things speak and exhort and rebuke with all authority. Let no man despise thee" (Titus. 2:15).***

Is there any exception in using our power and authority? God's instructions to us in the book of *Romans* made it very clear that we ought to be careful as not to misuse our authority, and to abide by the principles of order and discipline in the Church. **"Let every soul be subject unto the higher powers. For there is no power but of God: the powers that be are ordained of God" (Rom. 13:1).** Consequently, we need to establish discipline and structure in the Church, as designed and purposed by God. Our God-given authority and power ought not to be exercised in isolation from ordained ministers, pastors, and the elders of the Church. The effectiveness of our authority against Satan depends on our own ability to submit ourselves to the authority of ordained ministers, pastors, and the elders of the church. It took me quite some time to realize the truth that our God-given authority can be easily stripped away from us, just by refusing to abide by the rules and principles concerning order in the Church, as set by our Heavenly Father.

Developing a healthy relationship with our pastors starts with seeing them in the light of their assignments. Pastors have a direct command from God and are appointed by the Lord, to feed and protect, not harm the flock. As we begin to honor our pastors, we will see it fit to deliberately submit to their God-given authority. ***"My sheep wandered through all the mountains, and upon every*** *high hill: yea, my flock was scattered upon all the face of the earth, and none did search or see after them. Therefore, ye shepherds hear the word of the Lord" (Ezk. 34:7-8).* What an enormous responsibility pastors must heed to the instructions of God to gather the lost and scattered sheep and to feed them. Submitting to the authority of the pastors, allows the ministers, laymen, worship leaders, etc., to flow mightily into their full potential, as this creates a culture of order and discipline in the body of Christ. In an atmosphere of order, ministers can operate efficiently under the pastors' oversight, as they ensure to follow the leading of the Holy Spirit and consult with their pastors before taking any ministerial decisions. For instance, when a minister feels led of the Lord to go anywhere to minister, it is a most honorable thing for him to humbly approach the pastor about it and ask for his covering and blessing.

The dimension of God's power is limited by our unwillingness to do the following: take God's command for what it is, submitting to His authority by submitting to those he places above us, and abide in humility.

God commands us to: *"Remember them which have the rule over us, who have spoken unto us the word of God..." (Heb. 13:7).* This is not to be interpreted as a rule of force; but as a gracious way to demonstrate reverence and honor towards our pastors. *"Obey them that have the rule over us and submit ourselves: for they watch over our souls, as they must give account..." (Heb. 13:17).* Pastors carry the most self-sacrificing responsibility to watch over our souls, as they must answer and give account to God. Therefore, it is best that we refrain from passing judgment over our pastors. I have heard some very harsh criticisms of pastors; some claim it is the pastors' fault that they are losing respect among the flock. It is everyone's responsibility, including ministers, to obey God's command, which is to kindly submit to our pastors, as they are in a spiritual position of higher authority over us. If they were to fail in the performance of their duty, it would therefore be up to God to reprimand, correct or chastise them accordingly. A pastor's failing should never justify any contempt or disrespect towards them.

There are plenty of talented and gifted young people in various areas of ministry in the church. During this great wealth of gifts, however, there is great disorder. The problem is not in the abundance of talent, but in the lack of respect that some gifted ministers demonstrate towards their pastors. One may be very gifted in leading worship, but there are still ministerial boundaries to honor and principles to adhere to. In the following fictitious scenario, Jessica is a great worship leader, but the problem lies in how and where she uses her gift. She is all over the place ministering from church to church, exercising her gift in way that is out of order with her assigned ministry at her local church. The pastor rarely, has any idea as to what she is doing or where she is going. Many times, Jessica is asked to minister at a variety of churches, and almost all of the time, she naively accepts every offer without doing any background research on the church denomination or beliefs. She finds herself ministering at so-called churches that, in fact have nothing to do with Christ. Sadly, often, her belief is in direct contradiction with those of many churches where she gullibly accepts to minister. What conflict and spiritual confusion she could have easily avoided, had she checked in with her pastor prior to accepting any invitation to perform anywhere else outside her local church. This may only be a fictitious scenario, but it is far too common in our churches today. The fact is, when ministers perform outside of the order of God's principles, they remove themselves from under the umbrella and spiritual covering of their pastors, leaving themselves spiritually vulnerable to the attacks of the enemy. Therefore, my advice to every minister, is to be very careful not to hinder the flow of God's anointing, and to wisely submit to the authority of their pastors.

This pertains not just to ministers, but to all church members. Recently, I met one of our church members coming from a prayer meeting at another church. She asked me: "why I didn't attend?" My response to her was "I have fasting and praying at my own church; I cannot leave my house dirty to go clean someone else's house." The problem with many church goers nowadays, is in the lack of order by not considering the advice of their pastors, and getting up and taking part of any prayer meeting that is taking place anywhere across town. They neglect the need of their own local church, in order to attend to the needs of some other churches, without the pastor's consent.

At times it appears, especially during bible study, that pastors are only teaching to the pews, as the members have left them empty. When things go wrong, however, those same members return to their churches asking for a quick prayer or an instant miracle. Well let me be among those Christians of principle, who strongly believe that we must restore order in God's house. Pastors everywhere should not allow themselves to be accustomed to letting their members behave in ways that are not consistent with the Lord's plan and purpose for order in the Church. Pastors should not be so afraid to lose members, to the point where they begin to compromise on what they know to be solid truth and spiritual ethics by which every church member and minister should abide. Let us, therefore, be on guard not to give access to the enemy because of insubordination to the authority of our pastors and elders in the church. Let us be prompt to serve honorably in perfect agreement with our overseers.

In 2011, I experienced the demonstration of God's power in my life in a tremendous way. It was a very cold and snowy winter day, a Friday morning as I clearly remember. I woke up early to go to work, but it was so extremely cold that I was debating whether I should go; the streets and sidewalks were so slippery that everyone was on guard. My husband, on the other hand, had already decided that he would take the day off; he suggested that I, too, should do the same. For some odd reason I felt compelled, however, to go to work anyway. At around five O'clock in the morning, I got up, dressed myself up and decided to leave. Even as I was stepping out the door, my husband kept insisting that I stay home; he said that it was crazy for me to go to work in this kind of weather. I pushed my way, however, out through the door which was covered and blocked with snow. I took my first step, and my legs quickly sank all the way to my knees into a pile of snow. I slowly fought my way through this brutal weather, and cautiously walked down the streets through tire tracks, all the way to the Flatbush Avenue subway station.

When I got there, they announced that all trains were delayed, but they gave no information as to when the next train would be arriving. As I was standing on the station platform waiting for the train, I realized that on the bench behind me, sat a mid-aged woman with two adolescent girls seating next to her. For some reason, she randomly initiated a conversation with me, and began to relate to me that school was cancelled, and that she thought it was unsafe to leave her daughters all alone at home; and consequently, she decided to take them to work with her. The train finally arrived, and we sat next to each other. I sensed immediately that she was distressed, and she had a lot on her mind. She began to disclose her many fears and troubles, confiding in me that she was sexually abused by her uncle when she was a little girl. She had so much on her chest to divulge, that I knew I needed to quietly listen to her stories. She then went on talking about her horrible experiences in her marriage. I could very much relate to a lot of her turmoil, as I, myself had lived through similar experiences in the past. It was as though she was reminding me, somewhat of my own past. I immediately sympathized with her situation; and we exchanged numbers.

When I got to work that day, it was hard for me to concentrate on my work, as I was incessantly thinking about that poor and distressed woman. The random encounter, earlier that day, just left me with a deep desire to reach out and help her. I figured that meeting her was, perhaps, not a random encounter after all. Could it be that the Lord had arranged that we crossed path? I considered it as something I should not take lightly. I kept thinking about my own past stories in comparison to hers. I recalled how in the past; God had purposely placed in my life strong women to mentor me and help me through many of my struggles. Now, I thought to myself, it was my turn to reach out and help. I tried to reach her by phone, but unfortunately, the number was incorrectly written; and I could not find her. I prayed to God and asked, if it should be His will, to make it possible for her to reach out to me that same day.

On my way home, I was still very absorbed by her stories; I could not get them out of my mind. At around nine o'clock, I was home in the kitchen preparing a meal, but I was prayerfully hoping that I would hear from her. Just as I was expecting, my phone rang, and sure enough, it was her. We talked about how God had set us up in allowing that we met earlier that day. I told her about how I wanted to hear from her and expressed to her that I needed to help her the best I could. I took her phone number again and this time I made sure that it was correctly printed. I thought that it would be a good idea for us to meet for a counseling session as soon as possible. I advised her not to delay, and she agreed to meet with me the following day. We were supposed to meet at 10 AM, but she did not show up then. When I called her, she explained to me that one of her daughters strongly objected to her meeting with me again. I spoke to both her and the child; and I suggested that she should take control of the situation while I prayed for her.

At around 12 o'clock the bell rang; my husband rushed downstairs to open the door; it was her along with her two daughters. Startlingly the girls jumped with joy at the sight of my husband and rushed to embrace him. To my surprise the lady knew my husband from a prior church which they both used to attend. She marveled that I was the wife of someone she knew from the past. That surely made her rather comfortable, and that I was not a total stranger after all. My husband chatted with them a little and went back upstairs. I fed them lunch and invited the girls to go play and watch TV in the basement. The lady and I sat at the table with Bibles in hand, as we were ready to begin our counselling session. Just when I attempted to start, the

Holy Spirit changed the plan around, and directed me to the piano. As I began to worship the Lord in songs, she got up and joined me. I felt the prompting of the Holy Spirit for me to continue singing; so, I sang, and sang, and sang, and sang some more. She began to sing along, our voices beautifully blended in perfect harmony.

Suddenly, she stopped singing. Immediately, demonic spirits began to manifest in her. This lady was possessed with many demonic spirits. She began crawling under the table and crying like a baby. The Holy Spirit directed me to remain calm and to continue worshiping in songs. I sang my heart out. Again, the spirit of a rebellious teen began to manifest itself. She became very rude and aggressive towards me, as she tried to distract me from my worship. I commanded her to be still, and out of her came sharp screams. She ran towards the front door, to run away from me. All the noise and the screams got the children's attention. They rapidly ran upstairs to see what was going on, but I stopped them from coming to their mother, and commanded them to go back downstairs and remain still. All the while my husband was upstairs, totally unaware of what was happening. I anointed her with oil and cast out those evil spirits in the name of Jesus. After she was settled, she had no clue as to what had happened; I had to explain everything to her.

This battle had just begun. For the following months, the lady would call me any time of day or night, asking for prayer. During that period, I had very little sleep, but God granted me the grace and courage to make it through the days. She called me one night, asking me if she could carpool with me on her way to work the next morning; my husband and I generously agreed. So, she met with us early that morning, and we got on the FDR Drive towards Manhattan. Normally, my husband and I used our travelling time to pray; and as we were already engaged in our routine prayer on the road, the demonic spirits began to manifest out of her once again; but this time the evil spirits attempted to strangle her to death.

Imagine the horror of this scene: travelling on a highway, through rush hour traffic, and having to deal with demonic spirits manifesting right there in the car you are travelling in. It wasn't a pleasant situation, but I had no fear whatsoever; and I prayed that the Holy Spirit take control. We determined that we were going to continue driving, since it didn't make sense to stop the car and pull over. While my husband was focused on driving, I unbuckled up so it could be easier for me to turn around in order to attend to her, and to deal with the demonic spirits. I tried repeatedly to get her to say the name of Jesus, but she was unable to; she was mumbling her words instead. The evil spirit began to speak, making threats that he was going to kill her, just as he had killed her mother; and that before killing her, he was going to send her, first to a mental ward. It was clear to me that those were serious threats, which I didn't take lightly. I began to make declarations of faith, boldly speaking the word of God, to cast the demons out of her. The Holy Spirit intervened powerfully as she started to weep uncontrollably; a sign that she was experiencing deep deliverance.

Her full deliverance, however, was a long and gradual process. She continued to meet with me for several months for prayer and counselling. One evening, as I was praying with her at the church, a demonic spirit started to rage out of her, saying "I am not going to let her go." The Lord then revealed to me, that there had to be an open door in her life which gave access to those spirits to come in and torment her that way. I knew right then and there that I needed to address this situation differently. I began to speak boldly to the demonic spirit, asking "Why are you here?" The spirit replied, "Because she let me in." I rebuked that foul spirit and continued to pray fervently. After a long prayer session, she finally got back to herself, and she went home. But I knew in my spirit that I needed to get to the bottom of this whole thing. I needed to find out what was giving access to those spirits to torment her that way.

In the following counselling session, I had with her, she began to share with me that she was having a hard time forgiving her husband who had been emotionally and verbally abusive to her over many years, and that he was also unfaithful in the relationship. I explained to her how important it was to let go of all past hurt, and to close all doors to those demonic spirits. She admitted that she just could not find in herself any desire to forgive him. I brought her attention to the word of God and showed her how to reverse that way of thinking: ***"she could do all things through Christ which strengthens her" (Phil. 4:13).*** I knew it was not going to be easy for her; I patiently continued to work with her, knowing that one day she would be completely set free. However, she abruptly stopped coming to the prayer and counselling sessions. I continued to pray for her nonetheless; and in my prayers, I asked the Lord to allow me to see the fruits of my labor with this woman.

One Saturday in March 2014, almost two years since our last meeting, as I had just gone up to my office to catch up with some unfinished work, my husband called me to let me know that someone was here for me. Normally, I prefer not to be interrupted while I am working, and my husband was very much aware of my discipline. However, given the fact that he knew about my deep concern for the lady, he specified that it was her who came by to see me. I stopped what I was doing and ran downstairs to honor her visit. I immediately noticed that she was not carrying the heavy bags that she would normally carry everywhere she would go. We sat and talked for a moment; and then she began to testify that her deliverance was made complete because she finally realized how important it was to forgive her husband. It was truly amazing to witness this great transformation. She experienced a complete turnaround, and my heart was filled with joy. I began to praise God for His wondrous work in the life of this woman.

There is so much to learn from this story. A "chance encounter" evolved into multiple deliverance sessions and concluded with a victorious ending. However, the catalyst of all that was just a song of worship. There is something about our singing that ushers in the presence of God. Demons tremble when we worship; and they flee far away from us. Our worship is powerful and can set captives free.

Demonic spirits, as stubborn as they pretend to be, cannot stand against us, when we confront them in spiritual warfare and with songs of deliverance and worship. We are powerful people who have access to the whole armor of God. ***"Put on the whole armor of God that ye may be able to stand against the wiles of the devil" (Eph. 6:11).*** Every victory gained is the result of the power of God in us. We cannot face the enemy, based on our own limited abilities. Let us then clothe ourselves appropriately. As much as we understand the importance of dressing up physically, in like manner must we dress up spiritually, to always be on guard to defend ourselves against the wiles and traps of the devil. We should therefore face the power of evil: ***"By the word of truth, by the power of God, by the armor of righteousness on the right hand and on the left..." (II Cor. 6:7).***

The armor of God consists of six ornaments— prayer as a bonus makes seven to reinforce it. (1) the girdle of truth; which represents acknowledging of Jesus Christ as the final reality of redemption; (2) the breastplate of righteousness; which figuratively means to stand and operate on what is upright; (3) the preparation of the gospel of peace; which implies that we ought to always be ready to spread the gospel of peace; (4) the shield of faith, which is the protection against false ideas and doctrines; (5) the helmet of salvation, which is the confessing of Jesus Christ as the only way to salvation; (6) the sword of the Spirit; which is the word of God, a double-edged sword to cut off all work of the enemy; and (7) all sorts of prayers; our way of communicating with God, and interceding for others.

Christ, in obedience to His Father's command, was anointed to set the captives free. In a similar manner, we are also appointed to set the captives free. The Lord truly got my attention when He demonstrated that His liberating power works perfectly through the ministry of singing. I take no pleasure in boasting about my singing, but I do love to boast about the power of God. As the Psalmist said, ***"But I will sing of thy power; yea, I will sing aloud of thy mercy in the morning..." (Ps. 59:16).*** God can use our gifts to set others free. But, sometimes, we fail to act submissively and obediently, as it relates to our calling and gifting. We procrastinate, and put off for the future, what we are called to do in the present; not realizing that even our physical well-being can be inversely impacted by our lack of obedience. We would be amazed to know that some forms of sickness and ailment could prove themselves to be the result of our own doing. An act of disobedience may be as passive as procrastinating, but conversely, its result may cause some serious detriments to our health.

The Consequence of My Disobedience to God's Command:

In 2004, a message was delivered to me by Sister Marie, who is mentioned in a previous chapter in this book, as someone I led to Lord through my singing ministry. She called me one day and related to me, that the Lord had given her a special word on my behalf, she affirmed to me that "The Lord charged me to tell you to take your singing ministry seriously and concentrate on your recording project." In fact, I had been working on the recording project for so long, that I lost all desire to finish it. Instead of taking heed to Marie's message, and going back where I left off, I just passively didn't listen, and put my singing ministry on hold. I was rather preoccupied with going to school and pursuing a degree in Psychology.

The more engrossed I was in my studies, the more I lost interest in my singing ministry. I gave priority to other things rather than the assignment that God had given. During my second year in college, I began to experience sore throats and breathing problems. The symptoms were like those of a cold, but it was not that at all. Gradually, my vocal cords began to shrink, to the point where I started to experience major throat pain, especially when I tried to talk. I was then working as a payroll accountant, and the use of my voice was vital to my workflow, as I had to be in constant oral communication with other employees. Losing my voice was insane; and the condition progressively worsened over the years to come.

My doctor had to put me on allergy medications and treated me with some injections bi-weekly. There were times that I longed to worship God in songs, but I just could not muster enough strength in my vocal cords to produce much audible sounds. After several years, nothing has changed; I decided to get a second opinion from a different doctor. Alarmed by the gravity of my condition, the doctor immediately ordered that my throat be x-rayed and scanned. The results were heartbreaking; my vocal cords had deteriorated so overly that the doctor prohibited me from ever trying to sing again. He explained to me that any forceful use of my voice would damage my vocal cords beyond repair. He looked at me in the eyes, and told me, point blank, that I would never be able to sing again. He referred me to a speech therapist who put me on bi-weekly visit for at least two years. I was devastated; I cried my heart out on my way home. It was just so overwhelming; however, I was able to collect enough strength to rebuke the devil and determined that I was not going to lose my voice.

This situation took me to a new dimension with God. I began to refuse to accept the doctor's report as a life sentence; I knew in my heart that God desired to restore my relationship with Him and heal my vocal cords just as well. However, one day, the Holy Spirit brought to my attention that my condition was due to my own disobedience, and refusal to take my music ministry seriously. He reminded me of Sister Marie's message which clearly instructed that I needed to focus on the recording project rather than pursuing other things of lesser importance first. The Spirit of God began to deeply convict me of my disobedience; I quickly got on my knees, and with a heart full of repentance I asked the Lord to forgive me. For it is written that: **"God is good and ready to forgive; and plenteous in mercy unto all them that calls upon Him" (Ps. 86:5).** My singing ministry was a valuable instrument in the hands of God. I was a lead vocalist, and worship leader at the Beraca Baptist Church in Brooklyn, New York. I have participated in several recording projects; singing is my ministry, it's my passion, my life. Even as my condition worsened, I managed to travel two to three hours by train, to attend choir rehearsals. I could not sing, but I forced myself to learn the songs quietly.

One day God, in his mercy, gave me grace to lead some songs with the choir under His anointing, and then, immediately after, my vocal cord gave out again. The Lord allowed me to perform that way for another year. I acknowledged that even though God's grace was still upon me, the consequence of my disobedience was so great, that I truly began to value, more and more, and day by day the gift of singing as a treasure.

The Healing: During the year 2009, I was miraculously healed. Pastor Benny Hinn came to New York City to minister at Madison Square Garden. I exercised my faith and called in to sign up to take part in the mass choir that was being put together for the event. I knew in my heart this was going to be a breakthrough opportunity for me to get healed. I totally believed without any shadow of doubt that God was going to heal me while I worship. I scheduled to leave my job early for those three nights. The first two nights had gone by, yet my vocal cords were still closed, and I could not sing.

"This was my time!" so I thought to myself. I persisted in faith, as I was not about to miss out on God's healing power for me on that very last day. That night, I checked in early, and promptly assumed my assigned position in the choir. With great expectancy in my heart, I knew I was going to be healed that same night. As the event was about to unfold, Pastor Benny Hinn turned suddenly to us and asked, "Are you ready choir?" We all replied, "Yea." He shouted, "Receive it," and all choir members fell, all at once, backwards. The musicians began to play their instruments creating a rumble of sound, the sound of worship; and it filled the room as much as my heart. I was overtaken by this great anointing in the room, and my spirit inside of me began to worship. I found myself regaining my ease and ability once again to produce audible sound without any discomfort. The more I sang the louder I could hear myself. The Holy Spirit took over and my healing was complete until this day; and to this day I am forever grateful to God for healing me and restoring my gift of singing. It is evident that was not the work of man, nobody touched me. Although I am eternally thankful for his ministry, Pastor Benny Hinn didn't lay hands on me; but the Lord saw the pain of his precious daughter, and the burning desire inside of her to take back what she had lost for some many years. He touched me and I was instantly made whole. Right now, I can humbly say that the anointing of God is even greater upon my life, as I cherish every opportunity I get, to use my gift of singing, if only to bring comfort to the broken hearted, and healing to the sick.

Security/Hope: *"For I know the thoughts that I think toward you, saith the LORD, thoughts of peace, and not of evil, to give you an expected end" (Jer. 29:11).* When God calls us to serve, He promises security for our ministry. Taking God at His words gives us faith and courage to condemn and dismiss any doubts that could hinder our sense of security. Over the years in ministry, I had to learn to put my hope in God and God alone. I have helped many churches with their ministries throughout the years. As a result of that, I was hoping that those that I helped loyally in the past, would in due time, return reciprocity. Although this way of thinking makes sense in terms of human logic, it is inconsistent with how the Lord wants us to relate to each other. I must admit that this erroneous way of thinking had brought me many disappointments.

Excited about my second chance with my singing ministry, I rushed back to my recording, and started to work hard to make things happen rather quickly. I knew that for me to complete this recording, I would need to raise some funds. While I was talking to a sister friend of mine, a sudden thought came to my mind about raising funds for the project. I immediately shared the idea with her, and she encouraged me to go along with it; I did not wait another second. I picked up the phone and talked to my husband about it, and he too quickly encouraged me to go along with it just as well. It did not occur to me to seek God's counsel concerning his own plan for this project. I was supposed to consult Him first; but I thought this was my season to bloom. My idea was for me to utilize my strategies to come up with the funds necessary to finance the project. I scheduled a concert for December 2012, in Philadelphia at a local church where I had been ministering on a yearly basis. The congregation knew me well; however, it wasn't so, for the other neighboring churches within that same community. Nevertheless, I had some friends with whom I had worked in the past, who offered to help me promote the concert. I figured with two or three churches gathering, I could raise enough money to continue with the recording project. I did not have in mind to sell tickets, but only to collect a love offering at the event. A month prior to the concert, I got a phone call from the First Lady of the Church, who advised me to come over two weeks prior to the concert, to visit a few neighboring churches in the area; so that way they would have a better idea about my ministry. Although that sounded like a perfect plan, I could not honor the invitation, however, due to conflicting schedules on my part. Besides that, my workload and responsibilities did not allow me to do so. In lieu of the church visits, however, I did radio interviews, promotional spots, and played samples of my music for the listeners to get acquainted with my ministry.

On the actual day of the concert my husband and I drove for hours, and we made it there early Sunday Morning, for us to participate in the Sunday worship service. As a late request, I asked the church youth choir to minister at the concert, as opening act; an invitation which they gladly honored. And promptly at 5:00 pm, as scheduled, we started off the concert with the youth choir, whose performance was truly a blessing. However halfway through the concert, I noticed that the attendance in the church was still in very small numbers; nonetheless the presence of the Holy Spirit was with us and working mightily. The Lord was just about to teach me a lesson. I presented the cause of the fundraising to the people, and we passed the collection plate around. My expectation of reaching my financial goal failed miserably; we collected less than three hundred dollars. Imagine the disappointment I felt that day, and how the enemy tried to use that against us. We spent more than we had collected. We didn't even have enough funds to pay the camera guy who insisted that he get compensated immediately after the concert.

On our way back home that night, my husband and I decided not to talk negatively about the mishaps and shortcomings of the concert. We instead renewed our faith in the Lord; and we were confident that God would deliver his promises of a good future to us. Although the enemy tried to use this situation to bring doubts into my heart, the presence of the Holy Spirit had a greater influence on me, as he redirected me to continue to have faith in Him. What Satan did not know is that I was counting my blessings that night, regardless of what happened: (1) I received the love of those who were blessed and edified by my ministry; that alone was encouraging to me. (2) I received my husband's support because; he never passed any blame on me. His presence was rather comforting and reassuring to me. (3) I received hope from God through the presence of His Holy Spirit. (4) My faith in the promises of God increased greatly, knowing that He is faithful and loving towards me.

Our works for the Lord can never be in vain. Reaching higher faith is reaching higher goals. My hope was renewed, and I was determined to continue with the fundraising plans. I came back to Brooklyn, New York and scheduled for both a concert and a dinner banquet. As I continued to reach out to those who I helped in the past, I asked the Pastor of one of the churches at which I ministered over the years, to allow me to use his facility. He kindly allowed me to use both the church sanctuary and the reception area, all at no cost to me. I was excited, and very grateful for his generosity towards me, as I did not have much money to start with. I thought since I was not a total stranger to most of these peoples, I expected the church to respond in full. The concert was suitably promoted by the Pastor of the church; I was optimistic that we were going to have a great turnout.

It was snowing the night of the concert, but not to the point of needing to cancel it. I consulted the Lord in prayer about cancelling the concert, but He did not allow me to do so. We intentionally did not start on time due to the weather conditions, to give enough time for those on their way to show up. I knew in my heart that for everything we do for God, whether great or small, it must be done well. I had spent many nights listening to the voice of the Holy Spirit who directed me at how the concert should go. The Lord had put it in my heart to prepare a PowerPoint of a prayer and healing scriptures for those who He had planned to heal and deliver that night. I had confidence that this concert was going to be a success both materially and spiritually. I gathered all who were scheduled to minister in this concert and asked them to remain in prayer. I went and sat behind the door next to the pulpit instead of sitting on it. It was clear that the people of that very church did not come out to support me. Only four individuals out of six hundred members of that church attended the concert. But I refused to let that bother me, as I had an intense desire to release the blessing of God over those who had attended. That was the source of my strength and hope to carry on. God had something to tell them through me, and I could not dare return home, leaving His people empty handed, without delivering this message of hope to them.

God had already sanctified me and prepared me for this glorious night. The precious Holy Spirit embraced me, and I could no longer focus on those who were not there. It was most beneficial for me to be still and allow God to minister through me. When it was time for me to begin to minister in song, I felt embraced by the Holy Spirit, and ushered into a greater dimension of his anointing. The glory of God covered me, His presence filled the atmosphere. An event that was planned out as a concert, changed into a spontaneous worship experience. Everyone in the room was touched by God's presence, they all began to join me in singing and praising God. Then I shared my testimony about how the Lord miraculously healed my vocal cords. I display the medical result through images of CAT scans and X-Rays on a PowerPoint as proof of God's miracle working power. The miraculous work of the Lord as displayed on the PowerPoint left them in amazement. I believe that many of those who did not show up heard about the marvelous work of God that night. At that point, money or the turnout did not matter to me anymore. My joy was made complete, as I witnessed how the Lord just intervened and greatly blessed those in attendance that night.

But the next day after the concert, the fleshy part of me began to feel let down by those who didn't show up to support me. I felt that I did not deserve that treatment, because I had invested many years in supporting them loyally. Just as I was about to fall in the enemy trap of disappointment, the Holy Spirit came to my rescue, and pointed out to me, my insecurity and ungratefulness. I fought back those demonic thoughts with a vengeance, Satan could not succeed in making me feel like a failure. I began to reflect on the generosity of the Pastor who had allowed me to use the church free of charge. I began to play back the tape of this awesome night virtually, in mind; and I resolved that Satan was not going to make me feel like a failure. In the eyes of God and those that were in attendance that night, the concert was a total success. I refocused my energy back on the Lord who helped through my bout of insecurity. ***"Hitherto have ye asked nothing in my name: Ask, and ye shall receive, that your joy may be full" (John 16: 24).*** I asked God to forgive me for my ungratefulness, and I immediately felt forgiven. I cannot describe how the tenderness of God's love covered me, as I embraced His comfort.

My hope for a greater future was renewed; and immediately afterwards, I started to plan for the dinner banquet. Promoting it, however, was extremely hard and taxing. I spent hours on the phone, each night making phone calls. I sent out emails to as many people as I could reach. But out of that came an unexpected blessing. A very good friend and sister in Christ who lives in Dallas, Texas, miraculously opened her email and saw my invitation. I say "miraculously", because I had not heard from her for a very long time; she recounted to me how she was led by God to open her emails. I shared with her the vision and purpose of the fundraising event; and she quickly embraced the project as if it were her own. She dedicated much of her time to helping me improve the flyer's graphic design. She went as far as paying for the printing cost and mailed them out to my address in New York. How beautiful is the manifestation of love in her.

The enemy, however, strongly stood against the promotion of the banquet. After my friend had put all her effort into ensuring that I received the flyers on time, he held them back for several weeks. I did not receive them through the mail until the week of the banquet. Besides that, he tried to discourage me, when money was not coming in for me to cover all necessary expenses. My friend acknowledged the battle, and she too was attacked. The Holy Spirit reminded me about putting on the whole Armor of God and I rested on the assurance of God's word. The word of God sustained my faith, and I kept on trusting Him. I came to realize that the condition of laboring for God rests in the hope of His promises." *... **My presence shall go with thee, and I will give thee rest" (Ex. 33:14).***

To offset the work of the enemy, the Lord allowed me to have a brand-new testimony for the banquet. It just so happened that a week prior to the event, the Lord led me to reconcile with my first born and only son, after thirteen long years of separation. The enemy just could not block the flow of God's blessing in my life; and I knew deep inside of me, that the banquet was going to be a success. Indeed, all went well; we were able to raise a fair amount of money; part of which was spent on paying for all the expenses accrued for the event. I then allocated the rest of the money, roughly twelve hundred dollars, towards the recording project. I still had a long way to go since it would take me a substantial amount of money to finish the recording. I expected greater and mightier things to come, and that hope alone settled it for me. ***"For Thou art my hope, O Lord God: Thou art my trust from my youth" (Ps. 71:5).*** Carrying God's promises in our hearts is the key to the door of victory in the ministry. For this very reason, ministers need to keep these promises alive in their heart, so as to be able to stand steadfast in the face of trials and tribulations.

The Contest Between Satan and the Believer:

Through my "Can I be the One?" journey, of hard-earned knowledge and wisdom about ministry. All Christians must aspire to serve in a ministry to one extent or another. However, it is equally important for believers and aspiring servants of the Lord to beware of some critical spiritual realities regarding ministry. Simply stated, being in ministry constitutes a declaration of war against Satan. There is warfare going on against all ministers, who are perceived by the enemy as a direct threat to his agenda. Satan is after every man and woman who dedicates their lives to the work of the ministry. It is a never-ending conflict that originated with Satan's revolt against God's authority in heaven. He unsuccessfully attempted an overthrow of God's sovereign kingdom. He failed miserably and paid the ultimate price; he was stripped of all authority and honor. He, along with an army of rebellious angels, were cast out of heaven. Seeing the failure of his attempt, Satan vows in his pride and arrogance to stand against God's plan and purpose for mankind, as he attempts to establish his evil government here on Earth. What the adversary had lost from God will never be retrieved.

Given the fact that we are clearly aware of the adversary's plans, we must therefore refuse to operate in fear of him. He is not king, never had been, and never will be. The Bible refers to him as this world's prince, whose authority has been stripped away. ***"...Now shall the prince of this world be cast out" (John 12:31).*** Satan, who was once referred to as the "Angel of Light" had been evicted from his position of authority. He was disqualified to serve and revoked from his ministry of worship. He is mad and enraged with jealousy and cannot stand the sight of anyone who faithfully serves and ministers to the Lord. Satan is out to steal, kill and destroy as many ministers as he can, who are dedicated to serving God and glorifying His name here on Earth. Satan's intention is to deceive Christians with lies and illusions, trials, and persecutions. Satan uses whatever strategy or scheme at his disposal, to distract ministers away from the focus of their ministry. He transforms himself as an angel of light to mislead God's people if they let him. ***"And not marvel; for Satan himself is transformed into an angel of light" (II Cor. 11:14)***.

Ever since the fall of Adam, Satan, the devil, has been trying relentlessly to impose his so-called kingdom on mankind, by assigning evil spirits and demonic forces to do his dirty work here on the planet. In the wilderness, his arrogance and crude audacity pushed him to the point of tempting Jesus and trying to coerce the Lord into bowing down and worshipping him. How disturbing is such haughtiness. Let us remember that Satan is a fallen being who is totally defected and corrupted; he is tormented and consumed by his own pride with a perpetual obsession to be worshipped. His egotistic nature causes him to employ whichever tactic, to lie and seduce, or threaten whomever he can, just so the beast can viciously sip in moments of stolen worship. He will do anything to get homage from anybody. ***"And the devil said unto Him, "All this power will I give thee, and the glory of them: for that is delivered unto me; and to whomsoever I will give it. Therefore, if you will worship me, all will be yours" (Luke 4:6-7).*** Let us pause and dissect the elements of this verse for a minute. ***"All this power will I give you."*** Power is what most people are chasing after. Giving power to man has always proven to be Satan's most effective way to force him into perfect submission. **"Glory"** in this context, represents material possessions, fame, and money, or just about anything that mankind commonly lusts after. It is often said: "Give a manpower and money, and his true worth of character is soon revealed." Satan uses the same old trickery, he sets the same old traps; and sure enough, he finds the next victim, lurking around to be preyed on.

We must therefore be rooted and grounded in the truth of the Word of God, to guard our heart and keep our conscience pure. Let us be reminded of the fact that we stand on the winning side; Satan is nothing but a rebellious angel who has drifted away from the truth. He is the Father of lies, and void of all truth. Jesus is the first begotten son of God; He is the way, the life and the truth. **"And let all angels he saith and let the angels of God worship Him." Jesus' throne is established forever." Therefore, we ought to give the more earnest heed to the things which we have heard, lest at any time we should let them slip" (Heb. 1:6, 8; 2:1).** Jesus laid the foundation of the world, yet He uses the Word of God to rebuke Satan, the devil. **"And Jesus answered and said unto him; Get thee behind Me, Satan: For it is written, 'thou shalt worship the LORD thy God and Him only shalt thou serve" (Luke 4: 8).** We ought to do the same; let us exercise the authority of the Word over Satan to overcome him. Jesus demonstrated His higher authority, using God's Word, as the One and only, who is worthy of worship, and is no match for Satan. Satan's confrontation was miniscule, compared to our Savior's imposing power and authority over everything. **"Jesus in the beginning has laid the foundation of the earth; and the heavens are the works of His hands" (Heb. 1:10).** Every believer must be persuaded of the fact that the Lord will continue to use his people, to tread on scorpions and serpents and proclaim victory over the adversary as He came to destroy the works of Satan. **"...For this purpose, the Son of God was manifested, that He might destroy the works of the devil" (I John 3:8).**

Where is your heart when it comes to worshiping God? It requires absolute spiritual discernment, to fully understand what is at stake when one is involved in ministry. Hence the reason why the minister must know for sure that God is with him, and that he needs to be in a continuous mode of worship. All the enemy needs are an open portal to our hearts, through which to have access to our life, unnoticed. We are in this race to win. However, Satan is looking for every opportunity possible to snatch away our victory from us. The enemy is constantly trying to win over our faith. Therefore, we must always be on guard. We must walk continually in obedience to God. The enemy will try persistently to cause us to lose our faith, and stray from our commitment to love the Lord, and one another. But he will not succeed, if we stand strong against his every move. We must be in constant alert of Satan's strategies, and never should he retire his weapons of warfare against the enemy. We must win this race!

How does the believer win this race? Spiritual sobriety is one of the determining factors to winning the race against Satan. A sober mind takes the believer to the finish line. The Bible instructs us to **"Be sober, be vigilant; because your adversary the devil as a roaring lion walketh about seeking whom he may devour" (I Pet. 5:8).** Our capacity to triumph over the forces of evil requires sobriety, and a perfect reliance on God's strength. **"Blessed is the man whose strength is in Thee... They go from strength to strength..." (Ps. 84:5-7).** As we remain sober, and totally dependent on God's strength, we will overtake the enemy and celebrate our victory.

How do we remain sober? One who is under the influence of liquor, obviously, does not have a sober mind, because his behavior is greatly impacted by the elevated alcohol content in the blood. A drunkard cannot make rational decisions, even if his speech is incoherent. As ministers of the gospel, we are called, however, to a superior kind of sobriety. For us ministers, sobriety is synonymous with mental and spiritual freedom. Our mind must be free of ungodly thoughts, our hearts clear of envy, jealousy, and pride. This is far superior to being sober only as it pertains to blood alcohol level. It's the kind of sobriety that keeps one spiritually composed and always ready to fight the good fight of faith. This superior kind of sobriety has three components to it: a sound mind, sympathy, and self-control.

*A **sound mind,*** which is the total opposite of insanity, is always sober as it is always filled with peace that comes from the Holy Spirit. Our mind is a battleground on which many wars are fought. Therefore, the mind must be clear and sane, not troubled, or tormented. A sound mind, however, is not produced overnight, but it is the product of a progressive process of deep transformation in our thinking. It is only when we heed to God's Word and submit to his instructions, can we begin to develop the sober mind of Christ in us. ***"For if anyone thinks himself to be something, when he is nothing, he deceiveth himself" (Gal. 6:3).*** Any prideful thoughts that cause us to think of ourselves as being higher than others should be eradicated. Satan deceived himself into thinking of himself as being higher than God, his creator. He lost his mind, and his sanity cost him his job and caused his eviction far from Heaven's glory. Therefore, let us stand steadfast against the seductive spirit of pride; let us all be of a sound mind. ***"For who hath known the mind of the Lord, that he may instruct him? But we have the mind of Christ" (I Cor. 2:16).***

Compassion, which I believe to be an important component of sobriety, is lacking greatly among Christians nowadays. It seems as if we are getting colder and colder, towards each other. Sadly, it appears that it has become easier for Christians to pass judgment on each other than show compassion towards one another. We are rather quick to "crucify" those who transgress and fall behind, but we are slow to show compassion. ***"Brethren, if a man is overtaken in a fault, ye which are spiritual, restore such a one in the spirit of meekness; considering thyself, lest thou also be tempted" (Gal. 6:1).*** Brothers and sisters, let us remember that we are born after the image of God, and God is loving and compassionate. It is not our place to convict and condemn others for their wrongdoing. We should rather be agents of love and restoration. Our sobriety is incomplete without compassion and love for others. Remember we too, were once in the same position, and we needed someone to reach out and show grace. From this day forward let us stop the bashing, and obediently get with the program of showing compassion, and being sober.

One day after our worship service, a lady who had visited our church for the second time asked me if she could have a word with me. After service, all church members normally sat together around the table to fellowship and share a meal together. The woman stood there at distance from us, she hesitated to come join us at the table. As I observed her closely, I discerned that something was deeply troubling her. I left the table and sat with her; and then we began to talk. She confided in me that she was guilty of idolatry, and that she was sorry for straying so far away from God. She confessed that she had consulted a voodoo priest about some marital problems she was dealing with. Since then, the burden of guilt on her has been overwhelming; it has been consuming and eating her alive. She felt horrible, and unworthy of God's forgiveness. She admitted that she was just moments away from committing suicide.

I asked her if she had shared this incident with anyone else. "No," she said. I explained to her that there was no need to share this with any other person; however, she needed to confess her sin to God alone. I then asked her if she was ready to make that confession before God, and to ask for forgiveness, she said yes. Before we prayed, I explained to her, that she had to take full responsibility of her action, and to openly confess her sins to God in prayer. She prayed her heart out, to the Lord, pleading for forgiveness. I was deeply moved, and my heart was filled with compassion for her. At that moment, I could just imagine that God must have been moved with great compassion towards her just as well. **"Nevertheless, when one shall turn to the Lord, the veil shall be taken away" (II Cor. 3:16).**

Satan tried his best to crush this woman with the burden of guilt, preventing her from returning to the Lord. You see, the opportunity had afforded me by God to help this lady "run the race" and win. My brothers and sisters, we are indeed in a race, and we need each other to get to the finish line. As I recalled my past sins, I prayed for her with compassion. My shortcomings may not have been the same exact ones, but I too, had fallen behind. We can't treat sin as though one weighs more than the other. We must be fair, uplifting, and compassionate to each other. We ought to be compassionate to those in need, coach them with words of wisdom, and help them to finish their race with dignity.

Self-control is an essential component of sobriety, as it is one of the characteristics of the fruit of the spirit. Self-control is in fact a spiritual resource from which we draw our strength to run the race. Satan knows about our vulnerabilities, and he is sure to create circumstances around us to trouble our heart and cause us to lose our sense of balance and control. It is therefore crucial that we build in us this important component of sobriety, through prayer and fasting, and dwelling in the presence of God. Self-control is produced in us only when we connect with God, as we keep ourselves in a continuous relationship with the Lord.

Having self-control prepares us to put on the garment of Christ. ***"But put on the Lord Jesus Christ, and make not provision for the flesh, to fulfill the lust thereof" (Rom. 13:14).*** The first time I read this verse, it just caught my attention, as I was eager to know what it means to "put on Jesus Christ." After meditating on it for a while, I have come to realize, that it is to be dressed up spiritually, wearing the spiritual garment of Christ. It began to sink in, that it is of utmost importance that every Christian, regardless of age or gender, "put on Christ." We must first remove the garment of the flesh with its old habits and lust. Then we ought to dress ourselves up with that new garment, which is Jesus Christ, himself. To put on Jesus, in essence, is to put on the Word; for the Word is Jesus himself. With all sinful garments removed, we are now ready to be dressed up properly, in the spirit to defeat the devil. There is no way the believer can face the devil wearing a sinful garment. All Christians must be uniformly outfitted with the same garment of Christ. We are part of the same army, the same team wearing the same uniform. Our uniform becomes our identity. That uniform terrifies the devil because it reminds him of the resurrected Christ. A sober Christian who puts on Christ is surely sets himself on the right track to win the race.

Winning the race is not a *logical* approach, but rather a *spiritual* one. It is based on our obedience, commitment, dedication, and reverential walk with God. Christians let us be reassured that we are poised to win this race, knowing that we are not in this alone. God is with us through every step of the way. Beware, however, that the enemy will try to use his old tactics against us. He brings flattery to some, money, and fame to others; however, at the end of the day the only thing he is really concerned about is distracting us and leading us astray.

The love of flattery always leads to pride, which then brings disappointments and leads to destruction. The Bible recounts that, while Apostle Paul and Barnabas were in the synagogue preaching the gospel of Jesus Christ; standing there was a crippled man, desiring to be healed. Paul turned his attention to him and commanded him to get up and walk; and miraculously he got up and walked. When the people saw what happened, they were amazed, and cried out with a loud voice: "the gods are come down to us in the likeness of men." They were ready to worship Paul and Barnabas, whom they passed for gods. Paul and Barnabas were appalled by their ignorance; they tore their clothes and shouted to the crowd with horror, as they rebuked them so as not to think of them as gods. Paul and Barnabas redirected the crowd's focus away from themselves and turned it rather to God instead **(Acts 14:8-18).** It's important that we learn to do just the same.

Let us be humble in our ministry, never taking God's glory for our own. This will save us from all trouble. You see, these people were assigned by Satan to deceive Paul and Barnabas, so they could take

God's glory for themselves. Taking God's glory for our own, inflates the heart with pride and block the flow of God's anointing in our lives. Let us therefore be calm and self-less when we minister; knowing that it is never about us, but always about the Almighty God of whom we are just mere servants.

We race to make it to the finish line, and Satan races to stop us from getting there. Satan's temporary reward is to win us over; however, his permanent punishment is eternal damnation in the lake of fire. In the other hand, the believer who makes it to the finish line will earn the eternal reward of everlasting glory. ***"Know ye not that they which run in race run all, but one receiveth the prize? So run, that ye may obtain. And every man that striveth for the mastery is temperate in all things. Now they do it to obtain a corruptible crown; but we for an incorruptible crown" (I Cor. 9:24-25).***

As we continue to run this race, we also grow in faith and experience God's unfailing love. While the adversary is never tired of running against us, we however, should not lose courage in our walk with God. Disobedience is the path of least resistance; but our obedience to God's leads us to the way of righteousness. Know that periods of trials and testing will come, but they serve the purpose of shaping us into great men and women of ministry. ***"For Thou, O God hast proved us: Thou hast tried us, as silver is tried" (Ps. 66:10).***

The Apostle Paul, in his teachings, warns us about trials to come. Some of these trials are harsh, but they are no match for God. ***"For we would not, brethren, have you ignorant of our trouble... that we were pressed out of measure, above our strength, insomuch that despaired even of life... But we had the sentence of death in ourselves, that we should not trust in ourselves, but in God which raiseth the dead" (II Cor. 1:8-9).*** If God is the winner of this contest, then we, too, can absolutely partake of this victory. Therefore, I urge all believers to stand steadfast, in perseverance, continuing in the exercise of God's given gifts faithfully.

In doing so, we can now rest in faith, believing that God will never reject the prayers of those who serve in reverence and humility. Let Satan remain a liar, and let God stand always as the truth. ***"Being confident of this very thing, that He which has begun a good work in us will perform it until the day of Jesus Christ"*** (Phil. 1:6).

SESSION THIRTEEN

A Glimpse at the Victory Over Oppositions & Persecutions

Opposition One:

As time went by during the process of both the recording and the writing of this book, opposition increased exponentially; I must say they were countless. It might have been difficult having to deal with so many oppositions, but at the end, as this recount will prove, they all culminated into a common purpose, which was to bring me from glory to glory, and triumph to triumph.

At one point in time, I was under serious spiritual attack, I was emotionally drained out. I felt I was being robbed of my peace and joy; I was filled with worries. The plan of the enemy was to sabotage my work and hinder me from using my gifts effectively. The series of attacks that were to follow, happened all within a period of six months. This account is to strengthen your faith as you go through your own set of oppositions.

As I was still in a fundraising phase for the recording, Reverend Honoré, who lives in Jacksonville, Florida, offered to help me find a location in Florida for my next concert. John connected me with a friend of his, who in turn introduced me to the music director at a church in Orlando, Florida. He requested that I send him a demo of one of my songs, which I promptly did. After auditioning the demo, the music director contacted me immediately, letting me know of his interest to promote my ministry.

For quite some time, we were in constant and perfect communication with each other. Suddenly, I stopped hearing from the music director, and I decided to call him. During our conversation, he revealed to me that I needed to have a "name"; which meant, I was not popular enough, and that they were not ready to grant me access to use the church for my concert. However, the Lord was about to do something new in my life. I called Pastor Rousselin Allonce a friend of mine, who knew me very well from New York City, and asked him if I could use his church in Fort-Lauderdale. He was very excited about the idea, but he said that the church didn't have the seating capacity to accommodate hundreds of people. However, Pastor Allonce generously connected me to his Father, who then helped me find another church.

The concert was scheduled for November 24, 2012, in Fort-Lauderdale, Florida. I worked day and night to plan that event. In the process of looking for a local artist in Florida to take part in this concert, Don, the event promoter linked me up with a well-known local artist by the stage name: "Brother J." Pastor Allonce also suggested that I get in touch with Brother J. I took his advice and called him immediately. When I called and asked him if he would accept my invitation to be one of my guest artists for the night, with an open heart, he accepted it, and promised to call me back.

One week later I got a call from Brother J; but the conversation took an unexpected turn. Brother J. said to me "Can I ask you something?" And I said "yes." He proceeded and asked: "Did you live in Freeport Grand Bahamas before?" Then Brother J mentioned my mother's name." I paused, and then I said "Yes." He started laughing hysterically. Then he asked, "Do you remember Pastor Francis Joseph?" and I said "Yes." In fact, Pastor Francis Joseph had given me guitar lessons when I was an adolescent." "Well, Pastor Joseph was my Father." Brother J replied, he then added "I knew you since you were a teenager." He told me: "As we are talking, I am having flashbacks of the night when my Father took me to one of your concerts with The Salt of the Earth Gospel Band. The people were so blessed by your performance that they honored you with a bouquet of roses. I always wondered what had happened to you. I cannot believe that I found you. This is God's doing." He caught my attention, and that's when I realized that God was up to something different. During our trouble, God is always there to give us reassurance that He is with us. Could you imagine how thrilled I was? After over three decades, God was reuniting me again with old friends who appreciate my ministry. So, you see, if I did not experience that rejection by the other church, I would have missed the opportunity to be reunited with people who know me and truly appreciate my ministry. Now, let's find out what happened prior to the concert so I could take you through the various sets of opposition I endured.

Although JFK Airport is only a half hour drive from where we lived, we left two and half hours early. But prior to our trip to Florida, I had spent three days and nights fasting and praying, preparing to minister there. Those days and nights, as you will see, proved themselves to be one of the best ministerial decisions I have made. We arrived at JFK Airport that morning and parked our car at the garage then proceeded to check in.

I stepped into the escalator with both my luggage and carry-on bag; my husband was ahead of me, and an elderly woman was behind me. There was a line of people on the lower steps. I am not sure how it happened, but all I knew is that I totally lost my balance and fell backward and began to roll like a ball down the escalator; all the while, the moving escalator caused the luggage and carry-on to roll over me. Of course, everybody who was there totally panicked; and my husband who was too far ahead of me, didn't fully realize what happened. Besides, the upward motion of the escalator would make it impossible for him to run back towards me, as that would put him also in danger. What made the situation worse, was the fact that the elderly woman behind me was so afraid of the domino effect that could result from my falling, that she started screaming at the top of her lungs. Fortunately, an airport officer who was watching the scene unfold on his monitors ran quickly to the area and stopped the escalator. By then, I had some severe palpitations, and it felt like an earthquake was running through my chest. My heartbeat was racing hysterically. My husband rushed to get me up and asked me if I was alright. I couldn't provide him with a coherent answer, as I was so frightened. I was shocked, in pain, and worried; I wanted to know what on earth had just happened.

As a precaution, the Police Officer insisted that I file an accident report. I knew that if I did file a report, they would have to take me to the hospital; and that would automatically cause me to cancel my trip. So many things were going in my mind, it just didn't make sense as to what caused me to lose my balance and sustain such a fall. But then again, I thought that Satan is the invisible enemy, who will try anything to create oppositions against those who are assigned to do God's work. I began to express my gratitude to God for his miraculous protection that kept me from any danger. I could have been badly injured or even died from this accident, but He protected me. So, I decided to trust God, and I refused to neither wait for the ambulance nor file a report. I resolved therefore, that I was not going to let anything come in my way of what I believed was going to be a life transforming event for many: the Florida concert. I proceeded with our trip to the Sunshine State and claimed my victory over this situation.

When we face a situation where we must choose between God and the easy way out, our will must play a very important role in the decision process. The struggle between self-will and God's will, is essentially how our battles begin. However, we must not allow adversities to negatively impact our own faith, even to the point where we feel like giving up. I looked at my husband, and said, "I do not mind dealing with the hardships of the trip, as long as we make it to Fort-Lauderdale, Florida." I was determined and willing to suffer just to allow God to use me no matter what it takes. As a result of my determination and willingness to be obedient to God, He opened new doors for my ministry, and I was able to see the manifestation of God's power on the night of the concert. Had I not surrendered my will to God for him to have His way, I would never have experienced the benefits of His blessings that night. I accepted to suffer in exchange for the honor there is in serving the Lord and giving glory to His name. ***"Yet if anyone suffer as a Christian, let him not be ashamed; but let him glorify God on this behalf" (I Pet. 4:16).***

Some might think that it was a foolish decision to not have pursued a lawsuit against the Airport for my fall. They knew I needed money to complete the recording project. But I was determined that nothing would take my focus away for the mission that I was set to accomplish. I believe that only those who put their trust in God, can defeat the works of the enemy. The servants are not greater than God's son, Jesus, the Master. God did not spare His son's life who suffered greater oppositions to fulfill His plan of salvation. Likewise, sometimes God might not spare us from certain situations because He has a better plan for us.

I had great longing to complete the recording project, but so much had happened that I began to lose the desire to continue working on it. Waiting in despair for a breakthrough, on October 6, 2012, prior to my accident at the airport, the Lord sent me a powerful message through a sister in Christ named Junie Pelissier. I met her in Brooklyn, New York when I was one of the lead soloists for Beraca Baptist Church Choir. It was about 6:30 pm when I arrived home from work. Junie called me and asked me if I had received a package? I replied, "No." She kindly said, "You should have received it already, at least by 7 pm." Then I said that "I must have been special to receive a package at a time such as this." Junie replied, "Yes, you are because it's coming from me." However, being so occupied in the kitchen, I somewhat forgot about our conversation.

Early the next morning, my husband found, at our doorstep, a beautiful vase containing fresh spring flowers. I still have the vase to this day. This beautiful gift was breathtaking. God knows about my passion for nature and decided to cheer me up with flowers. The gift was priceless, as it gave me the reassurance and the comfort that God is watching over me. The message on the card was just that powerful: *"Myrtha, remember the battle is not yours. This is not about you. It's about the Word, Jesus; just rest in God. Love Ya, Junie."* How precious were those words? It was exactly what my spirit needed to hear. I was totally encouraged and uplifted. I was filled with Joy, just to know that God was thinking of me. It was through this tough period of my life that God's love sustained me the most.

I said to my husband, "Look how God used sister Junie to comfort me." Sister Junie knew nothing about what I was going through, but God, the love of my life, knew just what I needed. He always brings joy at the end of sorrow. God surely knows how to cheer up His children. How wonderful it was to have experienced such beautiful show of God's kindness. ***"But glory, honor, and peace to every man that worketh good..." (Rom. 2:10).*** I acknowledged how deep the love of God is for me. I honor Him, every chance I get, for His perfect love for me. The devil does not send flowers to comfort people. He came to steal, kill, and destroy. On the contrary, God is always in the business of restoring our joy and peace. The Savior of my soul wanted me to have this abundant joy, even in time of trouble. He used Junie to surprise me, just when I needed it the most. Perhaps, Junie had no idea how blessed she was to have been used by God as a vessel of honor. Her obedience is proof that we can truly exercise the love of God towards one another, just by listening to God's voice. What a wonderful feeling that was!

Putting the pieces of the puzzle together, it becomes certain as to why it was vital not to cancel my flight to Florida. It was God's will, after all, for me to continue the work of the ministry, as He made it crystal clear that "it was not about me, but about His Word" which I had to bring forth. A precious soul who was more valuable than money was awaiting me so I could share the good news of the Gospel of Jesus Christ with him or her.

I finally boarded the airplane, I must say, this was exactly where my mission unexpectedly began. Sitting at my left, next to the window, was an elderly Jewish lady. Out of the blue she initiated a conversation which led to a biblical discussion about salvation. Though she knew a lot about God, however Jesus, the son of God, was a mystery to her. Having to share the word with this lady made the flight beyond pleasant and worthwhile. Apparently, the Lord was already doing His work through me. I am not sure if she ever accepted Jesus as her personal Savoir later. All I know is that I did what I was supposed to do, which was to plant the seed of the Word in her heart. I guess, I'll find out when I get to heaven, whether she did receive the message of the gospel.

After all, it was satisfying to know that I made the right decision by not cancelling the concert, which later proved to be a great success. I was not able to raise much money to help me with the recording, but I was contented and blessed with the positive feedback that I received from those who attended. It was totally inspiring and uplifting to them; I had fundraising in mind, but God had fishing of-souls in mind. God was teaching me that He is a great provider, and all these fundraising activities were in fact unnecessary; perhaps for the simple reason that no one could boast or exercise pride in taking credit for God's marvelous works.

Putting your personal will and agenda aside, to allow God's will to take precedence, requires a great deal of discipline. Discipline will increase resistance, resistance, in turn, builds up endurance, and endurance affects our will and ability to consistently make the right decisions. The lesson to learn from all of this, is to know that even when things don't go the way you plan it in your ministry, God will sustain you with His perfect love, and will give you peace of mind. Therefore, when you have the assurance that you are secure in God's love, you can face any opposition.

Opposition Two:

The Bible teaches that: ***"The thief cometh not, for to steal, and to kill, and to destroy..." (John 10:10).*** After failing to distract and discourage me from my purpose in his first bout of opposition against me, the enemy went about attacking me through a second round of opposition. This time it felt like he was aiming at me with a fiery dart, or an arrow of destruction. Three weeks after returning to New York City from the Florida trip, I began to experience serious opposition once again. I certainly hope that the recount of what was to follow help you see how important it is to be steadfast in your faith during adversities. When the enemy attacks with oppositions, DO NOT panic. Panicking is never the solution. Standing in faith, however, is what gets us to the finish line.

It so happened that the company that I worked for decided to upgrade their computer operating system to the latest Windows, for security reasons. They determined that even personals drive must be encrypted. Not knowing the ramification of that change; I complied with their demand and allowed them to encrypt my personal external hard drive. One day, as I attempted to use the drive, a message popped up, indicating that there was an error on the drive requiring my attention, and prompting me to click "yes" if I wanted to fix it. So, I clicked yes. That click was the *"second arrow."* The arrow of destruction that wiped out the entire hard drive and permanently deleted every piece of information on it, including the first draft of this book. I just couldn't believe it. I held my hands up, and gave a "mental" scream: "Can this be happening to me?" It was a dreadful attack of the enemy; and I must admit it shook me to the core. I was struck with disbelief, it was surreal. I did not know what to do at that moment. One of my co-workers, noticing the panic on my face, asked me if I was okay. My eyes were filled with tears; I was speechless. It took me a while before I could compose myself and tell her what happened. Several attempts were made to recover the information, but nothing worked.

When the enemy is shaking our faith, he will destroy what is the most precious and valuable possession we have. His ultimate plan and purpose are to bring us discouragement to the point of letting down our guard. Hence the reason why we need to maintain our faith in God, no matter what tomorrow brings. Grieve, but do it with faith. Mourn, but with hope. Cry, but with trust in God that He will intervene on your behalf and pull you through your troubles. Giving up is not an option, because when God's plan is already in progress, no devil or demons on earth can stop Him from accomplishing His purpose through His people.

After the destruction of the external drive, I can sincerely confess that discouragement knocked hard on my door. I began to think about the loss of the book, and all the time and energy I had already put into it. If I can be transparent, as I promised that I would be, I undeniably, took a nosedive into crippling fear and anxiety. Sadness filled my heart. I questioned why I was under attack once again. I knew deep down inside my heart that God was here with me, but it was hard for me to accept the reality of the loss of something so precious. I was grieving, not out of total despair, but with the hope that the Lord would make a way, and bring his glory out of this situation.

During a conversation with Professor Rocco Dormarunno, one of the editors of this manual, I inadvertently told him about the hard drive, and the loss of the book. However, it didn't even occur to me to inquire of any possibility of him having a copy of it. That was when he said to me "I have a good amount of the first draft you sent to me." "I will send it back to you, and we'll take it from there" he reassured me. That was the "best" news I had heard all my life. Professor Dormarunno perhaps had no idea that the Lord was using him as a channel to bring forth His plan. It was a dark moment in my life; but God turned on the light of hope again, by using someone else to demonstrate His faithfulness towards me. My spirit was restored, and my joy renewed. Professor Dormarunno forwarded what he had, which was about half of the book; and I was immensely grateful.

Later that night, I anxiously downloaded the file and saved it to my computer. I noticed that the version that he sent me was already formatted for editing, and I could not convert it back to an editable version. That was a bit frightening, but I never doubted the favor of God in my life. I called Professor Dormarunno and asked him if he could reformat the file so I could continue the work on it. He said that he would call me back to let me know whether that was possible. When he called back, sadly the answer was no. I prayed about the situation for at least two weeks and expected a miracle from God.

One night in the silence and serenity of a moment with the Lord, as I was laying on my back, I began to have a heart-to-heart conversation with my Master about my concerns. In my conversation with my Heavenly Father, I simply allowed His voice to speak to me and His word to govern my thoughts. I quoted Psalms one hundred an thirty-eight to myself, ***"The LORD will perfect that which concerneth me: Thy mercy, O LORD endureth forever: forsake not the works of thine hands" (Ps. 138:8).*** Soon after I made this simple prayer, the voice of the Holy Spirit spoke softly to my heart saying "I want you to get out of bed, open the file, copy and paste it to a new page. It was about two o'clock in the morning. I got up quickly without disturbing my husband in his sleep, went downstairs, and did just what the Lord had instructed me to do. I copied the entire file and pasted it to a new page; however, there was no change.

I went back to bed but could not stop thinking about the voice I heard. Early the next day, I got up and went to work, and I still could not stop thinking about the clear instruction that was given to me the night before. I was convinced that I should try it again. Even when everything seems to go wrong in your ministry, just believe that God is in control and do what He instructs you to do. If God tells you to do it again, be sure to do it as many times as it takes to get results. That's exactly what happened with the recovery of this manuscript. I felt strongly that God would not fail me, and that my breakthrough was near. So again, I copied and pasted the file to a new page. And there it was: my newly recovered file was as intact as when I sent it to Professor Rocco. What a Mighty God I serve! Though oppositions are set to keep us from reaching our goals, God ironically uses these very same oppositions to demonstrate His love and faithfulness towards us. I want to encourage you by letting you know that God never overlooks His servants during their troubles. He wants us to always rely on His promises, because He will never forsake or leave us. Even if an army were to revolt against you, be assured that the Lord would fight for you, and ensure your victory.

Our Heavenly Father does not want us to be ignorant about-facing opposition or persecutions in our ministry. That is why God assigned me to share my experiences with you. I hope that you are giving some type of priority to this message. God also wants us to be vigilant and ready to strike back, but not with our own ability and strength, but with a fearful attitude towards God. *"He will bless them that fear the LORD, both small and great" (Ps. 115: 13).* After Satan threw several arrows to oppose my ministry from moving forward, he did not stop there, however. Remember, Jesus fasted for forty days and nights before the Devil took many strikes at Him, to win Him over; but the bread that sustained Jesus, the word of His Father, secured His victory over the enemy. Likewise, the word of the Lord sustained me when the adversary launched his fiery darts and arrows of destruction at me. He tried robbing me of my gift, but the Lord would not allow him to do so. Ironically, his attempt to destroy the writing of this book gave me double for my trouble. Not only God allowed me to retrieve the first draft of the manual, but He also used my testimonies in the book to bring deep conviction in the heart of Professor Rocco, even as he was reading and editing the manuscript. Professor Rocco confessed to have received Jesus as his personal savior, and that the book played a major role in making this decision. Therefore, brothers and sisters, be comforted by these words. *"For in that he himself hath suffered being tempted, he is able to succour they that are tempted" (Heb. 2:18).*

Opposition Three:

We have an enemy out there, who is loos, and after us. This should be a reality that every Christian ought to come to term with. None of us is exempt from his attacks and opposition. The plain and simple fact is that Satan does not want us to acknowledge our gifts and talents as being provisions coming from God. And furthermore, he totally despises us when we use our special abilities to honor the Lord. The adversary, the Devil, wants to keep us shackled and paralyzed in our thinking, so he may shift our attention from serving God, and seize our focus. We should not give the enemy access to rob us of our legitimate right to utilize our gifts.

Right after the second round of opposition, in December 2012, I was struck again with a third episode. I received a call from Milot Eliassaint, a renowned and highly gifted music producer and engineer who had been diligently working with me to bring the recording project to completion. He didn't bring good news; he told me "The external hard drive that contained the audio files of the recording was defective and therefore inaccessible. I thought: "How could that possibly be?" This news made me tremble; and I could not believe what I had just heard, again. I could have played the blame game and assign fault to anybody who was involved in the project, but I didn't, because the Lord reminded me of the truth of His Word as resonated in the sixth chapter of the book of Ephesians, that ***"my warfare is not against flesh and blood" (Eph. 6:12).***

As I mentioned before, it took me over twenty years to finally reach 85% of this recording. Now this? At this point, many thoughts came rushing into my mind: "What would people think about me? How do I deal with this situation? How am I going to break this news to my husband? How could I continue to work on this manual since it explains how the songs came about?" Could you relate to those questions? Consequently, the door of my writing inspiration was shut up, the shade of my hope was pulled down, and my heart was shattered in solitude. I isolated myself from everyone because I did not want people to know what had happened. Besides, I just could not explain it.

I was so overwhelmed by this opposition that I became inflated with the feeling of uncertainty. I was oppressed by a panicking spirit beyond my wildest dream. As a result, I could not focus, and it affected my work performance. And much more, I came close to losing my job; however, the Lord intervened on my behalf by using two co-workers to back me up. I had a very difficult time singing. Just thinking about what had happened turned the volume of my voice down. My vocal cords became rusty, and I just did not have the desire to do anything. Reader, I want you to know that I had no time to fool around with oppression. I needed a quick double dose of faith to revive my spirit. I went on a three days and nights fasting immediately.

All along, God had the answers to all my questions. While I was confronted by these attacks, God again assigned five women to minister to me. Sister Brunette Marthorn, a prayer warrior, Reverend, Dr. Ghislaine Herard, a mentor to me, Sister Esther Reynold who prophesized over my life, Sister Minerva Morisseau who provides financial help, and Sister Junie Pelissier, one with the gift of encouraging. Sister Marthorn called me one morning at work, just to pray with me. She told me that she felt strongly compelled to pray for me, and she could not resist the voice of the Holy Spirit prompting her to do so. Though she had no clue what was going on in my life at that point in time, but God knew all about my struggles.

Take note, believer, no matter what types of adversities we are confronting in our ministry, as we submit ourselves to God's purpose in our life, He will straighten our paths and complete the work He has started on our behalf. ***"And make straight paths for your feet, lest that which is lame be turned out of the way; but let it rather be healed" (Heb. 12:13).*** During this new episode of opposition, I quickly armed myself with two powerful weapons of choice: prayer (my key to have access to God), and the Word of God (my double-edged Sword). In fervent prayer I began to aggressively cut off any negative influence in my life. Prayer pulled me away from all spiritual distraction and took me in into a place of needed isolation. I plugged my mind into the outlet of God's word (Hebrew: 11,) and began to remedy my faith. The word of God redirected my mind on things spiritual. Every day, while commuting to work, I loaded my mind and heart with scriptures, even memorizing entire chapters. Consider my case for a moment: What else was I supposed to do as a servant of God, but to seek Him diligently? In these verses, God gave me the prescription for a shattered heart, as He reassured me that His power can overcome all oppositions.

And, finally, I regained the courage to share the news with my husband about the defective hard drive. What I thought would be terrifying to him, was received as ordinary news. A couple of months after Sister Marthorn prayed with me, I tried to contact Milot to advise him that I was coming to Montreal, where he was then residing, and to see him about the defective hard drive; but I could not get in touch with him. Courageously, my husband and I drove eight hours to Montreal; and when we got there, we were able to reach him by phone. My husband and I arranged to meet up with him to pick up the defective hard drive. Check this out: it so happened, as Milot was handing out the defected drive to my husband, it slipped out of his hand and hit the floor. That meant the degree of damage became worse than before. On the road back to New York, my husband suggested that, if I had backed up the audio files of the recording on a separate hard-drive, I wouldn't have to deal with this problem; however, I did not say much to reply to his comment, to not create any reason for any unnecessary arguing. I knew my fight was spiritual. After all, I was sure that God would victoriously put an end to this warfare.

I then took the damaged external hard drive to a Best Buy location in New York City to be evaluated. They required a $250.00 deposit just for diagnostic. Besides, I was told that repairing the hard drive could cost up to $5,000.00, depending on the degree of damage to it.

While they did not guarantee full recovery of the files, they assured me that they would call me back with an estimated repair cost. I paid the required deposit, and anxiously waited for the call. Meanwhile, I continued to unite myself with the word of God and allowed my faith to take precedence over the situation. You must know that when the adversary strikes against your ministry, uniting yourself to the word is the only way to conquer oppositions.

The anticipation surrounding the outcome of the external drive had become rather burdensome, but I braced myself for any outcome, whatever it might be. As the Best Buy agent promised, three weeks later, I received a voice mail message asking me to call back about the condition of the external hard drive. When I heard the message, honestly, anxiety filled my spirit again, and I was somewhat reluctant to call back. I waited for three days before I was able to muster the strength to call. It was twelve O'clock that day, during lunch time; I sat at my desk, fighting a strong stint of anxiety. For a moment great fear came upon me again; I was terrified to pick up the phone and call. I felt I was losing control over a battle that God had already won. During this moment in time, I was discrediting God for what He could do, and what He has already done. Under such conviction, I acknowledged that the source of my fear was based on lack of trust. The Holy Spirit impressed in my heart to confess my shortcomings. Under such conviction, I decided to boost myself up with the spiritual vitamin of faith confessions. I surrendered all fear, anxiety, and discomfort to God. Having God on our side is a reality that every minister should experience.

Great victory is reserved for those who resist the snares of opposition. While sitting at my desk tracing through my thoughts, the Holy Spirit triggered Hebrews eleven back to my memory. And out of my mouth I began to speak the words concerning faith: ***"But without faith it is impossible to please Him: for he that cometh to God must believe that He is, and that He is a rewarder of them that diligently seek Him" (Heb. 11: 6).*** That claim immediately freed me from anxiety. I declared and decreed that ***"My hand is upon the neck of my enemies" (Gen. 49:8).*** Soon after, I picked up the phone and called Best Buy. The news that I received was negative; the verdict was that I needed to come up with a great amount of money for them to start working on the hard drive. But the good news was that God gave me victory over my anxiety and the fear of failure, and I set my mind again on trusting and waiting on Him. Glory to God! Can you picture this victory? There is no greater joy to me than to have the privilege of sharing my stories with you. I hope this episode encourages you to be steadfast in your trusting of God.

I am perfectly fascinated with God's patience towards me as He always reaffirms that He is with me every step of the way. I began to spread the news about the defective drive to some of my friends, even asking them if they could help with the cost of repairing it and recovering the recording on it. However, some concerned friends were able to help; yet I was never able to recover any of the data from the hard drive. God allowed me to go through this experience, so He could show me how patient and loving He is towards me. Yes indeed, God is patient with me because, despite all my downfalls, He is still faithful enough to come through for me. The heavenly hosts stand with us to prepare us in standing firm in the days of oppositions. If you are one of those to be quick to doubt God, caught in discouragement, and fearful of oppositions like I was, please, pause here for a moment; take a minute to pray and settle this matter at once. Confess your weaknesses to God, and He will deliver you just as He delivered me. Know that through it all, God is patient enough to uphold you with His perfect love, and to fill your cup with the oil of peace and joy.

Though the obscurity of oppositions may seem stronger than our faith, never doubt that God is a fair Judge. He will render justice to all who trust in Him. Yes! Satan did attempt to destroy my faith in God, but in the end, all oppositions were shifted to absolute victory. In God's own time, He brought about God's plan for both the book and the recording to be completed. The blessings came through not because of the attempted fundraising that I pursued, or because of charitable contributions I made in the past, and not because of my reputation. It was because God does not want anyone to boast about the victory that He only is able to win on our behalf. When man reaches to the end of his limitation, God takes over and finishes what man cannot accomplish*. **"Not that we are sufficient of ourselves to think anything as of ourselves; but our sufficiency is of God"** (II Cor. 3:5).*

While I continued to trust God for a breakthrough, the power of prayer shook the ground of oppositions, and opened doors, making it possible to retrieve the first sessions and drafts in MIDI format of the recording. God began to work in the heart of his servant Milot, the music producer and engineer of the album. One day, I received a call from Milot telling me that he found the MIDI files that contained the "skeleton" of the work from an old drive and thought that it was worthwhile to continue the work from there. Isn't God's amazing love and patience beyond our imaginations? That is why the Apostle Paul reminded us in Romans 8:35 ***"Who shall separate us form the love of Christ? Shall tribulation, or distress, or persecution, or famine, or nakedness, or peril, or sword?" (Rom. 8:35).*** By now, we should be persuaded that the same love applies to all of us. Often when confronted by opposition in our ministry, we ought to know that there should be no excuse based on discrediting God for allowing it to happen.

The lesson learned in the process of both the recording the songs and the writing of this manual is to have steadfast confidence in God by ***"Looking unto Jesus the author and the finisher of my faith..." (Heb. 12:2).*** Even after long and serious attacks of oppositions, life went on, the work continued; all while I was being entirely sustained by the faithfulness of God. Most definitely, faith and obedience were in the treasure box that held my precious work together. Knowing this increases my hope in God daily. After all, what is left for me to do but to put my confidence in God who had called me to serve? It is important to note that our reluctance in using our gifts can greatly delay the release of God's blessing in our ministry. Sometimes, we fail ourselves because of our own misconception or misinterpretation of how God works. As we grow in maturity and understanding of who God is and how He operates, we need to assess how we utilize our gifts to redirect them back to the Lord.

Serving God with our gifts must not be an openly publicized affair to please men, but rather an act of personal and intimate obedience to the calling unto ministry, and the edifying of the body of Christ. ***"Even so ye, forasmuch as ye are zealous of spiritual gifts, seek that ye may excel to the edification of the church" (I Cor. 14:12).*** It is okay to consult our Master and inquire about things that we do not understand. It is true that some of us misused our gifts, but that is my purpose for sharing this information in this book. It is not too late to please God. All we must do is to grasp the intentions of God for giving us both natural and spiritual gifts and talents. As we have come to understand God's principles about the given gift (s); we can truly remain in faith even under fierce oppositions.

Opposition Four:

While remaining in faith under fierce oppositions, things had shifted from worst to horrible. My faith was continuously being tested. In the silence of waiting on God, something terrible happened to my voice once again. For many years I felt as though my voice was losing its quality. I had to turn down many invitations to do outgoing ministry because of this issue. This was a tremendous challenge for me because I had several episodic nightmares about some gummy and sticky stuff, like mucus stuck in my throat that I could never get rid of it. After having these repetitive nightmares, I felt compelled to share my concern with my friend, Dr. Ghislaine Herard, who was so overwhelmingly concerned about my condition that she began to spend countless hours in intercessory prayer on my behalf. I thank

God for giving me a prayer warrior friend in the person of Dr. Herard. From her mouth to God's ears, she made her request known. Soon after, the awful repetitive dream had stopped; it seemed however, as though God was not yet ready to attend to the specific request to restore my voice. Nonetheless through it all, I held on to my faith and perseverance in the Lord.

It was my perseverance that caused me to continue to minister in our local church despite my struggles and health condition. Besides the voice issue, I became ill for several years to the point that I was given a cane to walk; doctors suggested that I should have several surgeries. My long suffering and painful hours had caused the appearance of excessive wrinkles on my face. Even though I was young, I felt as though I was over ninety years old. I was physically weak and had long lost my joy; but I persevered. Perseverance held my hand like a friend and helped me cross over the bridge of afflictions. The Holy Spirit reminded me that **"the branch cannot bear fruit of itself, except it abide in the vine..." (John 15:4).** I kept my appointment with the Lord for several months at three o'clock in the morning. My attic, which I called my prayer room, was my place of warfare to combat against these satanic challenges. Suddenly, at the end of 2018, the swellings in my hands and legs began to decrease miraculously and my suffering disappeared. Praise God! I never had to experience the risks of being surgically operated on. Obviously, my healing was the fruit of my perseverance in prayer.

Though I rejoiced in the Lord for my healing, the anxiety concerning my voice continued to greatly disturb my peace still. Prior to my illness, I had recorded the single of "Can I be the One", but I felt in my heart that God did not approve of it because of the location at which the song was mixed. I regretted my disobedience and decided to remix the song. I continued to persevere, but still the work of the recording had been interrupted.

I kept declaring the word of God over my life. In my intimate conversations with the Lord, I told Him that I was willing to let go of my fear and allow Him to have His way. I declared that no principalities or power were above God's power, and nothing could stop God's work from moving forward. ***"For by him were all things created, that are in earth, visible and invisible, whether they e thrones, or dominions, or principalities, or powers: all things were created by him, and for him" (Col. 1:16).*** Then I continue to wait and persevere. It took me seven years of perseverance before the Lord finally gave me His approval to move on with the work of the recording; even though there was no change in the condition of my voice. The Lord sealed his approval by directing the man who did the musical arrangement of the songs to get in touch with me. He said that he had not heard from me for so long and wanted to know how I was doing. That call reinforced my hope that it was time to resume the recording. From that point on, all my fears and insecurity fell flat before me. I continued with the work of the recording as directed by the Lord. I came to realize that, in essence, God had little to do with the recording being interrupted for so long. He was just waiting on me to let go of my fears, and to trust Him entirely.

Ministers, I want you believe that no opposition is greater than God's love. Turn your focus towards Him during your times of trial. Stick with trusting God and wait on Him patiently. Surely, God will bring an overall shift in your life, just when you least expect it. Through it all, He has upheld me with His love and everlasting strength. The work continued until both the recording and the manual were completed. When the storm of oppositions and persecutions are raging, I know for sure that I have an anchor. My boat will never sink with God as my anchor. ***"Persecuted, but not forsaken; cast down, but not destroyed" (II Cor. 4:9).*** Halleluiah! MY VICTORY IS COMPLETE IN JESUS CHRIST MY SAVIOR!

Inspiration Twelve

 * Blessed are those servants whom the Master when he comes, will find watching...

* Make sure that no one misses out On God's wonderful kindness.

* Now if we died with Christ, we believe that we shall also live with Him.

* For it is God who commanded the light to shine out of darkness who has shone in our hearts to give the light of the knowledge of the glory of God in the face of Jesus Christ.

* Therefore, you also be ready, for the Son of Man is coming at an hour you do not expect.

(Luke 12:37; Heb. 12:15; 2 Cor. 4:6; Luke 12:40)

I'LL Be There

1- Soon and very soon the roll will call in heaven. Will you be ready to meet the Lord? Are you washed in the blood, the blood of the Lamb? Is your name listed in the book of life? Being justified by faith, you'll praise His holy name forevermore; singing Holy, Holy, Holy is the Lamb.

Chorus

Yes! I'll be there, be there when Jesus calls my name. I will be there in heaven when Jesus calls my name. O yes! In God's presence I will be. Yes, I'll be there with the glorifying Lamb.

Holy, Holy, is the Lamb! (3)

Holy is the Lamb!

 2- There are many souls to reach, the foundations are already laid. We must work together as God's Church. Holding steadfast in the Lord, no matter what it takes with Jesus-Christ, our leader to follow. Let us press toward the goal to win the prize for which we have called; we will conquer in the Lord.

3- Be watchful and ready and awaken when the trumpet sounds. Be faithful as Disciples of Christ. Reaching lost souls and bringing them to the light. Spread the gospel's seeds in every heart. As laborers for the King, our reward is awaiting in Heaven, with a glorious crown. I've been redeemed, justified, and sanctified by the blood. I'll be there when Jesus calls my name. And my name is listed in Lamb's book of life; I'll be with the glorifying Lamb.

Heavenly Hope and Inspiration for and the Congregation:

The original subject of "I'll Be There" is **Assurance and Hope** in which I am addressing my beloved brothers and sisters in Christ. It fits in the category of **Edification.** To declare, "I'll be there," (Heaven) one must understand that there are five (4) requirements that lead to the glory of this rewarding place. These include:

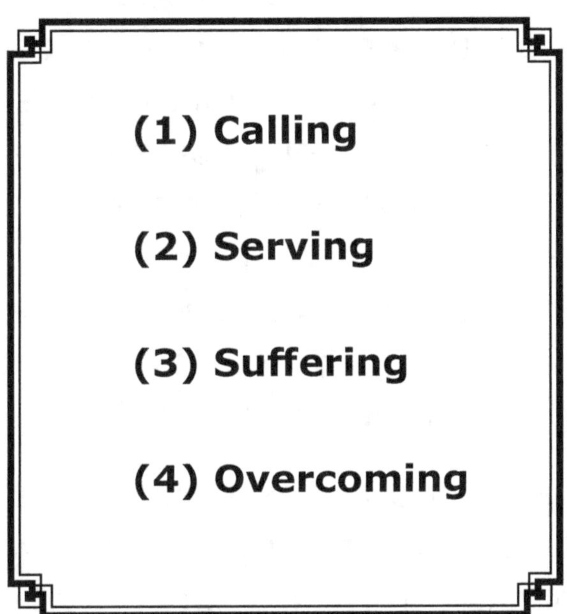

The **calling** starts with receiving the gift of salvation. Salvation pertains to those who are created in God's image (human beings) and not all creations. When receiving the gift of salvation, it opens the door to becoming children of God. As children of God, we are called Disciples of Christ. Disciples are trained to work in the kingdom of God, as they look forward to their reward in heaven. The kingdom of God is where we live now (Marc 1:15). And the kingdom of heaven is where we are looking forward to spending our eternity with our Heavenly Father (Matt.3:2). The church, who is God's bride, has the responsibility to work together as one body in the increasing of God's kingdom here on Earth. As stated in the word, the church belongs to Christ. **"And I say also unto thee, Thou art Peter, and upon**

this rock I will build my church..." (Mat. 16:18). Understanding these concepts, the church, needs to carry on with this assignment as required by our Master, as each one of us in the house of God stands for an individual rock that completes the church structure.

"I'll Be There" is very personal to me, but when I wrote it, I was leaning more towards the duties and responsibilities of the church. God uses the church to **serve** as a channel for the spreading of the gospel, which is more important than any other assignment on Earth. It is not sufficient that we should be satisfied with just being saved. It is a requirement that we should bring forth fruits (souls). To bring forth greater fruits in our *service,* it is essential that we should present our work together, in unity. Unfortunately, sometimes, it's too often not the case. Why is that? Being placed in the position of leadership, I believe it is because some of our leaders think that the God's church is their personal possession, rather than to see themselves as God's vessels for His purpose. Such a perception leaves a big gap among the workers and creates delays in the growth of the church.

There are conditions attached to the calling. The church must remain steadfast to the Lord even through **suffering**. Remaining steadfast includes being obedient to the instructions of God, standing firm and defending our faith, walking in love, letting our lives shine, and, most of all, being ready when the trumpet sounds. Each member of the church will have to stand before the Master and answer for his or her services. The intent of the lyrics in this song is to get the church's attention and to remind her of the duties that come with the calling. I embrace my calling to work together with my fellow brothers and sisters. My hope is to see the church attract people to the kingdom of God, in the beauty of loving one another. The quality of our work sets our reputation. Godly reputation is in God's plan to be follow by victory when we listen to God and do what is pleasing unto Him.

I often hear how some of our beloveds are discrediting each other while they are working together. God did not call us so we could be in enmity with each other. We are to encourage each other because we share the same heavenly hope and the same eternal life in Jesus Christ. ***"For what is our hope, or joy, or crown of rejoicing? Are not even ye in the presence of our Lord Jesus Christ at his coming" (I Thess. 2:19).*** This is more the reason; I urge the church in this song to walk in the image of Christ. Christ was in perfect harmony with His Father. Christ charged us to be His imitator. If we imitate Christ, He will restore righteousness and truth in our midst. Therefore, if we must suffer for one another while working together, it will be worth the price. ***Overcoming*** our differences, our mourning, and our dark moments are the evidence of the fruits of good works. I pray that God will restore love in His church that we may reflect His divine image of love. Our Lord and Savior, Jesus Christ, expects us to be ready when He comes. What a comfort that is to know that our merit is to be together rejoicing in God's presente, dwelling in a peaceful habitation, and wearing the crown of ***glory***. I'll see you there.

LITERATURE REVIEW:

Ammerman, N T, Jackson W. Carroll, Carl S. Dudley, and Williams McKeinney, Studying <u>Congregations A New Handbook Nashville, TN</u>: Harper Collins publisher, Inc. (1998).

Capaldi, N, Eugene Kelly, and Luis E. Navia <u>Journeys through Philosophy, A Classic Revised Edition</u> Buffalo, New York: Prometheus Books publisher (1982).

Moore, B *Giving Christ First Place*: Gospel Light publisher Printed in the USA (2001).

Lovin, R. W, *Christian Ethics an Essential Guide* United States of America: Abington Press publisher (2000).

Pamphile, L.D *The Mind of Christ Your Weapon of Victory* Nashville, TN: Thomas nelson, inc., publisher (2006).

Orsi R.A *God of the City* Indianapolis, Indiana: Bloomington University Press (1999).

Barker, G.A *Jesus in the World's Faiths* Maryknoll, NY: Published by Obis Books, (2007).

White, S J. *Foundations of Christian Worship*: Louisville, Kentucky: Published Westminster John Know Press (1997, 2006).

Charles Spurgeon Spiritual *Warfare in a Believer's Life*: Published by Emerad Books Lynnwood, Washington (1993)

Ed Rainer Sainvill *Tambours Frappés Haitïens Campés*: Printing by Book Masters, Inc. (2001).

Wayne G. Boulton, Thomas d. Kennedy, and Allen Verhey From *Christ to the World Introductory Reading in Christian Ethics*: Published by: Wm. B. Eerdmans Publishing Co. Cambridge CB3 9PU U.K (1994).

Rev. Dr. Alfonse Wyatt Leadership *by Numbers:* Published by: The Power of Hope Press Scottsdale, Arizona (2016)

Obery M. Hendricks, JR. *The Politics of Jesus*: Published by: Three Leaves Press, Random House, Inc., New York (2006).

PREFACE/ INTRODUCTION NOTES:

Preface:

"I will instruct thee and teach thee in the way which thou shalt go: I will guide thee with mine eye" (Psalm 32:8).

Introduction

"God Opens the ears of men and seals their instructions" (Job 33:17).

"My my words shall be of the uprightness of my heart: and my lips shall utter knowledge clearly" (Job 33:3).

"Not that we are sufficient of ourselves to think anything as of ourselves; but our sufficiency is of God" (II Cor. 3:5).

"But the Comforter, which is the Holy Ghost, whom the Father will send in my name, he shall teach you all things, and bring all things to your remembrance, whatsoever I have said unto you" (John 14:26).

Session Notes

Part I

Session One...Behind the Theme

"Having then gifts, differing according to the grace that is given to us, whether prophecy, let us prophesy according to the proportion of faith; or ministry, let us wait on our ministering: or he that teaches, on teaching..." (Rom. 12:6-7).

"My heart is inditing a good matter" (Ps. 45:1).

"I am the righteousness of God in Christ Jesus" (II Cor. 5:21).

"If they obey and serve Him, they shall spend their days in prosperity, and their years in pleasures" (Job 36:11).

"Moreover, whom He did predestinate, them He also called..." (Rom. 8:30).

"Let no man say when he is tempted, I am tempted of God: for God cannot be tempted with evil, neither tempteth he any man" But every

man is tempted, when he is drawn away of his own lust, and enticed." (James 1:13-14).

"And immediately His fame spread throughout all the region around about Galilee" (Marc 1:28).

"Then when the lust hath conceived, it is finished, bringeth forth death" (James 1:15).

"He will make our names to be remembered in all generations..." (Psalm 45:17).

"Dearly beloved, I beseech you as strangers and pilgrims, abstain from fleshly lusts, which war against the soul" (I Pet. 2:11).

"Glory in men..." (I Cor. 3:21).

"For a good tree bringeth not corrupt fruit; neither doth a corrupt tree brings forth good fruit" (Luke 6:43).

"And confident that thou thyself art a guide to the blind, a light of them which are in darkness, an instructor of the foolish, a teacher of babes..." (Rom. 2:19, 20).

"...Whosoever shall confess me before men, him shall the Son of man also confess before the angels of God" (Luke 12:8).

"Now no chastening seemeth to be joyous, but grievous: nevertheless, afterward it yieldeth the peaceable fruit of righteousness unto them which are exercised thereby" (Heb. 12:11).

"Him that is taught in the word communicateth unto him that teacheth in all good things" (Gal. 6:6).

"Now thanks be unto God, which always causeth us to triumph in Christ, and maketh manifest the savor of His knowledge by us in every place" (II Cor. 2:14).

"God is faithful, by whom ye were called unto the fellowship of His son, Jesus Christ our Lord" (I Cor. 1:9).

"Every good gift and every perfect gift is from above, and cometh down from the Father of lights, with whom is no variableness, neither shadow of turning" (James 1:17).

Session Two................. Crossing over the Bridge of a fairy-tale Destiny

"Now therefore hearken unto me, O ye children: for blessed are they that keep my ways" (Prov. 8: 32).

"Marvel not, my brethren, if the world hate you" (I John 3:13).

"Be not thou afraid when one is made rich, when the glory of his house is increased; for when he dieth, he shall carry nothing away: his glory shall not descend after him" (Ps. 49:16-17).

"The foolishness of man perverteth his way: and his heart fretteth against the LORD" (Prov. 19:3).

"The foolishness of man perverteth his way: and his heart fretteth against the LORD" (Prov. 19:3).

"If ye then be risen with Christ, seek those things which are above..." (Col. 3:1).

"If we say that we have not sinned, we make Him a liar, and His word is not in us" (I John 1:10).

"Even the Spirit of truth; whom the world cannot receive because it seeth him not, neither knoweth Him..." (John 14:17).

"And whatsoever we ask, we receive of Him, because we keep His commandments, and do those things that are pleasing in His sight" (I John 3:22).

"And the prayer of faith shall save the sick, and the Lord shall raise him up; and if he has committed sins, they shall be forgiven him" (James 5:15).

"But whoso looketh into the perfect law of liberty and continueth therein, he is being not a forgetful hearer, but a doer of the work, this one will be blessed in his deed" (James 1:25).

"Serve the Lord with gladness: come before His presence with singing" (Ps. 100:2).

Is Confession Necessary in Ministers' lives?

"He that covereth his sins shall not prosper but whoso confesseth

and forsaketh his heart shall fall into mischief" (Prov. 28:13).

"For what man knoweth the things of a man, save the spirit of man which is in him? Even so the things of God knoweth no man, but the spirit of God" (I Cor. 2:11).

"For as the body without the spirit is dead..." (James 2:26).

"I the LORD thy God am a jealous God..." (Ex. 20:5).

"Love the Lord our God with all our hearts, and with all our souls, and with all our strengths, and with all our minds" (Luke 10:27).

"Which shew the work of the law written in their hearts, their conscience also bearing witness..." (Rom. 2:15).

"When God shall judge the secrets of men by Jesus Christ according to His gospel" (Rom. 2:16).

"When God shall judge the secrets of men by Jesus Christ according to His gospel" (Rom. 2:16).

"Casting down imaginations, and every high thing that exalteth itself against the knowledge of God, and bringing into captivity every thought to the obedience of Christ" (II Cor. 10:5).

"Hearing ear, and Seeing Eye, the LORD hath made even both of them" (Prov. 20:12).

"Whosoever committeth sin transgressth also the law: for sin is the transgression of the law" (I John 3:4).

"If we confess our sins, He is faithful and just to forgive us our sins, and to cleanse us from all unrighteousness" (I John 1:9).

"And ye put on the new man, which after God created righteousness and true holiness" (Eph. 4:24).

"Repent therefore of this thy wickedness, and pray God, if perhaps the thought of thine heart maybe forgiven thee" (Acts 8:22).

"Then they that gladly received his word were baptized: and the same day there were added unto them about three thousand souls" (Acts 2:41).

"If we confess our sins, He is faithful to forgive us our sins and to cleanse us from all unrighteousness" (I John I: 9).

First: Hearing the call (Mark 28:19; Rev. 3:20).

Second: Answering (Rom. 10:9).

Third: Come forth (Is. 55:3).

Fourth: Deliver (Matt. 6:13).

"And he fell to the earth, and heard a voice saying to him, "Saul, Saul, why are you persecuting me?" (Act. 9:4).

"...Who are thou Lord" (Act. 9:5)?

"And Ananias went his way and entered into the house; and putting his hands on him..." (Act. 9:17)?

Religion vs. Salvation

"That if "Thou shall confess with thy mouth the Lord Jesus, and shalt believe in thy heart that God hath raised Him from the dead, thou shalt be saved" (Rom. 10:9).

"God shall bring every work into judgment, with every secret thing, whether it be good, or whether it be evil" (Job 12:14).

"This people draweth nigh unto me with their mouth, and honor me with their lips; but their hearts is far from me, but in vain they do worship me, teaching for doctrines the commandments of God" (Matt. 15:8-9).

"If any man among you seem to be religious, and bridleth not his tongue, but deceiveth his own heart, this man's religion is in vain" (James 1:26).

"And these shall go away into everlasting punishment, but the righteous into life eternal" (Matt 25:46).

Answer to Question Two

"For all have sinned and come short of God's glory" (Romans 3:23).

Part - II .... Session Three

The Establishment of the Principles

"My meat is to do the will of Him that sent me, and to finish His work" (John 4:34).

Description of these principles (Hebrews 5:12).

The Five Gifts of the Acts of the Principles

"But without faith it is impossible to please Him..." (Heb. 11:6).

Identifying the principles in the use of the gifts

"Nevertheless, brethren, I have written the more boldly unto you in some sort, as putting you in mind, because of the grace that is given to me of God" (Rom. 15:15).

"Partakers of the divine nature" (II Pet 1:4).

"...God resisteth the proud, but giveth grace unto the humble" (Jas. 4:6).

Principle to Question One:

"Submit yourselves therefore to God. Resist the devil and he will flee from you" (James. 4:7; Luke 4:1-7).

"Submit yourselves therefore to God. Resist the devil and he will flee from you" (James. 4:7).

"God's will be done on earth, as it is in heaven" (Matt. 6:10).

"If we live in the Spirit, let us also walk in the Spirit" (Gal. 5:25).

"I must be subject to my masters with all fear; not only to the gentle, but also to the forward" (I Pet. 2:18).

Principle to Question Two

"Delight thyself also in the LORD; and He shall give thee the desires of thine heart" (Ps. 37:4).

"The works of his hands are verity and judgment; all his commandments are sure. They stand fast forever and ever and are done in truth and uprightness" (Ps. 111:7-8).

"For the hope, which is laid up for you in heaven, wherefore ye

heard before in the word of the truth of the gospel; which is come unto you, as it doth also in you, since the day ye heard of it, and knew the grace of God in truth" (Col. 1:5-6).

Presenting our gifts as a cup of blessing: "BEHOLD, bless ye the Lord, all ye servants of which by nightstand in the house of the LORD" (Ps. 134:1).

Being thankful for the anointing: "THE Spirit of the Lord God is upon me; because the Lord hath anointed me to preach good tidings unto the meek; he hath sent me to bind up the brokenhearted, to proclaim liberty to the captive, and the opening of the prison to them that are bound" (Is. 61:1).

Enriching our songs with God's word "Uphold me according unto thy word that I may live: and let me not be ashamed of my hope" (Ps. 119:116).

Walking in the righteousness of God "And the fruit of righteousness is sown in peace of them that make peace." (James. 3:18).

Seeing our voice as a precious stone. "To whom coming as a living stone, disallowed indeed of men, but chosen of God and precious" (I Pet. 2:4).

"Now unto the King eternal, immortal, invisible, the only wise God, be honor and glory forever and ever A-men" (I Tim. 2:17).

Principle to Question Three:

"LORD, who shall abide in thy tabernacle? Who shall dwell in thy holy hill? He that walketh uprightly, and worketh righteousness, and speaketh the truth, in his heart. He that backbiteth not with his tongue, nor doeth evil to his neighbor, nor taketh up a reproach against his neighbor" (Ps. 15:1-5).

Principle to Question Four

"For whom He foreknew, He also did predestinate to be conformed to the image of His Son, that He might be the firstborn among many brethren" (Rom. 8:29).

"For the Lord taketh pleasure in his people: He will beautify the

meek with salvation" (Ps. 149:4).

"Praise Him with the sound of the trumpet: praise Him with the psaltery and harp. Praise Him with the timbrel and dance: Praise Him with stringed instruments and organs. Praise Him upon the loud cymbals: Praise Him upon the high-sounding cymbals" (Ps. 150:3-5).

"Our works should be done in the meekness of wisdom" (James 3:13).

"The way of a fool is right in his own eyes: but he that hearkeneth unto counsel is wise" (Prov. 12:15).

"If ye have bitter envying and strife in your hearts, glory not, and lie not against the truth. This wisdom decendeth not from above, but is earthly, sensual, devilish" (James 3:14-15).

"To Him who alone doeth great wonders...." To Him that by wisdom made heaven. To Him that stretched out the earth above the waters. To Him that made great lights: the sun to rule by day, the moon and stars to rule by night..." "Such knowledge is too wonderful for me; it is high, I cannot attain unto it"* (Ps. 136:5-9; Ps. 139:6).

"There is no searching of His understanding" (Is. 40:28b).

*"God hath chosen the foolish things of the world to confound the wise... (I Cor. 1:27).

"In God are hid all the treasures of wisdom and knowledge" (Col. 2:3).

"Mine eyes prevent the night watches that I might meditate on Thy word" (Ps. 119:148).

"Beware lest any man spoil me through philosophy and vain deceit, after the tradition of men, after the rudiments of the world, and not after Christ" (Col. 2:8).

"If any of you lacks wisdom, let him ask of God, who giveth to all men liberally, and upbraideth not; and it shall be given him" (James 1: 5).

"Who is a wise man and endued with knowledge among you understanding among you? Let him show out of a good conversation

his works with meekness of wisdom" (James 3:13).

Principle to Question Five

"We then that are strong ought to bear the infirmities of the weak and not to please ourselves" (Rom. 15:1).

"For whatsoever things were written, aforetime were written for our learning, that we through patience and comfort of the scriptures might have hope" (Rom. 15:4).

"But my God shall supply <u>all</u> your need according to His riches in glory by Christ Jesus" (Phil.4:19).

(Rom. 2:14, 15; II Cor. 5:17).

"He would put His laws in their mind and write them on their hearts; and He will be their God, and they will be His people" (Heb. 8:10).

"Neither be ye idolaters as were some of them; as it is written..." (I Cor. 10:7).

"If we live in the Spirit let us also walk in the Spirit" (Gal. 5: 25).

"We are the light of the world. A city that is set on a hill cannot be hid" (Matt. 5:14).

"So then every one of us shall give account of himself to God" (Rom. 14:12).

"But when ye pray, use not vain repetitions as the heathen do.... For your Father knoweth what things ye have needed of, before ye ask Him" (Matt. 6:7-8).

"It is written; man shall not live by bread alone, but by every word that proceeded out of the mouth of God" (Matt. 4:4).

"That which we have seen and heard declare we unto you, that ye also may have fellowship with us: and truly our fellowship is with the Father and with His Son Jesus Christ" (I John 1:3).

"A son honoureth his Father, and a servant his master: if then be a Father, where is mine honor? saith the LORD of hosts unto you...?" (Mal. 1:6).

"Ye cannot drink the cup of the Lord, and the cup of devils; ye cannot be partakes of the Lord's Table, and of the table of devils. "Do we provoke the Lord to jealousy? Are we stronger than He?" (I Cor. 10: 21-22).

"For they that are after the flesh do mind the things of the flesh; but they that are after the Spirit the things of the Spirit" (Rom. 8:5).

"Are not five sparrows sold for two farthings, and not one of them is forgotten before God?" (Luke 12:6).

"Now the just shall live by faith: but if any man draw back, my soul shall have no pleasure in him. But we are not of them who draw back unto perdition; but of them that believe to the saving of the soul" (Heb. 10:38, 39).

"Ye are the salt of the earth: but if the salt have lost his savor, wherewith shall it be salted?" (Matt. 5:13).

"Let no man despise thy youth; but be thou an example of the believers, in word, in conversation, in charity, in spirit, in faith, in purity" (I Tim. 4:12).

"For the love of money is the root of all evil: which while some coveted after they have erred from the faith and pierced themselves through with many sorrows" (I Tim. 6:10).

"We brought nothing into this world, and it is certain we can carry nothing out." (I Tim. 6:7).

"Order my steps in thy word: and let not any iniquity have dominion over me" (Ps. 119:133).

"In all things, showing thyself a pattern of good works: in doctrine showing incorruptness, gravity, sincerity" (Titus 2:7).

"That ye may walk honestly toward them that are without, and that ye may lack of nothing" (I Thes. 4:12).

"God is greatly to be feared in the assembly of the saints and to be had in reverences of all them that are about Him" (Ps. 89:7).

"Do we provoke the Lord to jealousy? Are we stronger than He?" (I Cor. 10:22).

"Even as I please all men in all things, not seeking mine own profit, but the profit of many, that they may be saved" (I Cor. 10:33).

"Hearing of thy love and faith, which thou hast toward the Lord Jesus, and toward all the saints; that the communication of thy faith may become effectual by the acknowledgement of every good thing which is in you in Christ Jesus" (Phim. 1:5, 6).

"For bodily exercise profiteth little: but Godliness is profitable unto all things, having promise of the life that now is and of that which is to come" (I Tim. 4:8).

"Awake to righteousness, and sin not: for some have not yet the knowledge of God" (I Cor. 15:34).

"Be not deceived: evil communications corrupt good manners" (I Cor. 15:34).

"For therein is righteousness of God revealed from faith to faith: as it is written, "The just shall live by faith." "Who knowing the judgment of God, they which commit such things are worthy of death, not only do the same, but have pleasure in them that do them" (Rom. 1:17; 32).

Principle to Question Six

"And it came to pass, when the evil spirit from God was upon Saul, that David took a harp, and played with his hand: so Saul was refreshed, and was well, and the evil spirit departed from him." (I Sam. 16: 23).

"That at what time ye hear the sound of the cornet (horn), flute, harp, sackbut, psaltery, dulcimer, and all kinds of music; ye fall down and worship the golden image..." (Dan. 3:5).

Part- III............. Session Four

The Motive Outside God's Intent

"Whatever I say to you in the dark, you must tell in the light. And you must announce from the housetops whatever I have whispered to you" (Matt. 10:27).

"As every man hath received the gift, even so minister the same

one to another, as good stewards of the manifold grace of God" (I Pet.4:10).

"For the gospel's sake, that we might be partakers of it" (I Cor. 9:23); (John 7:4—17).

Faithful: (Rom. 15:17-19).

Diligent: (I Cor. 15:10).

Meek: (II Tim. 2:25).

Impartial: (I Tim. 5:21).

Obedient: (I Sam. 15:22, 23).

Spirit-filled: (Act. 1:8).

Compassionate: (Heb. 5:2).

Prayerful: (Acts 6:4).

Sincerity: (II Cor. 4:1-2).

"Love my neighbor as I love myself" (Mat. 19:19).

"For the time is come that judgment must begin at the house of God..." (I Pet. 4:17).

Does God Approve or Disapprove the Ministers' Works?

Ownership, Love, and Obedience

"BEHOLD, what manner of love the Father hath bestowed upon us, that we should be called children of God: Therefore, the world knoweth us not, because it knew Him not"

"In this the children of God are manifest, and the children of the devil: whosoever doeth not righteousness is not of God..." (I John 3:10).

"But that world may know that I love the Father; and as the Father gave me commandment, even so I so..." (John 15:31).

"Little children, let no one deceive you: he that doeth righteousness is righteous, even as He is righteous" (I John 3: 7).

Session Five:

The Dispersion of Worship & Praise

"God the Father is looking for true worshipers to worship Him in spirit and in truth" (John 4:23).

"Give unto the LORD the glory due unto His name" (I Chr. 16:29).

"Thou shalt not bow down thyself to them, nor serve them: For I the LORD thy God am a jealous God, visiting the iniquity of the Fathers upon the children unto the third and fourth generation of them that hate me" (Ex. 20:5). (Matt 2:10-11).

"For thou hast possesses my reins; thou hast covered me in my mother's womb. I will praise thee; for I am fearfully and wonderfully made marvelous are thy works; and that my soul knoweth right well" (Ps. 139:13-14). (Mark 2:8; John 4:24).

"How art thou fallen from heaven, O Lucifer, son of the morning...? For thou hast said in thine heart, I will ascend into heaven; I will exalt my throne above the stars of God... I will be like the most-High..." (Is. 14:12-14).

"For whom he did foreknow, he also did predestinate to be conformed to the image of his Son, that he might be the first–born among many brethren" (Rom 8:29).

"For the wrath of God is revealed from heaven against all ungodliness and unrighteousness of men who hold the truth in unrighteousness: Because that which may be known of God is manifest in them; for God hath shewed it unto them" (Rom. 1:18, 19).

PART- FIVE............ Session Six

The Five Acts of the Ministerial Gifts

"Neglect not the gift that is in thee which was given thee..." (I Tim. 4:14).

"Put on the whole armor of God, that ye may be able to stand against the wiles of the devil" (Eph. 6:11-18).

"But without faith, it is impossible to please Him, for he that cometh

to God must believe that He is…" (Heb. 11:6).

"For the perfecting of the saints, for the work of the ministry, and for the edifying of the body of Christ." (Eph. 4:12).

Gift: -1……………Apostle

"By whom we have received grace and apostleship for obedience to the faith amoung all nations, for His name." (Rom. 1:5).

"And when it was day, He called unto him His disciples: and of them He chose twelve whom He named apostles" (Luke 6:13).

"But when the Comforter is come, whom I will send unto you from the Father, even the Spirit of truth, which proceedeth from the Father, he shall testify of me" (John 15:26).

Gift: -2……………Prophet

"To Him give all the prophets witness that, through His name, whosoever believeth in Him shall receive remission of sins" (Acts 10:43).

"But the prophet, which shall presume to speak a word in my name, which I have not commanded him to speak, … shall die" (Deut. 18:20).

"And all these blessings shall come on thee, and overtake thee, if thou shalt hearken unto the voice of the Lord thy God" (Deut.28:2).

"For God is not the author of confusion, but of peace, as in all churches of the saints" (I Cor. 14:33).

"…And they rest not day and night, saying, Holy, holy, holy, Lord God Almighty" (Rev.4:8).

"Come unto me, all ye that labor and are heavy laden, and I will give you rest." (Matt. 11:28).

"Come boldly unto the throne of grace, that we may obtain mercy, and find grace to help in time of need" (Heb. 4:16).

Gift: -3…………… Evangelist

"But you be watchful in all things, endure afflictions, do the work of an evangelist, fulfill your ministry" (II Tim. 4:5).

"The salt of the earth" (Matt. 5:13).

"...O prepare mercy and truth, which may preserve him" (Ps. 61:7).

"For God so loved the world, that He gave His only begotten Son, that whosoever believeth in Him should not perish, but have everlasting life." (John 3:16).

"Exhorting one another: and so much the more, as ye see the day approaching" (Heb. 10:25).

"If we should lift up the Lord, He will draw men unto Him" (John 12: 32).

Gift: -4...............Pastor

Gift: -5...............Teachers

"The LORD requires of us to do justly, and to love mercy, and to talk humbly with Him" (Mic. 6:8).

"Giving no offense in anything, that our ministry may not be blamed" (II Cor. 6:3).

"Some indeed preach Christ even of envy and strife; and some also of good will" (Phl. 1:15).

The Benefit Attributes of Teaching to the Congregation:

"Let the word of Christ dwell in us richly in all wisdom, teaching and admonishing one another in psalms and hymns and spiritual songs, singing with grace in our hearts to the Lord" (Col. 3:16).

"Teaching is a direct command with a promise from our Lord and Savior Jesus Christ." *(Matt. 28:20).*

"His soul, wait silently for God alone, for his expectation is from Him. He only is his rock and salvation" (Ps. 62:5).

Session Seven........... Our Audience

GOD, The Ultimate Individual Audience:

"God is greatly to be feared in the assembly of the saints and to be had in reverence of all of them that are about Him" (Ps. 89:7).

"I will love thee, O LORD, my strength. The Lord is my rock and my fortress, and my deliverer; My God, my strength, in whom I will trust; My shield and the horn of my salvation, my high tower. I will call upon the Lord, who is worthy to be praised" (Ps. 18:1-3).

"Always bearing about in the body the dying of the Lord Jesus, that the life also of Jesus might be made manifest in our body" (II Cor. 4:10).

"We are wonderfully made by Him" (Ps. 139:14).

Inspiration Expression to GOD, the Ultimate Individual Audience:

"Give ear, O LORD, unto my prayer; and attend to the voice of my supplication. In the day of my trouble I will call upon Thee; for Thou wilt answer me" (Ps. 86:6-7).

"I sought the LORD, and he heard me, and delivered me from all my fears." (Ps. 34:4).

"Cast thy burden upon the LORD, and He shall sustain thee; He shall never suffer the righteousness to be moved" (Ps. 55:22).

"Thou art my hiding place; "Thou shalt preserve me from trouble; Thou shalt compass me about with songs of deliverance" (Ps.32:7).

God, the Incorporated Audience:

"It shall blossom abundantly, and rejoice even with joy and singing..." (Is. 35:2); (Rom. 5:12).

"What we do is not to please men, but to please God which trieth our hearts" (I Thess. 2:4).

Inspiration Expression:

"O praise the LORD, all ye nations: praise Him, all ye people. For His merciful kindness is great toward us: and the truth of the Lord endureth forever. Praise ye the Lord" (Ps. 117).

"Because thy loving kindess is better than life, my lips shall praise thee" (Ps. 63:3).

"Declare His glory among the heathen, His wonders among all

people. For the LORD is great, and greatly to be praised: He is to be feared above all god" (Ps. 96:3).

"And again, Praise the LORD, all ye Gentiles; and laud Him all ye people" (Rom. 15:11).

"The wages of sin is death; but the gift of God is eternal life through Christ Jesus our Lord" (Rom. 6:23).

"Study to show myself approved unto God, a workman that needeth not to be ashamed, rightly dividing the word of truth." (II Tim. 2:15).

The Unsaved Targeted Audience:

"What do people say about the Son of Man?" "Some people say you are John the Baptist or maybe Elijah or Jeremiah or some other prophet" (Matthew 16:13-b; 14).

"He was in the world, and the world was made by Him, and the world knew Him not. He came unto His own, and His own received Him not. But as many as received Him, to them gave He the power to become the sons of God..."(John 1: 10-12).

"Behold! The Lamb of God, which taketh away the sin of the world!" (John 1:29).

And He came and touched the bier: and they that bore him stood still. And He said, "Young man, I say unto thee, arise." And he that was dead sat up and, began to speak. And He delivered him to his mother" (Luke 7:14-15).

The Congregational Selected Audience:

"And all the ends of the world shall remember and turn unto the LORD: and all the kindreds of the nations shall worship before Thee...." (Ps. 22:27, 28).

"Train up a child in the way he should go: and when he is old, he will not depart from it" (Ps. 22:27, 28).

"Lo, children are a heritage of the LORD: and the fruit of the womb is his reward" (Prv. 22:6).

"Suffer the little children to come unto me, and forbid them not: for of such is the Kingdom of God" (Ps. 127: 3a).

"All thy children shall be taught by the LORD, and great shall be the peace of thy children" (Mark 10:14).

"All your children shall be taught by the LORD, and great shall be the peace of your children" (Isa. 54:13).

Session Eight

Performing vs. Ministering:

"All power is given unto me in heaven and in earth. Go ye therefore, and teach all nations, baptize them in the name of the Father, and of the Son, and of the Holy Ghost: teach them to observe all things and whatsoever I have command you..." (Matt. 28:18- 20).

PART FIVE .... Session Nine

Inspiration One "Can I be the One"?

"And He hath put a new song in my mouth, even praise unto our God: many shall see it, and fear, and shall trust in the LORD" (Ps.40:2).

"Ye have not chosen me, but I have chosen you, and ordained you, that ye should go and bear fruit, and that your fruit should remain that whatsoever ye shall ask the Father in my name, He may give it you" (John 15:16).

"The harvest truly is plenteous, but the laborers are few; pray ye therefore the Lord of the harvest, that He will send forth laborers into His harvest" (Mat. 9: 37-38).

"Defend the poor and Fatherless: do justice to the afflicted and needy. Deliver the poor and needy; do justice to the afflicted and needy: rid them out from the hand of the wicked" (Psalm 82:3-4).

"And your feet shod with the preparation of the gospel of peace" (Ep. 6:15).

"I will sing unto the LORD as long as I live: I will sing praise to my God while I have my being" (Ps. 104:33).

Inspiration Two: "This is my Reason"

"Love the LORD your God with all your heart, soul, and mind. This is the first and most crucial commandment" (Mat. 22:37-38).

"I will love You, O LORD, my strength" (Ps. 18:1).

"The LORD is my rock and my fortress and my deliverer" (Ps.146:2).

"While I live I will praise the Lord; I will sing praises to my God while I have my being. Before I was afflicted I went astray, but now have I kept Thy word" (Ps. 119:67-68).

"Thou hast also given me the shield of Thy salvation: and Thy right hand hath made me great. Your gentleness has made me great" (Ps.18:35).

Inspiration Three: "The Lost Sheep"

"Fear *not, little flock; for it is your Father's good pleasure to give you the kingdom" (Luke 12: 32).*

"All we like sheep have gone astray; we have turned, everyone, to his own way" (Is. 53:6 a).

"I say unto you, likewise joy shall be in Heaven over one sinner that repenteth, more than over ninety and nine just persons, which need no repentance" (Luke 15:7).

"I will seek that which was lost, and bring again that which was driven away, and will bind up that which was broken, and strengthen that which was Sick..." (Ezek. 34:16).

"They profess that they know God; but in works they deny Him, being abominable, and disobedient, and unto every good work reprobate" (Titus 1:16 a).

Inspiration Four: "It's an Honor"

"And Jesus said unto them, come ye after me, and I will make you to become fishers of men" (Mark 1:17).

"I have taught thee in the way of wisdom; I have led thee in right paths" (Prv. 4:11).

"Even a child is known by his doings, whether his work be pure, and whether it be right" (Prv. 20:11).

"Train up a child in the way he should go: and when he is old, he will not depart from it" (Prv. 22:6).

"Ye therefore, beloved, seeing ye know these things before, beware lest ye also, being led away with the error of the wicked, fall from your own steadfastness" (II Pet.3:17).

"It is the spirit that quickeneth; the flesh profiteth nothing: the words that I speak unto you, they are spirit, and they are life" (John 6:63).

"The Rich Young man story" (Matt. 19:16-23), the story about "The Three servants" (Matt. 25: 14-28), and the story about "The Great Banquet" (Matt. 22:15-21).

"And He said, unto you it is given to know the mystery of the kingdom of God: but to others in parables" (Luke 8:10).

Inspiration Five: "From Tears to Laughter"

"To appoint unto them that mourn in Zion, to give unto them beauty for ashes, the oil of joy for mourning, the garment of praise for the spirit of heaviness; that they might be called trees of righteousness, the planting of the Lord, that He might be glory" (Is. 61:3).

"They that sow in tears shall reap in joy" (Ps. 126:5).

"Come to Me, all you who labor and are heavy laden and I will give you rest" (Matt. 11:28).

"Satan himself is transformed into an angel of light" (II Cor. 11:14).

"The God of all grace, who hath called us unto his eternal glory by Christ Jesus, after that ye have suffered a while, make you perfect, stablish, strengthen, settle you" (I Pt. 5:10).

"For Thou, LORD, art good, and ready to forgive; and plenteous in mercy unto all them that call upon Thee" (Ps. 86:5).

"Therefore, all things whatsoever ye that men would do to you, do ye even so to them: for this is the law and the Prophets" (Matt. 7:12).

Inspiration Six: "Let Freedom Reign!"

"For, brethren, ye have been called unto liberty; only use not liberty for an occasion to the flesh, but by love, serve one another" (Gal. 5:13).

"Stand fast therefore in the liberty where Christ hath made us free and be not be entangled again with a yoke of bondage" (Gal. 5:1)

"Then the earth shook and trembled; the foundations also of the hills moved and were shaken, because He was wroth. He bowed the heavens also and came down: and darkness was under His feet. The LORD also thundered in the heavens, and in the Highest gave His voice; hail stones and coals of fire..." (Ps. 18:7, 9, 13).

Inspiration Seven: "For His Glory"

"Holy, holy, holy, is the LORD of hosts; the whole earth is full of His glory!" (Is. 6:3B).

"For thus says the LORD, who created the Heaven; God himself that formed the earth and made it; He hath established it, He create it not in vain, He formed it to be inhabited: I am the LORD; and there is none else" (45:18).

"All thy works shall praise thee, O LORD; and thy saints shall bless Thee. They shall speak of the glorious majesty of Thy kingdom. Thy kingdom is an everlasting kingdom and Thy dominion endureth throughout all generations" (Ps. 45:10-13; 145:10-13).

PART SIX:.............. Session Ten

Ministers' Contribution to the Development of the Given Gift:

"According to my earnest expectation and hope, that in nothing I shall be ashamed, but with all boldness, as always so now also Christ will be magnified in my body, whether it be life or by death" (Phl. 1:20).

"The mouth of righteous speaketh wisdom and his tongue talketh of judgment" (Ps. 37:30).

"Don't *neglect* the salvation of others. *"How shall we escape, if we neglect so great a salvation, which at the first began to be spoken by* the Lord, and was confirmed unto us by them that hear Him" (Heb. 2:3).

Teaching should not be *burdensome to the minister*. "*Laying up in store for themselves a good foundation against the time to come, that they may lay hold on eternal life*" (I Tim. 6:19).

Ministers should have *no tolerance* for laziness. "*This witness is true. Wherefore rebuke them sharply, that they may be sound in the faith*" (Titus 1:13).

Use the opportunity with *confidence* in order to see a positive result "*But continue thou in the things which thou hast learned and hast been assured of, knowing of whom they have learned them*" (II Tm. 3: 14).

Learn how to approach people with *love* in a *non-threatening way*. "*In all things showing pattern of good work: in doctrine showing corruptness, gravity, sincerity*" (Titus. 2:7).

Build up potentiality by *disclosing* our own weaknesses. "*That the communication of thy faith may become effectual by the acknowledgement of every good thing which is in you in Christ Jesus*" (Philem. 1:6).

Teach others that the gift *is about stewardship for the kingdom of God* and not about personal gain. "*And let ours also learn to maintain good work, for necessary uses, that they be not unfruitful*" (Titus 3:14).

Show people that their *weaknesses are part of their growth process*. "*And this I pray, that your love may abound yet more and more in knowledge and in all discernment.*" (Phil. 1:9).

Proclaim the *fear* of the Lord to people in the early stage of their new birth in Christ. "*The Lord gave the word: great was the company of those that published it*" (Ps. 68:11).

Try to win their trust by making people comfortable. "*But avoid foolish questions, and genealogies, and contentions, and strivings about the law; for they are unprofitable and vain*" (Titus 3:9).

Allow people the opportunity to discuss what they have learned openly. *"All things are lawful for me, but not all things are not expedient; all things are lawful for me, but not all things edify not"* (I Cor. 10:23).

Can the Gift Become Ineffective?

(Mat. 13:24-30).

"Wherefore comfort yourselves together, and edify one another, even as also ye do" (I Tim. 5:11).

Criticism, insecurity, discouragement, fear, scar, and secession:

"And the serpent said unto the woman, ye shall not surely die." (Gen. 3:4).

"And he said, I heard thy voice in the garden, and I was afraid, because I was naked; and I hid myself" (Gen. 3: 10).

"...The LORD hath put wisdom, even everyone whose heart stirred him up to come unto the work to do it" (Ex. 36:2).

"But ye that is spiritual judgeth all things, yet he himself is judged of no man" (I Cor. 2:15).

"Give therefore thy servant an understanding heart...that I may discern between good and bad..." (I Kings 3:9).

"And He commanded us to preach unto the people, and to testify that it is He was ordained of God to be the judge of quick and dead" (Acts 10:42).

"But put ye on the Lord Jesus Christ, and make not provision for the flesh, to fulfill the lusts thereof" (Rom. 13:14).

"Be ye not unequally yoked together with unbelievers: for what fellowship hath righteousness? And what communion hath light with darkness?" (2 Cor. 6:14).

"Let as many servants as are under the yoke of count their own masters worthy of all honor, that the name of God and His doctrine be not blasphemed" (I Tim. 6:1).

"I have set you as a light to the Gentiles that thou shouldest be for salvation unto the ends of the earth" (Acts 13:47b).

"Wherefore let them that suffer according to the will of God commit the keeping of their souls to Him in well doing, as unto a faithful Creator" (I Pet. 4:19).

The expectations that follow the ministerial work:

God expected that Jesus would fulfill the Father's will. *(Luke 4:18).*

God expected Jesus would teach and preach about His kingdom to everyone *(Luke 4:43).*

God expected that Jesus would have many followers *(Luke 9:12).*

God expected that Jesus' message would awaken the heart of men. *(Luke 5:8).*

God expected that Jesus would teach His disciples how to be true servants. *(Luke 22:27).*

God expected that Jesus' works would bring healing to those who are ill *(John 5:47).*

God expected that his son would have *many enemies (Luke 6:11).*

God expected that people would acknowledge the work of Jesus *(Luke 19:37).*

God expected that Jesus' disciples to tell the truth about Him *(John 5:31-32).*

God expected that Jesus would pray for His *(Luke 22: 31-32).*

God expected that His son would be denied even among His followers. *(Luke 22:57).*

God expected that Jesus would testify about the doctrine of His kingdom *(John 7:16).*

God expected that Jesus would be betrayed by one man *(Luke 22:22).*

God expected that Jesus would face many challenges, even the death of the cross. *(Luke 23:21).*

"...For unto whomsoever much is given, of him much shall much required: and to whom much has been committed much, of him they

will ask the more" (Luke 12:48).

Self-Challenging & Offensiveness Expectations:

"Thou shalt never wash my feet" (John 13: 8).

"Lord, not my feet only, but also my hands and my head" (John 13:9).

"Get thee behind Me, Satan! Thou art an offense unto: for thou savorest not the things that be of God, but those that be of men" Matt. 16:23).

"Even as I please men in all things, not seeking mine own profit, but the profit of many that they may be saved" (I Cor. 10:33).

"He shall come down like rain upon the mown grass: as showers that water the earth" (Ps. 72:6).

"Blessed are the meek: for they shall inherit the earth" (Matt. 5:5).

"Many will receive the words as from God and not from men" (I Thess. 2:13).

"He that receiveth you receiveth me, and he that receiveth me receiveth Him that sent me. He that receiveth a prophet in the name of a prophet shall receive a prophet's reward" (Matt. 10:40-41).

PART VII.............. Session Eleven

Defeating Satanic Challenges:

"Verily, verily, I say unto you, he that entereth not by the door into the sheepfold, but climbeth up some other way, the same is a thief and a robber" (John 10:1).

"Having therefore these promises, dearly beloved, let us cleanse ourselves from all filthiness of the flesh and spirit, perfecting holiness in the fear of God" (2 Cor. 7:1).

"For if any be a hearer to the word, and not a doer, he is like unto a man beholding his natural face in a glass: For he beholdeth himself, and goeth his way, and straightway forgetteth what manner of man he was" (James 1: 23, 24).

Defeating unforgiveness:

"Father, forgive them; for they know not what they do" (Luke 23:34).

"Forgive our sins; for we also forgive everyone that is indebted to us…" (Luke 11:4).

"Deliver thyself from as a roe from the hand of the hunter…" (Prv. 6:5).

"Lead us not into temptation; but deliver us from evil" (Luke 11:4b).

Defeating accusation:

"The disciple is not above his master, nor the servant above his Lord" (Mat. 10:24).

"The Lord is faithful, who shall establish me and keep me from evil" (II Thess. 3:3).

"Nay in all these things I am more than conquerors though Him that loved me" (Rom. 8:37).

"But whoso hearkeneth unto me shall dwell safely and shall be quiet from fear of evil" (Prv. 1:33).

"But the comforter, which is the Holy Ghost, who the Father will send in my name, he shall teach you all things" (John 14:26).

"…Fear not: for God is come to prove you, and that His fear may be before your faces, that ye sin not" (Exd. 20:20).

"For God hath not given us a spirit of fear; but of power, and of love, an of sound mind" (2 Tm.1: 7); (Prv. 5:21).

"Let us hold fast the profession of our faith without wavering, for He is faithful that promised" (Heb. 10:23).

"I cried with my whole heart; hear me, O LORD: I will keep Thy statutes" (Ps. 119:145).

"In my distress I called upon the LORD and cried unto my God: He heard my voice out of his temple, and my cry came before Him, even into His ears" (Ps. 18:6).

We must believe always in God's promises *(I Cor. 10:13)*.

We must trust always in God: *(Ps. 42:5)*.

We must accept God's chastisement: *(Heb. 12:11)*.

We must cast our burdens upon the Lord: *r you" (I Pet. 5:7)*.

Demonstrations:

"...Who is greatest in the kingdom of heaven" (Mat. 18:1).

"...Why say the scribes that Elijah must first come" (Mark. 9:11)?

"Why could not we cast him out?" (Mark 9:28).

"Thou hypocrite, First cast out the beam out of thine eye; and then shalt thou see clearly to cast the mote from out of thine brother's eye?" (Matt. 7:5).

"Wherefore lay apart all filthiness and superfluity of naughtiness, and receive with meekness the engrafted word, which is able to save your souls" (James 1:21).

"We then that are strong ought to bear the infirmities of the weak and not to please ourselves" (Rom. 15:1).

"Let everyone of us please his neighbor for his good to edification" (Rom. 15:2).

"That we may be in one mind and one mouth glorifying God, even the Father of our LORD Jesus Christ" (Rom. 15:6).

"Be doers of the word, and not hearers only, deceiving your own selves" (James 1:22).

"Set a watch, O LORD, before my mouth; and keep the door of my lips" (Ps. 141:3).

"Above all, taking the shield of faith, wherewith ye shall be able to quench all the fiery darts of the wicked" (Eph. 6:16).

"Pray for us: for we trust we have that we have a good conscience, in all things willing to live honestly" (Heb. 13:18).

"And who is he who will harm you if you, if ye be followers of that which is good" (I Pet. 3:13)?

"...Be ye therefore sober and watch unto prayer" (I Pet. 4:7).

"For what glory is it, if, when ye be buffeted for your faults...? But if when ye do well, and suffer for it, ye take it patiently, this is acceptable with God" (I Pet.2:20).

"Sanctify the Lord God in my heart: and be ready always to give an answer to every man that asks me a reason of the hope that is in me, with meekness and fear" (I Pet. 3:15).

"Casting down imaginations and every high thing that exalts itself against the knowledge of God and bringing into captivity every thought to the obedience of Christ, and having in a readiness to revenge all disobedience, when your obedience is fulfilled" (II Cor. 10:5-6).

"Are filled with the fruits of righteousness, which are by Jesus Christ, unto the glory and praise of God" (Phil. 2:11).

"All things are possible with Him" (Matt. 19:26).

"Trust in Him at all times, ye people; pour out your heart before Him; God is a refuge for us" (Ps. 62:8).

"The salvation of the righteous is of the LORD; He is their strength in the time of trouble. And the LORD shall help them from the wicked, and save them, because they trust in Him" (Ps. 37:39-40).

Session Twelve:

God's Promises with the gift:

"Behold, I give unto you the power to tread on serpents and scorpions, and over all the power of the enemy: and nothing shall by any means hurt you" (Luke 10:19).

"And God said, let Us make man in our image after our likeness: and let them have dominion over the fish, of the sea, and over the cattle, and over all the earth, and over every creeping thing that creepeth upon the earth" (Gn. 1:26).

"But the fruit of the tree which is in the midst of the garden, God hath said, ye shall not eat of it, neither shall ye touch it, lest ye died" (Gn.2:17).

"When the righteous are in authority the people rejoice: but when the wicked beareth rule, the people mourn" (Prv. 29:2).

"Forasmuch then as the children are partakers of flesh and blood, he also himself likewise took part of the same: that through death he might destroy him that had the power of death, that is, the devil" (Heb. 2:14).

"These things speak and exhort and rebuke with all authority. Let no man despise thee" (Titus. 2:15).

"Let every soul be subject unto the higher powers. For there is no power but of God: the powers that be are ordained of God" (Rom. 13:1).

"My sheep wandered through all the mountains, and upon every high hill: yea, my flock was scattered upon all the face of the earth, and none did search or see after them. Therefore, ye shepherds hear the word of the Lord" (Ezk. 34:7-8).

"Put on the whole armor of God that ye may be able to stand against the wiles of the devil" (Eph. 6:11).

"By the word of truth, by the power of God, by the armor of righteousness on the right hand and on the left..." (II Cor. 6:7).

"But I will sing of thy power; yea, I will sing aloud of thy mercy in the morning..." (Ps. 59:16).

"God is good and ready to forgive; and plenteous in mercy unto all of them that call upon Him" (Ps. 86:5).

Healing, Security, Hope:

"For I know the thoughts that I think toward you, saith the LORD, thoughts of peace, and not of evil, to give you an expected end" (Jer. 29:11).

"For Thou art my hope, O Lord God: Thou art my trust from my youth" (Ps. 71:5).

The contest Between Satan and the Minister:

"And not marvel; for Satan himself is transformed into an angel of

light" (II Cor. 11:14).

"...Now shall the prince of this world be cast out" (John 12:31).

"And the devil said unto Him, "All this power will I give thee, and the glory of them: for that is delivered unto me; and to whomsoever I will give it. Therefore, if you will worship me, all will be yours" (Luke 4:6-7).

"And Jesus answered and said unto him; Get thee behind Me, Satan: For it is written, 'thou shalt worship the LORD thy God, and Him only shalt serve" (Luke 4 :8).

"...For this purpose, the Son of God was manifested, that He might destroy the works of the devil" (I John 3:8).

"Be sober, be vigilant; because your adversary the devil as a roaring lion walketh about seeking whom he may devour" (I Pet. 5:8).

"Blessed is the man whose strength is in Thee... They go from strength to strength... " (Ps. 84:5-7).

"For who hath known the mind of the Lord, that he may instruct him? But we have the mind of Christ" (I Cor. 2:16).

"For if anyone thinks himself to be something, when he is nothing, he deceiveth himself" (Gal.6:3).

"Brethren, if a man is overtaken in a fault, ye which are spiritual, restore such a one in the spirit of meekness; considering thyself, lest thou also be tempted" (Gal. 6:1).

"Nevertheless, when it shall turn to the Lord, the veil shall be taken away" (II Cor. 3:16).

"For Thou, O God hast proved us: Thou hast tried us, as silver is tried" (Ps. 66:10).

"For we would not, brethren, have you ignorant of our trouble ... that we were pressed out of measure, above our strength, insomuch that despaired even of life... But we had the sentence of death in ourselves, that we should not trust in ourselves, but in God which raiseth the dead" (II Cor. 1:8-9).

"Being confident of this very thing, that He which has begun a good work in us will perform it until the day of Jesus Christ" (Phil. 1:6).

Session Thirteen:

Opposition One:

"Yet if anyone suffer as a Christian, let him not be ashamed; but let him glorify God on this behalf" (I Pet. 4:16).

"But glory, honor, and peace to every man that worketh good..." (Rom. 2:10).

Opposition Two:

"The thief cometh not, for to steal, and to kill, and to destroy..." (John 10:10).

"The LORD will perfect that which concerneth me: Thy mercy, O LORD endureth forever: forsake not the works of thine hands" (Ps. 138:8).

"He will bless them that fear the LORD, both small and great" (Ps. 115: 13).

"For in that he himself hath suffered being tempted, he is able to succor the that are tempted" (Heb. 2:18).

Opposition Three:

"My warfare is not against flesh and blood" (Eph. 6:12).

"And make straight paths for your feet, lest that which is lame be turned out of the way; but let it rather be healed" (Heb. 12:13)

"But without faith it is impossible to please Him: for he that cometh to God must believe that He is, and that He is a rewarder of them that diligently seek Him" (Heb. 11: 6).

"My hand is upon the neck of my enemies" (Gen. 49:8).

"Not that we are sufficient of ourselves to think anything as of ourselves; but our sufficiency is of God" (II Cor. 3:5).

"Who shall separate us form the love of Christ? Shall tribulation, or distress, or persecution, or famine, or nakedness, or peril, or sword"

(Rom. 8:35)?

"Looking unto Jesus the author and the finisher of my faith..." (Heb. 12:2).

"Even so ye, forasmuch as ye are zealous of spiritual gifts, seek that ye may excel to the edification of the church" (I Cor. 14:12).

Inspiration Twelve: "I'll be There"

"Blessed are those servants, whom the Lord when he cometh shall find watching" (Luke 12:37a).

"Now if we died with Christ, we believe that we shall also live with Him" (Heb. 12:15).

"For it is God who commanded the light to shine out of darkness who has shone in our hearts to give the light of the knowledge of the glory of God in the face of Jesus Christ" (Heb. 12:15).

Therefore, you also be ready, for the Son of Man is coming at an hour you do not expect" (II Cor. 4:6; Luke 12:40).

"And I say also unto thee, Thou art Peter, and upon this rock I will build my church..." (Mat. 16:18).

"For what is our hope, or joy, or crown of rejoicing? Are not even ye in the presence of our Lord Jesus Christ at his coming" (I Thess. 2:19).

Opposition Four:

"The branch cannot bear fruit of itself, except it abides in the vine..." (John 15:4).

"For by him were all things created, that are in earth, visible and invisible, whether they e thrones, or dominions, or principalities, or powers: all things were created by him, and for him" (Col. 1:16).

"Persecuted, but not forsaken; cast down, but not destroyed" (II Cor. 4:9).

Words of knowledge & Wisdom:

You are a guide to the blind (Rom. 2:19, 20).

Be aware of the hatred of the world toward you (I John 3:13).

Beware about worldly glorification after death (Ps. 49:16-17).

Keep the ways of the Lord to obtain success (Prov. 8: 32).

Seek things which are above the world (Col. 3:1).

Beware that lust is a spiritual illness (I John 1:10).

Do things that are pleasing to God's sight (I John 3:22)

Serve the Lord with gladness (Ps. 100:2).

Those who covered their sins shall not prosper (Prov. 28:13).

You can Know the heart of God through the Holy Spirit (I Cor. 2:11).

You must love God with all their hearts (Luke 10:27).

Don't use your gift to transgress the law of God. (I John 3:4).

Exercise putting the new man in obedience to God, to walk in righteousness and true holiness (Eph. 4:24).

Repent often for your wickedness (Acts 8:22).

Your assignment is to do the will of God, and to accomplish His work. (John 4:34).

You can't please God without faith in Him (Heb. 11:6).

You are chosen and ordained by God to go and bring forth fruit (John 15:16).

Submitting to the Holy Spirit is what makes you partaker of the divine nature of God (II Peter 1:4).

Submit yourselves to God to resist the devil… (James. 4:7).

Obey God rather than men (Acts 5:29b).

Be subject to your master with all fear (I Pet. 2:18).

The Holy Spirit shall teach you how to use the gift in obedience to God's will." (Luke 12:12).

Recognize the gift as Gods' Grace (Col. 1:5-6).

Present your gifts to God as a cup of blessing (Ps. 134:1).

Always be thankful for the anointing (Is. 61:1).

Remember to sow the gift in the righteousness of God (Jas. 3:18).

See your voice as a precious stone in the building of God's church (I Pet. 2:4).

Be not conform to the likeness of the (Rom. 8:29).

You were created God for His own pleasure. (Ps. 149:4).

Perform your work *in the meekness of wisdom (James 3:13).*

It is foolish to depend solely on your natural wisdom (Prov. 12:15).

Guard your heart from bitter envy and strife in their hearts (James 3:14-15).

Beware lest any man spoil your ministry through philosophy and vain deceit... (Col. 2:8).

If you are lacking wisdom, you should ask God in prayer...

(James 1: 5).

Remember, you are a new creature in Christ (II Cor. 5:17).

Beware that music is also used as instrument to accomplish evil missions (Dan. 3:5).

You must believe that God shall supply all their need... (Phil.4:19).

Keep God's promises in their mind and write them on your heart (Heb. 8:10).

You are the light of the world. A city that is set on a hill cannot be hidden (Mat. 5:14).

You should not live by bread alone, but by every word that proceeded out of the mouth of God (Matt. 4:4).

Remember, fellowship with God and His son Jesus-Christ includes suffering (I John 1:3).

Keep your mind after the things of the Spirit not of the flesh (Rom. 8:5).

Beware that the love of money is the root of all evil (Tim. 6:10).

You are the salt of the earth; you must not lose your flavor because of immorality (Mat. 5:13).

Let God order your steps by His word (Ps. 119:133).

Show a pattern of good works, showing incorruptness, gravity, and sincerity (Titus 2:7).

Walk honestly toward them that are without that you may lack of nothing (I Thes. 4:12).

You must feel deep respect to God while using their gifts (Ps. 89:7).

Seek not your own profit, but the profit of others, that they may be saved (I Cor. 10:33).

You must be incorruptible and trustworthy in integrity (Philem. 1:5).

Know that those who profess to know God; but in works deny Him, will be disqualified by God (Titus 1:16).

Beware that bodily exercise profits little: but Godliness is profitable unto all things (I Tim. 4:8).

Use your gift to release the message of the Lord as commanded by Jesus-Christ (Matt. 10:27).

Be good stewards of the manifold grace of God through your gifts (I Pet. 4:10).

Don't use the gift simply for retailing purpose because the purpose is already established by God (I Pet.4:10).

You are God's children, and you should not let anyone deceive you with while using the gift (I John 3: 7).

You should not make your gift an idol because God is a jealous God (Ex. 20:5).

Use your gift to worship God in spirit and in truth (John 4:23).

You are assigned to go and make disciples of all nations, baptizing them in the name of the Father and of the Son and of the Holy Spirit (Matt. 28:19).

Understand that all gifts were given for the perfecting of the saints, for the work of the ministry, and for the edifying of the body of Christ (Ep. 4:12).

Your primary commission is to represent Christ (John 15:26).

You are fully equipped for the work. (Rom. 8:29).

Don't use offensive lyrics to condemn anyone (Heb. 4:16).

Use your gift to lift the Lord, He will draw all men unto God (John 12: 32).

Remember your audience is your flock and should be treated with care (Ps. 23:1).

You are required by God to do justly, to love mercy, and to talk humbly with Him (Micah 6:8).

Beware not to bite and devour one another in their lyrics (Gal. 5:15)

Give no offense to anything, that your ministry may not be blamed (II Cor. 6:3).

Don't use the gift out of envy and strife; but in good will (Phil. 1:15).

Wait silently for God alone for your expectation is from Him (Ps. 62:5).

Use your gift in fear and reverence in the assembly of God (Ps. 89:7).

Love the Lord with all your strength (Ps. 18:1-3).

Your life must be made manifest in Christ (II Cor. 4:10).

Give to the Lord the glory due unto His name (Ps. 96:8).

Let your gift blossom abundantly and rejoice even with joy and singing (Is. 35:2).

Your works are not to please men, but to please God who knows your heart (I Thess. 2:4).

Beware, your adversary is not flesh and blood. You to wrestle against the rulers of darkness of this world... (Eph. 6: 12).

Study the Word of God to show yourself approved unto God (II Tim. 2:15).

Let the word of Christ dwell richly in you in all wisdom (Col. 3:16).

You are assigned to go and teach all nations with your gift... (Matt. 28:18- 20).

Sing unto the LORD as long as you live: while you have your being" (Ps. 104:33).

Beware lest you also be led away with the error of the wicked (II Pet.3:17).

Your strength is quickened by the Word and the Spirit; the flesh profits nothing (John 6:63).

Treat others as you expect them to treat you (Matt. 7:12).

Be not ashamed but use the gift with boldness... Christ should be magnified in their body, whether it be in life or by death (Phil. 1:20).

Pray for Godly wisdom while using the gift (Ex. 36:2).

Be wise enough to judge all things, even yourself (I Cor. 2:15).

Be rooted and built up in God and established in the faith, as you have been taught (Col. 2:7).

You are set as a light to the unsaved that they too may be saved through your gift (Acts 13:47b).

Beware you must suffer according to the will of God and commit the keeping of your soul to Him in well doing, as unto a faithful Creator (I Pet. 4:19).

Believe that all things are possible with God ((Mat. 19:20).

You must always trust God (Ps. 62:8).

You must forgive others as God forgives you (Luke 11:4).

You must be humble and understand that you are not above their Master... (Matt. 10:24).

Know that you are secured, protected, and established by God through His faithfulness. (II Thess. 3:3).

You must hold fast to the profession of their faith without wavering. (Heb. 10:23).

Call unto God in your distress, and He will hear your voice out of His temple (Ps. 18:6).

You are not given the spirit of fear but of power, and of love and, of a sound mind (II Tim. 1:7).

Don't be a hypocrite. Be sincere to yourself as helping others (Matt. 7:5).

You must lay apart all filthiness and superfluity of naughtiness, and receive with meekness the engrafted word, which is able to save your soul (James 1:21).

Be doers of the Word not hearers of the Word (James 1:2).

Your gift should be harmless if you are followers of that which is good (I Pet. 3:13).

You must be sober and watch unto prayer (I Pet. 4:7).

Learn to cast down imaginations and every high thing that exalts itself against the knowledge of God and bring into captivity every thought to the obedience of Christ (II Cor. 10:5-6).

Believe that all things are possible with God (Matt. 19:26).

You must always trust in God and pour out your heart before Him because He is your refuge (Ps. 62:8).

You have been given power to tread on serpents and scorpions, and over all the power of the enemy (Luke 10:19).

You could do all things through Christ which strengthens them (Phil. 4:13)

You must put on the whole armor of God that they may be able to stand against the wiles of the devil (Eph. 6:11).

You must always face the power of evil by the word of truth, by the power of God, by the armor of righteousness on your right hand and on the left (II Cor. 6:7).

Know the thoughts that God think toward you: thoughts of peace, and not of evil, to give you an expected end (Jer. 29:11).

You must believe that the presence of God will be there to give them rest (Ex. 33:14).

You should not marvel; for Satan himself is transformed into an angel of light (II Cor. 11:14).

You must be sober and vigilant because their adversary the devil is a roaring lion walking about seeking whom he may devour
(I Pet. 5:8).

You are blessed because your trust is in God. You will go from strength to strength (Ps. 84:5-7).

 Think not of yourself to be something, when you are nothing, you will deceive yourself (Gal.6:3)

Use your gift to restore those that are overtaken by a fault... lest also you too will be tempted (Gal. 6:1).

Be confident in everything, that God which has begun a good work in you will perform it until the day of Jesus Christ (Phil. 1:6).

You will suffer while using the gift, but don't be ashamed; but glorify God on your suffering. (I Pet. 4:16).

Beware that the thief comes only to steal, and to kill, and to destroy (John 10:10).

Use your gift to make path for your feet... (Heb. 12:13)

Have faith in God. It is impossible to please Him without faith (Heb. 11: 6).

You are not sufficient of yourself to think anything as yourself, but your sufficiency is of God (II Cor. 3:5).

Be zealous of spiritual gifts, so that you may excel in the edification of the church (I Cor. 14:12).

Your hope is the joy of receiving the crown of glory in the presence of Lord Jesus Christ at his coming (I Thess. 2:19).

Believe that your power and authority has been restored through Jesus Christ (Luke 10:19).

Know that authority must be operate in the guideline of God's righteousness (Prv. 29:2).

Believe that Jesus can destroy the power of the devil using your gift (Heb. 2:14).

Beware not to subjective to higher authority (Rom. 13:1).

You must win the contest between you and Satan (2 Cor. 11:14).

Beware not to fall into repetitive temptations (Luke 4:6-7).

Be confident that God can finish the work in you (Phil. 1:6).

Believe the Lord will bless those that fear him (Ps. 115:13).

Know that without faith it is impossible to please God (Heb. 11:6).

Know that God alone is sufficient for you (2 Cor.3:5).

Let nothing separate them from the love of God (Ro. 8:35).

You must not adopt the spirit of flattery (Acts 14:8-18).

Remember those who rule over you (Heb. 13:7).

Obey those that have authority over you (Heb. 13:17).

You must put on Jesus Christ to win the race (Rom. 13:14).

Face opposition in your ministry courageously (1Pet. 4:16).

Understand that Satan come to steal, killed, and destroy your ministry. So, don't let him (John 10:10).

Believe that the Lord will make perfect your concerns
(Ps. 138:8).

You are in a race, run to receive the prize (I Cor. 9:24).